BLADE RUNNER ™ ④

Also by K. W. Jeter in Victor Gollancz/Millennium

Blade Runner™ 2: The Edge of Human
Blade Runner™ 3: Replicant Night
Noir

BLADE RUNNER ™ ④

EYE & TALON

K.W. JETER

VICTOR GOLLANCZ

LONDON

The right of K. W. Jeter to be identified as the author
of this work has been asserted by him in accordance with the
Copyright, Designs and Patents Act 1988.

This edition published in Great Britain in 2000 by

Victor Gollancz
An imprint of Orion Books Ltd
Orion House, 5 Upper St Martin's Lane, London WC2H 9EA

To receive information on the Millennium list, e-mail us at:
smy@orionbooks.co.uk

A CIP catalogue record for this book
is available from the British Library

ISBN 0 575 068655

Typeset by Deltatype Ltd, Birkenhead, Merseyside

Printed in Great Britain by
Clays Ltd, St Ives plc

To Patrick Gyger

Out-Take

MEDIUM SHOT, a small airless room, two chairs with a table between them. A ceiling fan turns slowly through strata of blue-gray cigarette smoke, like knifeblades through ghosts. A cop stands peering out through a horizontal slit of a window, as narrow as though it were at the surface level of some underground bunker.

THE COP'S POV. What the cop sees: the narrow window doesn't look out at the ground, but rather from above, down towards the lights of some massive nocturnal city, stretching out toward the horizon, like an inverted mirror of the sky that can no longer be seen past dirtied, rain-heavy clouds. As the cop watches, the mottled undersides of the clouds turn reddish-orange, tinged by gouts of flame that blossom like the tongues of dragons from needle spires stitched through the dark. The dragon-hiss sounds of the jetting flames are answered by the quick traces of police spinners cutting the night city into quadrants and smaller, asymmetric sectors. What the cop sees is dead space, from the pulsing neon streets intertwining with each other below, to the rain-driven ashes miring the crests of the jumbled towers. What the cop sees is Los Angeles.

A MAN'S VOICE: 'Okay if I talk?'

The cop doesn't turn away from the narrow window. 'Talk all you want,' says the cop.

REVERSE ANGLE, showing the window slit from the outside of the building. CLOSE on the cop's face, CLOSE on the cop's eye, CLOSE on the dark center of the eye, until the eye's mottled pupil fills the screen.

PULL BACK, all the way to LONG, showing the window's narrow slit of light, like the cut of a knife in the sloping exterior wall of the building's massive pyramid shape.

'I kind of get nervous when I take tests.'

The cop turns away from the window and looks at the man – heavy-set, muscular, not too bright – sitting at the table. The cop's brow creases; something is already wrong. Or rather, not right, off in

I

some almost invisible but important way. It can be felt in the heavy, oxygen-depleted air filling the small room.

Something's always wrong. The cop walks over and sits down at the table, opposite the big, stupid guy. The cop smiles, even though she knows the smile comes across as creepy and unpleasant on her face.

'Don't move,' says the cop.

The room is empty except for the two of them. The room is silent except for the muted whisper of the ceiling fan, slowly and ineffectually moving the blue-gray smoke around.

There's something else in the room with them. It sits on the table between them, a machine slowly breathing in and out, silently, its fan bellows moving back and forth, breathing in the molecules of sweat and fear in the room.

CLOSE on the Voigt-Kampff machine. A camera lens points toward the big, stupid guy; a tiny screen mounted on a metal stalk is turned toward the cop. Another eye fills this screen; if the big, stupid guy moves, it'll spoil the focus that the cop is painstakingly adjusting.

'Sorry.' The name stitched on the front of the big, stupid guy's coveralls is LEON. He's not so stupid-looking that there isn't a trace of brutish cunning visible in his stubble-jawed, weak-chinned face. Somebody watching him might have easily figured that he was trying to screw up the whole procedure. But now he sits still, with his hands clasped in his lap. 'I already had my IQ test this year and I—'

The cop cuts him off. 'Reaction time is a factor in this.' Her voice is severe, admonishing. Face attractive, even beautiful – eyes large, skin of porcelain fineness, contrasting with the red artifice of her lips; dark hair arranged in a retro fashion both severe and oddly delicate – but with an expression of cold hauteur. 'So please pay attention,' she continues, 'and answer as quickly as you can.'

Pay attention. She falls silent, as though troubled by the words. They hardly sound like her own, or even spoken in her own voice. She has to wonder whose words they really are.

CLOSE on Leon. He sulkily nods his head.

'A man,' says the cop. She leans back in her chair, watching the trembling fluctuations of the eye magnified on the Voigt-Kampff machine's tiny screen. 'Goes into the desert. He's walking along in the sand when he looks down and sees—'

'What one?'

CLOSE on the cop. She looks annoyed. 'What?'

'What desert?'

'It doesn't matter . . .' She stops, searching for the right words. As though she has to remember them, bring them up from somewhere else. Somewhere outside of herself. 'It doesn't make any difference,' the cop says at last. 'It's completely hypothetical.'

'How come he'd be there, then?'

She knows he's trying to screw it up, to throw her off balance, to blow the test, render the results useless. *So that tells me right there*, thinks the cop. *That he's a replicant.* The cold look in her eyes indicates the thoughts behind them. And as any cop would know, there's nothing dumber than a dumb person trying to be smart. She might as well just haul out the big gun from inside her jacket and blow him away, right now. Why wait? But the cop knows that there are steps to be gone through, departmental procedures, and that asking the questions is part of all that. Necessary, even though at this moment, she couldn't figure out why.

'Maybe he's fed up.' The rest of the words come a little easier to her, though she still doesn't know from where. 'Maybe he wants to be by himself.' That is what the cop wants right now; her pulse pounds at her temples and the small room seems to be getting even smaller, constricting around her like a fist. 'Who . . .' She concentrates fiercely, bearing down on the words and the magnified image of the eye in the little screen. 'Who knows?'

'It's okay,' says Leon softly. The big dumb guy's words are wrong, out of character, as though he had managed to perceive the cop's attack of nerves. 'Take it easy.'

The cop glares at him. She doesn't need his help. She'll get through this.

'Anyway' – she snaps the word out, viciously – 'this man looks down and sees a tortoise.' The words come faster, pushed out by the anger that makes her pulse beat even faster and harder at the limits of her skull. 'Looks down and sees a tortoise crawling towards him—'

'A tortoise?' Leon's back in sync, and in character. 'What's that?'

'You know what a turtle is?'

'Sure.'

'Same thing,' says the cop. The small room is closing around her again, pressing the breath from her lungs. She skips ahead, not caring about the missed dialogue. She just wants to get out of here. Before anything else goes wrong. 'The man reaches down and flips the tortoise over on its back.'

3

CLOSE on the machine in the middle of the table. The needles quiver on the dials, just as the cop knew they would.

CLOSE on Leon's big, sulky face. 'Do you make up these questions,' he asks, 'or does somebody write 'em down for you?'

The cop doesn't seem to hear him. Her lips move slightly, as though reciting different words, another question, from some other time and place.

Is this testing whether I'm a replicant . . . or a lesbian, Mr Deckard?

Leon whispers to her: 'Come on . . .'

The cop rouses herself, emerging from her own vague, insubstantial memories. Leon's words seem to irritate her, even though she had known somehow that he would ask that of her.

'They're just questions, Leon.' She leans back in her chair, making the effort to regain control, to seem cool and in charge. A thin, unpleasant smile shows on her face as she reaches out to the only other object on the table, closer to her, an ashtray with a hand-rolled cigarette trailing a gray thread up to the other smoke at the low ceiling. Real tobacco, black-market goods, the kind of thing that only a cop would be so open about indulging in. The cop inhales, blows out the smoke, all the while coldly regarding the bulky figure across from her. 'That's all. Don't sweat it.'

Leon glances nervously about the room, then back to the cop. He knows that things are going wrong, have gone wrong, will always go wrong. But they won't end, either; he has to ride it out, just as she does.

'Okay,' says Leon slowly. 'About the turtle—'

'Forget the turtle.'

CLOSE on Leon. His brow creases. 'But the turtle's important—'

'No, it's not.' The cop picks up the cigarette again and takes a long drag on it, almost burning her knuckles as the hot end comes close to her hand. 'Forget the fucking turtle. It doesn't matter now. I'll ask you another one.'

Leon heaves a deep sigh, both agitated and resigned. 'Go ahead.'

CLOSE on the cop. Her gaze turns away from the figure on the other side of the table, away from the little screen with its magnified image of his eye, and toward some place deep inside herself. Where her thoughts have turned wordless and strangely calm, no longer apprehensive and unsure. But absolutely certain now, of what was going to happen next.

EXTREME CLOSE. She gazes at the burning cigarette stub

between her fingers, then slowly and carefully sets it back down in the ashtray. The thread of blue-gray smoke cuts a vertical line through the air. The cop turns her gaze back toward Leon, focusing on him once again.

'Let me ask you,' she says, 'about . . . your mother.'

'My mother?' Leon acts puzzled, though the cop knows he understood the question.

'Sure.' The cop nods, her smile encouraging and even friendly. Or as much so as is possible under the circumstances. She feels better now; it'll be over soon. 'Just tell me in your own words . . . everything good you remember about your mother.'

'My mother . . .' Leon's expression darkens, like the lowering clouds filling the night sky outside the little room and the pyramid-shaped building. 'I'll tell you about my mother.'

The cop knew what was going to happen. She wasn't surprised when the shots tore through the surface of the table, fire erupting from the gun in Leon's hands, hidden below. It made no sense that he would have the gun, that he should have been able to sneak it into the interrogation. Where were the security procedures? But at the same time, it made perfect sense. It had to happen that way . . .

A diagonal line, from the gun to her. The bullets struck the cop, slamming her back into the chair, slamming the chair backward against the flimsy pre-fab wall, the bullets' force smashing the chair through a corona of splinters and dust. The chair toppled over, spilling the cop onto the floor and onto her back. She looked up, with eyes already starting to de-focus and film over.

All wrong, she thought. And exactly the way it had to be.

Time stopped, dilated, spread around the cop like the cooling puddle of blood beneath. The room seemed vast to her now; it contained whole universes. She was just conscious enough to be aware of two other figures coming into the room, and Leon looking up at them and asking, *Was that all right?*

You were fine, answered one of them. *Don't worry about it.* But the cop could hear the disappointment in his voice.

Even more so, when the figure came and stood over her and she could hear him speak to the other, in the last infinite second of her dying.

This one didn't work, either. In the unfocused dark, the cop could make out the slow shake of his head. *We'll have to try another one . . .*

PULL BACK to LONG SHOT.

ELEVATED ANGLE, the dead cop on the floor.
And FADE TO BLACK.

1

She loved her job.

Iris knew she was good at it. Even at a time like this, when she also knew that she could die any second, and that her death would be her own fault – even now, the conviction burned within her, a white-hot spark at the center of her gut, that there was nobody better at this. Most of the other blade runners – or at least those who had been at the game as long as she had – were already dead or burnt out.

Wimps, thought Iris, as she stepped through the woman's face, luminous white.

The geisha image was all around her, a substance tangible as the foggy mists that rose between monsoon bouts from the stagnant lagoons that had once been the San Pedro freight docks at the edge of the city, where LA's sprawl was terminated by the gray, oil-shiny waves of the Pacific Ocean. Iris had childhood memories of the docks and the dead, decaying sea – from not that long ago; the street orphanage had unlocked and taken from her ankle the coded radio-emitter band, the magic circlet that had enabled her to check into the safety of the hivelike, hexagonal sleeping shelters every night, just a few years ago, when she had passed her twenty-first birthday. That was when she had been legally entitled to sign away enough bodily security rights to join the LAPD's basic training program. The worst part of joining up had been lying in a departmental hospital chamber for a week, with a thermal-reduction blood substitute filling her veins while all of her drained-off real blood was being scanned for trace elements and metabolites of the few toxically thrilling chemicals that the lab's filtrons were sensitive enough to detect. She remembered through all that time, with her body core hammered down to 78 degrees Fahrenheit, dreaming of icebergs, blue and glowing like summer moonlight, marching in ponderous slow-motion through the LA streets, sweeping them clear, leaving them pure and englaciated, like the diamonds she had felt growing along her spine. When the department medics in their bloodstained blue scrubs had woken her up, and she had blinked away the ice crystals from her eyelashes, she had been almost sad to see the dirty city again, washed no cleaner by the fever-laden tropical rains . . .

Giant red *kanji* marched through the enveloping cloud, spelling out the brand name of whatever wideband tricyclic the geisha was so happily placing on her tongue. The ideograms and the face faded a bit, enough that Iris could see a narrow swath of stars through a break in the bigger, darker nightclouds above. And enough that her prey might be able to spot her; with the bulky black metal of her gun filling both her hands, and poised barrel-upright along the side of her head, Iris drew back into the building's shadow. Under her bootsole, fragments of the concrete ledge crumbled and fell, dropping like cold, dead stars the twenty stories to the street's crowded, neon-shimmering wetness. The rain creeping down the building's exterior slunk through the neck tendrils of her close-cropped black hair, and down inside the collar of her Kevlar®-stranded leatherite jacket. Her knuckles were studded gemlike with drops of the same rain; wet, the gun's muzzle looked like carved and polished obsidian, a little totem of violence raised aloft by one of its worshipers.

All right, thought Iris. *Where is it?* The adrenaline in her veins was making her impatient. She wanted to bag this one before the chase-exhilaration that revved her pulse modulated to a slower pace, marathon-running mode rather than a sprinter's full-out push. Half the pleasure in replicant-hunting came with sighting down on one, with her heartbeat so strong in her throat that she had to fight her own body to keep the gun from trembling in her grip, and the quarry turning and locking its fated gaze with hers, so they both knew exactly what was going to happen next, what moment of terminal intimacy they were about to share, only the small motion of a curved finger away, trigger and release, all the way up her braced arms and into that small, private room beneath her breastbone . . .

The other half of the pleasure came with getting paid a blade runner's bounty. She could use the money. The gun in her hands wasn't regulation LAPD-issue, but something she was still making payments on, herself.

A little motion fluttered the damp cloud pressing around her, a motion that wasn't caused by minor meteorological shifts, wind currents or a ventilator shaft's purge-release cycle. Something human, Iris knew, had done it. Or something close enough to human to run like one, far enough from human to be legal prey.

8

Come on . . .

She slid her foot along the narrow ledge, the heel of her boot scraping against the ancient brick facing. Carefully, with each small movement timed to her own pulse, she made her way to the building's corner. The sweat of her palms mingled with the rain inching along the grooves of the gun's incised grip.

At the corner, with its blunt knife's-edge against her spine, she could look down and discern through mist the broken, rusting skeleton of the blimp that had used to cruise past the buildings' upper reaches, with its spiky, sea-creature-like antennae and swiveling pinlights, its pixel-swarm display of tantalizing off-world vistas, and synthesized voice boomily extolling the virtues of emigration to the stars. Rep-symp terrorists had brought the service-ad blimp down some time after Iris had gotten out of the LAPD's advanced training immersion compound, and she had been starting to make her mark in the blade runner unit, with an effective kill ratio knocked down from a straight one-thousand only by winging some pedestrian who had panicked in the wrong direction when she had started emptying her clip down the length of Figueroa Boulevard. Off-duty and narcotized asleep, Iris hadn't seen the blimp go down; from what some of the uniformed bull cops had told her, it'd looked like an ignited whale, as though Captain Ahab had traded his harpoon for a flame-thrower. The dead seas held no more whales; their bones rotted in the marine trenches, covered with oil. Only in bad dreams and televised news could you see one fall from the sky with such slow, sad grace.

There.

She'd spotted it, the target she'd been pursuing all the way from the hovel burrows beneath the old Angel's Flight tracks, in the densely humid and compacted core of the city. The troglodyte denizens, pale as cave fish and blinking at even what little sunlight was available during LA's monsoon season, had managed to excavate a dome-like space in the earth beneath the stacked-up office towers, lit it with bootleg current tapped off one of the main trunk lines, and had been selling tickets for an entertainment uniquely attractive to the bodyguarded residents of the fortified Beverly Hills and Brentwood enclaves. Most of the show was the usual tawdrily choreographed sex thing, retro Vegasy glamor from the empty spot in the desert on the city's edge where Vegas used to be, tit spangles mixed with sinister black-leather military kitsch straight out of genetic

memories of Fosse-ized Weimar Berlin. But the star of the underground show, the singular sensation, had been something truly, sickly
intriguing—

A replicant impersonator.

That's entertainment, Iris had thought when she'd heard about it,
down at the station's plain-clothes briefings. Show biz and flash, a
genuine human being imitating an imitation of a human being. The
ultimate drag queen, not transformed from one sex to the other, but
deeper than that, from real flesh and blood, man born of woman, to
synthesized, born of the old Tyrell Corporation's production lines.

Supposedly Art Enesque's act – that was the rep impersonator's
stage name – ran the gamut from a funny interrogation bit, with
wink-nudge answers over a prop Voigt-Kampff machine and leering
asides to the audience clustered around the tables and their watered
drinks, to a hardcore demo, with half the chorine troop as assistants,
of how much physically stronger replicants were than humans – in
every department. And the finale, where the impersonator took a
mock bullet in the head from a cliché blade runner, all dead eyes and
grubby trench coat, was supposed to be a stone riot.

'Let the vice squad shut it down,' had been Iris's answer when
she'd been told by the squad's captain to scope the show. 'If it's over
the line, they can take care of it.'

'Nothing's over the line,' the captain had replied. 'Not in LA. Just
check it out.'

So she had, sitting hunched over an unsipped drink that her
departmental expense account had paid for, inhaling the sour,
mingled sweat odors of the laughing civilians around her. A tour bus
full of Cambodian businessmen, face-masked and giddy from their
Customs Division full-body searches, had swarmed in behind her; Iris
could hear them all through the show's clanking, sax- and gamelan-
heavy stroke music, their laughter and gasps like softly muted bells.
She had mastered the art of ignoring them by the time the headliner
came on.

None of Enesque's jokes had struck her as particularly funny.
Wasting my time here, she'd decided, the glass's sweat chilling her
fingertips. Then the interrogation bit had started, and she had
realized why she'd been sent there. The prop Voigt-Kampff machine
had huge gauges mounted on it, big enough for the audience to see
from their tables in the subterranean club; part of Enesque's shtick
had been his twitching in synch with the needles on the dials, as the

straight man playing the cop had run through the questions. Halfway through the familiar catechism, Iris had felt the fine, dark hair along her neck tighten and rise. *It's real*, she had thought. *It's a real V-K machine*. The rest of the audience might have thought it was just a dummy prop, a wheezing accordion bellows and some phony dials and lights, but she had known different. Which had meant . . .

She had knocked over the glass sitting untouched in front of her, as she had reached inside her leatherite jacket. Even before she had pulled out her gun, Art Enesque's sharp gaze had snapped around from his partner in the act, and had locked onto hers. The classic split-second moment of realization had passed between them, like a bullet or a thrown kiss, in which cop and prey, blade runner and replicant, recognized each other for what they really were.

It'd been a good disguise, she had to admit. Maybe the best possible: for an escaped replicant on the run, hiding out in the center of the city, what better front to assume than as a human pretending to be a replicant? Too clever, though; his own answers had given him away. Or if he had used a real fake Voigt-Kampff, instead of one he must've stolen from an outlying police station or that had been fenced to him by some former blade runner, burnt-out and on the skids, hard up for money. But to use a real one, and pump up his tiny physiological responses so that the needles jumped from side to side, but with that crucial little lag time, measured in milliseconds, that only a trained V-K operator could spot, and which was a critical factor in IDing replicants.

That was a mistake. Or sheer bravado, or simple death wish. Which Enesque had compounded by grabbing the gun of his partner in the act, the one playing the cop asking the questions. The gun turned out to be real as well; the club's patrons had realized that as soon as he had started firing. They all hit the floor, tables and chairs overturning, as Iris had been left as the only one standing, arms extended and hands locked on the grip of her own gun, coldly firing off enough rounds to send Enesque running for a backstage exit.

By the time Iris had emerged from the same upwardly sloping tunnel through which her target had fled, she had slammed another full clip into her gun. The usual milling crowds that filled the streets of LA, like a slow, shuffling sea of nocturnal sunglasses and chanting, saffron-robed millennial cults, had been shoved apart by Enesque's furious onrush, then had closed behind him. Iris had had to scramble on top of a police *koban*, quickly scanning the throng of heads and faces for any sign of her target. A disturbance in the crowd's flow, something crouched down to remain unseen, but obviously pushing its way past the slower bodies around it, had signaled the replicant's escape route to her. With gun held aloft, she had leapt from the *koban*, flattening a pair of unfortunate pedestrians to the sidewalk, then kneeing them aside as their pallid hands had clutched at her.

That had been the real start of the chase, the kind she knew and liked, a scrambling predatory run across any impeding vehicles stalled in the streets, losing sight of the target and then spotting it again. The adrenaline rush in her blood blotted out all sensory input except for the focused, radar-like scan of her vision, locked onto the back of her target like some ancient military heat-seeking missile.

She would run it through her mind again later, when she was savoring these memories on top of all the ones that had gone before it. Standing on the narrow, crumbling ledge at the corner of the building tower, she focused on the precious moment before her. She and the escaped replicant were in end-game mode; above and below her, the building's maze of retrofitted power conduits and ventilation shafts thrummed hollowly with their own blind, nervous energy, as though in sympathetic motion with the blood pulsing tighter and faster from her heart.

Maybe on whatever off-world colony from which he'd escaped, Enesque had been some kind of high-steel construction drone, expendable and trained for altitude maneuvers. Maybe it was where he felt safest, that far above the ground; so when the chase had eaten up the last of his rational thought processes, reduced him to a thing of gasping anger and fear, that was where he had naturally scrambled to. Iris had spotted him clambering up the side of this building, using the exterior pipes as hand- and footholds, heading for the giant geisha-and-pill ad projected onto the low, artificially generated clouds. *At least he can't take a shot at me now.* She'd also spotted that the replicant had had to stash his gun inside his jacket, to leave both hands free for climbing. Iris had tucked her own gun away, into the silicone-greased shoulder holster beneath the leatherite, and had started after him.

Part of the magnified geisha's face blanked out, as Iris took another slow step along the ledge, rounding the building's corner and coming in front of one of the projector units. Each breath was sharp with the distinctive metallic tang of the microscopic water droplets, ion-charged so the pulsing magnetic field could sculpt the mist cloud into a smooth enough surface for the animated image. The pulses made the gun lying so close to Iris's heart seem almost alive, as though it also had started beating with the chase's excitement.

Another wind gust split the cloud, so she could see across the empty space above the street to the old, dead billboard from which the geisha had used to smile and beckon. The projector behind her cast Iris's shadow, twenty times larger than life, onto one corner of the flat, gray rectangle; its shadows wavered with the rain sluicing down the deactivated pixels.

A different shadow moved on the billboard, at the opposite corner; a shadow with human form which Iris knew didn't belong to anything human. As the mists sealed up again, she turned her head and could discern, through the geisha's enveloping smile, the escaped replicant Enesque, spine and hands flattened against the side of the building.

He was less than ten meters from her, and with nowhere left to go. The ledge came to an abrupt, sheared-off end, with nothing beyond it but empty night air. In the distance beyond him, the lights of a police spinner blinked and faded away, as though scared off by a sudden gout of flame.

Maybe the rep wasn't used to heights; maybe it had been only fear that had driven him this far up. Iris could see he was petrified by the greater fear, the emptiness and the falling that lay a couple of inches in front of him. He couldn't even move one hand away from the wall, to reach inside his jacket for his gun. An agonized face turned toward Iris, sweat and rain drawing chalky rivulets through his clown-white stage makeup.

'Don't . . .' The voice that had brayed and cracked jokes inside the subterranean club was now a dry rasp. 'Don't you have to . . . read me my rights? Or something?'

'Get real.' The ledge was plenty wide enough for Iris to turn away from the building's wall and face directly toward Enesque. 'You know that only applies to humans.' She reached inside her own jacket and pulled her gun from its holster, leveling it easy and slow toward the replicant at the end of the ledge. The wet slickness of the concrete on which they both stood was enough that a too-quick move could have thrown her over and down to the street below. The thought didn't cause her any nervousness, but she knew she had to be careful.

'Or questions?' The escaped replicant was pleading for anything that would give it a few more seconds of life. Iris admired that fierce desire in them – but not enough to let one go. 'You're supposed to . . .' Enesque's voice rose to a scream, cutting through the blurring mist. *'You're supposed to ask me questions!'*

'Just one,' said Iris. She stared along her outstretched arm and the barrel of the gun, locking her gaze once again with that of the target. 'How do you want it?'

There were just enough guts left, underneath the replicant's quivering fear, for him to answer the question. The only way left to him.

The artificially generated mist had thickened sufficiently to make the geisha's immense face seem almost ghostly solid, blurring Enesque's outline behind it. So when he leapt toward Iris – hands outstretched for her throat, the rep-enhanced strength of his legs carrying him the entire distance – he seemed to burst Athena-like from the illusory woman's powdered forehead, becoming real and distinct, his own face snarling with the desperate anger of cornered prey.

A smaller birth blossomed from the replicant's brow, a red flower flecked with minute bone shards and bits of pinkish-gray brain tissue. Iris fired another quick pair of rounds, one tearing open Enesque's throat, the other hitting him in one shoulder, so that he spun around as his hurtling body crashed into her.

Enough fierce energy was left in the replicant, so that his hands locked upon Iris, fingers digging hard into her biceps. Blood-spattered, Iris was pinned to the ledge by the weight of Enesque's corpse. His face pressed close to hers, as though in his last moment of dying he had wanted a kiss, perhaps of absolution, rather than mere life.

Sharp, convulsing muscle spasms shook the replicant's body. Iris had to let go of her gun, pinned between her breast and the flailing weight of the body on top of her, and scrabble a hold with her fingertips, into the crevice between the ledge and the building's exterior wall, to keep from toppling over the crumbling edge, locked in the other's embrace.

Enesque's eyelids fluttered open. 'You think . . . you're so smart . . .' His voice was a weak, fading rasp. 'You don't even know . . .'

'Know what?'

He didn't seem to hear her. 'You think . . . you've got a choice . . .'

'Did you say "choice"? Hey—' She turned toward his face, trying

14

to make out the words, as if they mattered. 'Or "chance"? Was that it?'

No answer came from the dead replicant.

Jerk, thought Iris. She didn't know why she'd bothered. The words had already been dismissed from her memory.

She managed to work her other hand between herself and the corpse, and drag out her police tight-cell unit. It lit up as soon as it was in her grip, already keyed into the LAPD dispatch desk. 'Get me a clean-up crew out here.' She'd let the dispatcher read out the building's address from the tight-cell's built-in satellite tracking and position system. 'I've got somebody who's about ready to take the dive.' A glance over her shoulder, past the concrete edge, showed that a group of gawkers, attracted by the gunfire, had already congregated below, separate from the milling street traffic. 'Get 'em here *now*.'

The crew showed up, long after she was bored with having a dead body lying on top of her; only a few minutes, in clock time. She heard the sirens down at sidewalk level. She didn't bother to check whether the crew had cleared a landing zone; the corpse's grip had loosened enough that one good upward shove was enough to send it toppling below.

Iris pulled herself up into a sitting position, leaning back against the building. 'Damn.' Looking down at herself, she saw that Enesque's blood had not only gotten all over the leatherite jacket – that could be wiped off – but had also seeped onto the subtly monochrome, cactus motif silk cowboy shirt she wore beneath. That meant dry cleaning.

It was one of the few drawbacks to what she did for a living. She didn't even mind the evil, slit-like glance of the head of the clean-up crew when she had made her way down to the street and had registered the details of the kill.

'You get off on this kind of thing?'

Iris looked right back into the bull cop's jowly face, as the rain spattering across the shrouded corpse on the gurney cart had also sluiced the blood from her clothes into a feathering red puddle around her boots.

She smiled at him. 'I *love* this job.'

2

'Christ, look at this place.' The squad captain shook his head in disgust. 'How could anybody work in conditions like this?'

Iris stood in the doorway of the office, watching her boss – Meyer was head of the LAPD's entire blade runner division – shuffle through the tides of old paper and strata of various crap in the too-small room. Dust sifted down from the ceiling, a darkly beamed and faceted space somewhere above the open-topped walls, like the beginnings, the first tiny specks, of some pollution-grayed snow flurry. The captain's revulsion was evident in the way he hunched his narrow shoulders and kept his arms tight against his ribs, as though he could prevent the contamination of decay and slow withering from touching him. *Hopeless*, thought Iris. *Give it up.*

She spoke aloud. 'You owe me money.' She leaned against the side of the doorway. 'There was a double bounty on that last one.'

Meyer ignored her. A stack of yellowing newspapers, true antiques from vanished days of general literacy, toppled with a kick from his mirror-polished shoe. 'Beats me how Bryant could've put up with it. I mean . . . *look* at this junk.'

It wasn't an order, but Iris did it anyway. She followed her boss into his predecessor's office and its shadowy pools of dim light, away from the greater darkness surrounding it. Meyer's words were still echoing somewhere out there, in the lofty caverns of the empty police station; ratlike pigeons cooed from their droppings-whitened perches, then settled back down like blinking old women in rags.

Iris picked up a lamp, fallen onto its side on the desk. The piece might have been worth something, if anybody still cared about things as old as that. In LA, nobody did; just yesterday was already too old, broken and forgotten. She held the lamp higher, studying the little photographic scenes imprinted on its parchment shade. Hunting scenes, grinning bwanas posing with their massively calibered rifles beside the corpses of real elephants and water buffalo. If there was a real elephant left anywhere in the world, it wouldn't have been on the

African plains, but dully anesthetized in some dingy holding cage right here in LA's own animal trading *souk*. Things like that were too valuable to be left wandering around; that was why they were all dead by now.

She reached with her other hand under the shade and found a small button. Low-wattage light seeped out of the bulb, transforming the monochrome pictures as though with the dim sunshine of other days. It wasn't likely that any of the pictures could have been of Bryant himself, even as a young man. Maybe they were family mementos, images of his grandfather or even farther back, a long line of gun-toting men with bad smiles, who had the knack of making wild, escaping things fall down and be dead.

Other, smaller but brighter lights cast their shifting glow around the office, from below Iris's knees. A troop of scanitorial autonoms, little more than lenses and caterpillar treads and tiny, claw-tipped grappling pincers, had filed into the office as well; each one had the insignia of the LAPD's data preservation unit stenciled on its cylindrical power source. One of the scanitors crawled ratlike over the toe of Iris's boot, as it seized an empty, square-sided Scotch bottle and turned its lens upon the faded label; a bright red line swiftly read down the words and a sepia image of some vanished Highland glen, and that data had been transmitted and dumped to some catch-all file in the cellars of the new police station, along with every other scrap of information left behind in the office. None of it meant anything, not now: lists of escaped replicants that had been hunted down long ago, procedural memoranda, junk food wrappers with built-in flash heating elements, blackmail dirt for pressuring 'retired' – meaning burnt-out – cops into picking up the gun again, cryptic notes that Bryant had written to himself, back when he'd been heading the blade runner division . . .

One of those, a sticky-backed yellow square, was stuck to the mouth of the empty bottle. Iris idly reached down and plucked it like a minimalist blossom between her thumb and forefinger; straightening up again, she kicked the little scanitor away. The machine and the bottle flew together and smashed against the nearest wall; from out of the shards of glass, the scanitor crawled, looking for more things to read and file away.

When every murder seems the same, it's time to quit.

Iris looked at the words scrawled on the note, in Bryant's messy, alcohol-loosened hand. She wadded it up and flicked it away. That was something the former head of the blade runner division didn't have to worry about anymore. Or anything else, for that matter: he'd been killed right here in this office, blown away by a gun as big as those carried by the cops who had been under his command. The piece Iris carried was both smaller and deadlier than those hulking cannons; she didn't need to feel like a big man to get her job done. Whoever had taken Bryant out – Iris wasn't sure of the details; she never paid much attention to locker-room gossip – had done just as good a job on the former division captain. Quitting time had been arranged for him, whether he'd really wanted it or not.

That was the main reason the small office smelled the way it did. Like bottled-up death, even though its ceiling was open to the rest of the empty station. The whole building stank like that, of police business and administrative termination orders. The memos and day orders could refer to it as 'retirement' or any other euphemism; it still meant the same thing. And which also meant that the smell of a top cop's death wasn't going to fade away, either.

Or any of the other indicators left behind: another scanitorial unit had cleared away enough paper scraps to expose the spatter of dried blood across the floor – Bryant's blood – and was now busily scanning and recording the dark-brown marks, as though they were the hieroglyph of some forgotten, omen-laden language.

'You said I owe you money?'

Iris looked up when the new division captain spoke. 'That's right.'

'Not me.' Meyer shook his head. 'Payroll takes care of that.' His fine-boned, almost hairless hands pawed through the messy stacks on what had been Bryant's desk. 'Put in your voucher and wait, like everybody else.' He picked up a single sheet of paper, studied it for a moment, then discarded it with the rest on the floor. 'You got a confirmed kill, you'll get paid.'

Iris felt her eyes narrowing as she watched the man. 'You could front me,' she said quietly but firmly. 'If you wanted to.' He'd done it before, often enough – and not only for her – that it was close to standard procedure for the division.

'Could do all sorts of things.' Meyer poked a finger through a crack-rimmed porcelain sake cup, filled with paper clips. He fished one out and uncurled it into a straight line. 'But I'm not going to.'

'Why not? I've got expenses.'

'We all do, cupcake.' Meyer held the bit of soft metal between both his thumbs and forefingers, looking across it at her. 'It's a rough old

18

world out there, and nobody loves our asses the way we do. Things are happening right now, so it would behoove both you *and* me to keep our noses clean. Shiny, even.' With one point of the metal, Meyer scratched his chin, deep enough to draw a white line across the skin. 'So I'm not bending any rules for you. And you shouldn't be asking me to. Not if you're smart.'

That worried her. Not much else could, but departmental politics were a jungle to her, darker than any back alley in LA. 'What do you mean? What's going on?'

Meyer regarded her skeptically. 'You haven't heard?'

'Come on. You know I don't listen to this kind of stuff. I got better things to do. Like my job, for one.'

'Yeah, well, your job is what it's about. Your job and mine.' Meyer righted the swivel chair from behind the desk and sat down in it. 'I feel,' he said, 'like I should offer you a drink or something.' He laid his hands flat on the desk blotter, with its overlapping ring marks left by all the glasses that had been sat on it, like the ghost residues of the bottle's brown contents. 'That's what Bryant always did, when he was telling one of his crew some kind of bad news. Just an excuse to have one himself, the poor old lush.'

'Screw Bryant.' The dead didn't interest her; not if they weren't one of her income sources. 'Something's going on with the division, right? What is it?'

'Big reorganization coming down,' said Meyer. 'All through the department. Not just our little blade runner division, but top to bottom, through the entire LAPD.' He leaned back in Bryant's old chair, hands folded across the vest buttons of his Brooks Bros suit. 'Think ants in a jar. Then think about somebody picking up that jar and shaking it. Shaking it *good*. So when the jar gets set back down, the ants are tearing at each other.' Meyer nodded slowly. 'That's what it's going to be like, all over the new headquarters.'

She'd seen ants; they were one of the survivor species, like rats and cockroaches and pigeons, that went on living and crawling around, no matter how bad conditions got. And like human beings.

'What brought this on?'

'Who knows?' Meyer shrugged. 'For this town, money problems are like the rain: they come in and kick your ass on a regular basis. And if you spend too much time looking up and wondering where it's coming from, you'll drown. Probably the last revenue bond issue tanked; let's face it, there are twenty different languages spoken in

LA, and half the population are monoglots – they don't speak to anyone else. You're going to get those people to vote for more money for the police? Fat chance.'

For a moment, Iris felt as though she were standing out in the edges of the ocean, the one she remembered from when she was a child, and the tide was sucking at her skinny-kid legs as it receded and exposed the sharp rocks hiding below the waves. Then she realized it was the scanitor units going about their business, the tiny machines scurrying about and dragging out of the office the paper they had already recorded and filed away. A bigger cleaning module would come by later, and sweep up and incinerate the hard-copy pieces of the late Captain Bryant's existence. In the meantime, the edges of the battered furniture and the corners of the room were gradually becoming visible.

'What about the UN?' Iris tilted her head, indicating the world outside the empty building. 'I thought we got some kind of peacekeeping grant from them. This being the front line and all.' She didn't have to say what the front was up against, what war was going on. The whole reason that the LAPD even had a blade runner division was because this was where the escaped replicants came. Their birthplace. 'Isn't that worth something to them?'

'Yeah, it's worth something. It's worth taking over, that's what it's worth. Pure power-grab time.' The expression on Meyer's boyish face turned sour and cynical, making him look like a life-embittered old man. 'What I hear – and I've got pretty good sources, right into the Secretary-General's office – is that the UN's emigration program is majorly screwed. They're not getting the outgo exit numbers they need; emigrant recruitment's creeping along at the one to two percent level. Doesn't mean *bupkis* against the birth-rate escalation, even in a toxic dump like this town. Still enough live births to jack up the population versus food-source ratio. If things don't improve, you and me are both going to be standing on the streets in full urban-combat gear, along with the regular bull cops, trying to keep the carbohydrate riots down to a low roar.' A corner of his mouth twisted into an ugly partial smile. 'And we won't be succeeding, either.'

Iris gave a single nod of agreement. In LA, things could get ugly – or uglier – in a matter of seconds, especially where food distribution was concerned. If the city's lid came off, there wouldn't be enough private security forces to keep the fortified enclaves from the torch.

'All of which makes a perfect opportunity,' continued Meyer, 'for the UN's Pacific Rim Tactical Command to raise its profile *just* a little, especially with the local Chamber of Commerce and the various non-guilded industrial councils. They'll sell out the city government in a heartbeat rather than see their factories and *primomaquiladores* go up in smoke. If the UN's military wing takes over, they're not going to need a police department anymore; this place will be under direct martial-law administration. Tanks in the streets, curfews and no-go zones, insurrection pre-profiling sweeps . . . the works.' Meyer gave a noncommittal shrug. 'Of course, that could be a good thing for the city, at least in terms of cleaning this mess up. But a little hard on people like you and me.'

No shit, thought Iris. The fear that she didn't feel when chasing escaped replicants now assaulted her, right down in the sinews in the backs of her knees. She and Meyer, and the rest of the LAPD's brass and uniformed and non-uniformed grunts alike, would be more than out of their jobs. They'd be dead. Anybody doing police work in a pressure cooker like Los Angeles inevitably wound up with a list of grievances against him, grudges carried by his opposite numbers, crooks and other scum, who would feel they had died and gone to heaven, to have their shots at former cops without departmental protection to keep them alive.

'Yeah,' said Meyer, 'that'd be one way of going.' He'd read her thoughts, visible right on the page of her face. 'But not the only one. United Nation military types don't like to leave a lot of dangling loose ends around when they set up shop in a new territory. Too much coup potential, if you know what I mean; disgruntled former public employees with weapons experience can be a little volatile. They try to keep it out of the media, but death-squad mode is the usual agenda. And those blue-capped sonsabitches can be *real* efficient. Peacekeepers, right?'

'Check.' And who didn't know that the dead were the most peaceful of all? It came with the cop territory. Iris sat down on the corner of the desk, feeling cold.

'Hey – don't worry about it.' At the edge of her vision, Meyer's sickly smile floated. 'You'll be okay. You and me both.' He leaned forward and patted her with deserved familiarity on the thinly padded jut of her hip. 'Trust me on this one.'

'How do you figure?' Neither his words or his touch had made her feel any better, so far.

'As I said.' Meyer's hand lingered a moment before drawing away.

'Reorganization. The whole LAPD is going to get leaner and meaner. Do more with less. What we'll lack in funding, we'll make up with sheer orneriness.' The unintended rhyme seemed to inspire him. 'Violence works wonders, when properly applied. The department will clamp down on this city so hard, somebody pees against a wall, he'll be dancing on the end of a monadnack.' Meyer moved his loosely clenched fists through parallel small arcs, miming the motion of the standard-issue, double-handled nightstick coming into contact with a human – or non-human – face. 'The mayor's office and the city council will be happy to let us do whatever we need to, rather than have the UN come in and boot them out the door. It'll be pure rock-'n'-roll, believe me.'

A thin ray of hope penetrated the gloom inside Iris's thoughts. 'Really?'

Meyer nodded. 'Trust me on this one. I know how city hall works. The police department's already the heavies for most of this town's population; it's not like we've got a lot of positive PR to lose. So the powers that be will let us off our leashes. Finally. Better that than having the whole dog-dish taken away, for everybody.'

'Solid on that.' Iris echoed her boss's nod. 'So our division is going to get thinner, too. Thinner and tougher.'

'You got it.' Rolling the swivel chair back, Meyer swung his feet up onto his dead predecessor's desk. 'You know some of the clowns you've been working with, the old slow ones? The burnt-out cases, all the way down to the far end of the Wambaugh Curve, drawing their pay but doing jack for it?' This time, it was a hard, sharp shake of his head. 'They're not going to make the cut. They're history. They can retire early, on half-pension. We won't need 'em.'

Half a cop's pension, Iris knew, without bonuses or bounties, didn't buy much in this town. 'What if they don't want to retire?'

'They can retire . . .' Meyer's voice went soft and ominous. 'Or they can *be* retired. *Comprende?*'

She understood. The slang term for killing replicants could be stretched to cover humans as well. Especially the ones who were supposed to be the killers, if they still had the guts for their job.

'Who decides . . .' Her words came out slowly. 'Who makes the cut . . . and who doesn't?'

'That's up to you.'

'What?'

'You and every other blade runner in this division.' Meyer reached forward and knocked a speck of dust from his glossily polished shoes. 'Let's just call it . . . performance review. Okay? Meaning that you're going to be watched pretty damn close – just during this little reorganization period.'

'What the hell for?' Iris's temper flared, extinguishing whatever was left of the apprehension she'd felt earlier. 'You know what kind of work I do. What I *can* do, that the others can't even come close to. I'm the best you've got in this division.'

'Sweetheart. *I* know that; *you* know that.' Meyer spoke with elaborate patience. 'But *they* don't know that. The ones up above me. I'm hanging from the same chain of command that you are, if maybe a couple links higher. That only means I've got farther to fall. The brass want to make sure I'm not cutting you any special favors.' He smiled, eyes half-lidded. 'Which of course I'd be otherwise inclined to do, just to keep you around. For old times' sake.'

'Thanks a lot.' *For this, I slept with the putz?* 'And what happens if I don't make the cut? Anybody can screw up, at least once.'

Meyer wasn't smiling now. 'Then you go down with the rest. Whether you want to or not.'

'I see.'

'You should. I've got my own ass to save. If I can save yours, too, I will. But if you *are* going down, I'm not going with you.'

Iris nodded again. A certain kind of peace came over her, a darkly grim one, that resulted from knowing what the score was.

A little see of resolution crystalized in her heart. *One of these days,* thought Iris, *I'll have his job. And he'll be asking me to do him a favor.* Who would go down then – him or her – was something pleasant to contemplate.

But later. 'So what do I have to do?'

'What I tell you to,' said Meyer. 'That's all.'

'I did that before. And look where it got me.'

'No, I just mean take the assignments.' Meyer put his feet back down on the floor. 'Take them and do them – you know how, right? – and make yourself look good. And no bitching about 'em, okay?'

Her turn to smile. 'That'll be the hard part.'

'You're telling me. Because good assignments are scarce right now.' He shook his head in disgust. 'What a stupid business. Working a crew of blade runners is for idiots. If they're no good, they get killed on the job, and if they know what they're doing – like you – then they're constantly drying up the market.'

'Which means?'

'Not a lot of action right now.' Meyer's shoulders lifted in a fatalistic shrug. 'What can I tell you? We're not getting a lot of escaped replicants showing up around here.'

Iris frowned. 'Where are they going, if not LA?'

'Nowhere, that I've heard of. Maybe the word's finally gotten to them, out in the far colonies. See Earth and die. You can't go home again. Something like that. Let's face it, their lifespans are short enough already. I mean, if *you* only had four years or so to kick around in, would you blow a big portion of what you got by coming to LA and getting sniped off by some blade runner who needs to pay his rent? I wouldn't.'

'But don't they . . . ?' Her words faded; she felt herself groping in the dark. Iris didn't often wonder about what went on inside the heads of her targets – it was a waste of time – but every once in a while, when she woke up in the middle of the night, sleep would elude her as she wondered about whatever drove them toward a rendezvous with her and a bullet. 'Don't they have some special *reason* for coming here?'

'Who knows? Who cares? Whatever it is, it doesn't seem to be a good enough reason right now.'

'Something they want.' She puzzled further over it. 'Something they need to know.'

'They should read a book next time. All the answers you'd ever need, right there. And you don't have to die for them.'

Iris shook her head. The feeling, that something intangible had started to become solid enough for her to wrap her fist around it, had already faded away. 'Maybe,' she said, 'they did find the answers. The ones they were looking for.'

'*Mazel tov*,' said Meyer bluntly. 'I'm happy for them. But whatever the reason, what it boils down to is that just when we need them the most, to come here and show off their happy little faces so we can strut our stuff and kill them, *that's* when they decide not to come around.'

'Not at all? Like none?'

'Maybe not that bad,' admitted Meyer. 'There's still a few showing up. We haven't managed to totally work our way out of our jobs yet. But that Enesque character you bagged – he was the first really good one in a long time, an escaped replicant that'd gotten past our perimeter defenses and gone into deep cover. That was why I steered you on to him. One, I knew you could do the business with him, and two, I wanted you to get the kill credit.'

'I appreciate it.' Her heart warmed a couple of degrees; the division's boss might be a sonuvabitch, but he had a few redeeming qualities. 'That was kind of a fun one.' It would be even more fun when she got paid for the job, but she decided not to press that point.

'Yeah. Too bad we don't have a couple dozen more – hell, a couple hundred – going down like that. We could use 'em, if we're going to make a case for keeping our departmental funding up to a decent level. Plus, you know the way the universe works.' A brooding resentment showed in Meyer's narrow face, as though he'd seen God personally kill his puppy. 'We go through a dry spell and our budget gets slashed to the bone, I'll be trying to run this division out of my hat and with my best runners gone – and *that's* when the reps will start showing up. I swear they will; it'd be just like the bastards.'

Iris regarded him with amusement. 'Maybe that's the answer that they found out. The best way to yank your chain.'

'Typical,' said Meyer. His disgust was genuine and unfeigned. 'It goes to show that replicants really do lack the empathic function; that's what distinguishes them from us humans. If they had any concern for others at all, they damn well *would* show up here and get themselves killed. Hard times for blade runners, otherwise. I mean – *look* at this place. You think I'd be cleaning this dump and setting up shop in it, if I had a choice? But it's a quarter of the budget allotment that my corner window office in the new police building went for, so I'm making the sacrifice. Cutting right down to the bone, Iris; to the *bone.*'

She'd been wondering why he'd told her to meet him here, in the old and otherwise abandoned facility, rather than the shiny new LAPD headquarters. Plus she knew he had a natural aversion to the place where a former division captain had bit it. That death smell wasn't only a matter of molecules drifting in the air, ready to be inhaled; it seeped out of the dingy, ill-lit corners and yellowing stacks of paper, right into one's soul.

Another of the scanitorial units crawled across the toe of Iris's boot, carrying an outdated departmental memo about ammunition expenditures to the incinerator-prepped pile beyond the door. All the time the humans in the room had been bitching and moaning, the swarm of small machines had been swiftly and efficiently going about their business; the stacks and tides of old paper had already been

25

considerably diminished, like a dry, dead sea being drained away. That was, Iris supposed, what made them better than both humans and replicants. *They don't,* she thought, *bitch about their lot in life.*

"'Go to the ant, thou sluggard.'" She spoke her next thoughts aloud. "'Consider her ways.'"

'What?' Meyer had pulled one of the desk drawers all the way out and had been dumping its contents into an empty cardboard box. He looked up at her in puzzlement.

'Nothing.' She didn't know what she had been quoting from, either. The disconnected scrap of memory faded away. 'Look,' said Iris, 'I don't care about the quantity or quality of the jobs out on the street. You want me to kick ass, I'll kick ass. That's what I do. Just give me what you got.'

'All right.' Meyer slid the empty drawer back into the desk. 'But you might think it's a bit out of your line.' He rummaged in his jacket's inside pocket and drew out a couple of folded sheets of paper. 'Here you go.'

'What the hell's this?' The top sheet wasn't the usual rep-hunting data. The only name given was 'Scrappy'; there were no bio details, no list of identifying physical characteristics. And the height given – 64 centimeters – was absurd. She'd blown away some small-statured replicants in her time, usually female ones, but nothing so tiny as to be in the two-foot-tall range. That would have to be a child, an infant – and there were no baby replicants, she knew. Replicants couldn't reproduce.

'Look at the photo.'

She flipped to the next sheet. The picture was in grainy black and white, but clear enough for her to make out what it was.

'This is a joke, right?' Iris lowered the sheets of paper in her hand and glared at Meyer. 'Real funny.'

'No joke, sweetheart. That's the job.'

Iris looked again at the second sheet. The photo of a bird – an owl, with large circular eyes – looked back at her.

'I hunt replicants.' Iris angrily tossed the sheets of paper onto the desk. 'You want a bird, go down to the *souk*. They got plenty of artificial ones there.'

'This isn't a fake bird,' said Meyer. 'It's a real owl.'

'Sure it is. A real, living owl? In LA? Try it on somebody else. The only real birds left in this town are those ratty pigeons you find at the tops of the buildings.'

'Nevertheless.' Meyer reached into his jacket again and pulled out an unlabeled data-tab. Holding the small square between his thumb and forefinger, he deposited it in the palm of Iris's hand. 'Here's some more info on it. Enough to get you started, at least.'

She felt like flinging the small black square back into his face. 'I don't do birds.'

'Oh?' Meyer raised an eyebrow. 'Even when there's a bounty on one?'

That stopped her. 'How much?'

Her heart ticked a little faster when he told her. The bounty was even more than the double whack for which the Enesque replicant had gone. Way more. 'How come so much?'

'That's not your concern,' said Meyer. 'Not mine, either.' With the back of his hand, he knocked aside a scanitor that had climbed onto the desk, aiming for the two folded pieces of paper. 'The only question is – you want the job?'

'I don't know . . .' A rare feeling of self-doubt walked around inside her gut. 'It's not really the kind of thing I do . . .'

'Let me put it this way.' Meyer's voice turned colder than she had ever heard it before. 'The alternative is turning down the assignment, at a time when there aren't a lot of assignments going around. I bumped you ahead of some others on the list, to give you that Enesque job. I'm doing the same on this one with the owl.' He shook his head. 'You turn it down, and I won't be able to guarantee you that I can get you another job, not for a while, at least. And sitting on your hands, doing nothing, is not where you want to be when the departmental reorganization comes down. I'll have a hard enough time keeping my own neck off the chopping block. I'm not going to stick it out there for yours.'

Iris nodded slowly; she'd never had any illusions about the nature of the relationship between the two of them. 'That's the way it is, huh?'

'You got it, sweetheart.'

She closed her fist around the black square. 'I'll take it.'

3

The neon had gotten into her apartment again.

'Shit.' With hands planted on her hips, ring of door-lock swipe cards dangling from one crooked finger, Iris looked around in disgust at the colors brightly threading through the dark living room. The stuff was like kudzu, the creeper vines that she'd once read about; maybe in some place far from Los Angeles, real kudzu still existed, greenly extending its leafy, serpentine tendrils across the otherwise empty landscape. That crawling neon was what one got in LA only confirmed the city as some fallen and degraded sphere of existence.

Iris closed the door behind her – a vertical row of LEDs flashed from green to amber to red, as the locks shot home in sequence – and fumbled for the lights. She had to dig her fingers under a parallel set of flickering glass tubes and snap them loose from the wall, before she could reach the switch. The overhead glow from the expensive full-spectrum fluorescents came on dimmed and filtered violet and blue; Iris looked up and saw that the fixture in the center of the water-stained ceiling had also been engulfed by the neon tubing, like a bird's nest besieged by luminous snakes.

She threw the ring of cards onto the utility table she had left folded out from the efficiency apartment's wall; the neon hadn't yet completely taken over that horizontal space. The stuff grew fast; she could see the tips of the softly glowing tendrils assembling and extending themselves farther, a darker string of liquefied silica along each tube supplying the raw materials, and a translucent surface-effect sheath providing the power to light up the gas pumped inside. A probing lead tendril must have been prying away at the exterior of the apartment building, searching for some hairline chink between the gray cement blocks that it could wriggle through. One time before, when the neon had gotten in, Iris had traced the main stem, big around as her forearm by then, back to the bathroom toilet, where it had come up, urban-legendlike, from the underground sewers. That had happened while she was asleep; she had woken to find herself in the middle of a bad dream of advertising, her walls pulsing in the night with *pinyin* ideograms and the flesh-colored outlines of stylized strip-club dancers, blinking red dots for nipples.

None of the stuff on the apartment's living room walls looked as bad as that had been; this time, most of the neon ads appeared to be in Anglo-Cyrillic, with obscurely labeled bottles outlined in the brightest reds. She wasn't curious enough to puzzle out a translation of what was being hawked; as far as she could tell, most of the products might not even exist. The neon was programmed to generate words and brand names and even skin emporia addresses, all from randomizing syllabic algorithms; the way LA was ceaselessly reinventing itself, the chances were good that at least some of the advertisements would turn out prophetic.

I'll clean up this mess later. Iris didn't have time to screw around with it now. She'd need safety goggles to deal with the broken glass tubing, and a mask and portable oxygen supply to keep from being suffocated by the vapors that would be released. That was way too much trouble, even when the pressure wasn't on her.

The neon hadn't swallowed up her genuine-vintage, naugahyde La-Z-Boy® recliner; the crawling tubes preferred covering the hard surfaces in a locale before taking on anything as soft and cushy as that. As Iris lowered herself into the armchair's enveloping depth, letting it elevate her aching feet, something warm and rubbery climbed into her lap.

'It's been hell around here,' announced her pet chat. Its complaint was voiced in a relentlessly perky voice. 'Lookit this place.'

'I'm not blind.' Iris automatically stroked the chat's bare head. 'I can see it.'

'What're you going to do about it? Huh?' The chat's voice shifted into wheedling-nag mode, a barely perceptible underlay of sawtooth waveforms filtering its words. 'How'm I supposed to sleep with everything lit up like the MacArthur Park towers?'

'Shush.' Iris's fingertips had started to go tingly-numb, as the chat's endorphic, *fugu*-derived neurotoxins started to seep beneath the skin. A metal taste, like licking the top of a flashlight battery, slid beneath her tongue; the world outside the apartment's multi-locked door already seemed less dark and forbidding. 'I'll take care of it. But Mom's got work to do right now.'

The chat perched on the arm of the recliner and watched as she fished out of her jacket the datad Meyer had given her. 'Wuzzat?'

29

'Stuff about a job.' Iris placed the tiny black square into the chat's paws and pushed it toward the surresper machine's intake mouth. 'So Mom can pay your cable bills; all those weep-'n'-fight springerthons cost money, honey. Go on; be a pal.'

'For you,' said the chat. It climbed down from the recliner and waddled to the waffle-textured globe in the middle of the living room. The surresper's rubbery lips sucked the datad from the chat's paws; the show began unfolding even before the chat could scramble back up into Iris's lap. 'Yi-eee!' It looked behind itself just in time to see the three-dimensional projection of the owl, yellow eyes glowing and talons extended, come swooping toward it. *'Gott im Himmel!'*

'Freeze image.' With the chat cowering against her stomach, Iris dropped her voice to the surresper's instruction band. The insubstantial owl stopped in mid-air, its broad, powerful wings buckled at the beginning of their upstroke. 'Roll-out context twenty meters, then processor standby.'

'Don't let it get me . . .'

'Come on; you know it's not real.' Iris peeled the chat away from her midriff and let it climb down from her hands to the floor, before she got up from the recliner. 'Sit over there in the corner, okay? I've got work to do.'

The surround-esper had cost a lot of money, some of which she was still making monthly payments on to the police department's credit union. But compared to the cheap-ass flat-rez espers that were standard issue for the department, working with something like this was worth the debtload. Iris stood face to face with the owl; the projector's feed-in loop set a convex reflection of her image at the dark center of the creature's eyes. 'Magnify,' she told the surresper. 'Two ex.'

A second of pixel blur, then the owl's image doubled in size. The chat squeaked in alarm and dived beneath a pile of dirty laundry. Iris stepped closer to the owl, being careful to duck her head beneath its outspread wings. She hated the sensation of any body-part moving through apparently substantial objects. It made her feel like a ghost, as though she were the unreal one.

She was looking for something in particular, a bright bit of metal. *If this thing's valuable,* she had figured, *then somebody must own it.* She found the proof of that logic in the band on the owl's leg, above one set of splayed, scimitar-curved claws. 'Isolate quarter-meter section, enlarge another two ex.'

30

The owl's foot doubled in size again, like a display of a device efficiently designed for the seizing of prey. Iris felt a chill around her heart, the last of the fuzzy warmth from the chat's topical exudations breaking down in her bloodstream. She leaned in toward the claws, close enough to read the incised markings on the owl's band.

'Memo record.' The string of digits was probably no more than a private ID code, but she recited them one by one anyway. The other words, at the lower edge of the metal band, were the more significant ones. 'Property,' Iris read aloud, 'of the Tyrell Corporation.'

That explained a lot, right there. Specifically about why her boss Meyer had had this particular assignment to hand out. Anything to do with the company that made the replicants the blade runners hunted down – even if that company was now out of business – was of interest to the division. Even a bird.

Iris stepped back from the image. 'Resize one-one.' The owl, caught in mid-flight, zipped back to the size it would have been in reality. She turned away from it and scanned the context in which the image had been captured, that the surresper had now laid over the confines of her own apartment. Faintly, the glowing lines of the neon creepers could still be seen, as though they were the secret words and glyphs of a dreaming world beneath the one in which she found herself.

The image of the owl hadn't been caught out of doors; that figured, for such a valuable piece of property. Whoever had owned it – not only the Tyrell Corporation, but somebody inside the company – would have made sure to keep it indoors, safe not only from its own natural tendency to fly off into the open skies and freedom, but also from anyone who would've wanted to lay hands on it for sinister purposes. *Birdnappers*, supposed Iris. There was an ongoing trade in exotic animals, or at least the simulations of them, in the crowded, maze-like *souk* near the city's heart. In a toxic pit such as LA, sights of any living creature – other than survivor species – were so rare that a biophiliac hunger was generated thereby, which could be assuaged by expensive fakery. Replicants, but of animals rather than human beings. Rumors sometimes circulated, through the *souk*'s shabby booths and security-gridded storefronts, of real animals, fabulously rare species caught in some dwindling environmental niche far from Los Angeles, passing from buyer to seller for dizzyingly astronomical prices. A real owl – it was hard to imagine that any of them still existed in the wild, let alone in the city – would be worth a fortune.

Whose fortune, though? The big question, Iris figured, was who the owl belonged to now, given that the nominal owner, the Tyrell Corporation, was defunct. Who had the ownership of the owl passed to? She'd have to root around a little, find out who the survivors and heirs to the Tyrell Corporation were.

'Who, who, who.' Iris spoke the words like the owl's own hooting cry, and smiled. The bird was a hunter like herself; she could admire the sharpness of its claws.

She couldn't make out the details of the high-ceilinged room that the surresper had laid over her own; the light from that other space, dim and fragmentary, cast anemic, wavering shadows with too little strength to keep from being swallowed up by a larger, surrounding darkness. 'Enhance ambient light levels,' Iris instructed the surresper. 'Fifty pink lumens.' She always started a bright-scaled visual scan in the pink zone, the spectrum band that the human eye could perceive. Going white, into the full-bandwidth spectra, added more information, but rarely anything useful. *What the eye can see*, Iris repeated a basic police-training adage, *the eye can find*. The corollary being that what the eye couldn't see wasn't important. 'Another ten. Stop and edge-sharp boundaries, probable physical objects, max detail def.'

The high-ceilinged room that the surresper had called up now seemed flooded with daylight, as though the other building's roof had been torn off during some season when the city wasn't being pounded with monsoon rains. Banks of candles, guttering in crystal dishes or antlered in horizontal arcs by the arms of cathedral-style candelabra, had their small teardrop flames almost eclipsed by the multiplied light filling the summoned room.

At the same time, the owl – arrested in its flight, yellow eyes and clawtips gleaming – seemed to shimmer for a moment, as each feather leapt into unnaturally high definition; the effect was as if a rough crayon sketch had suddenly been re-done with a single-hair brush, honed engraving needle, and infinite patience. The outspread claws looked sharp as hypodermics.

The winged creature held her attention again. 'Fact-check basic, taxonomic on down.'

A neutered, dispassionate voice sounded from the surresper. '*Bubo virginianus*, commonly known as great horned owl. Adult size varies, generally within range of sixty-three to sixty-six centimeters; wingspread one point four meters. Largest, best-known variety of common owls; former range in wild extending throughout all parts of Northern America—'

'Urban areas?'

It took a second for the voice to switch to another text section of its built-in encyclopedic function. 'On occasion, particularly in areas adjacent to open country or with large, densely forested park zones with small prey opportunities.'

So, thought Iris, *it could live in a city.* But it'd been a long time since LA had had anything like a park in it, at least in the sense of green, growing things and small edible creatures running around. *Other than rats.*

The voice picked up again. 'Range in coloration: nearly white in Arctic areas, to dark brown and gray, mottled and streaked markings below.'

'Yeah, I got that much.' Iris regarded the owl, suspended in mid-air, once again. 'Current population status?'

'Extinct in wild, certainty level one hundred percent. Last captive breeding program terminated, DNA samples discarded as non-viable. Some unsupervised trading suspected among private collectors; no official priority level established for tracking.'

That was pretty much as Iris had suspected. Government agencies, from the local level right through to the UN, had enough on their hands without worrying about *bubo virginianus.* In this world, people were an endangered species. It might not have seemed like that, when pushing your way through the packed streets of Los Angeles, but outside the remaining population magnets – LA, Mexico City, Jakarta, the Euro-Disney Workers Paradise, New Beijing – the human gene-pool dried up rapidly. The cities were like the last, luridly fluorescent night-blossoms on a dying bush, roots withering in polluted soil; if humanity didn't get transplanted successfully to the star colonies, then it would be as extinct as the owl and every other creature that didn't make the cut in a toxin-rich environment. Hard to imagine what collectors would be around to trade the last few members of the otherwise dead breed.

Iris knew all that, and didn't care. She had the same comforting belief system as the generations before her: *I'll be gone before the shit comes down.* Gone in the sense of no longer being alive. No matter how good she was at the blade runner trade – and deep in her heart, she knew she was the best that her boss Meyer had at the moment – she knew it was a short-lived profession. She wasn't worried about the

Wambaugh Curve, the burn-out cycle that tripped up most runners – only wimps and whiners let themselves get tweaked about killing replicants. But eventually, as in any contact sport, even a long-term champ would feel her step slowing by a fraction of a second, the gun in her hand weighing a fraction of an ounce more, coming up and aiming a hair's-breadth too late and a sliver of a degree wide of the fatal mark on the chest of its target – all of which would give that faster, harder and younger target the micro-second gap in time for turning, aiming and firing before she could get her own shot off.

That was the unfair thing about replicants, and why hunting them was, eventually, like betting against the house. They were always, *de facto*, at their prime; their four-year lifespan, as much as some of them griped about it, meant they were always at the top of their own efficiency curve, at their fastest and smartest and deadliest peak. *At least*, thought Iris, *they don't have to worry about losing a step as they get older*. And many of the replicants, especially the ones designed for military combat, had a lot on the ball to begin with; they were to humans as the owl was to the small furry creatures that it seized in its scything talons and tore apart with the cruel machinery of its hooked beak. It was no wonder that the authorities tolerated having blade runners, the next step up in the prey-and-predator chain, running around the streets and firing off cannon-sized weaponry in the midst of the taxpayers and citizens; the alternative was even bleaker. Fat chance of getting the human race to pack up and move out to the stars, with the negative advertisement of escaped replicants, who were supposed to be mankind's slaves and servants in the far colonies, proving how much tougher and more dangerous than their masters they were. In that regard, there was a real PR value in blade runners blowing away the escapees in as public a manner as possible: it showed that everything was still under control, that the gone-bad replicants would be eliminated before they could crush too many people's heads like eggshells. *As long*, mused Iris bitterly, *as they let us do our jobs*. Which, as her boss Meyer had indicated to her, was a matter up in the air for the moment.

That was just more shit destined to come down someday, like the oil-dark rains burdening the black clouds above the city. With any luck, Iris figured, she'd have made her wad by then, rolling up the bounties and socking them away in her retirement accounts, and she'd be able to chill out in her comfy apartment, reminiscing about how good a bullet-warmed gun had felt in her hand, back when she'd been in the game, and watching on the broadcast news as the city's streets filled with blood.

'So much for the bird.' Iris spoke aloud. From the corner of her eye, she spotted her pet chat creeping out a few inches from its hiding place and regarding the frame-stalled image with acute suspicion and loathing. Iris turned her attention back to the surroundings that the surresper had summoned up, a ghost-walled room now more brightly lit than her own.

Expensive, as she had figured it would be: wood paneling from some close-grained tree species that was probably reduced to a few acres in New Guinea by now. If in fact the last of the breed hadn't been leveled to provide the board footage for the illusory chamber in which Iris stood. Common knowledge that a lot of high-level corporate execs, with money to burn, indulged in the luxury of species extinction, giving their material comforts a true *Après moi, le déluge* thrill. It wasn't a complete wipe-out unless any surviving genetic material was taken from deep cryo storage and destroyed, to make sure nobody came along later and recreated one's unique and private possessions. That was probably what had happened to *bubo virginianus*'s DNA samples as well: nothing enhanced the collector's market like scarcity, and nothing enhanced scarcity like death. For animal collectors, extinction – or as close to it as one could get while still leaving a specimen or two alive – was a desirable quality.

And for the rich, the dead past was a treasure trove as well. The illusory space that the surresper had conjured up was tastefully – not her taste, but someone's – and expensively appointed with true museum-level antiques, bits and pieces from the dead centuries before this dying one. Even with only an optical feed to her senses, Iris could just about smell the hand-rubbed *matte* patina on the ornately inlaid writing desk standing against one wall on curved legs with gilt-clawed feet. Above it, a circular, convex mirror, surrounded by stylized golden sunrays, showed her own face's image; the surresper's simulator programming had spliced that bit of the real world's data into the illusory one.

There was another image in the mirror, of someone approaching from a dark hallway on the opposite side of the high-ceilinged room. The hallway's shadows, even with the light enhancement she had ordered from the surresper, all but concealed the figure of a short and slight man frozen in midstep as he headed toward her. The only detail that the light was able to pick out was its own reflected gleam upon a deep silver bowl he carried in one hand.

'Resume action, half-speed.' Iris stepped back from the room's center, so the man's reconstructed image wouldn't overlap with her own physical presence. 'Maintain enhanced light levels.'

Even before she had finished giving the surresper its instructions, the owl's wings swept into motion. Iris ducked reflexively as two slow-motion beats, like the furling and unfurling of a magician's feathered cape, brought the creature over her head and onto a metal perch, away from the small flames of the candelabra. The owl's claws seized onto the perch's crossbar; its feathers smoothed into place as it drew the broad wings close to itself. Golden eyes, perfectly round as coins, turned their fierce, unblinking gaze toward the approaching image.

The man's image, carrying the silver bowl, stepped slowly into the illusory room, where Iris could see him.

Her first thought was that he looked like death. Her second was that death would look better.

'Freeze image.'

The image halted, unmoving as the owl in mid-flight had been. Iris stepped up close to the image, examining the man's face almost nose to nose.

Between the man and the owl were certain similarities. The man's eyes were magnified by black-rimmed, rectangular-lensed glasses, giving him an owlish look, avidly staring, as though some small prey had been spotted in the patterned Oriental rug that the surresper had laid out underfoot. Skin of wrinkled parchment was stretched tight across the facial bones; the city's rains might never have come in this man's lifetime, leaving him to wither in the deracinating sun beyond the clouds. One corner of the man's mouth had already lifted into a smile as he had entered the room; the kind of smile, it struck Iris, that a person got when they were about to indulge in some small, private pleasure. *Pleasant for him*, thought Iris. *Maybe not so much, for anything else.*

She stepped back from the man's image and instructed the surresper again. 'ID male subject.'

The surresper was silent for a few seconds longer than usual. 'Process failure,' the machine announced. 'No identity file on record for subject in view. Redact command?'

'Really?' Iris glanced away from the image, and over her shoulder toward the surresper. 'All banks trawled?'

'Trawled, indices and by-file mode. Still negative.'

The chat had overcome some of its fear of the owl, and had crept out close to Iris's ankle. 'Wuzzat mean?'

'Means this guy's one rich sonuvabitch.' *Or maybe was*, Iris corrected herself. There was always the chance that he was dead already. Either way, it took a lot of money, and the power that went with it, to keep one's personal information out of the LAPD databanks. Tyrell Corporation power? Iris slowly nodded. The odds were in favor of it.

'Facial scan,' said Iris. 'Block and grid, left profile, left three-quarters, full face, right three-quarters, right profile. Index all possible recognition points for brute-force trawl—'

'Excuse me.' The surresper interrupted Iris's orders. 'But brute-force ID trawling was made illegal by United Nations Justice Court administrative decree code MMH, executive number 13–4583, reaffirmed on appeal number 565–8891. Adopted as procedure standard by Los Angeles Police Department, command level alpha-alpha-zero-point-twelve.'

'Wow.' Strings of numbers always impressed the chat. 'What's *that* mean?'

'Figure it out,' Iris answered irritably. She spoke louder, so the surresper would be sure to hear. 'Override on personal authority. Execute command as given.'

'Must advise: all override instructions are reported to departmental supervisor.'

As if I didn't know that. Iris felt a thin smile show on her face. The surresper would fink on her, she knew already; it was wired straight to the LAPD switchboard. Which meant that a piece of paper with her name on it somewhere would land on her boss Meyer's desk. He could either round-file it, or keep it handy for some blackmail possibilities against her. She didn't care which; nobody worked in the blade runner division for very long without racking up a fat file folder of black marks.

'Proceed,' instructed Iris.

A job like that would take some time, not in the scanning of the image's face, but in cranking through the match-up with the details of any person, human or replicant, outside the regulation ID bank. With the chat tagging behind her, Iris headed for the apartment's kitchen module to scrounge a cup of something warm. The illusory room's wood paneling had been laid over the door; she walked through the optical data of the burnished woodgrain, not even blinking as the

37

sensory feed passed across her face. The chat had to pluck up its courage and dive through, eyes closed. Tucked into a ball, it rolled against the kitchen module's wall, then scrambled onto the solitary chair at the fold-down table.

She'd remembered to bring her ring of swipe cards with her; she needed them to get into the freezer compartment of the wall fridge. *This is going to be a tough one* – that conviction had come over her, even before the surresper had come up blank on the regulation ID process. *Better fortify myself.* When the LEDs of the freezer locks had blinked to green, Iris opened it and took out the unmarked cylinder of black-market coffee. It wasn't the caffeine levels, way above what the UN's health police allowed, that she wanted so much as the reaffirmed knowledge that she had pulled off tough jobs in the past, and had raked in enough bounties that she could afford a pricey, sold-by-the-gram luxury like this.

'Can I have some?' The chat perched on the back of the chair, its eyes widened into a hopeful expression. 'Please?'

'Sure.' A thimbleful was all it took to hop the little construct up more than it already was. Any more than that would blow out the tiny teflon-valved heart in its chest. 'You watch it for me, okay?'

At the sink end of the kitchen module's countertop, Iris carefully defurred and sterilized the interior of her favorite yellow mug, an only slightly chipped antique that read BEANS AND MACHINES – SEATTLE around the side. It'd been a while since she had spent any major relaxing time in the apartment; the last two jobs, the Enesque rep and the one before him, had been practically back to back, with no break between. That was her preferred mode of operating, to stay on the hunt as long as possible, pushing the fatigue barrier away with pure strength of will. But it did tend to shoot the crap out of her housekeeping; entropy moved into the place during her extended absences, and silted the corners with gray, ageless dust.

As her hands busied themselves in the sink, Iris looked into the tiny mirror, spattered with minute dots of toothpaste and hazed with steam, that she'd hung there when she'd first moved in. She wiped it clear with her sleeve and leaned closer to her image, studying it as she had the one in the illusory room summoned by the surresper.

'Lookin' good,' Iris whispered to herself. The city hadn't crept under her skin yet, loosening the threadlike sinews that connected her flesh to the bones beneath. *Still young and hard.* She smiled and nodded. Most people in LA looked as if they had been chewed on by invisible teeth, then spat out, more or less in one piece. Even street punks and trench cases, whole tribes younger than her, and the glossy retro strippers down in the clubs – under the subdermal thin-film silicone frosting of both the real females and the artful transies, the rot had nearly always set in; you could see it in their eyes. This town aged people, as though there were an epidemic of Methuselah Syndrome rolling down the streets; it was a wonder that anyone, human or otherwise, had more than a four-year lifespan.

Maybe I'll get out, thought Iris. *Before I'm that way, too.*

She carried the coffee back into the apartment's front room, and into the illusory chamber that filled it for the time being. 'Results?'

'Process terminated,' replied the surresper's overly calm voice, 'when exact match found. Male subject in view is identified as one Doctor Eldon Tyrell.'

Iris managed to find the arm of the recliner and sat down on it. 'Details?' As she sipped at the cup, the chat wandered from the kitchen module, paws wiping its ration of coffee from the round cheeks of its face.

'Former CEO of Tyrell Corporation. Now deceased.'

She wasn't surprised. 'Mode of death?'

'Homicide.' The word as uninflected by emotion as any other in the surresper's vocabulary. 'Perp conclusively identified as one Roy Batty, escaped replicant. Perp retired.'

Cop talk. Humans were murdered, but replicants were retired. Both were equally dead afterwards. Iris wondered which blade runner had gotten the bounty for this Batty job. *Must've been a tough one*, she figured. If the replicant had managed to penetrate the security systems of a major outfit like the Tyrell Corporation, he would've had to have been smarter – and more dangerous – than the average escapee. *Whoever took him down*, thought Iris, *should've gotten a bonus*. When she got some free time – hardly likely – she'd have to root around in the department records and find out which one of her colleagues it had been.

So the owl had very likely belonged to Dr Tyrell; a personal pet, funded as a corporate write-off, like the high-ceilinged room's other expensive furnishings, no doubt. Typical exec perk. But if the good doctor was dead, then it wasn't him wanting the owl back. Somebody else at the Tyrell Corporation, maybe; they could probably sell off the bird and make enough to meet the company's payroll for a couple of weeks. But it was her understanding that the Tyrell Corporation was as dead as the doctor who had run it. So there wouldn't be anybody left at the company who'd want to get such a valuable asset back into its possession. Which meant that some third party knew about the creature, knew what it was worth, and naturally wanted to grab it. But if they were using official police channels to track the owl down, instead of going through some private operation, they must have some powerful political connections. *Not*, figured Iris, *the kind of people you want to screw around with.*

The job was getting uglier, and more interesting, at the same time. Which must have been why her boss Meyer had given it to her, rather than some lesser-skilled blade runner. The feeling grew larger inside her gut that the missing owl had more importance than just its money value to black-market real animal dealers and collectors. Which also meant that the process of tracking it down might have some deeper and darker risks attached to it; if somebody as protected as the owl's original owner, the late Dr Eldon Tyrell, could get himself iced, then the chances were good that the creature was flying around out there in the night, over some dangerous territory.

Cool, thought Iris, nodding to herself. Maybe Meyer really was her pal, after all. This wasn't some hoke job that he'd shuffled off onto her; it was starting to smell like something much bigger. Which meant that there'd be all the more bonus points for her, maybe not in the form of hard cash money, but in recognition from both the higher-ups in the department and from the invisible, string-pulling forces that they served – *if* she pulled it off.

'Don't worry.' She turned her thin smile toward the frozen image of the owl sitting on its perch, circular yellow gaze as avid as before. 'I'll find you, all right. You can count on it.'

The chat echoed her self-confidence pump, bobbing itself up and down in a corner of the room. 'Yeah! You can do it! Know you can!'

Iris ignored the chat. 'Resume action,' she instructed the surresper. 'Normal speed.'

Dr Eldon Tyrell's resurrected image, with its unpleasant partial smile, passed by Iris. She watched as the image carried the silver bowl in its hands over to the antique writing desk, and set it down. The image looked over its shoulder, still smiling, toward the owl on its perch. For a moment, a tiny spark of something close to recognition passed between the two images, as though each saw in the other's magnified eyes its own reflection.

The man's image spoke aloud. 'Hungry?' The recorded voice struck Iris as being as mockingly cruel as the smile on Tyrell's face.

Iris had a good idea of what was going to happen next. *Feeding time.*

She wasn't disappointed. An artificial owl could be kept going on all sorts of things, including a fresh set of batteries inserted under some feathered hatch between its wings. But a living one had a predator's appetite, for other, smaller living things. She didn't need the surresper's encyclopedic function to tell her that. It was the way of the world, this one or any other.

She saw the image of the owl rising higher on its perch, spreading its broad wings partway open, then settling them capelike around itself again. The aroused hunger was apparent.

That's an expensive meal, thought Iris; she watched as Tyrell's image lifted a white rat by its pink, hairless tail from the silver bowl. The gray and brown vermin that scuttled through the strata of LA's rubbish-filled alleys weren't worth much, but one like that, a real one, could command a good price among the dealers at the *souk*. The white rat was bent into a soft C shape by its pink feet having been bound together by a tight circle of what looked to be nylon thread. A high-pitched, terrified and terrifying squeal sounded in both the illusory room and Iris's surrounding apartment as the dangling creature wriggled and jerked like a hectic, spring-driven toy.

'Is this what you want? Hm?' Tyrell lifted the struggling white rat higher. The owl on the other side of the paneled room responded by leaning hungrily forward on its perch, a stroke of its outfurled wings maintaining its balance.

I don't need to see this, thought Iris.

With a snip of a tiny pair of scissors from the writing desk's top drawer, the image of Dr Tyrell cut the circlet of thread around the white rat's feet. Its frantic gyrations turned wilder, almost pulling the hairless tail from Tyrell's grasp.

With a flick of his hand, Tyrell tossed the white rat into the center of the room. The rat's image landed a few inches away from the tips of Iris's boots and froze in place, its bright red beadlike eyes fastened on what it had spotted across the illusory space.

'Run,' Iris spoke aloud, though she knew it would do no good. 'Under the desk.' What she was watching happen had already happened. 'It won't catch you there.' And what had happened couldn't be changed.

She turned her own gaze, hearing the audible displacement of air as the owl's image spread its great wings and leapt from its perch. The owl appeared to fill the center of the room, with no magnification necessary from the surresper that had summoned it into being. Its claws spread apart, into the perfect machinery of capture and death. Beneath the owl's swift shadow, the white rat crouched down, too far into the paralysis of fear to do otherwise.

'Okay, stop.' Iris closed her eyes. 'I mean, freeze. Freeze action.' She didn't open them as she gave more instructions to the surresper. 'Search for other discrete sequences, time separate from current display.'

The apartment was silent for a moment, as the surresper probed the rest of the data she had fed into its soft mouth. 'Found,' it announced at last. 'One sequence. Commence playback?'

'Sure.' Whatever it was, it couldn't be worse than the coldly smiling Dr Eldon Tyrell. 'Commence.'

Another illusory room snapped into perceived existence, laid over the more solid walls of Iris's apartment. It looked just as luxurious, dipped in the Tyrell Corporation's endless well of money. The image of a man stood waiting in the center of the room; younger than Tyrell, as just about anybody living would be. A long, shabby-looking coat, that he'd probably slept in on more than one occasion, dark hair cropped close, almost to a buzz coat, utilitarian and unfussed with; not bad-looking, Iris judged, with a small, faded scar on one side of his chin, and intense, angry eyes. His disgruntled, world-sick expression made him appear harder and more mean-spirited than he really was. Iris smiled to herself, spotting the thinness of the man's tough-guy façade. *Scratch a cynic*, she thought, *and wound a romantic*. She didn't bleed that particular way, herself.

She could see where it would've been a problem for this guy, whoever he was or had been. The image standing in the center of the newly summoned illusory room was obviously a cop; even without spotting the bulge of his high-calibered gun under his coat, Iris had been sure of that much. And a cop with soft notions about the world, about what could and couldn't be expected in it, was already bound hand and foot to the breaking arc of the Wambaugh Curve. This one was already burnt out; even with only the optical sensory data, and no actual physical presence to work from, Iris could just about smell it on him. *Must've reached his limit*. Iris peered closer at the man's image, as though she were a coroner examining a specimen stood upright on a vertical slab. *But kept going, anyway*. She frowned; it usually took a lot of pressure to get some curve casualty like this out on the job again. *Somebody in the department put the screws to him.* Who?

'Freeze image,' Iris instructed the surresper. 'ID male subject in immediate view.'

The answer was in the open-access files, coming back at her within milliseconds. 'Last name of male subject,' the surresper spoke flatly, 'is Deckard. First name, Rick.'

'LAPD?'

'Affirmative. Male subject, Deckard, Rick, last known employment with Los Angeles Police Department.'

Last known? Something had happened to the poor bastard. Things usually did, when a burnt-out case didn't care what happened to him. 'What division?'

'Male subject, Deckard, Rick – attached to replicant escapee, detection and interception.'

Iris hadn't been expecting that. 'This guy's a blade runner?'

'Slang designate recognized for indicated departmental division.' The surresper's vocabulary parsing functions stepped through the rest of their logic. 'Thus, affirmative.'

Thought I knew them all. Iris put the tip of her forefinger to her lips, mulling over this revelation. She was familiar with all the currently active blade runners, inasmuch as they represented the competition she needed to stay on top of. And the inactives, the dead or no longer functional – either burn-outs or those who had managed to get themselves safely promoted or transferred out of danger, usually in the form of sticking the barrels of their own guns into their mouths – were in her mental database as well. Or so she had thought. But this Deckard person was an unknown, a blank in that record. Which meant that she had either overlooked him somehow – she immediately dismissed that possibility – or something else had happened to him, a data erasure of some kind. And it had happened at the division level, figured Iris, instead of farther up; if the deliberate hole in the data had been created by a departmental action, by the real and spooky powers above her boss Meyer, then they would have taken out this Deckard's regulation profile as well, instead of leaving his name and divisional affiliation behind to ID him with.

'Interesting,' mused Iris aloud. 'Very . . .'

'What is?' The chat, now stationed by her ankles, looked up at her.

'The only thing more curious than a hole, where something should be, is a *partial* hole. You know?' She smiled down at the chat. 'If

43

somebody's got the power to remove it, they should have the power to remove it all the way, without leaving little pieces behind. And if they *want* to remove it in the first place, why wouldn't they want to remove it all?'

'Dunno.' The chat shook its head. 'Cuddle?'

'Later. I'm still working.' The tingling, subdermal numbness in her fingertips had already ebbed away, along with whatever woozy endorphins had been produced by handling the chat. That was fine by Iris: figuring out a new assignment's intricacies, sniffing the trail of the tiny and fragmentary data and where they led to, gave a better high.

This Deckard thing . . .

She had the sense, down in the base of her gut, that it was important. Though what a partially deleted blade runner could have to do with tracking down an escaped pet owl, she didn't have a clue on yet.

'Resume playback.'

The owl showed up again, in the surresper's current discrete sequence. Only for a moment, sitting on a different metal perch, but with the same alert and round, golden eyes, scanning the territory in front of it. Which this time included the image of a woman coming into the illusory room. She looked even colder and harder than the blade runner Deckard, though she was obviously younger and, by objective standards, prettier. The woman looked as if she had been dipped in money as well, gilded by its transforming power into another piece of the Tyrell Corporation's expensive furnishings. Her dark hair was done up in some kind of retro fashion, like the brittly unpleasant rich girl in an ancient black and white movie; the image's makeup had the over-precise, controlled sexuality that Iris associated with virgins and mental patients. Iris shook her head and looked away, giving in to her own deep, instinctive dislike of the young woman, without bothering to figure out what about her had triggered such a quick aversive reaction. *Maybe she reminded me of somebody . . .*

In the illusory room, in the surresper's brief snippet of reconstructed past, the two images exchanged a few words – and then it was over. 'Sequence terminus,' announced the machine.

'That's it?'

'Affirmative.' The circuitry inside the surresper didn't care, one way or the other. 'Loaded data contains two chron sequences, optical and auditory representation. Viewing of first sequence aborted before terminus, upon command; second sequence played through.'

Not much to go on, grumped Iris to herself. There had been only a quick glimpse of the owl, looking exactly as it had in the other sequence, and a few words exchanged between the images of the woman and the cop named Deckard. She had barely paid attention to what the two had said; she'd been paying attention to the owl, over at the side of the reconstructed space. The bit had been so brief and uninformative that Iris had to wonder why Meyer had included it in the first place.

'Play it again,' suggested the chat, sensitive to her mood.

This time, she listened to what the two images said.

Do you like our owl? That was the first thing the woman said to Deckard, as she'd walked into the room and caught him looking at it. The woman's use of the word 'our' confirmed what Iris had already surmised: the owl belonged to the Tyrell Corporation itself.

It's artificial? Deckard had asked an obvious, and logical, question in return. Owls of any kind weren't seen every day.

Of course –

'Freeze sequence,' Iris instructed the surresper. Now that she'd heard it correctly, it didn't make any sense. 'Back five seconds, resume sequence action.'

The woman's image said it again, in her cold, unemotional tone: *Of course.*

Meaning that the owl was artificial, as Deckard had asked. Or that the woman had believed, at that time, that it was.

Iris listened to the rest of the image's dialogue.

Must be expensive. Deckard again.

Very, said the woman's image.

Iris halted the surresper's playback once more. The words, these in addition to the others, made even less sense than they had before. She stepped closer to the woman's frozen image, studying it, trying to figure out if that one word had been either a deliberate lie or a simple mistake. An artificial owl of this quality would have been expensive, all right, but not enough to brag about. Larger and more complicated avian simulacra, emus and ostriches and the like, even down to nanotech-stuffed hummingbirds, could be obtained easily enough, at the *souk* in the center of LA. A noodle stand could afford a mascot like that; Iris herself patronized one down the street that had a brace of artificial fresh-water arawanas swimming in a tank behind the cash

45

register; those fish had never been anywhere near the Amazon where their biological prototypes had been sourced. Whereas a genuine living owl, sitting on a perch at company headquarters, would have really been something for a Tyrell Corporation representative to brag so haughtily about; that kind of expenditure, on top of the already lavishly appointed surroundings, would have indicated a whole other level of wealth and power.

'Thinking?' The chat tapped at her shin with one of its tiny paws.

She nodded. ''Tis a mystery.' Her words were followed by a shrug. 'But that's the kind of thing I get paid to figure out.'

There was one more scrap of information to be gotten out of the second discrete sequence on the surresper. At the very end of the bit, the image of the woman spoke her name. Iris played it back, to make sure she got it right.

I'm Rachael.

That was what the woman had told the cop named Deckard. Iris mentally filed the info away, and forgot about it for the time being. She had more important things to worry about right now, such as where this missing owl had gotten to. This woman in the data she'd fed to the surresper, Rachael whoever, had probably been caught up in the collapse of the Tyrell Corporation, along with everybody else who had been connected to the replicant-manufacturing company. Not a big deal – at least that part wasn't.

'Go back to the first discrete sequence.' The room with the cop named Deckard and the snotty young woman disappeared, replaced by the other illusory one that held the owl and the late Dr Eldon Tyrell. With his silver bowl on the antique writing desk, and the white rat he had tossed onto the center of the room's intricately loomed Oriental rug . . .

This time, Iris watched the sequence all the way through. The owl did what its own biological nature had programmed it to do. *The claws that catch*, Iris found herself thinking, remembering some scrap of a nonsense poem. It wasn't nonsense to the white rat, whose programming was to die.

The image of the owl flapped to its perch, where it bloodily disassembled its meal. Still coldly smiling, the image of Dr Tyrell watched, then picked up the empty silver bowl and carried it away, back into the darkness from which it had emerged.

'Sequence complete,' announced the surresper.

Whatever, thought Iris. 'Terminate session.'

The illusory room, with its candlelit, cavernous spaces and glossy, expensive wood paneling disappeared, restoring Iris's own, smaller apartment.

The neon had died.

It happened sometimes. Iris found herself in darkness, relieved only by the horizontal slots of blueish streetlight coming in through the apartment's small shuttered and barred windows. The chat was freaked by the sudden gloom, and clung to her ankle, shivering. The neon's power source, usually a parasitic tap on a main feeder circuit, had probably gotten over-extended and had snapped at some critical corner junction. That left only the pencil-thin glass tubes covering the walls and nearly every other hard surface, to be broken up and swept away, ghost-like vacated letters and pictographs.

I'll just clear off the bed, thought Iris. If she woke up surrounded by shards and needles of broken glass, it wouldn't be the first time.

'Residual data left,' announced the surresper. 'From encyclopedic function.'

At the bedroom door, still hobbled by the frightened chat, Iris glanced back at the machine. 'All right,' she said. 'Give it to me.'

'"Large, varies in color, nearly white when found in Arctic conditions, mottled dark gray and brown otherwise . . ."'

'I already heard that bit.' Iris shook her head. 'So it's a bird,' she said disgustedly. 'That's all it is.'

There was more: '"Once thought to possess supernatural powers, due to ability to see in the dark; solemn, prepossessing aspect gave rise to being considered as symbols of wisdom or occult knowledge." End of data.'

'Even better,' said Iris sourly.

But the surresper had switched itself off, and wasn't listening.

4

The *soukmeisters* were clever bastards.

Gotta hand it to 'em, thought Iris. She stood in the neon-stitched darkness and let herself be buffeted by the jostling crowd around her. The people who ran the marketplace in artificial animals, the shadowy figures who collected the rents on the densely packed stalls and storefronts, had gone to the trouble and expense of making the place smell as if real animals were being bought and sold in it; the zone was interspersed with scent-emitter units protruding from the sewer grates that gave off a cycling olfactory parade of sweaty barnyard odors, moldering grain feed mixed with the riper, nastier tang of unswept fecal droppings. Iris could see that the dealers' customers obviously went for it; the sensory impression filling their nostrils added to the illusion of purchasing a real, biologically living animal, rather than some battery-powered replicant sheathed in fake fur or feathers.

Careful not to step in any of the more realistic props that had been deposited in the street, Iris pushed her way through the crowd toward the open-fronted, double-wide stall with the sizzling neon above that read WINGS OF GOLDEN SMILE. An animated sparrow, twenty times life-size and outlined in glowing blue, flapped its wings through a stuttering, three-step drill, over and over.

'What can I do ya for?' The half-dozen staff behind the stall's counter looked like brothers of a single family, a genetic mélange like any other in LA; this specific one could have been a third-generation cross of Hmong and Vladivoski squareheads. 'How 'bout a canary? It'll sing you to sleep. If that doesn't work for ya' – the lead counter guy winked at her – 'then you and I can make other arrangements.'

'Put it back in your pants, pal.' Iris leaned forward, looking past him and into the depths of the stall. The other staff turned from their workbenches and abacus, regarding her with impassive silence and ink-black pupils as she scanned the wares on the dangling perches and inside the wire cages. Most of their stock consisted of smaller birds, but there was a pair of ravens – bigger than she had expected them to be, hulking like sullen murderers on a rusting steel perch – and even a redtail hawk, staring at her with one glittering yellow eye. So maybe the tout at the edge of the *souk*, who Iris had queried and then tipped with a pre-devaluation titanium quarter, had been right about this being the place for predatory birds. 'I'm looking' – Iris leaned away from the counter guy's *kimchi*-scented breath – 'for an owl.'

'Owl, huh? You mean a regular horned owl or something more exotic, like a winter-plumage snow owl? Doesn't matter.' He turned and shouted over his shoulder to one of the other staff. 'Francesco – c'mere a minute.'

The other man approached, wiping his hands on an oil-stained rag. 'Nice shirt,' he said, indicating Iris's chest. Like the rest of the staff, he was wearing a modified Stetson knock-off and shiny neoprene bondage *lederhosen* that exposed his yellowish and scabby knees. 'I collect Autreys myself. Lariat motif, mainly.'

'Lady wants an owl,' said the first counter guy. 'What's the line on that?'

Francesco nodded slowly. 'Yeah . . . we can do an owl.' His face was longer and sadder than the other staff's. 'It'd have to be a special order, though. We don't keep that kind of body frame in stock.' He pointed his thumb back toward the stall's interior. 'We do mainly the smaller *columbidae* and *psittacidae* – you know, pigeons and parrots. That's what people can afford around here. And maybe a couple of the bigger *accipitridae* – hawks – three or four times a year. For the collector's market. But we can swap around a lot of the basic structural elements on those. An owl, though . . .' He shrugged. 'Different configuration; kinda stacked up vertical, you know what I mean?'

'Right,' said Iris. 'But that's not what I'm talking about. I mean a *real* owl.'

Both men stared at her in silence for a few seconds.

'Lady . . .' The lead counter guy spoke up, shaking his head in disgust. 'If you walked into a Seven-Eleven and asked for a diamond necklace, you might *get* a diamond necklace – but it wouldn't be a real one.' He turned and waved his hand at the stall's stock. 'See these? See how they go chirp chirp, flap their wings and stuff? They're fakes. That's what we *do*.' He turned back to Iris. 'Did you *think* they were real?' He glanced over at his longer-faced colleague. 'Lady thinks we deal in real birds.'

'I understand,' said Iris slowly, emphasizing each syllable, 'that you have, in fact, done so. On occasion. Dealt in real birds. True?'

'Who told you that? One of those putzes out on the street? Tell me which one, point him out, and I'll kick his ass.' The counter guy crossed his arms and scowled. 'Real animals are restricted. Even birds. You can get into a lot of trouble dealing in 'em without a license.' One of his thin eyebrows raised. '*You* got a license?'

'I don't need one.' Her eyes had adjusted further to the gloom inside the stall; she could make out a few more birds tucked away into the corners and on top of a pile of packing crates. 'So nobody's come around lately, offering you a deal on a hot owl?'

'Yeah, right. Who'd have one? Tell me that.'

'You hear of any other dealer in the *souk* who's got one?'

The counter guy turned surlier. 'How would I know?'

Iris decided to take another tack. She reached into her jacket and pulled out the hard-copy photo she'd had the surresper print. 'Ever see this person?'

The counter guy's gaze flicked down for only a second, to the photo of the cop named Deckard, then back up to Iris's face. 'You a cop?'

'What makes you think that?'

'Lady . . . that's what cops *do*. Pull out a picture and ask you if you've ever seen him. Jeez.'

Iris left the photo sitting on the counter, so she could pull something else from inside her jacket.

Both men nodded when they saw the gun in her hand. 'You're a cop, all right,' said the lead counter guy.

She let the gun rest flat on its side, on her palm. She touched the cold black metal with the tip of her other forefinger. 'We could go downtown,' she said, 'to that nice, shiny new station where all the other cops hang out, and talk about this some more. And on the way, I could take you and this into an alley and beat the crap out of you. Or we can talk now. Your choice.'

The counter guy picked up the photo and gazed at it. Iris replaced her gun in its shoulder holster and waited.

'Hey, this is weird. You know what?' The counter guy lowered the photo and smiled at Iris. 'I do remember seeing this guy before. He's some other cop, right?'

Iris said nothing.

The counter guy's gold-capped smile faded. He turned the photo toward his colleague. 'Remember him?'

'Kinda.' Tilting his head to one side, to see the photo better, Francesco scratched at the hinge of his jaw. 'But he didn't come here. I mean, to our shop.' He straightened and pointed to another stall, visible several yards away through the milling crowd. 'He was over there. Asking something about a fish. I dunno what, though.'

'That's right.' The lead counter guy nodded vigorously. He looked relieved. 'Go talk to the fish woman.'

It turned out not to be a fish. At least, not that the cop named Deckard had been looking for. The tiny Asian woman at the artificial fish dealer's stall gave Iris a story about the man in the photo having come around with a scale in a tiny plastic evidence bag; she'd put the scale under her microscope, read off the serial numbers and species reference, and then had pointed him toward one of the storefronts where a fez-wearing, upmarket Arab type, who'd never come any closer to making his *hegira* than the average LA infidel, dealt in the larger herpetoids.

'A snake?' Standing in the Arab's shop, Iris tucked the photo back into her jacket. 'He was asking about a *snake*?'

'Yes; he was.' The Arab dealer kept a handrolled cigarette, filled with ersatz and legal tobacco, cradled in the fingertips of his upside-down hand. One corner of his lip curled with disdain. 'Very unpleasant enquiries they were, too. An *ugly* man; violent and cruel.'

'That was his job,' said Iris. She didn't give a rat's ass about Deckard, but she didn't care for civilians slagging off on cops.

'Nevertheless; if a police officer, he was a servant of the general population, not its master. An honest businessman such as myself naturally resents paying taxes and the expected schedule of bribery only to be abused by such a creature.' The Arab dealer took a deep drag off the *faux* cigarette, then contemplated the blue-gray cloud he expelled a moment later. 'I have heard tell,' he spoke meditatively, 'that the individual in question is dead. As the Prophet might have put it, payback is a bitch.'

'The Prophet can stick it.' A bad mood rose inside Iris, like the polluted tide coming in over the oil-stained beaches to the west of the city. The Arab didn't irritate her so much as the sinking realization that she had come to a dead end, scrabbling around for leads here in the hotly fetid-scented marketplace.

'You don't look well,' said the Arab, with no apparent concern.

The man's cologne, star anise mixed with unnatural flowers, flared Iris's nostrils and left a sour taste on her tongue. As she watched him pick up a foot-long baby coral snake and adjust the action of its flickering tongue with a twelve-power jeweler's loupe and a hair-thin watchmaker's screwdriver, she felt the shop closing tighter against her shoulders, as though one of the artificial anacondas in back had managed to escape and wrap itself around the storefront, squeezing the air out of it.

'No more questions?'

Iris heard the amusement in the Arab's voice, so she didn't need to glance over her shoulder to see his oily smile. She pushed her way out of the shop and back onto the crowded, jostling sidewalk. The tinge of nausea she'd felt at the base of her stomach abated a little as she drew in a deep breath of the rain-scrubbed air.

'You're wasting your time.' Another man's voice came from behind her.

'Think I don't know that?' Iris hadn't recognized the voice; she turned to see whoever it was that had spoken.

She didn't recognize his face, either. A nearly lipless smile slashed a horizontal line across the knife-sharp projection of his facial bones; the angular ridge of his nose and brow gave him as avid and predatory a look as the hawks inside the bird dealers' stall. He must have been waiting for her, out in the rain, for some time; his raven-black hair, cropped to a millimeter buzz, and the shoulders and back of his unbelted duster were soaked wet.

'What *do* you know?' His smile widened.

'Not your name, for one.' Iris didn't return his smile. 'I like to know to whom I'm talking.'

'Must be a cop thing,' said the tall figure. He extended a long-fingered, large-knuckled hand. 'Vogel. And you're Iris Knaught. Just in case you've forgotten.'

The rain, which had diminished to a sulky drizzle when Iris had first arrived at the *souk*, squalled harder now. Through the monsoon downpour, she could see a pair of jumpsuited simul-wranglers using sharp hooksticks to prod a half-completed baby elephant, a flop-eared head and snaking gray trunk fastened to an articulated steel skeleton, safely under cover before the pistons and servos of the exposed machinery got damaged. Iris locked her grip on this Vogel character's forearm and pulled him against the window of the Arab snake dealer's shop, under the minimal protection of its retractable overhead awning. She could already feel a couple of damp rain tendrils trickling under the collar of her leatherite jacket and down her back.

She let go of his arm, like dropping a rat, either real or artificial. 'I don't like,' said Iris flatly, 'people who know more about me than I do about them. Makes me nervous. Like I'm being watched.'

'I imagine so.' Leaning against the security-tempered window glass, Vogel watched his own hands busily and efficiently rolling a cigarette. 'And it just wouldn't *do* to have someone like you get fidgety.' He extended the papers and bindle of artificial tobacco toward Iris, then shrugged and put them away inside his duster when she shook her head. 'Especially with the caliber of that piece you carry around with you. The way you blade runners are so given to firing your arsenal off in public, it's amazing that LA has any population crunch at all.'

'Hilarious.' The artificial tobacco smelled as though one of the more realistic props in the *souk*'s gutters had been scraped up, dried and set on fire. 'But we only do it for a reason.'

'Sure you do.' Vogel flicked a scrap of ash toward the glistening street. 'People – and replicants – can be *so* uncooperative. Especially when you're trying to, um, "retire" them.'

'But not you,' said Iris. Her gaze narrowed as she studied the figure standing beside her. 'Something tells me that you're motivated by some burning desire to be of help to me.'

'You got that right, cupcake.' One side of the man's face was lit in detail by the light spilling from inside the Arab snake dealer's shop; the other side was blue-shadowed by the flickering neon threaded above the *souk*'s stalls. 'I'm the answer to all your prayers.'

'I've heard that from guys before.'

'Really?' Vogel leaned his head back and exhaled more gray smoke. 'Did it work?'

'Not yet.'

'This time, I promise you, it'll be different.' There was no remnant of his smile left as he leaned close to her. 'You really think you can find what you're looking for by just coming around a place like this and asking for it?'

'Depends.' Iris met Vogel's hard gaze with her own. 'But then . . . I know what it is I'm looking for. Do you?'

'Let's not screw around.' His knuckles were lit fiery orange by the cigarette's burn. 'You're looking for an owl.' He raised his eyebrows.

53

'You know? Big kind of a bird. Flies around and pounces on little mice.' He made a grabbing motion with one hand. 'Too bad if that's what you are.'

A chill, colder than the rain, crawled the wrong way up Iris's back. *If he knows what I'm here for*, she thought, *then what else does he know?*

'Yeah, too bad.' Iris nodded slowly. 'Lot of people come around here, looking for owls?'

'You're the only one.' One corner of Vogel's smile returned. 'Everybody else knows better.'

Two possibilities formed themselves in Iris's mind, like the thin rain puddles gathering at her bootsoles. Either this person, whoever he was, had spotted her when she'd first arrived at the *souk*, and had been following her around, asking the stallkeepers questions about the questions she'd been asking – and that was how he'd found out about her owl inquiries – or he'd known about this particular quest before she'd even got here. *Which would mean,* figured Iris, *that he's in on the loop, way more than I am.* Inasmuch as this Vogel knew all – or enough – about her and what she was doing, whereas she didn't know jack about him.

Either one of those possibilities didn't please her. But since the latter of the two was the worse, it was good practice to assume it was the case. And then do something about it.

'We need to talk,' said Iris. 'In private.'

'Who's listening in around here?' Amused, Vogel glanced at the crowded street and the narrower passageways between the stalls. A pair of Latter-Day Berbers, their mouths and aquiline noses swathed with indigo-dyed cotton, herded a small flock of replicated black-faced ewes toward a gated pen. 'These people have got their own business to take care of. They're not interested in yours.'

'Nevertheless.' She pointed with her thumb toward an unlit alley tucked behind the Arab's shop. 'Just to make me comfortable, all right?'

'Sure.' Vogel followed her into the alley. 'Whatever you want—'

His words were cut off by the air being violently expelled from his lungs, the result of Iris's small but rock-hard fist landing in his gut. He doubled over, far enough that Iris could grab the back of his head with both hands and smash his face against one upraised knee.

Iris threw him back up against the alley's damp brick wall, with enough force that he stayed there instead of slumping to the debris-littered ground.

'You *are* . . . a full-service cop . . .' Vogel's expression turned into a red sneer as he wiped the blood from his mouth and nose onto the palm of one hand. 'Some people pay extra for this kind of treatment.'

'Then you're getting a real bargain.' Iris reached up and pushed the man's shoulders against the wall. 'Because I've got more of it.' Rain trickled down her exposed wrists and along the inside of her jacket sleeves. 'So like I said. Let's talk.'

'About owls?' Vogel's sneer, dripping red, curled tighter. 'Buy a book.'

Her hands turned into fists, locked on the zippered front of his coveralls. She turned on her heel, yanking him away from the wall and sending him skidding on one shoulder across the wet paving. Before Vogel could shake off his stun, Iris had reached down and dragged him to his feet again.

'Yeah,' she said. 'Let's talk birds.' She thumped his spine against the wall opposite from where they had started. 'Let's talk about this one owl in particular. Former property of the Tyrell Corporation. They named it "Scrappy", God knows why; it's not that cute.' Another thump, this time with the back of his head against the bricks. 'What do you know about it? Other than that I'm looking for it.'

'I know lots, sweetheart.' Vogel rubbed more blood off his angular chin. 'Lot of stuff you'd never find out in a million years, wandering around the *souk* asking stupid questions. The kind of thing you're looking for isn't exactly the everyday merchandise they deal in here.'

'It was worth a shot,' grumped Iris. 'Where the hell else was I supposed to go?'

'Exactly my point.' Vogel spat a red wad onto the ground, then reached into his mouth and tested a wobbly tooth with the ball of his thumb. '*You don't know where to go*. Haven't even started, and already you're out of your league.'

If she'd wanted to, she could've finished taking him apart, disassembling him like a meat-filled store dummy. Or a faster method: when she had first slammed him against the wall, she'd done a quick frisk while he'd been dazed almost unconscious, and had found that he wasn't carrying any armaments, licensed or otherwise. She could take her own cannon out of the holster inside her jacket, brace its snout against his forehead and put him to sleep for good. 'Interference with official police business' didn't even merit paper-work down at the police station; the department's clean-up squad wouldn't list it as a reportable death, only as cartridge expenditure.

55

And at the same time, she felt a dark-blue thread of fear underneath her heart. *He's right*, thought Iris. *I don't know.* Whatever level of confidence she had going for her when she was running down an escaped replicant, whether it was on some crumbling building ledge twenty stories above the teeming LA streets, or in that fractional moment of stopped time when she had to get her gun up, aimed and fired before the rep could squeeze his finger around the trigger of the weapon in his hand – that had been chilled and diminished now, confronted by the unknown. Her secret dread: not knowing what to do next. Hunting down replicants was simple compared to finding an owl, a real one, in a city where everything was fake.

'That's why you need me.' Vogel's words broke into her gloomy thoughts. 'I'm here to help you.'

Iris refocused on him; the center of his thin smile was still tinged with red. 'Meyer sent you?'

'Meyer?' Vogel shook his head in disgust. 'That putz? He's out of the loop, sweetheart. He can get you *into* trouble, but he can't get you out of it. Not the way I can.'

This sucks, thought Iris. She hadn't become a runner, gone through the grueling training involved, both from the department and in the cold, precise ordering of her mind, just so she could wind up under somebody else's control. Crap coming down the division's chain of command, from the shadowy ones on top and then handed out by Meyer to her and the rest of her colleagues, was something she'd been able to get used to. That chain was something she might be able to climb one day, and in the meantime the crap-to-gold ratio was weighted on the side of getting to do what she wanted. Which was to hunt escaped replicants, and not some frickin' bird. And especially not under the thumb of some civilian she could take apart in two seconds.

'You know –' Iris spoke slowly and gave him a practised hard stare. 'If you've got information I need, I've got ways of getting it out of you.'

Vogel returned the stare without flinching. 'No, you don't. Not this time. Not with me.'

This was a steel needle, a tiny cold element at the center of his eyes, tinged blue by the flickering neon light that had worked its way down the alley. Iris recognized the bit, not real metal but something just as hard and sharp; she'd seen it in the mirror, in her own eyes. So she knew he was telling the truth. She wouldn't be able to get it out of him.

'All right,' said Iris. 'You win.' She figured that if it didn't work out, she could hand him major payback, painful and final, later on. And then they'd be done, like other, even briefer relationships she'd had in the past. 'So talk.'

Another shake of the head. 'Not here.'

'*Now* you've got privacy concerns?'

'Like you said: it's a matter of getting comfortable.' Vogel dabbed another spot of blood away from his mouth, using a folded handkerchief he'd dug from the pocket of his duster. He held the red-stained cloth toward her, as though demonstrating stigmata. 'Now I got the moral right to insist on *my* turf. Plus I've got something to show you. So if you're done showing off your testosterone, let's go.' He turned and headed toward the mouth of the alley, then glanced over his shoulder at her. 'Coming or not?'

Iris could see past him, to the *souk*'s throng of dealers and merchandise. They all looked real; the trick was in figuring out which ones weren't.

'I'm with you,' said Iris, and started walking.

Intercut

'That was some good footage.' The remote camera operator nodded in appreciation. He leaned back in the swivel chair, so he could see more of the monitor screens arrayed in front of him. 'Got some good action off her.'

Somebody else was looking at the monitors; the camera operator had to swing his chair out of the way of the director, balancing himself with his hands against the edge of the control board. The director brought his face close to the icy glow of the screens, as though he wanted to see through the rows of pixels and into the darkness behind them.

'I don't know . . .' The director's face, tending toward jowly at the best of times, now grew even heavier with the weight of his thoughts. He reached out one broad-fingered hand and rolled the tracking ball in the center of the board; the monitor with the red ACTIVE indicator lit up above the screen, showing the backs of the female blade runner and the taller man walking beside her, filled with a closer angle on their images. The brighter, more lurid lights of the replicant-animal *souk* spilled past them. 'The details . . . you really gotta sweat the details . . .'

'You mean that?' One of the camera operator's fingernails tapped at the monitor's glass. The lower left corner of the screen's image had a splotch of blackish red on it, from where the force of the female blade runner's fist had sent a spattered drop of blood flying onto the hidden lens. 'We've got plenty of area and character texture that we can map and dub in. We can track the cover-fill to match the other cameras. It'll look just like the real thing.' He shrugged. 'Or as much as anything does, these days.'

'That's not what I'm worried about,' said the director. He chewed on the knuckle of one hand, while he waved the other dismissively at the blot on the screen. 'What the hell? Might as well leave that in. It's a nice effect; adds to the impression of realism. The audience will think we planned it that way. So it's better than real, even if that's all

58

it is. Real, I mean.' He punched up another camera, hidden at the edge of the alley's wall; another screen in the stacked ranks of monitors showed the female blade runner and her new companion heading out of the *souk*, shoving their way through the crowd and the phony animals. The angle caught a bit of a three-quarters profile as she walked by the unnoticed camera. She would have been pretty enough – in a coldly near-perfect way – to have starred in some other, more obviously fictional, kind of drama if she had occasionally smiled. But the director knew that would have spoiled the particular effect he was going for. 'What concerns me is the loss of control. That's the worst.'

'What do you mean?' The camera operator glanced over at him. 'Everything *is* under control.' He gestured at the monitor screens. 'There's nothing that can happen we're not going to get tape on.'

'Don't be an idiot. That's not the problem.' The director slowly shook his head. 'We're not using digitized actors here. Those lucasoids will do whatever you want, whatever you program them to do. That's their nature. But not these guys.' He gestured again at the screen. 'Especially *her*. We've introduced an uncontrolled element into our mix – and not only uncontrolled: *unforeseeable*. And that can be disastrous. Believe me, I'd know; I've worked this blade runner stuff before. Very sticky. And dangerous; people can get hurt. Bad hurt, as in dead.'

'Let's get rid of her, then.' The camera operator's shoulders raised in a shrug. 'We can do without her. Like you said, digitized actors are a lot more obedient. And let's face it' – his smile looked both sick and ugly – 'nobody will miss her. And we are in that kind of territory where we can get her ass iced pretty quickly. It's one of the simpler production problems.'

'Thanks for the advice. Now shut up.' The director's words turned vehement. 'You don't even have a frickin' clue about what we're doing here. This is *not* your usual production.'

'Whatever.' Obviously miffed, the camera operator folded his arms across his chest. 'You want to jerk around with real stuff, instead of taking the easy and better route? Not my problem. You're the boss.'

'That's right.' The director let his gaze wander across the myriad screens, a wall of images from the various camera feeds scattered around LA. 'Like God in His domain . . .' He reached out and placed his wide fingertips on the glass separating him from the images of the female cop and her new companion, pushing their way through the anonymous crowds. 'I call the shots.'

The camera operator raised an eyebrow as he glanced sidelong at the figure beside him, but said nothing. This job, he might have spoken aloud, was no worse than any other.

Just different.

5

A vast, oblivious deity seemed to smile down at them from above.

They weren't far from where the remnants of the escaped replicant Enesque had been scraped from the sidewalk. Iris could recognize the surrounding buildings from recently imprinted memory. The artificially generated cloud, lower than the darker and stormier ones above, remained clinging halfway up the towers, as though it had hissed steamlike out of the retrofitted ductwork. Looming overhead, as she and Vogel rounded one building's corner, was the geisha's immense image, smiling as mysteriously as before, daintily placing the tiny pill in her mouth, lips as red as her lacquered nails. The gesture had always struck Iris as vaguely sacramental, a sinister communion.

'You see? Lot less crowded around here.' Leading the way, Vogel glanced over his shoulder at Iris, his own smile less pleasant than that of the Asian woman above. 'Back at the *souk* you can hardly breathe. Not that you'd particularly *want* to.'

She had noticed the density of human bodies starting to thin out as they'd passed by the exact building where she'd had her final, elevated tussle with Enesque. Coming around to the opposite side of the building, the sidewalks were practically deserted. 'What's the deal?'

'Superstitious dread,' answered Vogel. He kept walking, hands in the pockets of his duster and shoulders hunched forward, as though leaning into a wind. 'That's a very powerful motivator for a lot of street types. They don't have the same kind of keen, logical, *scientific* minds that you and I do. So when something big happens in a specific place, an event with spooky overtones, they tend to get their fear and reverence impulses mixed up, and give the whole zone a wide berth. Like a reverse pilgrimage: the place is holy, so you *don't* go there.'

'What was so big that happened around here?' Iris didn't figure it could have been anything to do with her tracking down and retiring the replicant Enesque. That was too much of a business-as-usual event for anyone to get excited about it.

'See for yourself.' Vogel stopped at the corner of the next building and pointed ahead.

Iris caught up with him and looked where he was pointing. An open space stretched out among the buildings; not as big as the *souk*, but large enough to contain an impressive pile of wreckage. Curved steel girders, interconnected into a crumpled framework, darkened with both rust and ashy scorch marks, had gouged their way through the street's asphalt and concrete, drawing jagged trenches into the hidden soil meters beneath. Scraps of tattered metallic cloth fluttered from the metal, more like unraveling bandages than flags.

'Oh.' Iris had a notion of what the wreckage represented, what it had been before the crash. 'It's the blimp.' The fragments of cloth sheathing had been the tip-off, along with the spiky antennae that could be seen protruding from junction points on the steel frame. Underneath the limited spectra of the widely spaced mercury-vapor streetlamps, glass shards glittered jewellike on the ground, from the broken lenses of the undercarriage's swiveling searchlights. 'This is where it came down.'

'Correction. This is where it was *brought* down.' With one raised fingertip, Vogel traced a quick diagonal slash through the air. 'By the rep-symps.' He glanced inquiringly at her. 'Savvy the word?'

'Get real. This is stuff I got in basic training. You're talking replicant sympathizers.'

'Very good,' said Vogel. 'Glad to see you're up to speed on these things. I wasn't sure you would be, since we're talking history rather than current affairs. Nobody's seen a lot of the rep-symp groups recently.'

'Maybe they wised up.' Iris gave a shrug. 'Maybe the penny finally dropped for them, that replicants aren't anything to be sympathetic about.'

'Maybe.' Vogel slowly nodded. 'Or maybe somebody wised them up. Did their thinking for them, in a terminal way. So they wouldn't be bothering anyone else with their crazy ideas. Get what I mean?'

'If anybody iced those solid citizens, it wasn't the blade runner division. We've got more important things to take care of. Like the escaped replicants this crowd was so nuts about. Not that they accomplished anything on the replicants' behalf.'

'That's the official line, huh?' Vogel smiled indulgently at her. 'The rep-symps were just nuisances? Maybe so, but you gotta admit, some of 'em did a good trade at that sort of thing. Quite a spectacle when they brought down this UN advertising blimp. It'd been cruising around above LA for years, so long that when it crashed it had pretty much become a regular part of the urban landscape.'

'Sorry I missed the fireworks.'

Vogel kept smiling. 'There'll be more. Come on.'

He led the way, out from the relative shelter that the buildings' exterior had provided. The rains had picked up again, the monsoon liquefying above the entire Los Angeles basin. With her hair plastered against her skull and the back of her neck, Iris sloshed across the poorly drained asphalt behind Vogel. Approaching the blimp's wreckage produced a chill under her skin several degrees lower than the water seeping through her jacket's seams. It looked less like some corrosion-ravaged techno-artifact than a ruined, Gaudiesque cathedral wrapped in night shadows, the glaring streetlamps substituting for the appropriate cloud-streaked moonlight. Its angular net of shadows fell across Iris as she stopped and looked up the framework's elliptic curve. The crossing lines were like a sketch of a cage, superimposed upon her own elongated silhouette.

'Come on in.' Vogel had used some of the crumpled framework's lower crossbars, the ones that had cut angled trenches through the street's asphalt, as a rough ladder to the dead blimp's midsection. He lifted a flap of the metallic fabric and gestured to the darkness inside. 'It's cozy. You'll like it.'

Both statements were inaccurate. When Iris had climbed up after him, then down into the blimp's partially collapsed abdomen, she found that *cozy* translated to *claustrophobic*. 'Like being swallowed by a whale,' she said aloud.

'Not that bad.' Using a vintage World War II military-issue Zippo, Vogel started setting candles alight; fastened by their stalactite-like drippings, the wax tapers were studded all over the metal ribs surrounding him and Iris. The flickering ambient light they provided slowly increased as Vogel moved around the ramshackle space, bearing the tiny flame in one hand. 'I call it home.'

'Charming.' With her fingertips, Iris tested the curved horizontal rib behind her back; its edge was as sharp as a honed knife. Falling asleep here would be like nesting among razorblades. 'You must get interesting visitors.'

'You're the first.' Vogel flicked off the Zippo's flame and restored the small metal rectangle to his pocket. 'I'm not by nature a sociable creature.'

'I'm flattered.' Iris supposed she and Vogel had at least that much in common. She looked up to the tentlike vault of the space. Someone, probably Vogel himself, had stitched together enough of the blimp's tattered sheath remnants to shelter this small area from the weather. The rain drummed against the metallic fabric, then gathered in its folds and valleys, forming thick rivulets that sluiced along the wind-billowed sides. In the massed, yellowish candlelight, the effect was primitive and cavelike, as though this small pocket of LA had devolved even further to archaic times. 'But don't think you have to go to any special effort.'

'For you, sweetheart, it's no trouble.' Vogel tugged at a section of the fabric, draped over some large object beneath. 'God knows I want you to be happy.'

'What's this?' With the fabric removed and piled on the sagging floor, the object was revealed as a broken section of wall, extending farther than Vogel's height and covered with a regular pattern of minute, translucent bumps.

'Section of the advertising panel that used to be on the exterior of the blimp. Back when it was a going concern, pre-crash, the UN's off-planet emigration program used it to bombard the citizenry with all those lovely images of what life is like out in the far colonies. Along with that unctuous sincere voice spieling out those promises: *A chance to begin anew*, yack yack. Probably worth bringing this puppy down just to get rid of that particular bit of urban pollution. Life's hard enough in LA without being constantly told about how much better it's supposed to be somewhere else.'

'Suits me fine.' Iris shrugged, watching him plugging in a series of cables to the bottom of the panel. 'If you don't like it here, why not leave? Like you said, the UN's always looking for more emigrants.'

'I'm not that stupid.' Vogel's expression soured as he fussed some more with the cables. He licked the multiple-pronged end of a plug before sticking it into its matching socket. 'There are things,' he said darkly, 'I know about the UN emigration program . . . that you don't.'

'What kind of things?'

'Maybe you'll find out someday. If you're unlucky.' Sparks sizzled off the back of Vogel's hand as he twisted the plug and socket closer together. 'Besides . . . I can't leave. I've got work to do here.'

64

'So do I.' Iris found a spot she could lean back against without slicing herself. 'So maybe we should get down to it. Whatever you brought me here to see.'

'Relax,' said Vogel. 'Show's about to start.' He dropped the cable, connected to his satisfaction, and kicked it beneath the lower edge of the suspended panel section. With his thumb and forefinger, he snuffed out some of the candles he had so carefully lit only a few minutes before, dropping the panel into shadowed darkness. 'I'm sure you'll enjoy it.'

The panel lit up, eye-stinging bright, as Vogel jabbed the largest button on a fist-sized, portable data-playback unit that had been spliced into the tangled cables. From somewhere else in the blimp's crumpled steel framework, Iris could hear a gasoline-powered electrical generator cough and wheeze into chugging life.

She shaded her eyes against the sudden glare. 'Could you turn it down?'

'Just a second.' Vogel's blurred outline was visible against the light. 'The pixel elements have to run through a hardwired display cycle before we can get to the good stuff. The stuff that *I* put in.'

The glare shifted downward in intensity; through the fingers in front of her eyes, Iris could see shapes forming on the panel section. She dropped her hand and saw the pixels blurring together, then sharpening into the off-world vistas that the UN's advertising sections had used to entice potential emigrants. A disembodied male voice boomed from a tangle of cabinetless, raw speaker drivers that hung from one of the overhead steel ribs: '*A new life awaits you in the off-world colonies . . . the chance to begin again—*'

'Enough of *that* crap,' growled Vogel. The voice went silent as he punched another set of buttons on the portable playback unit. The panel went dark, then was instantly filled with another image.

That Iris had seen before. The bright golden eyes of Scrappy the owl, like fire-heated coins, glared out from the panel. Enough of its surroundings were visible, with the soft, shifting glow of candlelight against expensive wood, to show that its perch remained in the former Tyrell Corporation headquarters.

'Where'd you get this?' It hadn't been that long since she had seen this particular playback, summoned by the surresper in her own apartment. 'This data record is an official police document.' She didn't know that for sure, but it was worth assuming. 'Penalties for unauthorized possession can be pretty unpleasant.'

'I'm so scared.' With his lanky arms folded across his chest, Vogel slowly shook his head. 'If the LAPD got on the case of everybody who cracked into their files, that's all they'd spend their time doing. Let's face it, the cops don't have the money to spend on the kind of security systems that would keep the average twelve-year-old from going through their files, looking for celebrity dirt and fatal gun-wound photos from the autopsy archives. So I'm not sweating it. Besides' – one eyebrow raised – 'how do you know I'm *not* authorized?'

'Because,' said Iris, 'then you'd be a cop. Like me. And you're not.'

'Touché. I can see why they give you the hard jobs to solve.' With his thumb, he pointed to the panel behind him. 'Like your problematic owl.'

'I'm beginning to think it was less of a problem before you came along. Look, you said you had something to show me, some kind of information I could use.' Iris nodded toward the owl's magnified image on the panel screen. 'If you're only going to show me stuff I already know about – such as what an owl looks like – then I'm not impressed. I was doing better on my own.'

'Like I said. The good stuff's about to start.' Vogel punched another button on the playback unit. 'Settle back and enjoy the show.'

The image of the owl, in two dimensions rather than the 3D in which she had seen it at her apartment, was equally impressive as it unfurled its broad, powerful wings and took off from its perch. As the similarly flattened, coldly smiling image of the late Dr Eldon Tyrell watched, the owl flared its claws and pounced upon the white rat on the Oriental carpet, then flapped to its perch with its struggling meal.

'Seen it,' said Iris. 'Big deal.'

'Ah; of course.' Vogel gave a nod. 'I expected you had. But what you've seen is the owl in question, *as it was*. Where and when, in the past. But let me show you something new.'

Another punch of a button, and the scene on the panel changed. Subtly: leaning forward from the sharp steel rib behind her, Iris had to peer closely to make out any difference at all. The light in the scene had changed; it was different and more complete in its spectrum from the blimp chamber's surrounding candlelight. And it gleamed from the perch on which the owl sat, turning its avid predator gaze from one angle to the next. *Wood*, thought Iris. The perch at the Tyrell Corporation had been made of metal.

'Where was this recorded?'

'As I said. Something new.' Vogel had moved back from the panel and stood next to Iris, gazing at the image before them. 'In fact, current. At the present location of the owl in question. This is where it's at, the thing you're looking for.'

Iris glanced over at him. 'And you know where that is?'

'Again, as I said. I have useful information for you.' Vogel displayed his thin, mocking smile once more. 'You see? You're not sorry now, that you met up with me.'

'Maybe.' Iris regarded him with suspicion. 'Information doesn't do me any good, if it doesn't translate into action.'

'True. As wise men have spoken, the word is the deed.' Vogel ran his thumb over the buttons on the playback unit's remote control; a wire dangled from it and ran to the portable machine by the panel. '*Aber in Anfang war der Wort*: the word still comes first. Which you have now received. Or at least in part: you know that the problematic owl is not lost, except perhaps to you. *I* know where it is; too bad *you're* the one looking for it.'

'So we make a deal,' said Iris. She had been expecting as much. 'Tell me what it is you want in exchange for the owl's location.'

'Not as easy as that.' Vogel shook his head. 'Even if I told you what you think you want to know – which I have every intention of doing – it wouldn't do you much good.'

'Why's that?'

'You'll see; let me lay a little more information on you.' Vogel's thumb fidgeted over the remote control's buttons, punching in a quick sequence. 'You'll *love* this.'

Iris watched the panel screen. The image of the owl dwindled into the background as the camera angle pulled back to a wider shot. Now the image on the panel included a couple of bored-looking, hardfaced men, sitting on cheap folding chairs in front of the owl's perch. The floor around them was littered with battery-depleted pornoids, the glossy nude images gone gray and static, a set of discarded gin rummy hands and greasy Chinese take-out containers speared with disposable plastic chopsticks. None of that concerned Iris; what interested her was the matched pair of blackly gleaming automatic rifles, safeties off, lying across the men's knees.

'Who are these guys?' The men were wearing identical dark gray trouser-and-jacket outfits, with vaguely military overtones but no distinguishing insignia. 'Private security?'

'You might say that.' Standing beside her, Vogel regarded the screen. 'Not your average rent-a-cops, though.'

She nodded in agreement. 'Not with that kind of firepower on hand.' Iris recognized the make and model of the autos, pre-devolution Czech hardware, from having worked one during a training session at the LAPD's firing range. 'Shit like that, you'd expect from the UN peace-enforcement squadrons.'

'This gear's better; the registration finktags have been disabled. See where the transmitter bumps have been filed away?' Vogel pointed. 'They can fire off these puppies all they want, and the central ammo-discharge agency wouldn't know squat about it.'

Iris glanced over at him. 'That's a capital-class felony. Just being in the same room with illegally modded gear like that.'

'Exactly.' Vogel smiled at her. 'So these guys must be really stupid, or really motivated. Which do you think it is?'

'Who's paying them that kind of money?'

'Maybe nobody.' Vogel shrugged. 'Maybe they're ideological types. With some non-financial reasons for what they're doing and risking.'

'Wait a minute.' Her gaze went from the panel screen to Vogel again. 'So you *don't* know who they are. And who they're working for.'

'Does it matter?' A tinge of impatience sounded in Vogel's voice. 'Get real. What difference is it going to make, knowing what's in their heads or who's signing their paychecks, when you're looking down the business end of one of those automatics?'

She mused it over in silence. *This job*, thought Iris, *is getting hinkier by the minute*. What had that sonuvabitch Meyer steered her onto? Heavy people, that whole Tyrell Corporation bunch, had had the owl in the first place, and heavier people, unknown and mysterious parties, apparently wanted it. And seemingly heaviest people, who could hire gun-toters like the ones shown in the image on the panel, had the owl right now, and were very likely not going to give it up with a mere please and thank you. *It's that valuable?* – she couldn't figure how it could be. Rare and expensive, sure, but not something anyone guarded with an illegal army.

Though maybe there were only the two she had seen on the panel. 'How many others are there?' She gestured at the panel. 'Besides these?'

'That I know about? Maybe six or seven total, that I've seen

68

coming and going, including these two beauties. But I haven't been monitoring this feed – which is live, by the way – for very long, and I don't have access to any other video sources at this location. So there may be others.'

'That's not good.' There were a lot of variables that would have to be dealt with, all of them with lethal potential. The unknown made her uncomfortable; it was one thing not to know what to expect when running down an escaped replicant, a whole other thing when looking at an organized, well-financed operation such as this. A replicant's options, violence-wise, were limited and tending toward the diffuse, even when they ran in packs, as sometimes happened. Someone hunting a replicant faced the possibility of getting killed, all right, but if it happened it would be through the blade runner's own ineptitude or miscalculation or sheer bad luck. Iris had no worries along those lines; she was still, after all, alive. Which counted for a lot in this game. The dead were that way because they had been losers before they began. She had a hunter's black and efficient karma in her bones; she could feel it there, the same way the owl undoubtedly knew how sharp its own claws were. But she was also alive and in the game, she knew, because she had shrewdly picked her targets; escaped replicants were her natural prey, as mice and other small vermin were to the owl. *Go up against something larger and tougher*, she told herself, *and you're the one who gets retired.*

'You're wondering,' said Vogel astutely, 'if you can pull this one off. Since it's not quite the same as what you've handled before.'

Iris nodded. 'Maybe I'm out of my league here.'

'Over your head. And every other good coward-enabling cliché. That's the problem with you blade runner types. You have it too easy; hunting down replicants is a piece of cake. Just licensed slaughter; they've got no real survival skills. How could they? A four-year lifespan is long enough to get desperate, not smart.'

'You think it's so easy?' Iris glared at him. 'You do it, then. See how long *you* last at it.'

'Simmer down,' said Vogel. 'Replicants aren't the problem here, are they?' He indicated the panel screen with a jerk of his head. 'Deal with the problem in front of you. We're talking real human beings here, as tough and bad as you, if not more so. And with real weaponry, even bigger than that cannon you tote around next to your heart. They've got what you want. You can either decide to go for it, or not.' Head tilted to one side, he watched for her reaction. 'What's it going to be?'

She had to think. If her boss Meyer had known about this, that the owl wasn't just flapping around the city, scavenging rats out of the alleys in the dark, but was actually in the possession of some heavy-duty organization like this – and how could he have *not* known? – then it opened up all sorts of ugly conjectures. Including the possibility that the whole job he'd given her was actually some kind of set-up. She could have gone on poking her nose into things, letting the word get around that she was looking for this particular real-live owl – there were probably dozens of gossiping dealers at the *souk* who were aware of it by now – and generally making a target out of herself, ready for the thugs on the panel screen to pay their terminal kind of attention to her. Iris glanced up at the image on the panel. *I could've wandered right in there*, she thought. *'Got an owl?' And bang, I would've been sorted out but good.*

'I could've been in big trouble' – Iris glanced over at Vogel – 'if I hadn't run into you.'

'See?' Vogel smiled. 'I knew you'd get to like me. Or at least *appreciate* me.'

'Oh, I do. I even almost regret beating the crap out of you.'

'It's not the best way to get a relationship started.'

Iris returned his thin, humorless smile. 'Depends on who you're seeing. Like they say, some people pay extra for that.'

'I could do without it.'

'I'll try to remember that,' said Iris. 'Because we still haven't worked out all the little kinks between us, have we?'

'Oh?' One of Vogel's eyebrows lifted. 'Like what?'

'Like what the hell it is you exactly want.' Iris's gaze narrowed to slits. 'You know what I want.' She gestured toward the panel screen a few yards away from them. 'I want the owl. But I haven't got the least notion of what you'd be getting out of this.'

'As I said before.' Vogel's smile turned even more amused. 'I want to help you.'

'Your ass; this is LA. Nobody helps anybody else, without a reason.'

'O ye of little faith.' Vogel ruefully shook his head. 'You're really going to have to learn to start trusting people.'

'Not trusting *anything* is what's kept me alive so far. I'm not going to change my operational style just for your sake.'

'You're going to have to,' said Vogel. 'Because you don't have any choice. You already know that you can't get the info you need out of me any other way. You either trust me, or you punt on this job.'

Iris resisted the urge to hit him again. 'Tell me who you're working for. Whose side are you on?'

'You don't need to know that.'

Her words rasped out from between clenched teeth, 'Tell . . . me.'

'Can't.' This time, the shake of Vogel's head was hard and final. 'Not without getting you into even deeper shit than you're already in. There are some things you're better off not knowing. Let's just say that there are certain parties for whom it's as vital as it is for you that you succeed at the assignment you've been given. Parties – people, forces, whatever – that would prefer having this owl some other place than where it is right now.'

'Like in their hands.'

Vogel shrugged. 'Conceivably.'

'And they're using the police to get it for them.'

'That's one possible analysis. If it helps you in some way to believe that, then go ahead.'

'One more question.' Her white-knuckled fists trembled at her sides. 'Why me? If this thing is so important, than it wasn't just Meyer's idea to give me the job. Somebody told him to give it to me. Why?'

His expression became almost pitying. 'Maybe they've got more confidence in you – that you can do it – than you do yourself.'

Iris turned back toward the screen panel and looked at the image it presented. One of the two men with the high-powered automatic rifles had propped his weapon against the side of the folding chair so he could unwrap a processed food-substitute sandwich packet on his lap and start ingesting the contents. Behind him, the owl shifted on its wooden perch, the bright yellow eyes watching hungrily for its own living food sources.

'All right,' said Iris. 'But I'm going to need a little time. To get things ready.'

'Don't take too long.' Vogel pressed a button on the remote control, and the panel went blank and dead. 'They're not going to wait around for you. They've got plans of their own.'

Iris looked from the candlelit interior of the dead blimp, through the tears in its metallic sheathing, to the night's darkness outside. The rain had stopped, leaving the city streets black and glistening.

She shook her head. 'It's not their plans I'm worried about.'

71

6

'Bad night?'

The chat had greeted her as soon as Iris had walked in the door of her apartment. As the bolts of the automatic door locks snicked into place behind her, she nodded, eyes closed. 'Not the best I've had.'

She dropped her ring of swipe cards on the floor and lay out on the couch, striped by the first pearl-gray light of dawn sliding through the blinds on the barred window. The couch wasn't long enough to stretch out full-length; she had to curl her knees up into a semi-fetal position. Which suited her bleak mood.

'Tea?' The round face of the chat bobbed close to her own. 'Hot and minty-fresh?'

'No thanks.' Right now, she didn't feel like rubbing her hand across the chat's smooth head, either, and leaking a transdermal endorphin buzz into her central nervous system. 'I'm fine.'

The chat wobbled away and returned with a *faux* handstitched comforter, which it managed to tug into place over Iris. She helped it out, pulling the hem up under her chin, though her impulse was to pull it all the way over her head, sealing herself into a soft, dark womb.

'That's great.' She managed a wan smile at the worried-looking autonomic creature. 'Look, I'm okay. Really.'

'Sure?' The chat appeared dubious. It had never seen her like this before. She hadn't gotten the thing yet, when she had been going through the roughest parts of the departmental training and had been afraid she would wash out of the program and wind up back on the streets.

'Yeah,' lied Iris. 'Don't worry about me. Go get in your basket.' She pulled a hand out from beneath the comforter and pointed to the corner of the apartment's front room. 'Sleep and stand-by.' She watched as it reluctantly did as she had ordered. 'That's a good boy.'

She lay for a while longer, head turned so she could gaze unseeingly at the irregular islands and continents of the water-

72

damaged acoustic ceiling tiles. Then she raised her head from the sofa's saggy end-cushion and told the phone on the side table to get Meyer for her.

'Will do.' The phone ran through its security out-protocols, speed-dialed, then extended its headpiece toward Iris. 'Here you go.'

'What's the problem?' Meyer's voice, both harried and sleepy, sounded in Iris's ear. 'It better be good, calling at this hour.'

'Like you don't know.' She let the curved strap dangle loosely from her hand rather than snugging it tight across her skull. 'What the hell have you gotten me into?'

The phone was silent for a few seconds, before Meyer responded. 'Look,' he said, 'just do the job. Or don't. But don't ask any more questions, either.'

'You sonuvabitch.' From the corner of her eye, Iris saw the chat cringe in its basket, alarmed by the anger in its owner's voice. 'This is some kind of weird, deep shit you got me walking through, and if I'm going to get to the other side – *with* this stupid owl you're so hot on – then I'm going to need some help.'

'Like what?'

'Don't worry,' said Iris, her voice bitter in her own ears. 'I won't ask you for information. I've got another source for that. You know what I'm talking about, don't you?'

Meyer was silent again, for longer this time. 'Go with it,' he said finally. 'You can trust the guy.'

'Oh, *that* makes me feel a whole lot better. Coming from a lying sack of shit like you.'

'So this is what you needed?' Meyer's voice sounded more weary than angry over the phone. 'To dump on me? Fine, you got it. Anything else?'

'Yeah, there's something else. Jesus Christ. This job isn't going to be a piece of cake.'

'Didn't think it would be.'

'So I'm going to need a little hardware upgrade,' said Iris. 'Something bigger than I normally carry around with me. I'm going to need you to okay an armory draw.'

'No can do.' The emphatic shake of Meyer's head was almost audible through the phone line's real-time excrypt sequences. 'Look, Iris, we're trying to keep this whole operation on the quiet. If I let you pull out of the station armory the kind of equipment you're going to want – I know you, when it comes to stuff like this – then it's going to be all over the department in no time. That kind of paperwork gets redundantly routed to every division, every level. I can't do that for you.'

'You can't do it *officially*, then fine. I don't give a shit about the requisition forms in triplicate and the rest of the paperwork. Get the stuff out the back door to me. That's all I'm asking.'

'"That's all?"' Meyer exploded, his shout barking out of the phone. 'Are you *insane*? What you're talking about is misappropriation of departmental property – *secured* departmental property. That's an administrative felony, class alpha; sanctions for which include, but are not limited to, rank demotion, forfeiture of accrued retirement benefits and monetary fines.'

'Don't cite the rule book to me, Meyer. I've read it.'

'Then maybe you read the part about what *else* the internal investigations division could do to me. Which is basically to drag my sorry ass up to the roof of the station, put a bullet through my head and toss my body over the side. And they'd get a gold star in their own personnel files, for having taken care of the incident in such a neat and expeditious manner.' Meyer's voice simmered down a few degrees. 'You know the department runs a tight ship, Iris. They have to.'

Iris sat up on the couch, letting the comforter slide down onto the floor. 'And what do *you* have to do, huh? Tell me that.'

'What are you talking about?'

'I'll make it plain for you.' The phone sweated in her fist as she talked to her boss. 'Do you want this owl or not? If you do, then you're going to get me what I need, no matter what it takes. If you got a problem with that, then you can find somebody else to go bird-hunting for you.'

Another few seconds of silence, then Meyer spoke again. 'All right,' he said. 'I'll get the stuff out the back door to you. Give me a list.'

She had already been thinking about that. When she had finished telling Meyer her requirements, she held the phone away from her ear, expecting another explosion from him.

Instead, she got a weary sigh coming from the other end of the line. 'This is nuts,' said Meyer's voice. 'We'll both wind up taking a dive off the top of the station.'

'Don't worry.' Iris kicked the wadded-up comforter away from her feet. 'I'll return everything in good condition.'

'No, you won't.' Meyer sounded resigned and defeated. 'You'll get yourself killed, in as messy a way as possible. And I'll wind up holding the bag for it.'

'Spare me. Self-pity doesn't suit you.' She stood up from the couch and walked into the center of the apartment's front room, the phone trotting beside her so she could keep the tethered headpiece to her ear. 'Giving me this job was *your* idea, remember.' Standing beside the barred window, she looked out at the first of the day's rains soaking the crowded traffic in the streets below. 'How soon can you have the gear ready for me to pick up?'

'You think I'm handing this kind of stuff over to you in broad daylight? Get real,' said Meyer. 'Tonight – and it won't happen at the station. I'll ring you with a stash-point location. I'll be there when you swing by for it.'

'I'm not expecting anything from you, Meyer. Not anymore.' She killed the connection and the excrypt protocols, and tossed the headpiece to the phone waiting beside her. It climbed onto the side table, settling down and switching itself off.

'Play? Quality time?' The chat trotted beside Iris as she headed for the apartment's minuscule bedroom. 'Cuddle?'

'Not now,' said Iris. She had given the window blinds their programmed handsignal, shutting down the whole apartment into darkness. Dark enough by which to get some real sleep. 'Later. I've got to get some rest.' Inaction and fretting had tired her out more than a dead-run chase could have. 'Big job to do tonight.'

She was asleep and dreamless, as soon as her head hit the pillow. Outside, the hard LA sunlight, grayed by its passage through the monsoon clouds, turned the rain to steam against the window glass, but couldn't find her.

Intercut

'This should be good,' said the remote camera operator. 'She's got all the right toys now.'

The blue-tinged glow of the wall of video monitors turned the operations bunker into a subset of the neon-lit LA streets. Outside, night had consumed the rain-sodden scraps of day, pushing the city once more into its true and most authentic mode of being.

'Could be.' The director roused himself from his deep, meditative silence. 'She always had the right attitude. Smart enough to be scared, but too pissy to let it stop her.'

For the past quarter-hour, the camera operator and the director had been watching an interesting transaction take place, recorded and brought to one of the central monitor screens by a unit hidden in the exposed and cobwebby ceiling rafters of one of the abandoned Traction Avenue warehouses, down by the concrete ditch of the Los Angeles River. The monitor had shown the female blade runner they had been following, her black leatherite jacket glistening from the rain, accepting what looked to be two metal-cornered briefcases from her boss.

Watch out, the man named Meyer had told her, with a trace of sarcasm. *They're heavy.*

Even on the monitor screen, with the remote camera set to an elevated long angle, the slit-eyed look of disdain she'd given him had been apparent. *They're supposed to be*, she'd replied coldly.

It was as well for the director's purposes that the woman didn't pop open the lids on the flat cases and check out the lethal gear inside; the camera operator figured that the sequence they'd been able to catch at the police station, where Meyer had surreptitiously extracted the items from the armory lockers, established sufficiently just what weaponry was involved. Anything that the audience wasn't clear on would be made plain when the hard action started.

The camera operator pushed himself away from the angled control panel, reverse-arching his spine with his hands shoved against the small of his back. A similar crick had lodged itself in the hinges of his neck vertebrae. That was the problem with these marathon gigs: too long sitting, too long watching, all to catch the quick little moments that added up to the real story.

'At least she's not going to waste any time,' the camera operator said aloud. Up on the wall of monitors, one screen over from the one inside the abandoned warehouse, a wasplike motorcycle with bubble fairing and retrofit exhaust-waveform obliterators was picking up speed, silent and swift, heading back into the densely packed heart of the city. Cold blue streetlamps glistened from the metal corners of the cases, strapped behind the rider leaning over the insignia-less tank. The woman rode without lights or markings, the better to arrive at her destination before anyone else knew she was even on her way. The camera operator nodded in appreciation, for both the black-wrapped-in-darkness visuals that the monitor held, and the inadvertent convenience the female blade runner's haste provided. 'Maybe we'll have this part wrapped up in the next couple of hours. With any luck.'

'Luck doesn't enter into it.' Still watching the monitor screens, the director slowly shook his head. 'Only fate.' He turned his unsmiling gaze toward the camera operator. 'And once we've got that under control . . .' The director shrugged. 'Then our job's done.'

The camera operator didn't like the sound of that last bit. *This job*, he thought, *is getting way too creepy*. He looked back up at the monitor screens. And to the one screen in particular, that showed the place where the woman would soon arrive.

7

'Ever use anything like this?'

Iris watched as the figure in front of her lifted the automatic rifle in both hands, as though he were trying to judge its weight. 'Once or twice,' said Vogel. With a couple of quick manipulations, he snapped the folding barrel into place, pushed home the ammo clip and thumbed off the safety. He raised the gunsight to his eye, aiming down the empty alley in which he and Iris stood. 'This thing calibrated?'

She knew he was showing off, displaying his familiarity with the hardware she had taken out of the metal-cornered cases at their feet. 'You don't need it to be,' she told him. 'Not at the ranges we're going to be working at. This isn't exactly a sniper operation we're talking about. All indoors, up close and personal.'

Vogel gave her a wink. 'That's how I like it.'

Her own gaze rolled upward. *What the hell am I doing?* As far as Iris was concerned, the job was already out of control. Here she was, not only relying on possibly flaky information, but on the flake who'd provided it as well. *A good way*, she told herself, *to get killed.* For all she knew, this Vogel character had no more heavy armaments experience than what he'd picked up from male adolescent target-audience video feeds and game immersions. Soon as he pulled the trigger on what she'd equipped him with, he could be walking backward from the weapon's streaming recoil, lethally spraying everything in an expanding cone of fire, including herself. She'd be lucky to survive this operation, let alone retrieve an unshredded owl.

As if her premonitions had somehow leaked out into the real world, an amplified burst of gunfire sounded from the other side of the alley wall. The ground floor of the building was an original Golden-Era movie palace with dust-shrouded, burnt-out chandeliers hanging in the lobby behind the shell-scrolled ticket booth, once-red carpets worn through in widening patches to the concrete beneath, and stylized Art Deco murals under layers of grime and spray-can *placa*, depicting Los Angeles as a paradise studded with oil wells and golden citrus fruit. Now the buzzing neon marquee advertised a twenty-four hour rota of cheap, multi-*patois* Indonesian eye-gougers; half the audience, Iris knew, would be asleep, using the broken-hinged seats as flop-house bedding.

'Give me the layout again,' said Iris. 'Slowly.' Vogel had sketched a rough map in the alley's wet dirt, but she had already dismissed it from her mind. She preferred pure verbal input. 'How do we get upstairs?'

'Easy.' From above Vogel's brow, the drizzling rain darkened his close-cropped hair and trickled to the corner of his jaw. 'Service entrance behind the projection booth; there's a stairway that goes up to the next floor, which is all vacated insurance and old theatrical agency offices. Next floor up from that is where our friends are keeping watch on the owl. The elevator shaft will bring us up right in the middle of the layout.'

'What kind of alarms have they got rigged up?'

'All thermal detection, keyed to normal human body temperature.' Vogel nodded in admiration. 'Latest tech from Iblis Sicherheit Gesellschaft in Geneva, with full inductor-driven subsurface probe capability. Nice stuff.'

'Yeah, it's "nice", nice and impossible to get past,' said Iris. 'What were you planning on doing? Blowing out the electrical service to the building?'

Vogel shook his head. 'That wouldn't accomplish anything. They're running their gear on shielded isotope-decay power generators. Military equipment – these guys have some real heavy-duty stuff, besides the guns they're toting. Even if we pumped a disruptor wave through the building, we couldn't shut 'em down. So all that cutting the power feed to the building would do is let them know we're on our way in.'

'Then the job's over. Right now, before we start.' Iris looked at him in amazement. 'If we could sneak in there, we'd have little enough chance of pulling this off. Tripping the alarm circuits, we'd have *zero* chance.'

'So we don't trip them. Leave them running, and slide right past them.'

'And how do you propose doing that?'

'Simple.' Letting the automatic rifle dangle at one side, Vogel reached with his other hand inside his coveralls. His fist came back out, extended toward Iris, then unfolded to the flat of his palm turned upward. 'We use these.'

Iris looked at the two plain, unmarked gelatin capsules on his palm; inside them she could see a granular white powder, not much different from the other white-powder drugs she had seen before. She wasn't thrilled. 'What is it?'

'Slow death.'

They all are, she thought, then caught herself; she realized he meant something specific. 'Wait a minute,' said Iris. 'You're talking about . . .'

'Thermatos.' Vogel smiled, one corner of his mouth lifting. 'A bastard coinage, from *therm* and *thanatos*, meaning heat and death. A bastard word for an orphan compound, otherwise nameless. Since the pharmaceutical lab that first invented it didn't want to even talk about it.'

There was a reason for that, Iris knew. Of all the cumulatively lethal, supposedly pleasurable chemicals ever on the street, this was the worst. Pleasure being a subjective concept: she had never seen the attraction of anything that lowered one's biological functions by stunning and cutting the brain's paleocortex, the mammalian buffer layer between the evolved, higher-level neocortex and the primitive reptilian brain core, out of the central nervous system's *gestalt*. When Iris had been fresh out of LAPD basic training, and before she had managed to engineer her promotion to the blade runner division, she had gone along on a raid to clean out a nest of thermatos addicts, down in the warrenlike cribs of Old Chinatown. They had been using the stuff for so long that the drug's short-cut integration between their reptile cerebral sections, just above the brain stems that regulated the body's unconscious autonomic respiration and pulsatile actions, and the fully human parts just under the curved lids of their skulls, was no longer temporary but fused solid, synapse to synapse, neuron to neuron. Iris had had the sensation, upon looking into their cold, unblinking eyes, that the spaces behind the dark pinpoint pupils were no longer inhabited by anything human, but only by the usurping reptilian brain core itself. It had been like staring into a nest of vipers – real ones, not artfully crafted fakes – but with human faces and skin.

It was no wonder, then, that the thermatos compound had been made illegal, both in its manufacture and possession, and ruthlessly suppressed, at the same time that every other narcotic and stimulant was *de facto* available and even encouraged in LA. The authorities had enough trouble sorting out real human beings from fake ones – replicants that had been *faux* human from their inception date – without having to cope with people who had made themselves non-human. And worse, the inversion of the old Tyrell Corporation motto, *More Human than Human*; in the case of the thermatos addicts, less human than even the replicants were. So that the human condition, the definition of being human, was no longer a binary matter, yes or no, but something on a sliding scale, from way not-human to very human at the other end. Which meant that the blade runners, the enforcers of that definition, were playing the averages when they did so; when they put a gun to somebody's head, they were grading on a bell curve. Passing the test meant you got to live for another term. Flunking was death, the collapse of the scale into a simple, terminal on-off state.

Iris had wondered before, when remembering, what the response would have been if anybody on the raid had slapped a Voigt-Kampff machine on one of the thermatos users. Whether the gauges would have lit up at all, or the needles have moved from zero. And as the machine's little bellows pump had moved back and forth like a concertina playing a sad, silent waltz, sucking in and analyzing the test subject's exhalations and sweat molecules, the cold-eyed creature on the other side of the table would have done the same, flicking out a thin, black forked ribbon of a tongue, sniffing the air for traces of its prey, like even a phony snake did . . .

'Where the hell did you get this?' Iris regarded with repugnance the two colorless capsules in Vogel's palm. 'Nobody makes thermatos anymore; it's a capital offense.'

'Old stock,' said Vogel. 'From when they did.'

'Great.' Iris's voice soured with disgust. 'On top of everything else, it's stale.'

'Fresh enough. Carefully preserved, in a vacuum-extraction deep-cryo chamber. Like the corpses of dead rich people dipped in liquid nitrogen, awaiting the call, as in Bach's cantata 140, *Wachet auf, ruft uns die Stimme*.'

'"Sleepers, awake." But nobody wakes up from being dead,' said Iris. 'Which is what that stuff will do for you, if you're caught with it.'

'Worth the risk.' Vogel held the two pale capsules up between his thumb and forefinger. 'Since these are what will make it possible for us to go cruising past the alarm systems up there.' He nodded toward the building that formed one side of the alley. 'Among the other, less desirable effects, thermatos also has the useful physiological effect of slamming the normal human body temperature by about twenty degrees Fahrenheit. Those alarm systems our friends are using won't trigger on anything below eighty degrees. Which means that we'll be effectively invisible to their security perimeter.'

'Yeah, and we'd also be screwed up out of our minds, and moving at about the speed of an iguana on an iceberg. I've seen what that stuff does to people and their reaction times. It's a perceptual dilation effect: kiss your clocks, internal and external, goodbye. We get past the alarm systems fine, and then we'll be standing there like window-display dummies, not even blinking while these people walk up and dismantle us at their leisure.'

'I share your concern,' said Vogel with elaborate mock-patience. 'Which is why this stuff isn't straight thermatos. It's cut with a micro-encapsulated dosage of a high-powered niacinamide analogue; once the stuff is in your gut, and the thermatos has kicked in, the niacinamide's thin-film barrier is timed to evaporate exactly five minutes later. You'll feel the heat rush all over, because the molecular load will already have dispersed throughout your body. That'll purge the thermatos effects, like flipping a switch, and you'll be ready to rock-'n'-roll. We both will, 'cause I'll be standing right next to you.'

'Nice plan,' Iris grudgingly admitted. 'Except for one thing.'

'What's that?'

'Down the line, after this job's over – *if* we survive it – what happens to me if I *like* the effects of this thermatos junk? And I decide I want more of it?'

'Then you're screwed,' Vogel told her. 'That's a one-way avenue, sweetheart. Either you don't find a source for more of it, and you suffer, or you *do* find a source and you suffer more.' He turned his head slightly, regarding her from the corner of one eye. 'You really concerned that you might enjoy being less than human?'

'It's a concern. Some people dig it.'

'Tell you what, then. I'll make you a promise.' He lifted the automatic rifle at his side. 'If it turns out later that you're screwed up from the stuff, I'll come around and put a bullet through your head, and put you out of your misery. Deal?'

'You're all heart,' said Iris.

'I told you you'd be glad you ran into me.'

Iris looked at the capsules in the center of Vogel's extended palm. 'You know . . . I'm getting tired of people talking me into doing stuff.

Especially when I wind up doing it.' She reached out and took one of the capsules. 'What the hell?' She popped it into her mouth and ground the soft gelatin shell between her molars. Something gritty and stinging, like wind-sharpened ice crystals, spilled across her tongue. 'Let's go.'

'No time like the present,' said Vogel. He swallowed the remaining capsule, then knelt to fold up the automatic rifle and pack it into the open metal-cornered case sitting on the pavement. Smiling, he stood up. 'Or no time at all.'

The thermatos kicked in as they were crossing the theater lobby. Iris felt the deep cellular impact that the long-term users called the 'glacier' hit her in a cascading surge up her spinal column. Her free hand, that wasn't toting the other weapons case, spasmed open; the torn red ticket stub fluttered and sped from her fingers toward the darkly stained carpeting, as though pulled by some new, urgent gravity. Everything in the lobby, human or not, instantly assumed a jittering, vaguely menace-filled animation, as the optic processors behind her eyes shifted down to the red end of the available light spectrum. A small tribe of cinephile squatters, indoor-pallid beneath their habitual dirt, their own eyes like lemurs', peered out at her and Vogel from the makeshift tents they had erected between the broken door of the men's room and the constantly trickling water fountain. Even their slow movements seemed frenetic and sharp to Iris, as her own kinetic functioning fell closer to absolute stasis.

Only Vogel's motions, as he strode alongside her steps, seemed normal; the thermatos had hit him as well, putting him on the same long-wave temporal plane. With eyes half-lidded, as though an inner herpetoid nature were manifesting itself on the angles of his face, he smiled and held up one hand, fingers spread apart to indicate the number of minutes he and Iris had to reach and break into the fortified area upstairs.

Iris nodded. Something in her mouth, seeping from beneath her tongue, seemed to taste of both blood and metal, as the reptilian core at the center of her brain locked itself in a neural embrace with the higher thinking functions. *I can see* – the thought crystalized itself, in a dark room inside her skull – *why people get into this stuff*. The blood in her veins seemed to transform into a crawling, numbing substance, closer and closer to freezing, and eradicating all human pain. Better than any synthetic opiate, legal or illegal, that she had ever tried; Iris realized now that those had only obliviated the conscious and unconscious misery of the human and awaked condition, by flooding those sharp rocks with an oceanic endorphin tide. Whereas the thermatos had dissolved the rocks at the bottom of the sea, deepened the lightless trench in which she sank, to the extinguished core of her own being. *That's how you get hooked, all right . . . not by pleasure.* The words moved slower in the icy corridors inside her skull. *But by the true absence of pain . . .*

Even the metal-cornered case, dangling from one hand as she walked through the theater lobby, felt like a vacuum-filled semblance of form, nothing with real mass inside – like the perceived apparitions of real human beings that she and Vogel shouldered their way past. *Good shit for a blade runner,* mused Iris. The stuff played right into the cold attitude needed for the job; she knew she could have opened the case, pulled out its airy toys, and stacked the lobby with leveled corpses without feeling a twinge of empathy.

But that would mean . . .

'Pay attention.' Vogel's words, from some place outside of her, sounded wavery and muffled, as though the air between them had congealed as well. 'We've got work to do.'

That I'm no different. Her thoughts continued to move, slow and unstoppable. *From what I hunt . . .*

'And not much time.'

All a matter of degree . . .

'If the niacinamide analogue goes off,' grated Vogel, 'and we're still on the wrong side of the alarm system, we're screwed. And dead.'

Iris swiveled her cold gaze toward him. Her tongue felt heavy and stiff in her mouth; her jaws pried themselves open through the sheer force of her will. 'I don't care,' she said flatly.

'I know you don't; that's the hit you took.' Vogel's pupils were two black pinpricks surrounded by ice-blue. He had stopped and turned to face her. 'Look, you might *think* you're in some timeless zone . . . but you're not.' His words took seeming decades to arrive, one after another. 'The clock is ticking – out there.' He gestured toward the surrounding lobby and its press of impassively curious faces. 'So get with the program . . . and let's get a move on. I'm not fetching the stupid bird for you all by myself.' Vogel ducked his head so he could gaze straight into Iris's eyes. 'It's your *job*. Remember?'

That one word stirred something to life inside her, as though it were awakening from hibernation beneath meter-thick icefloes. She nodded slowly. 'All right. Let's do it.' With the metal-cornered case weighing a little more in her hand, she shoved past Vogel and toward the door marked, beneath tangled layers of graffiti, EMPLOYEES ONLY.

When they reached the top of the bare concrete stairs, Iris heard the clatter of an ill-adjusted projection machine. The door to one side of the landing was open a crack, enough for Iris to see the projectionist asleep in a wooden chair tilted back, his feet on top of the machine, the floor a foot deep in discarded snippets of film like segmented snakes pressed flat and writhing. A flickering cone of light, aimed out of a small square hole in the far wall, resolved into black and white ghost images on the theatre's sagging screen: dead actors, a man and a woman Iris would have had no way of recognizing, were locked in the embrace that had probably killed them, over and over.

'Here.' Vogel nodded toward the elevator doors on the other side of the landing. 'Come on . . . we're running behind.'

Against the low-thermal load of the thermatos in her system, Iris pushed into action. Standard police training enabled her to pry off the control panel, short out the wires, and bring the elevator down a few feet in its shaft. Sparks painlessly stung her hand as she cross-connected another pair of wires, pulled the elevator's dented doors apart.

Lugging the metal-cornered cases, she and Vogel scrambled up onto the elevator's exposed top. The doubled steel cables reached up to the machinery at the building's roof level.

'If we use this thing,' whispered Iris, 'they'll hear it running.'

'Doesn't matter.' Vogel shook his head. 'The theater uses it all the time, for clearing out the audience rubbish to the dumpsters in the basement. There must be twenty years of accumulated trash down there; nobody pays to haul it away. So our friends are used to the sound of the elevator; it's background noise to them.'

The darkness of the elevator shaft, like an underground tunnel turned on end and threaded through the building's vertical axis, smelled like dust and long-dead, enclosed air. Iris closed her eyes for a moment, re-savoring the thermatos's glacial effect on her perceptions. Distant voices of the film being shown in the theater seeped into her consciousness, like pleasing reminders of all the human concerns it had been so gratifying to leave behind, a shed skin with the unoccupied ghost of her own face printed on it.

She felt as if she could have stayed there forever.

But you've got a job to do. It was her own voice nagging her this time, instead of Vogel's. Maybe the thermatos was already wearing off, past its peak levels in her bloodstream.

Without saying anything aloud, Iris knelt down and found the control box connections a hand's-breadth away from the steel cables. There was no playing with the wires necessary; the red UP button was in plain view. She punched it and the machinery above growled and clanked, rustily grinding the elevator toward the next floor.

A push of the STOP button brought the top of the elevator within a few easy inches of being level with the doors and the exposed mechanisms that would slide them apart. Vogel touched Iris on the shoulder. 'Wait a minute.' He took a small device from one of his coveralls pockets and flicked it on. The tiny round dome of a variable-emissions LED pulsed red, then yellow, went dead, then pulsed back on as green.

'Perfect,' said Vogel quietly. He slid the device back into his pocket. 'We're past the alarm perimeter.' He smiled down at her. 'And it didn't go off.'

Iris stood up, keeping the toe of her boot ready on the doors' control button. 'How's our time?'

'About ready for the show.'

She felt a regretful premonition, as if the end of the stilled world of her perceptions was already in view. Being human wasn't pleasant to begin with; going back to it, after even this brief a vacation, was bound to be painful.

Vogel extracted and assembled the necessary gear from the metal-cornered cases, then handed Iris her weapons. 'Here it comes,' he said.

The niacinamide analogue hit her system like an internalized flame-thrower, as the dispersed compound shed its time-delay polymers in a millisecond rush. Her heart pounded in her chest – for a dizzied moment, she wondered if the people on the other side of the elevator doors could hear its drumlike stroke – as a fevered heat boiled through her veins. Her mouth was sucked dry by the kiss of an invisible sun; the sweat coursed from her brow and stung salt into the corners of her eyes.

Then it was over, body heat fading to a normal 98.6 degrees. The thermatos's glacier was gone as well, melted away and revealing the once-again human form it had so efficiently encased and numbed.

She glanced over at Vogel. Even in the elevator shaft's darkness, his sharp-angled face seemed luminous with sweat.

Vogel nodded toward the doors. 'Hit it,' he said.

'Glad to.' Action might distract her from the misery onslaught of the human condition. Iris stepped down on the control button.

The machinery's various interlinked metal struts and rust-covered springs creaked into life, drawing the doors apart. Light spilled into the shaft from the spaces revealed on the other side.

Good luck, in a way: the doors opened onto one of the figures she had viewed on the cobbled-together panel screen in the wreckage of the downed blimp. The man was walking past, automatic rifle slung by a strap over his shoulder, carrying a styrofoam cup filled with coffee from the hot-plate and pot sitting on a folding card table against the far wall. Iris blinked away the sudden glare from the overhead exposed fluorescents, swung up her own rifle and nailed him. The obliterator at the end of her automatic's barrel tumesced for a split second, swelling to soak up the shot's sonic impact, then converting and releasing it as a few degrees of heat that rolled back along the barrel and grip to her hands. Lukewarm coffee splashed across the cracked and scuffed linoleum, as the corpse folded around itself and fell.

Vogel and Iris stepped over the body, into the corridor beyond the elevator doors. The map of the floor's layout, that Vogel had drawn and described to her in the alley below, flashed inside her head and superimposed itself upon the spaces around them.

'That way,' whispered Vogel, pointing to one end of the corridor.

She was already in motion, sliding her spine along the wall, the automatic's barrel braced vertical against her shoulder. Before she reached it, things went awry: the other man from the panel screen appeared behind her and Vogel, stepping out of the toilet facilities and zipping up his fly. He was faster than the first one had been, and able to dive and snatch up the rifle he'd left propped beside the toilet doorway. A quick brace of shots fanned down the center of the corridor before Vogel's silenced bullet took off the corner of the man's head and sprawled him against the wall, marked red as he collapsed and slid down to the floor.

That was as efficient an alarm as any other could have been. The audible shockwave of the dead man's fire, and its slamming impact into the wall at the opposite end of the corridor, was still echoing inside the space like fading seismic thunder as Iris tossed a smaller piece of her gear into the open doorway beside her.

The long-sustain, notched-spectrum glare grenade bounced into

87

the center of the room, the same one that she had watched before on the panel screen. On its perch, the owl for which she had been hunting unfurled its wings, as the blinding light shot against every surface, annihilating all visibility. A panicked screech sounded from the owl as it leapt futilely from the perch, the chain fastened to the metal band above its claws tethering it from flight. The men in the room had similarly jumped to their feet, automatic rifles swinging toward the open doorway. Some of them had filter goggles on, quickly pulled up over their eyes from where they had been hanging around their necks, ready for just such an assault.

Iris and Vogel had brought their own optic filters into place as well, as soon as she had pulled the pin from the glare grenade. But unlike the goggles of the men in front of them, the LAPD devices were tuned to the specific, shifting notch in the grenade's output; the untuned filters tried to lock onto the notch, but were too slow to catch up with its randomized, skittering pattern.

Which meant that the goggled men in the room were as blind as the bare-eyed ones; in the ensuing chaos, Iris could hear them cursing and barking futile orders to each other. A barrage of automatic rifle-fire fanned through the doorway, wild enough to take out the man standing nearest to the door.

Iris dove to the floor, beneath the hot tracer lines of the others' bullets. Still standing, feet braced apart in the center of the corridor, Vogel returned fire with his own automatic, nailing two of the men in rapid order, sending them sprawling back towards the wall with the wooden perch shoved against it. The owl desperately flapped its wings to get away from the noise and light, but only managed to tug tight the chain fastened to its leg-band. The two remaining men in the room, though still blinded by the glare grenade, swung their rifle muzzles in Vogel's direction, forcing him to break off and fall back against the wall near the doorway as their bullets rattled past.

Flat on her elbows, Iris raised her rifle and took out one more with a quick burst. Before she could swing the muzzle around, the last one remaining leapt headlong in her direction, guided more by desperate instinct than anything else. His chest and shoulders pinned Iris's rifle against her body, the weapon trapped and useless as a broad hand shoved against the side of her face, bending her neck back to its snapping point. The man's fingers dislodged her goggles, and her sight was suddenly filled with white, annihilating light.

Blackness welled in the center of that illumination, then Iris felt the

88

man's body go into a spasm of convulsions; another rapid stitch of rifle-fire tore through one side of his ribcage, the exit wounds within centimeters of her own flesh, the bullet ripping through the pocket and the lower sleeve section of her leatherite jacket, leaving them in singed tatters.

Iris shoved the dead weight off herself. The room and the hallway had gone silent except for the fizzing of the glare grenade, its photo-explosive charge finally expended. Able to see now, without the goggles looped around her throat being necessary, she looked up and saw Vogel extending a hand toward her.

'Come on.' Vogel pulled her to her feet. 'We're not done yet. There's at least another two around here somewhere.'

'We'll deal with them on the way out.' Iris picked up the metal-cornered case she had left in the middle of the hallway, snapped it open and extracted a set of less lethal objects. 'First, let's get the merchandise we came for.'

In the room's stillness, the owl had settled down on its perch; the movements of its head, wide golden eyes staring, were still hectic and jerky. 'Take it easy,' crooned Iris softly, as she stepped over the bodies littering the floor. She drew on a pair of heavily padded gauntlets that extended past her elbows. 'We'll be going to a nicer place now . . .'

The owl tried to escape from her as she reached for it, but the chain and leg-band kept it within reach. Averting her face to avoid the blows of its powerful wings. Iris managed to get both her gloved hands upon its body; bringing it against her chest to pinion its desperate exertions, she got it under control.

Or at least for a moment. 'Give me a hand,' she snapped at Vogel. The sense of a living creature, straining to escape and survive, was palpable even through the padding that encased her hands and forearms. She could even feel its tiny heart racing, the quivering of the terrified predator whose shadow had terrified even smaller creatures. The scything claws raked dangerously close to her stomach, the razor point of one almost snagging the cloth of her cowboyshirt. 'Hurry up—'

With his automatic rifle slung over his shoulder, Vogel stepped up with a wide, elastic restraining band. The two of them struggled for a few moments with the animal, then at last managed to secure it, the band pressing its wings to its body. Iris slipped an oxygen-permeable bag over the owl, drawing its opening tight over the feet, rendering the claws safe for transportation.

'Let's go.' With one hand still in the heavy leather gauntlet, and the owl tucked in the cradle of her forearm, Iris nodded toward the door. 'Before whoever's left gets organized.'

Vogel preceded her, automatic rifle poised. He posted against the wall beside the doorway, peering cautiously out into the corridor. 'Clear.' He gestured with a tilt of his head. 'Go for the elevator shaft, and I'll be right behind you.'

Her rifle's shoulder strap was long enough that Iris could keep it at her hip as she carried the bound owl with her other hand and forearm. Emerging from the room, she ducked down and sprinted straight for the open elevator doorway, a couple of meters farther down and opposite.

Before she reached it, a brace of rifle-shots crackled from the far end of the corridor. She didn't take time to see what door might have popped open, and how many opponents were behind it; she launched herself toward the darkness of the elevator shaft, rolling her shoulder under her so that she would land on her back.

The exposed metal protrusions on the top of the elevator car dug painfully into her spine, but with both arms wrapped protectively over the owl, she managed to keep it clutched safely against her chest. As she scrambled onto her knees, Iris heard more gunfire coming from both directions in the corridor outside the elevator doors.

From well back in the open doorway, Iris peered out and saw Vogel with his back flattened against the opposite wall, pinned down by and returning the fire from the doorway at the end of the corridor. He saw her and gestured with a nod of his head.

'Over there!' Vogel indicated the doorway from which the remaining men were firing. 'You got a better angle. Push 'em back and I'll be able to make it to the elevator.' A few more shots dug into the floor near him. 'Then we'll be out of here.'

'Got a better idea,' Iris called to him. 'Thanks for the help, but I've got a job to finish.' She reached behind and hit the DOWN button on the elevator's control box. She heard more gunfire, and Vogel shouting something after her, as the elevator started down the shaft, leaving the open doorway above.

The projectionist was still asleep in his booth when Iris climbed down with the bagged owl from the top of the elevator. So many cheap action flicks had played in the theater that the continuing sound of gunfire, barely muffled from the floor above, had merely seeped into his muddled dreams.

Which was also the case with the audience in the movie theater, when Iris reached the bottom of the service stairs and stepped out into the crowded lobby. No one was alarmed by the sounds, fainter here, coming from above. That kind of thing was as common in the real LA as it ever had been in the illusory film world.

Then she was out in the street, with the merchandise tucked against her chest, away from the night rain. Iris quickened her steps, heading for her own apartment, rather than the police station.

8

Two owls perched in the living room of her apartment, regarding her with their preternaturally golden eyes.

'Cross-check items in view.' Iris spoke to the surresper, giving the machine its next commands. She had already ordered up its data-stored, three-dimensional image of the owl, from when it had been recorded in the late Dr Eldon Tyrell's office suite. Another few quick words had sized and placed the image next to the real, living owl, its claws wrapped around a perch that Iris had improvised from a broom handle and the backs of a couple of chairs. 'Match for specific identity.'

The living owl, extracted less than an hour ago from the room above the downtown movie theater, hooted in mild alarm and ruffled its speckly brown feathers as the surresper played a shifting grid of bright green lines across its form. Iris watched the dance of the lines, waiting for the machine's verdict. She was alone in the room, except for the two owls, the real and the illusory; the real one had frightened the chat even more than its previous re-creation had, sending the small, prey-resembling artificial creature scuttling into the safety of the apartment's bedroom.

'Check completed,' announced the surresper. The grid of lines, starting an inch or so apart then narrowing down to map finer details, had disappeared from the living owl. 'Specific identity confirmed; recorded and physically present items are same creature. Chronological back-displacement estimated at one year, probability estimate in plus-ninety percentage range. Identifying tally marks are as follows: texture-read and mapped analysis of feather pattern, striation of organic beak base-material, impact stress marks at edge and point of beak, fibrous ocular patterning—'

'Skip all that.'

'Idiosyncratic heart and respiratory at-rest impulses—'

'I said, skip it.'

The surresper fell silent. Iris regarded the two identity-matched owls, one framed by a small section of the opulently wood-paneled Tyrell Corporation headquarters, the other by the bare walls and window frame of her own apartment. 'End re-creation display,' said Iris. The illusory owl vanished, along with its summoned-up surroundings. She was left alone with just the living creature in front of her.

'*Now* what do I do,' muttered Iris aloud. She turned and walked into the kitchen module, ignoring the chat cringing under the table, and poured herself a glass of water at the sink. The tap continued to run as she drained the glass in one gulp, head thrown back; then she leaned forward, face lowered to the thin stream of water, and splashed it into her face. There were streaks of pinkish red swirling toward the drain when she took her hands away; not her own blood, but that of the men in the room above the movie theater. Face still wet, she turned from the sink and regarded her leatherite jacket which she had tossed across the kitchen's fold-down table when she had made her way back here to home.

'That's bad enough.' Iris spoke to no one else as she picked up the jacket by its collar and regarded the damage the bullets had done to it. 'Christ,' she said in disgust as she poked the fingers of her other hand through the rips and tatters underneath one sleeve and along the corresponding side-seam. The jacket was a signature piece for her, as much as the collection of repro cowboyshirts she'd always worn underneath it. She would have felt naked out on the streets of LA without it.

Even worse, the cheap-ass LAPD didn't reimburse for in-field losses and damages like this. The only way Iris would have gotten any money out of the department, she knew from experience, would've been if the bullets had been an inch or two lower and closer to the center, and had left her flesh in bone-splintered tatters as well. She had never been able to figure out exactly how much of a morale-booster for the troops it was supposed to be, that the department was so willing – even eager – to splash out on funeral services, but not on incidental expenses along the way. Just irritating, she'd always considered the practice.

She threw the jacket across the table again and leaned back against the sink, arms folded across her chest. The money thing irritated her to what she knew was an irrational extent; the jacket wasn't so much of a loss – she could always get another, but not one that had been so nicely broken-in as this veteran, almost a second skin to her – except that she was also aware of how much she was in the hole on this job, already.

The extraction operation at the movie theater had gone well enough, in that both she and the owl had gotten out intact; and losing that weird Vogel character, whatever his personal agenda had been, was a bonus as well. But the material cost, all the expensive gear she had promised to return to Meyer, had been high: to really keep him clear with the departmental armory, she would've had to have retrieved the casing for the expended glare grenade, as well as the automatic rifle she'd laid on Vogel. Now, she couldn't even call in one of the department's regular clean-up crews, who would normally have taken care of the messy details like that; the gear had come out of the LAPD armory's back door, via Meyer, and hadn't been authorized to be in her possession to begin with. The only way to have kept in the clear would've been to sneak the stuff back into the armory the way it'd come out, without anyone knowing about its little excursion. She and Meyer both were in the deep shit. Meyer might be able to pull them out, with his usual string-pulling expertise inside the department, but she would then be even further beholden to him than she had been before – and that was a situation definitely not to her liking.

Which was why, she knew now, she had brought the owl here to her own place, rather than immediately getting it off her hands by taking it to Meyer at his office, either in the shiny, new police station or the old, abandoned one where he had given her this funky bird-hunting job. She hadn't planned on doing that, either before she had gone to the theater hiding-place with Vogel, or immediately after, when she had been on her own again. Some instinct or half-formed rationale inside her head had turned her steps toward home, rather than going ahead and finishing the job – the easiest part of it – no matter how much she had thought she'd wanted to.

She refilled the glass from the tap and carried it out to the apartment's living room, where she sourly regarded the owl on its improvised perch.

'You cost me, sucker.' Iris took a sip, then stepped over and refilled the dish she had put within reach of the owl. There had been enough left of the chain attached to the metal band on its foot that she had been able to secure the creature in place. The chat was already terrified of the intruder merely being in the apartment; if it'd been free to swoop around, with predatory intent toward anything smaller than itself and reasonably alive-seeming, the chat would probably have blown its circuits out of sheer panic. 'I don't know how yet,' said Iris, 'but I know you did.'

The owl maintained its dignified silence, gazing back at her with its round, golden eyes.

Iris looked down at the *pinyin* newspapers she had spread beneath the owl's perch. The papers were soaked wet around the base of the dish, blurring the vertical columns of Chinese ideograms; when she hadn't been watching, while she had been in the kitchen, the owl must have slaked its thirst. She wondered exactly how owls did that; could they lap water up, the way real cats supposedly did? It raised another question, which had already been nagging at the back of her mind, about keeping the animal alive. 'I suppose you gotta eat,' said Iris. The owl blinked its golden eyes, but otherwise made no comment.

She didn't have a fresh – and real – white rat to give to the creature. *Little out of my budget*, thought Iris. She was in the hole as it was, with this job. Did owls eat only live kill, or was that snakes? A vague memory played through her mind, something she'd read, that real frogs and toads had eyes or circuits in their brains that could only recognize moving, buzzing-around insects; a frog could be surrounded by mountains of tasty, nutritious dead flies and bugs, and starve to death because it couldn't tell they were there.

This thing should've come with a manual, groused Iris to herself. Either that, or she should have asked some questions of a more practical nature when she had been down at the animal traders' *souk*. Or kept one of the men in the room above the movie theater alive long enough to have found out what they had been feeding the thing.

'Let me see what I can find you.' The owl blinked back at her.

Iris left the apartment's front door open, as she was only going to the end of the hallway. By the trash chute opening, the building's management had set out an array of traps for the scurrying brown mice that were a constant feature of life in LA – another survivor species, like the pigeons that fouled the ledges and roofs of the older buildings.

Underneath a bare lightbulb swaying at the end of a frayed cord, Iris poked the toe of her boot through the traps, sorting out three that appeared to have been sprung recently. The blood spattered from the tiny corpses was still wet and shiny. Wrinkling her nose in distaste, she knelt down and pried open the traps, gingerly extracting the dead

95

mice, their eyes like tiny black beads. She realized that she hadn't brought anything from the apartment to carry them with; when she stood up, she had a palmful of soft, dampish-feeling fur objects, their bare tails trailing over the side of her hand.

'Try these,' said Iris. She deposited the tiny corpses on the newspaper in front of the owl. As she turned away to re-lock the front door, she heard the powerful whap of the owl's wings against the air, and the scrape of its claws across the paper. She looked back and saw the owl disassembling one of the dead mice, the hook of its beak tearing through the flesh beneath the soft grayish-brown fur.

Either the owl didn't, by its own nature, reject food it hadn't killed itself, or maybe the late Dr Tyrell had trained it that way; maybe the living and expensive white rat she had witnessed in the surresper's data record had been a special treat. Even someone as rich as the head of the Tyrell Corporation had been wouldn't have been able to come up with goodies like that on a regular basis.

Making progress, thought Iris. For the time being, at least, the problem of keeping the owl alive was solved. There was enough vermin in the apartment building to feed the thing indefinitely. But she wasn't planning on keeping it that long in her possession; the owl was still desired by some powerful people and forces. The sooner she figured out what to do with it, and then proceeded to get rid of the thing, the safer she'd be.

'Get rid of it,' echoed a tiny voice behind her.

Iris looked down over her shoulder and saw the chat pressing close to her ankles, looking around her shins at the feeding owl; the expression on the chat's round features was one of active hatred.

'Can't just yet.' Iris picked up the chat and held it to her with one forearm, careful not to stroke its endorphin-producing head. 'Gotta think.'

'What's to think about?' The chat laid its tiny paws on her breast. 'Icky.'

'Couple of items.' She walked a familiar circuit, back and forth in the apartment's living room, steering well clear of the owl. It had always helped sort out her thoughts, speaking them aloud to the chat; it was one of the artificial creature's useful functions for her. 'One – I don't really know what Meyer's intentions are, at least as far as I'm concerned.'

'Who's Meyer?'

96

'Nobody for you to worry about.' A big worry for her, though. The whole job stank even more of a set-up than it had before.

Not good. Iris shook her head as she continued walking back and forth, the chat held closer to her. She'd had some residual measure of trust in Meyer before, no matter how much he'd jerked her around, even before this job; that was *his* job, as head of the division, to hand out crap to all the blade runners, herself included. But not to get them killed, or at least not deliberately. A set-up like the one she could have found herself in – that amounted to a departmental execution, as efficient as putting a gun's muzzle behind her ear and pulling the trigger. Hard to go on trusting anyone, even minimally, with an analysis like that.

'But what did he want?' Iris mused over the question, taking one step after another, back and forth.

'Who?' The chat peered up into her face.

'Meyer.'

'Him again,' said the chat, annoyed.

It was the big question. *Did he want the owl*, thought Iris, *or did he want to get me killed?* Maybe both, though she wasn't sure how that would have worked out. But if her death had been Meyer's objective, then it would be suicide for her to go to the police station and hand over the owl. If the owl was in fact something that Meyer wanted, and not just a pretext to maneuver her into a situation where she'd get killed, then as soon as he had the damn thing, he'd have no reason to keep her alive; people got iced all the time inside police stations, cops included. The entrance to the building, either on street level or up on top where the spinners landed, was sometimes a one-way door, with no exit other than in a box. But those cops who got executed by the department were nearly always ones who'd screwed up big-time, either by taking so many bribes from criminal types that the internal-investigations division had no choice but to get rid of them, or by reason of having run afoul of departmental politics, getting on the wrong side of one of the brass way above Meyer's rung on the ladder. Right off-hand, she couldn't think of any reason why anybody up above would want to eliminate her.

It's like being a replicant, thought Iris. Or to be more exact, like a replicant who doesn't know that it's not human. She'd never had to retire one like that – at least, not yet – but she'd heard of a few cases where the poor bastards thought they were human, and then, as though they'd been dropped into a Kafka novel rewritten by Mickey

Spillane, found themselves being hunted down by some armed and legal nemesis figure like Iris herself. *You wake up one day*, it struck her, *and somebody wants you dead. For no reason you've been told.* She felt a twinge of pity, not only for herself, but for those replicants who got killed without even knowing why.

'Screw it,' Iris said aloud. She didn't care what the reason might be; she just wanted to stay alive. Again, like those poor bastard replicants; all of them, whether they knew what they were or not. She was starting to feel a little sympathy for them – which was a dangerous road for a blade runner to go down. First mere sympathy, then empathy, the actual sensing and experiencing of another creature's sufferings; Iris couldn't figure how she'd be able to do her job if that happened to her. *I'd have to give up being a cop*, she thought, *and go for being a saint*.

'The way I see it,' Iris told the chat, 'is that I've got a couple of options.' Neither of them impressed her as very good. 'I could call up Meyer—'

'Hrmph.'

'And try to cut a deal with him. If he wants this owl – or if somebody above him does – then they're not getting it until I'm in the clear. Meaning that I walk away after delivery, and nobody tries to retire me.'

The chat hadn't understood what she had said, but nodded its round, bald head anyway. 'Sounds good.'

'Only if you're an idiot,' said Iris. 'Which I'm not, except to the extent I got myself roped into this mess in the first place. I already don't trust the guy; why should I trust him about keeping a promise to let me live after I hand over the owl to him?'

'Dunno.'

'Exactly. Besides, it might not be up to him. If he's merely the errand boy, following somebody else's orders, he could make all the promises in the world, have every intention of carrying them out, and I'd *still* get iced. He might, too, but that wouldn't do me any good.'

'Gosh.' The chat wrinkled its simple features in perplexity. 'Doesn't sound nice.'

'You got that right, pal.' Iris stopped pacing, nodding slowly to herself as she mulled over the various bleak possibilities in front of her. 'Which leaves the other option . . .'

'Is?'

Iris glanced over at the owl. 'I try to figure out what's so important about our guest here.' She pointed a thumb toward the creature. 'And exactly why some people seem to want it so badly.'

'Ee-yuck.' The chat scowled. '*I* don't. Get rid of it!'

'Wish I could.' A sigh moved up from her heart. 'You don't know how *much* I wish I could.' This whole business, symbolized by the owl, had gotten way more complicated than she would have been able to imagine at the beginning. Her former life, in which all she had to do was track down and kill escaped replicants, now seemed like some vanished paradise, graced with an innocent and leisurely charm. 'But I'm stuck with it. For the time being.'

'How long's that?'

Something in the chat's question raised the skin prickling along her forearms. 'What do you mean?'

'You know.' The chat pushed itself back from her chest, so it could look up at her, full-face. 'Until something happens.' It tilted its round head to one side, small button eyes appearing slyer. 'More guests?'

Every once in a while, the chat's simpler brain circuits hit it right on the mark, catching something she had overlooked. *Of course*, thought Iris. The base beneath her gut seemed to vanish. *Something is going to happen. And soon.* The guests would be coming, and their visit, while short, wasn't likely to be pleasant. Iris cursed her own stupidity, the amount of time she'd wasted fidgeting and fussing, right here where anybody looking for her would be sure to find her. And there would be people looking; too many possible connections were hooked up between her and what had gone down in the room above the movie theater for her to have gotten away scot-free. Meyer had known that something was going to happen as soon as he'd delivered the gear from the armory to her; when she didn't get back to him within a reasonable amount of time, he'd start his own investigation. He might not know where the action had been, but to find out if she was still even alive the first place he'd come looking would be right here at her apartment. The multiple coded locks on the door wouldn't slow him down; by departmental regulation, every cop had to log his or her code registry in the police station's personnel database, to facilitate surprise inspections for contraband and/or ongoing drug-usage violations. With his rank, Meyer would be able to pull those codes and come waltzing in here whenever he felt like it. And would he be happy to find the desired owl sitting here, instead of having already been delivered to him at the station? Probably not – and he was smart enough to flash onto the simplest explanation for that non-delivery, which was that Iris no longer trusted him. In as nasty a situation as this one was shaping up to be, personal problems like that were likely to be solved by simple termination. Not from the job, but from one's life.

And Meyer wasn't the only one she had to worry about dropping in on her unexpectedly. The armed and ugly men from whom she had lifted the owl had undoubtedly been working for somebody else; they'd had the Rottweilerish appearance of mercenaries, highly skilled and equipped ones, but still operating on somebody else's orders. Somebody who could very likely afford other hired thugs, who in turn would be able to do their job more efficiently than the last batch, as Iris would no longer have the element of surprise on her side. For all she knew, they were already on their way; the owl might have some kind of micro-seed tracer element planted in or on it that she would have no way of detecting without using the through-pulse scanners at the police station's security labs. Her apartment could already be in the center of a glowing red circle on a track-in-progress screen, with other ominous red dots moving in on it . . .

'Shit.' Iris pulled the chat off her and dropped it, squealing in protest, to the floor. She hurried to the kitchen module and pulled her damaged leatherite jacket off the shoulder holster she had previously draped across the fold-down table. From the holster she extracted her gun; its weight in her hands provided more comfort at the moment than all the chat's exudations could have.

Iris walked back out into the apartment's living room, with both hands wrapped around the gun's checked grip, its muzzle pointed down but ready to be swung up at the first target to present itself. From its perch at the side of the room, the owl regarded her with round-eyed impassivity, as she flattened her spine against the wall beside the window. She took one hand from the gun and spread the slatted blinds apart, enough to peer out through the barred window and down to the street below. Tendrils of active neon laced their reflections through the blue-black mirrors of the pavement, slick with rain; a formation of nocturnal bicyclists, masked and shrouded, splashed through and disappeared in the distance, intent on their mysterious group-errand or religious observation. Then the street was empty, except for the shades of her fears, unseen but sensed as they gathered closer.

You're being an idiot, Iris told herself. *Like they're going to come walking down the street and ring your bell in the building lobby.* More likely, given the resources that the thugs' employers seemed to have at their disposal, an unlicensed police-level spinner would land silently on the roof, the men with the guns would just as silently break through the access door's locks, and they would sift down through the stairwells and corridors like the unavoidable heat of an LA dry-season Santa Ana wind. One you didn't know was coming, until it hit you in the face and sucked the breath out of your lungs.

A little voice spoke, from down beside her ankles. 'You're scaring me,' said the chat in its tiniest-seeming, most fragile manner. It had rarely seen her gun inside the apartment, and never in her hand; Iris knew that the sight of the cold metal tended to upset the creature's delicately tuned sensibilities.

'I'm sorry, sweetie.' With her free hand, Iris scooped up the chat; she kissed it on its rounded brow, then set it back down on the floor. 'But this is a work thing, okay? Not just for spookiness. So I gotta do it. Understand?'

'No.' The chat shook its head. 'Don't.'

'You don't have to. Tell you what. Why don't you take your basket, and pull it into the closet? Nap time. Nice and quiet and dark. You'll be happier that way.' *No matter what happens*, Iris told herself grimly. 'Go on.' She pointed to the foam-padded basket in the corner of the room. 'Hop, hop.'

The chat continued to gaze up at her. 'But what about *you*?'

'Don't worry about me,' said Iris. *I'll take care of that.* 'You go bed down.' She let her voice take on a stern edge. 'Right now. Move it.'

Reluctantly, the chat did as ordered. When Iris was alone in the apartment's front room again – alone except for the owl, blinking its round, golden eyes, the source of all her recent troubles – she stilled her breath and heartbeat as far as possible, listening into the resultant silence for the slightest sound of intruders anywhere in the building. She heard nothing but the almost subliminal inhaling and exhaling of the structure itself, the mingled indicators of the living things, dreaming or awake, in the rest of its small rooms.

Iris was so intent on listening, as though she had been transformed into one of the small creatures pursued through night forests by owls and other predators, that she jumped from sheer nerves when an already-familiar voice spoke again. 'Cuddle,' demanded the chat.

'For Christ's sake.' She had swung around with the gun clasped in both her hands, aiming it straight toward the chat in the doorway to the apartment's bedroom. Her arms and shoulders de-tensed as she lowered the gun. 'I *told* you to go to the closet and take a nap. You're going to be in my way if you hang around here.'

'Will not,' the chat said stubbornly.

'I don't want you around. Okay? That's an order.' Iris had another reason for wanting the artificial creature to go to sleep. Her alternate plan, swiftly coalescing in her thoughts, was to get out of the apartment entirely, taking the owl with her somehow, and going on the run. Anywhere out on the streets would be preferable to a place where she could be tracked down so easily. If she did split – and that option seemed increasingly sensible to her – she didn't want the chat to pitch a fuss as she went out the door. Her hands would already be full with the owl bagged and tucked under her arm again, the way she had brought it to the apartment in the first place. 'Go.'

The chat shook its head. 'You need me.'

Iris let the gun dangle at her side as she gazed in exasperation at the small creature. Its persistence, cute at less pressing times, was seriously annoying her now. 'How do you figure that?'

'Come on.' The chat shifted its small weight from side to side, as though exhibiting its own impatience. 'You're stressed out. I can *tell*. Countering deleterious stress and its performance-degrading effects is why you got me. That's what I'm *for*.'

The creature had a point. It wasn't the same sort of mandatory equipment as her upgraded-from-standard-issue surresper, but at the same time she knew that a lot of cops, particularly those in the blade runner division, had artificial companions similar or identical to the chat in whatever places they called home. A highly recommended practice; a cop could get, if not a black mark, then a definite gray in his personnel folder from the departmental shrinks for not having a chat-like buddy on which to unload his griefs and tensions. Cop life was hard on normal human relationships; marriages were rare, divorces frequent, domestic homicides common enough to have merited their own slang reference: 'at-home retirement'. Chats and other substitutes for regular, civilian-type social interaction had one big advantage over the human type, in that an artificial talking companion, if it got on one's frayed nerves too badly, could be eliminated without legal entanglements. Which could be a satisfying, even therapeutic experience in its own way; there was still a dark scorch mark down by the baseboards of the apartment's living room wall, where this chat's immediate predecessor had exploded into nasty-smelling plastic shrapnel when Iris, grumpily exasperated by its small talk, had emptied her gun into its rounded belly. That had been before she had at least partially mastered her temper. She didn't go in for that kind of emotional catharsis anymore; even if legal, chats made for expensive target practice.

'Your nerves are shot,' continued the current chat. 'Shaky hands; you could get hurt!'

'Don't worry about me.' Iris tightened her grip on the gun hanging at her side. 'I'll be all right.'

'Yeah – but what about *me*?' The chat bobbed up and down in the kitchen doorway. 'This is a wick-wick-wicked universe we live in. Full of bad things! Gotta protect the ones you love.'

It struck Iris that the situation must be as grim as she herself had perceived it to be. She had never heard the chat speak at such length before. 'What do you propose, buddy?'

'Take one hit.' The chat hurriedly waddled over to her and stretched up on its pudgy legs toward her free hand. 'It'll calm you down. Then you can shoot *real straight*. Get the bad guys. I promise you.'

She considered the small creature's offer. In its own way, it was exhibiting more bravery than she was, given how terrified it was of the owl perched on the other side of the room.

'Just a little,' wheedled the chat. 'I'll tone it down. I will, I will! Mild and sweet, guaranteed to make you a better, more productive lethal agent. Come on . . . you *know* you want to . . .'

'All right, all right. Jeez,' said Iris, giving in. 'Nag, nag, nag.' She reached down with her non-gun hand and laid her fingertips across the top of the chat's head, already shining with its chemical exudations.

The jolt came up her arm like lightning, a straight shot to the top of her skull. Where it exploded in white, glaring radiance, blinding and felling. The last sensation she had before her knees went liquid and buckled from beneath her was her fingers flaring out from each other, rigid and spastic, the gun's warmed black metal dropping away like an inert, dead stone.

A micro-gap in consciousness ended when the side of her face struck the floor. Iris could feel her heart laboring inside her chest, and could focus on the door at the other side of the room, but no more than that.

Sparks danced outside her overloaded cortex as the vertical row of doorlocks melted through and gave way, one after another. A few points of light were still sizzling and dying from white to red, inches from her trembling, paralyzed hand, as the door swung open. The still functioning parts of her brain expected several intruders to walk through, but instead only one pair of dark-trousered legs was visible, striding unhurriedly toward where she lay prostrate.

'Useful things,' said an unfamiliar voice. Iris couldn't see the man's face. 'If you know what's inside them.' One hand and arm became visible, reaching down and picking up the chat from the floor. The creature was no longer active; its button eyes were dull and gray, as though the charge it had delivered had also burnt out the delicate circuits inside. 'But you didn't. Not this one, at any rate.'

A ringer, thought Iris. The amused tone in the man's voice irritated her, but not enough to overcome the residual paralysis in her limbs. *Somebody . . . must have snuck it in . . .*

The man stepped over her. For a moment, Iris expected to feel something else, the smooth circular business-end of a gun's muzzle being placed behind her ear. Which would've been the last thing she would have felt.

That didn't happen. Instead, she heard a noise from the other side of the room, like small metal being snapped apart, then the owl's hooting cry and the muffled flap of its broad wings.

'Thanks,' came the man's voice once again. 'I appreciate your hard work. You've saved me a great deal of difficulty. Retrieving this valuable merchandise would not have been quite as easy for me as it apparently was for you.'

With a convulsive spasm of will, Iris managed to thrash herself onto her back. She had only a brief glimpse of the owl, snugged inside the soft bag in which she had brought it to the apartment, and nothing of the man's face, before she found herself gazing up at the water-stained ceiling.

'Who are . . . you working for?' The words creaked and stumbled from Iris's dried mouth. 'Who . . . sent you?'

'Do you really need to know?' A smile was audible in the man's soft voice. 'Think about it. I've given you a little present. The most valuable one possible: time. Think about what you need. Because right now . . . you don't really know.'

Whatever time existed, there wasn't enough for her to try and ask another question. With her fingertips still quivering against the floor beside her, Iris heard the apartment's front door swing open. And then the footsteps of the man, carrying his prize with him, fading away in the corridor beyond.

9

'You should've brought it to me.' Hands clasped between his knees, Meyer leaned forward in the chair beside the hospital bed. 'Straight off. I could've helped you.'

It was still hard for Iris to talk. Her tongue felt like some formerly living part, which had been extracted and embalmed, then sewn back into her mouth. 'Now . . .' Overly sensitized, she could feel the muscles at the back of her neck contract and release against the starchy white pillow as she forced out one word after another. 'Now you tell . . . me . . .'

'For Christ's sake.' Meyer sounded both angry and disgusted. He picked up the paper cup from the table, fished out a thawed-smooth ice chip between his thumb and forefinger and placed it between Iris's lips. 'As if you didn't know already – or you should've known, if you hadn't been trying to be so fucking clever.'

'You're right . . .' Iris gratefully let the cold liquid trickle into her throat, still raw-feeling from the air-passage tube that the doctors had shoved down it, like an unpleasant sexual encounter. 'That's . . . my problem . . .'

'Your *problem*,' said Meyer, 'is not trusting people. Or at least the ones you *should* trust. Like me. No, instead you've got your brain jacked up into overdrive all the time, turning every little thing over and over like a monkey with a nut, looking for the way to crack it and find out what's inside.' He shook his head. 'You can't just deal with things on the surface; everything's gotta be a big mystery to be solved.'

'Come on . . . ease up on me.' Iris felt worse now than she had when the emergency paramedics spinner had dumped her off on top of the LAPD hospital tower. Then she had been doped up, an IV morphine drip fat as a baby anaconda needled into her wrist by one of the angels in their blood-spattered, lime-green surgical scrubs; the anesthetic had been in addition to most of her cerebral cortex having

105

been shut down by the jolt she had received from the booby-trapped chat. 'I already . . . feel like crap . . .'

'It's what you deserve,' grumbled Meyer.

'You're so . . . sympathetic . . .'

'Not my job to be. Like it wasn't your job to take that owl home and babysit the damn thing. What your job was, was to *get* it and bring it to me. And that's all.'

'Sorry.' Iris barely opened one eye, and watched as Meyer pushed himself up from the chair and began pacing back and forth in the small, equipment-crowded room. 'I screwed up . . .'

'No shit.' Meyer was as angry-looking as she had ever seen him. 'This one's gonna cost us both, big time. My ass is on the line in about twelve different locales – mainly upstairs at the police station. Major heat – and for what?' He had already crossed the room a half-dozen times; now he stopped and swung his dark gaze back at her. 'And what did you accomplish, with your flipped-out paranoiac ratiocination? *Nada.*'

'Less than.' She wondered how long he was going to go on chewing her out. 'I agree.'

'For Christ's sake, Iris, you had the goddamn bird in your hands.' Teeth gritted, Meyer let his own hands curl into fists, as though he were laying hold of the object under discussion. 'In the *bag*. All you would've had to do was drop it in my lap, just like that, and you and I would both be golden in the department, no matter what we'd done to pull it off. We could've cleaned out the armory and sold it to Uzbeki gunrunners, and nobody would've cared. Didn't I make that clear to you at the beginning? How important this stupid owl is? Or was I only talking to myself?'

'I heard you.' Iris managed a small nod. 'The first time.'

'You didn't hear me enough, then.' Meyer slowly shook his head, the anger visibly draining out of him, as though his choleric skin was no more than a punctured balloon. 'Not nearly enough.' He sat down heavily on the corner of the high hospital bed, barely clearing the monitoring wires and the tubes from the dangling plastic bags. 'I gotta tell you, Iris – I don't see the way out of this one.' His shoulders slumped forward, bearing the weight of his sorrows. 'There's not a lot of favors I've got left that I can call in. You and I were both pretty much overdrawn on those accounts, before we even got into this mess.'

'Wait a minute.' Iris managed to struggle a little higher on the pillows stacked behind her. 'What . . . are you talking about?' Her movements sent microscopic bubbles up through the clear Ringer's solution seeping into her body. 'I thought . . . I was number one. In the whole division.'

'Yeah, right; the fair-haired girl. Killing machines like you are always popular with the top brass.' Meyer's disgust was audible in every spat-out word. 'For a while, at least. But any time somebody goes on too long, being a little too good at what she does, then the supervisor types start getting nervous. You're supposed to burn out, hit the low end of the Wambaugh Curve, drop out of the division or kill yourself, or find some way to get killed on the job. If nothing else, it saves the department heaps of money it'd otherwise have to pay out in retirement benefits – I mean the kind of retirement where you're still living and breathing. That kind is expensive, compared to a good, clean suicide; it'd take a lot of money to keep all of yesterday's blade runners in some old folks' home, stocked with enough cheap booze and adult-incontinency undergarments so they didn't come back out on the streets, waving their guns around and embarrassing everybody.'

'Sure . . .' The image evoked a feeble, wry smile from Iris. 'Give me a break, Meyer. I don't think . . . the department's really worried about what I'm going to be like . . . when I'm eighty. If I make it that far.'

'You won't at this rate.' Meyer's anger had ebbed to the point that the expression on his face was almost pitying. 'Stupidity has a low survival value. Especially in this business.'

The thin fabric of the hospital gown shifted across her body as her shoulders lifted in a shrug. 'I've done all right.'

'Up until now,' said Meyer. 'But that's over.'

His words produced a chilling crawl of flesh beneath the bandages that kept the tubes in place. 'What do you mean?'

'Over – as in over for you. You're done. *Finito*.'

'All right . . .' Iris nodded. 'Whatever. I didn't care for this whole owl business, anyway. I'd rather be out on the streets, taking care of real blade runner business.'

'You don't get it, do you?' The pity in Meyer's eyes was even more obvious now. 'When I say "over", I mean all the way over. You're not just done, you're out. As in goodbye. Get the picture?'

Iris couldn't believe what she'd heard. 'You mean, out of the division?'

'The division, the department, the cop business – the whole nine yards.' Meyer reached over and gently patted her knee, beneath the hospital-bed blanket. 'You're busted, sweetheart. Right on your sweet ass. You'll be going back out on the streets, all right – the nurses told me you'd be on your feet again in a couple of days – but you won't be going out there as any kind of a cop. It's civilian time for you again. Little people—' The tenderness faded from Meyer's voice, and his hand squeezed viciously tight on her leg. 'Know what I mean?'

'Yeah,' said Iris. 'I sure do.' The anger surging up from her gut produced enough strength for a backhanded swing of one fist, connecting hard enough against Meyer's jaw to knock him against the bed's metal end rail. One of the rehydration tubes tore loose from the needle inserted in Iris's wrist, spraying clear fluid across the top blanket; a trickle of blood seeped from under the loosened bandage and through her knuckles. 'You sonuvabitch. You sold me out – or you set me up; I don't know which one's worse.' Fury turned the edges of her vision red, as though the blood had gotten into her eyes. 'This whole thing was a screw, right from the beginning.'

'Hey – you want to think that, fine.' Meyer rubbed the bruise at the side of his jaw. 'I'm glad if it makes you feel better about it. Because there aren't going to be a lot of bright spots in your life after this. And you know what I mean about *that*, too, I bet. Nobody works as a cop for very long, at least in a city like LA, without making more enemies than friends, both on the streets and inside the department. Believe me; I should know.' He took his hand away from his face and used it to lay a finger on the lapel of his tailored jacket. 'But now there's a difference between you and me.' The finger pointed in Iris's direction. 'I'm still a cop – and you're not. I've still got some protection going for me, at least as long as the department knows that it's a negative morale inducer for the troops to see some other cop get thrown to the street wolves. I might get ripped up pretty good over this owl fiasco, but I'm still on the inside, out of the rain – and in the rain is where you're going to be, when the hospital finally boots you. And that's a cold, wet place to be.' Meyer smiled, humorlessly. 'But don't worry. Ex-cops don't last long there. Your suffering will be over, relatively quickly.'

Her eyes drew into slits as she regarded her ex-boss. 'I'll do all right,' said Iris. 'Let's just say that my job skills are transferable.'

'Sure they are. And you'll be fine.' Meyer shrugged. 'You want to bullshit yourself about your survival chances, then I'm happy to help you. It's the least I can do . . . for old times' sake.' His smile became genuine, and regretful. 'We did some good work together, Iris; killed off a lot of things that look exactly like you and me – or at least close enough to pass as human. That's got to count for something, these days.'

'Spare me.' Iris folded her arms, dragging the still-attached tubes and wires with them, across the front of the hospital gown. 'If it meant so much to you,' she said bitterly, 'I wouldn't be getting tossed like last night's condom.'

'Well . . . that's business.' With a sigh, Meyer stood up from the corner of the bed. He stepped toward the room's door – not far – and laid his hand on the metal knob, then looked back at her. 'You didn't trust me, Iris. And you should have. The one time when you really needed to – for both our sakes – and you didn't.'

Watching him as he stood at the door, Iris found herself with nothing to say.

'Take care of yourself.' Meyer pulled the door open, revealing the bright-lit corridor beyond, and the murmuring, uneasy silence of the clicking machines and green-lined monitors inside other rooms, beside other beds. 'How about doing me a favor, though? Last one.'

Iris hesitated a moment, then nodded. 'Name it.'

'Whatever happens to you out there –' He indicated the city beyond the room's blank wall. 'Make sure I don't hear about it.'

'All right.' She gave another nod. *It means*, thought Iris, *that he really cares*. Whatever that was worth. 'It's a deal. I guess I owe you that much.'

'I appreciate it.' Meyer started to step through the open doorway, then stopped and turned back toward the bed. 'Got something for you.' He dug one hand through his outside jacket pocket. 'A souvenir. Something to remember your last official cop job by.'

'Like I'd want to?'

'Your decision.' Meyer shrugged. 'With this, though, you'll be able to say that at least you got your hands on it.' He tossed a small object to her. 'That's something, given the circumstances.'

She caught it between her palms, then opened them side by side to see what it was. For a moment, she had the bizarre notion that her old boss was proposing marriage to her: a metal ring lay in her hands. But it was too small, and made of some dull, lead-looking metal, rather than gold. As though it were part of some miniaturized bondage gear, a chain of even smaller links dangled from the metal.

Then Iris realized she had seen it before, on the leg of the owl. The band that had kept the creature tethered to its perch had been pried open at one side, presumably by its present captor, the one who had taken it from her.

'All that's left,' said Meyer. 'Left behind. Yours to keep now, for ever and ever. Or maybe a little less than that.'

Whether it was meant as cruel or tender – Iris didn't know. *And he doesn't know*, she thought. Not about the gift's intent, but the clue it contained, that she had felt when she rubbed her thumb inside the broken band. Something that broke the smoothness of the metal, like tiny microscopic scratches; Meyer could have drawn his thumb across them, and probably had, but hadn't felt them. *A woman's touch*, thought Iris. *That's what it takes.*

She didn't say anything about it, but closed the band and its dangling chain inside her fist. 'Thanks. I'll treasure it. Always.' A slow nod of her head. 'You don't know how much it means.'

'Don't go overboard,' said Meyer. 'And sarcasm's wasted on me. Like everything else.' He stepped out into the corridor and pulled the door shut behind him.

As soon as the sound of his footsteps had faded away, Iris was out of the bed, blanket and sheets thrown back, the tubes and wires yanked off her skin. Barefoot, she tugged open the closet tucked into the corner of the small room, beneath the unlit television on its wall-bracket, and found her clothes hanging inside. Even the leatherite jacket, with its bullet-torn sleeve; the paramedics must have scooped it up, along with her unconscious body. That was a lucky break, the only real one she'd had in a long time.

Adrenaline, and the effort of getting dressed before anyone discovered what she was doing, left her dizzy; she had to lean her shoulder against the wall until the dancing black spots disappeared from in front of her eyes. Then she was out the door, and down the corridor as silently as possible, past the beds. Nobody at the nurses' station looked up as she passed by them.

In the elevator, Iris had just enough strength left to punch the ground-floor button, then keep herself upright, slumped against one corner, as the machine descended to the dark city streets.

10

When she went looking, she found ruins.

Jesus Christ, thought Iris, impressed despite herself. One never had to go far in a city such as LA to come across the broken and monumental evidence of the past; the city's present incarnation was an unsuccessful retrofit, exposed wiring and ventilation ductwork snaking across the exteriors of the shabby buildings like so many sinews and tracheae exposed by God the Vivisectionist's scalpels. At some point – Iris didn't know when; it wasn't the kind of thing she thought about – the notion of the future, of things being new, had been abandoned. In LA, the future and the past had become one intertwined substance, like the gnarled roots of dead trees.

But what she saw now was different. And worse, because she had never seen anything like it before.

The dark, cloud-heavy night sky rolled above her as she stood at the edge of the cleared space, broken concrete shrapnel and tiny bits of heat-scorched metal beneath her bootsoles, that surrounded the ruins. Intact buildings towered behind her, separated by the streets and transit lanes by which she had reached this point; even before she had arrived at her destination, she had been able to see the hole in the skyline, the absence of a man-made structure somehow more imposing than any physical shape could have been. The other thing that Iris had observed as she approached the spot had been the street crowds thinning out, the density of massed human forms dispersing like oxygen molecules into a vacuum. So much so that in the last few blocks she had been alone, walking in the building's night-shadows, a few scraps of sodden, yellowing paper dragged by the wind against her ankles, then tumbling and dying in the debris-clogged gutters. A few slanted rectangles of light, gray-dimmed by low mists, had fallen upon her from above; she had looked up and seen faceless silhouettes regard her in anonymous silence. Then they had turned away, as though already mourning her passage, and the high windows had remained empty.

Dread had emptied the streets around the ruins, the primeval fear of those places where holy violence had been visited upon the earth. The monsoon rains, hot and nocturnal, started up again; the drops collected and trickled down to Iris's jaw and neck as she stood and looked up at the still-imposing bulk of shattered walls and twisted inner network of rusting steel girders. *Must've been big*, thought Iris, already realizing how simple-minded that thought was. The bigness of whatever the structure had been was obvious; even in this post-destruction state, the remains towered nearly as high as the surrounding buildings. If the structure hadn't been designed or forced to collapse inward upon itself – Iris had enough experience and departmental training to recognize the tell-tale signs of high-powered core charges – it would have taken out and leveled everything around it as well, perhaps for as far as a half-mile.

'Pretty impressive, huh?'

The voice startled her; Iris turned and saw a familiar face smiling at her. *Too familiar*, she thought.

'Why,' said Iris flatly, 'am I not surprised to see you here?'

Vogel shrugged, in an awkward, one-shouldered manner; his other arm was held by a sling to his chest. 'We have a common destiny, sweetheart.' The smile on his angular face widened. 'At least for the time being. Whither thou goest, so goest I.'

'Great.' Iris shook her head in disgust. 'I thought I got rid of you.'

This time, Vogel laughed aloud. 'You almost did. And after all the help I'd been to you.'

'That's the kind of girl I am. You can't trust me.' Iris pointed to his immobilized arm. 'Maybe you'd better leave before something worse happens to you.'

'What?' Rain darkened Vogel's buzz-cut scalp and the upper part of his nondescript coveralls. 'And miss the fun?'

'Believe me – I wish I could.' Iris's mood turned even bleaker. 'Just about all your "help" accomplished was to nearly get me killed. And then it *did* get my ass fired from the police department.'

'Yeah . . .' Vogel nodded. 'I heard about that.'

Iris gave him a harder look, but didn't bother asking how he would have known. He'd either lie about it, or she wouldn't believe him. What was the difference?

'But you're not laying that one on me,' continued Vogel. 'There are some things being done to you, and then others that you've brought on yourself. Like right now. I'd still be as friendly and helpful as before, if you hadn't left me to get iced back at that movie theater.'

'Doesn't seem to have happened, though.' She nodded toward the arm in the sling. 'Except for that little bit.'

'It's the thought that counts, sweetheart. And believe me –' Vogel waggled the arm slightly, like a pinioned wing. 'It took some doing to get away with only this much damage. Good thing for me, that I have fast reflexes. I would've hated to have missed this special moment with you. Right here and right now.' His smile showed again, lazily insinuating. 'But then . . . it was meant to be.'

In the distance, up in the night sky and through the steady, blood-temperature rain, the soft shriek of a police spinner vehicle was audible. Iris turned and looked over her shoulder at the streak of light, converging with others like it on some point at the city's edge. Searchlights, blurred by the layers of mist, swept downward like the attentions of predatory birds. *Some other poor bastard*, thought Iris, *is in trouble*. It was like LA's monsoon-season weather, always ready to descend upon and envelop someone.

Iris turned back to Vogel, standing beside her. 'How did you find me?'

'I can always find you,' replied Vogel. 'Better question: how did you know to come here?'

'This.' She reached into her jacket pocket, underneath the bullet-torn sleeve, and pulled out a scrap of interlinked metal. 'My boss – my former boss – gave it to me.' She held it out on the flat of her palm.

'Meyer?' With one finger, Vogel poked at the metal band and bit of chain that had once been fastened to the owl's leg. 'Why'd he do that?'

'No good reason. Not really.' Iris gave a shrug. 'He wanted me to have a souvenir – that's what he called it. He didn't know what it had inside.'

'Which is?'

Something in the tone of Vogel's words disturbed her, even more than the mere fact of his physical presence. It struck Iris that his questions were all of things to which he already knew the answers somehow; he knew, but had to ask her anyway, as though it were part of some barely perceivable ritual through which he was leading her. To where, she had no idea.

'Data. Information.' Iris decided to play along once again, with

113

whatever game this mysterious figure had initiated. 'Nothing too esoteric; there was some GPS coding micro-incised on the inside of the owl's leg-band. I figured it must've been put there by the owl's original owners – either the Tyrell Corporation, when it was still functioning, or maybe Dr Eldon Tyrell. Like a "Return if Found" message, only with the geophysical location co-ordinates instead of an address.'

'And that's why you came here?' Genuine amusement showed in Vogel's smile. 'You don't have anything to return to anybody. You lost it, remember? And' – he glanced over at the monumental ruins before them, then back to her – 'there's nobody here to return it to. Is there?'

'Right,' said Iris irritably. 'I can see that much.' The guy was getting on her nerves again, with his smugly mocking attitude. Her only regret about leaving him to get killed by the mercenaries at the movie theater was that the putzes hadn't been able to pull it off. 'I'm not blind, you know.'

'Maybe not.' Vogel gave a slow, judicious nod. 'But you're pretty much in the dark, though. You don't even know *why* you came here. Do you?'

'It was a lead. A clue.' Her own voice sounded sullen to her. 'Sure, I didn't know what I'd find, but I had to come here and look. That's my job.'

'No, it isn't. You keep forgetting things. You don't *have* a job anymore. You're not a blade runner now; Meyer fired you. You're on your own.' The edge of Vogel's sharp gaze seemed to peel back a layer of her skin. 'So whatever you do, you're doing it for your own reasons. You just don't know what they are yet.'

'And you do?'

'Maybe,' said Vogel. 'After all, there's all sorts of things I know that you don't. Important things. And not only about owls and stuff.' The hand that he could still use reached out and laid a fingertip on her rain-damp brow. 'Things about *you*.'

'Prove it.' Iris slapped his hand away from her face. 'Otherwise, I've got stuff to do.'

'You don't have anything more important than *this*.' Vogel's hand gestured, with exaggeratedly slow grace, toward the ruins. 'This means *everything* to you.'

'Are you kidding?' She sneered at both him and the mountains of rubble. 'I don't even know what this place is.'

'Exactly,' said Vogel. He turned his head slightly, peering closer at her. 'Don't you think that's strange? I mean – your not knowing about this place. It's a big surprise to you, isn't it? You've never seen it before.'

'No.' Iris shook her head. 'I haven't.'

'Yet look at the size of it.' Vogel turned and gestured expansively, with his one good hand. 'It's huge. Before its fall, it must have been the largest building complex in all of Los Angeles.'

'Maybe.'

'Trust me on this one. It was. And here's what's left of it, right in the heart of LA, and you don't know anything about it.'

'It's a big city. I can't be expected to know every square foot of it.'

'For a city girl, you've got some interesting gaps in your geography,' Vogel said. 'But never mind. Come on. I'll show you around.' He started walking toward the jagged floes of steel-reinforced concrete, like an Arctic explorer heading toward the jumbled forward edge of glacial ice. When Iris didn't follow, he stopped and glanced over his shoulder at her. 'What's the matter? You got a lot out of the last time. Why are you scared now?'

She didn't know. *But he's right*, she thought. *I'm terrified.* It was a new feeling for her, one so intriguing that she felt she could almost step outside her own skin and study it, like a close examination of her image in a mirror. She took her focus from her trembling soul and laid it upon the mounted ruins beyond the taunting Vogel. The rain had increased its slanting fury, the monsoon's leading edge having given way to the heart of the storm; both she and Vogel were drenched to the skin. Her eyes had adjusted to the fractional blue streetlight seeping out from between the intact buildings behind her; it glistened upon the crumbling edges of the broken mass, rivulets collecting and trickling from one irregular form to the next, spiraling down ridged loops of rebar and burst phone and electrical cables. The shadows deepened in the ruins' crevices, more lightless than the night sky tinged orange by the sudden gouts of flame, high above.

Gazing upon the storm-lashed ruins, Iris realized at least one reason why it so frightened her. It was the first empty place she had ever seen in LA; empty as in unoccupied by any human presence, real or artificial. Everywhere else in the city someone could be sensed, even if not visible: some low-level empathic reaction picked up on the slight noises of respiration, breath and heartbeat, so quiet as to be under the threshold of normal hearing, or on the soft electrical tides of catecholamines inside the skull. But there was always someone, watching or listening in turn. *Except here*, thought Iris. Even in as crowded a locale as LA, with its teeming streets and mingled human exhalations, with every possible hole inhabited, somehow these ruins had been left abandoned. Whatever the reason, it probably wasn't a good one.

'So what's it going to be?'

Vogel's words snapped her out of the dark reverie into which she had fallen. She looked up, taking a moment to reassemble the image of his face into something recognizable.

'You're going to have to make up your mind.' His voice turned sharper. 'I don't have all night. You know, you're not the only one with things to do. If I don't take care of my business with you involved, then I gotta get busy and find somebody else.'

It wasn't the first time that something said by Vogel had made her wonder exactly what his agenda was. The same disturbing perception struck her, of questions and answers planned in advance, like the catechism of some obscure, vaguely threatening religion – plus all the other ritual steps that had to be gone through, as though the ruins before which they stood were just one more point on the stations of the cross that had been laid upon the night streets of LA.

'All right,' said Iris. 'You're right; I don't really have anything else going right now.' She stepped forward, closing her eyes for a moment as though not wanting to see the cliff-edge in front of her. 'Lead on.'

The last of the streetlights' blue illumination fell away behind them, as Vogel brought her to a point some fifty meters or so around the edge of the ruins. Here, a pair of immense stone and metal slabs had jammed against each other, forming a triangular cavern with the ground. With his unencumbered hand, Vogel lifted a net-like skein of wires up from the unlit space's mouth, then ducked his head and entered. 'Come on.' He held the wires up for Iris. 'I can't show you what you need to see if you just hang out there.'

With her mind made up, fatal or otherwise, Iris didn't need any more prompting. She had already followed him into one destroyed and decayed locale, though the downed UN advertising blimp had been but the tiniest fraction of these ruins' immensity; perhaps this place would contain the answers to the questions raised by the other.

'I don't care for your taste in habitats.' With her head and shoulders bowed below the cavern's angled ceiling, Iris followed the darting beam of the small flashlight Vogel had taken from his coveralls' pocket. The ground beneath her feet was an inch deep in puddled water, seeping down from above. 'Why not get yourself a regular apartment?'

'What fun would that be?' Vogel glanced back at her, his smile malicious. 'Besides, the blimp was affectation; this is serious. This is where you *have* to be.'

Bet me, thought Iris grimly. The crude tunnel's ceiling had lowered even further, forcing both her and Vogel into a bent-kneed crouch as they proceeded into the dark confines. The air smelled musty and soggy-damp, and she had been wrong, technically, about the complex of ruins being unoccupied: the city's ubiquitous vermin, with eyes that glittered as yellow pinpoints in the beam of Vogel's flashlight, scurried ahead, their tiny, sharp claws pattering against the smaller chunks of rubble.

More disturbing noises, lower in pitch, came from the ruins themselves: soft groaning and grinding, as though the jagged slabs of concrete and twisted steel were about to go through some delayed seismic rearrangement, and come down collapsing upon her and Vogel's heads.

'Hey –' Iris's voice broke into echoes and died away. 'Is this place safe?'

'It's all relative.' Vogel glanced back at her. 'Considering how close you've come to getting killed out there.'

Their crouching progress caused Iris to lose track of distance traveled; she couldn't be sure whether they had gone a hundred meters into the tumbled ruins, switching from one narrow passage to another, or an accumulation of miles. The small reserves of strength she had managed to force together when she had slipped out of the hospital were now close to a final ebb; her heart was laboring in her chest as she steadied herself, with one hand clutching for holds on the rough surface of the tunnel wall.

Blind from exhaustion, Iris bumped into Vogel; he had stopped in the narrow passageway without her noticing.

'Careful . . .' With one hand locked onto her arm, he kept her from falling. 'We're right at the edge.'

Iris found that she could stand upright. At some point they had emerged from the tunnel into a larger space, though still roofed with the giant slabs of concrete and steel; she could sense their tonnage above, blotting out the night sky. She shook off Vogel's hand. 'Edge of what?'

'You'll dig this.' Vogel tucked the butt-end of the flashlight into his sling, so he could adjust the beam from narrow to wide. 'It's worth seeing.'

She watched as he played the light out to one side. The surfaces it struck were so far away that it seemed for a moment that she and Vogel were in some kind of subterranean cathedral, its vaultings and pillars constructed in pure brutalist fashion. The only thing missing was any semblance of floor or bare-earth ground a few feet from where they stood. A yawning chasm had opened up, almost bottomless in appearance as the flared beam of light angled down into it.

'What the hell is this?' Iris could see other shapes, complicated metal and transparent forms, all still interlinked, even though the destruction of the building complex above had obviously wrought major damage upon them. 'Some kind of factory?'

'You got it, sweetheart.' Vogel used the flashlight beam to pick out a few of the larger pieces of broken manufacturing equipment. 'This is the real heart of the late Tyrell Corporation – or some kind of major organ, at least. This is where the action went on, production-wise. All the assembly lines for the Tyrell Corporation's various replicant models were right here. We're talking about major bioengineering processes, building ready-to-ship units from cell cultures, all the way out to skin and hair; even the toenails. Everything except for a few bits and pieces that the Tyrell Corporation contracted out to specialist prototype developers, such as the eyes. Take a look.'

Iris stepped closer to the chasm's edge and looked down to where the flashlight beam slid across the jumbled-together factory equipment. A few of the transparent pieces of machinery revealed their contents: human-like forms, some merely skeletal, others with recognizable internal organs attached to the white frameworks. Adult figures, no children or infants; all were dead, but a few had obviously come closer to birth and life than others. To Iris, the contents of the chasm resembled a mass grave, torn open and exposed by whatever explosives had leveled the buildings above.

'Of course,' continued Vogel, 'this is just where they assembled the flesh and bones, the physical part of the product. There's a lot more to manufacturing replicants than that. Matter of fact, before Tyrell achieved a monopoly in the industry, there were other companies producing replicants. Not here in LA; most of the others were over in

Europe. What enabled the Tyrell Corporation to snap up the franchise for the UN's off-world emigration program – which was the big money – were the little extras, the non-physical stuff it put into its products. The programing; the stuff in the replicants' *heads*.'

Something about the dark vista in front of Iris, illuminated one piece at a time by the shifting flashlight beam, angered her. She could feel a surge of blood at the center of her skull, as the small bright oval assembled a deeply concave terrain of broken production equipment and pale human forms, dried and flensed by the heat of the explosions into twisted leather and protruding splinters of ivory, all of which would perish no further. An image came into her thoughts, of the Tyrell Corporation's production line as it had been once, brightly lit, sterile and efficient as a hospital operating room on a grander scale. Iris could see it all, as clearly as though the other image, the one produced by Vogel's flashlight poking about in the darkness, were something evoked on a phosphor-dot screen, pixels without substance or meaning. *This is the illusion*, thought Iris, closing her eyes to the world in front of her, watching instead the one that had sprung up behind the wall of her brow. That one seemed both more real and more alive, with the human-like forms stirring their limbs, awake and fully formed, right down to the memories inside them; an industrial birth, but nevertheless a true one. The gift of Dr Eldon Tyrell, no matter how limited or dark its intent. A four-year lifespan was still life.

Vogel's words broke into her thoughts. 'Most of that cerebral-content design stuff took place upstairs.' He sounded like a dispassionate tour-guide. 'The actual force-loading process was one of the last steps before the de-vatting—'

'Okay, okay.' Iris stepped back from the chasm's edge. 'I've seen enough. If this is what you wanted to show me, great, you've done it. But I'm ready to leave now.'

'No, you're not.' The beam of Vogel's flashlight swung back into the tunnel where they stood. 'The show's only started.' He started down another branch. 'Come on.'

The new path led upward, sometimes steeply enough that Iris had to scramble up tilted slabs and rubble piles to keep Vogel in sight. Despite the exertions necessary, her breath came easier to her, the air in the higher spaces less confined and rank; through a few overhead chinks, Iris managed to catch fragmented glimpses of the night sky.

'Here we go.' Vogel stopped at a level section. 'This is what you came here for.'

The flashlight revealed a surreal juxtaposition, an ordinary door set at a skewed angle into a scarred and crumbling wall of concrete and exposed girder-ends. For a moment, Iris felt like the heroine of some dimly remembered children's story who had followed a waistcoated rabbit down a hole in the earth, only to find just such deranged and prosaic furnishings.

'What's on the other side?' Iris could see that the door was made of richly polished wood, its dimensions both higher and wider than doors she had encountered in that other world, outside the ruins.

'See for yourself.' Vogel grasped the ornate brass knob, twisted it and pushed, then stepped back so Iris could go ahead of him. 'Make yourself at home.'

She walked into the further darkness, feeling the smooth difference of its floor, covered only with dust, compared to the rubble-strewn tunnels through which she and Vogel had traveled. Like the door, the room itself was tilted at an angle, as though it were an antique sailing ship run aground on a costal reef; without a wall immediately handy, to touch and steady herself against, Iris had to lean back a bit to keep her balance. As she watched, the room slowly took perceptible form, in wavering, massed candlelight. With the flashlight switched off, Vogel lit the ranks of tapers in several elaborate, floor-standing and wall-mounted candelabra.

'Behold,' said Vogel, his self-appointed task completed. He snuffed out the loose candle he had been using as a lighter, his one good hand pressing the wick against the front of his coveralls. 'Look familiar?'

I've been here before, realized Iris. Not in the flesh, the way she was now, breathing the room's captured air and seeing the actual, expensively wood-paneled walls behind floor-to-ceiling swaths of heavy, ivory-colored fabrics. But as good as; the surresper device in her apartment had summoned up an illusion of this room, complete with the shifting, moody light of the candles, from the datad that Meyer had first given her. Having walked through that illusion, superimposed over her apartment's living room, she already knew her way around in the reality of it. She glanced over to the wall at one side, farthest from the ranks of burning candles, and saw, as she expected, the empty perch on which the owl had wrapped its talons, golden eyes blinking and watching everything that went on.

'So I take it,' said Iris aloud, 'that these are the private quarters of the late Dr Eldon Tyrell?' Even in the room's precariously angled condition, with dust from the surrounding rubble having been sifted across every surface, the expensive luxury was apparent. 'Guess he really did have the bucks.'

'Enough.' Vogel gave an appreciative nod, surveying the expansive suite of rooms with an explorer's proprietary manner, as if by discovering them he had taken possession from their original owner. 'Let's just say that Dr Tyrell had a taste for the finer things in life, and he didn't mind spending what it took to get them. Case in point being a real live owl, of course. Besides –' A wave of Vogel's good hand took in the room and the ones beyond it. 'All tax write-offs; he'd get the Tyrell Corporation to pay for what he wanted. Not only luxuries, of course.' With one finger, Vogel pointed toward the intricately worked ceiling. 'The corporation also paid to have the good doctor's private quarters structurally reinforced, to withstand any kind of seismic or otherwise destructive event. Even explosions that took place within the building complex itself wouldn't have been able to touch this area. You get past that pricey wood on the walls, there's enough of a steel cage wrapped around these rooms, all strung on breakaway connector joints, to have withstood anything short of old-time thermonuclear warheads. Even the windows.' Another gesture, to the wall opposite. 'They had steel barriers, nearly a half-meter thick, that came slamming down like guillotine blades when the complex was destroyed. There was a self-contained oxygen supply that kicked in, running off power sources separate from the buildings' main grid. That subsystem has gone dead by now, though; the hermetic seals have retracted. But basically, if Eldon Tyrell had still been alive when his corporation went up, he could've ridden out the explosions with nothing more than a few bruises.'

'What happened to him?' Iris peered around at the candle-illuminated spaces. 'Why was he already dead when this happened? I mean . . . unless he died of old age or a heart attack or something.'

'Hardly.' Vogel shook his head. 'Somebody like Tyrell doesn't die like ordinary people; he wasn't an ordinary person. Let's face it; there's a certain amount of violence – maybe even what people used to call "evil" – inherent in the way the Tyrell Corporation made its money. You're talking about a commercial product – replicants – which is perfectly willing to kill to get its freedom, and which gets killed if it tries. One way or another, somebody – or some *thing* – is going to get hurt. Just because it was legal for you to do the hurting when you were still a blade runner doesn't change anything.'

121

'Spare me the lecture,' said Iris. 'Tell me what happened to Tyrell.'

'Poetic justice. Or karma – what's the difference?' Vogel lifted his shoulders in a shrug. 'One of his replicants, that'd come off the assembly lines right here in this building, came home from the far colonies to have a little talk with its creator. The replicant's name was Roy Batty, and he told Dr Tyrell that he wanted more life. That four years just wasn't long enough, for a creature like him, who was so hungry to survive and taste life. And then when Tyrell couldn't give him any more, things got ugly. Ugly and fatal: the replicant Roy Batty crushed Dr Tyrell's head between his hands like a big egg. Right here in this room.' Vogel had delivered the details in a flat, uninflected monotone. 'That's the way it goes, right? What goes around, comes around. All that built-in, suppressed violence walked in the door, and made itself at home.'

'You seem to know an awful lot about it.' Iris regarded him with even more suspicion than before. 'Like you saw it happen, or something.'

'In a way, you could say I did.' The glow from the massed candles wavered across Vogel's face as he smiled thinly at her. 'Funny thing is, a lot of people saw it. Maybe you're the only one – the only one in all of LA – who didn't.'

'What're you talking about?' The same unease came over her as before, when she and Vogel had been standing outside the ruins they had now penetrated, and he'd pointed out her ignorance of the place and whatever had happened to bring it down. It had been her job to know things other people didn't – you couldn't track down escaped replicants unless you were on top of things – yet there seemed to be whole worlds of which she had known absolutely nothing. 'How many people could have been here in Tyrell's private quarters, to have witnessed him getting killed?'

'No one was here,' said Vogel, still smiling. 'Or just about: the only actual witness was a little nerdy genetic engineer named J. R. Sebastian, who'd worked freelance for Tyrell before. And he got dinged up pretty badly by Roy Batty as well; the initial police report actually had him down as dead also, though that part turned out to be wrong. So other than him, there was only Dr Tyrell and the escaped Batty replicant here in the room when it all went down.'

'All right, then.' Iris spoke with elaborate, barely maintained patience. 'So how could everybody in LA – except me, of course – have seen this Batty rep kill Eldon Tyrell?' She gestured around at the wood-paneled walls. 'I don't exactly think that the head of a powerful outfit such as the Tyrell Corporation would allow video bugs to be planted in his private quarters. Execs like that usually have more of a taste for privacy.'

'That they do,' agreed Vogel. 'And Tyrell was more private than most. So it wasn't really here in this room that people got to see Tyrell's gruesome death. Let's say it was as good as here.'

Iris sighed wearily. Vogel's toying around wore her out more than the trek through the buildings' ruins. 'I'm not following you.'

'It was in the studio; that's where it happened. Or at least what everyone saw. Not Tyrell's real death – but as good as. Realer than real, as some might say. The *re-creation* of Tyrell's death. On tape.'

'Wait a minute.' Iris held up her palm, to stop any more words from coming. 'You're saying somebody made a video production, after the fact, of this Eldon Tyrell getting murdered?'

'You bet.' Vogel gave a single nod. 'Of that, and a whole lot else, besides. An epic, as it were, about this bunch of escaped replicants Roy Batty was part of, and the cop that got assigned the job of tracking down and retiring them. You know the one; the blade runner named Rick Deckard.'

'I've heard the name.' Iris shrugged. 'That's about it, though.'

'Now that's what I was talking about before. There are some real holes in your knowledge of what's been going on here in LA. Or beyond; this thing was broadcast throughout the world, and to the off-planet colonies. Don't you think it's a little curious that you're not aware of it?'

'What was it called?'

'*Blade Runner*,' said Vogel. 'That's all. *Blade Runner*.'

'Catchy title.' Iris searched her memory for a couple of seconds, then shook her head. 'Nope. Complete blank on anything like that.'

Vogel peered closer at her. 'And you don't find that strange? I know for a fact that it was pretty popular with a lot of LAPD rank-and-file.'

'No,' said Iris. 'Not really. I don't watch a lot of video stuff, broadcast or otherwise. I don't have time for it.'

'You should still know about this one. It was a big hit, just about everywhere; got very high ratings. And beyond; it's still got quite a cult following.'

'I told you. Never heard of it.'

'So I see.' Vogel's gaze wandered across the candlelit room for a

123

few seconds, then snapped back to Iris. 'Maybe you should watch it some time. Might learn a lot from it.'

She could tell where this was going. 'Maybe I should.'

Vogel's smile widened. 'Now's a good time.' His teeth looked like antique, yellowed ivory in the wavering candlelight. 'Real good.'

'You know, you're really losing your capacity to surprise me.' Iris put her hands on her hips. 'I already watched one of your movies. There at the blimp, that other grungy hangout of yours. Just because you've dragged me into this pile doesn't mean I'm in the mood for another one.'

'Ah, but that other one was a live feed. That was so you'd know what was going on with the owl, and who had it then. What I've got here for you is real cinema, something historic. Higher production values. So it's a lot better than mere reality.'

As if I'd know anything about that, thought Iris, *anymore*. The rabbit-hole feeling embraced her again; she felt the weight of the Tyrell Corporation's rubble pressing down upon her, as though the ruins were ready to extinguish the small, charmed bubble of existence inside it. Somewhere, in the wandering through the maze that had led her here, the thread leading back to the outside world had been broken; she didn't know if she would ever find her way out again. Or if that other world out there even still existed. Or if it ever had.

'You win,' said Iris. She knew she didn't have a choice about the matter. Even if she did emerge from the ruins' depths, she would eventually crawl back into them, just to find out what it was that Vogel had wanted to show her. Not out of curiosity, but the fear of not knowing. 'Where do we go for this flick of yours?'

'Follow me.' Vogel picked up one of the floor-standing candle racks and carried its pool of light with him to a farther section of the rooms. 'Here we go.' He pushed open a door concealed in the wood panels, revealing another dust-covered, expensively furnished chamber. 'Eldon Tyrell's private theater. He didn't use it much – more of a book guy, you know? – but it had all the amenities. Or at least enough of them for our purposes.' Vogel gestured toward a pair of vintage leather wingchairs. 'Have a seat.'

Real leather; Iris could tell the difference between the stuff and her own jacket as she leaned back in the chair and rubbed her hands along the fatly padded arms. The way Tyrell had gone through the endangered species of the world, converting scraps of them into personal luxuries, there eventually wouldn't have been anything left alive on the planet, except rats and replicants.

Behind her, Vogel fussed about with some ancient-looking machine on a rolling stand. Leaning around the side of the wingchair, Iris watched him threading a thin strip of something black and shiny through cogs and sprockets, from one spoked double-wheel to another above it. 'What the hell's that?'

'Film,' said Vogel. 'Pre-digital technology. Like they use at that movie theater, where we had our little party.'

'Okay . . .' Iris recognized the stuff now; there had been coiling masses of it on the floor of the theater's projection booth. 'But those were old movies. Nobody produces anything on it anymore. And you said that this was something recent.'

'Very recent. But Tyrell had discriminating tastes; nothing but the best. Which for him meant no cheap-ass digitized mass of pixels, like everybody else in the world has gotten used to watching – mainly because they don't know any better. So if whatever he wanted to watch wasn't on film to begin with, he'd have his guys in the lab do a cross-media conversion on it, using the old equipment and hoard of film stock that he'd stashed. Then they'd strike a one-off print like this, just for his eyes. Though this is one movie Tyrell never got to see. Since he gets killed in it – really killed – he wasn't around to see the final edit, and all the top-drawer technical work his employees did on it. Which is too bad, from a cinephile viewpoint, because they really did a good job – right up there with the rest of them.'

'The rest?'

'In Tyrell's private archive. In the vault next to this theater – there's racks of film cans stored away. This particular movie was the last to be logged in, after Tyrell's, shall we say, *sudden* demise. But like I said, they're all top quality. That's film for you, though – most people can't tell the difference; the percept systems in their brains have been degraded to the point that they think a bunch of dots is the same thing as reality. So an analogue medium such as this is just no big thing to them. Maybe you'll be able to tell, though.'

She couldn't. When Vogel turned out the lights and set the clattery machine running, a horizontal cone of light sprang from its bright lens, filling the screen in front of her. Points of light showed, a night-time vista of some sprawling city. When gouts of flame burst into the sky and a police spinner streaked past, she realized that the city was LA itself. It looked real enough to her, but no different from any digital depiction ever had. The knowledge made her uncomfortable, as though some subtle test had been put before her, like the trick questions used with the standard-issue Voigt-Kampff machine. And she had failed the test.

'When's the good stuff start?' Discomfort had turned to irritation. 'This looks pretty artsy so far, but not important. At least, not to me.'

'Keep your shirt on.' Vogel had made himself comfortable in the matching chair. 'It'll be worth it. I promise.'

With the projector softly clicking in the background, the film's angle changed from its elevation above the city to a tracking shot, zooming forward on a vaguely pyramidal building. Vogel leaned over the arm of his chair and pointed to the image on the screen. 'That's the Tyrell Corporation headquarters,' he whispered. 'What you're sitting inside right now. Before it went up.'

Then a room inside the building, with a ceiling fan lazily stirring the smoke from the cigarette held by a cop; Iris didn't recognize him, though it was clear he was supposed to be a part of the blade runner division. She didn't like the guy's style, too sneering and cold; it was no surprise to her when the interview, with some hulking low-intelligence type, didn't go well, and the cop wound up getting shot from under the table. The bullet's force smashed him back through the wall behind, as though it were so much pre-fab fiberboard.

'Who's this?' Iris nodded toward the screen. The claustrophobic office from the pre-ruins Tyrell Corporation building had been replaced by a nocturnal, outdoor shot, the city's constant monsoon-season rain battering a streetside noodle bar. A *gaijin* with dark, close-cropped hair, not quite as buzzed-down as Vogel's, was having a hard time getting his order; a lot of irritated pidgin and sign language went on between him and the *noodlista* behind the counter. 'Somebody else I should recognize?'

'Maybe not,' said Vogel. 'But you've heard his name before. That's Rick Deckard. So now you know what he looks like.'

'No.' Iris glanced over at Vogel. 'That's an *actor* playing Deckard. According to what you told me, at least, about this being a video reconstruction. Right? So I still haven't seen his face.'

'Wrong. That *is* Deckard's face up there. As docudrama recon-structions go, this is a high-class job; very thorough. The producer and director, somebody named Urbenton, is a real fanatic for detail. So he had his special-effects crew do some basic CGI texture-mapping and real-time animated tracking; they dubbed in the faces of all the major characters – the real people involved; no big deal to get that kind of identity data – over the faces of the physiology-matched actors Urbenton used. So what you wind up with on the screen is indistinguishable from what you would've gotten if you had been right there on the spot, taping as the actual events were happening. And in some ways . . .' Vogel shrugged. 'This is *better* than mere reality would have been. Inasmuch as it contains all the information available in reality – the faces, the places – but in an enhanced, editable form.'

Enhanced, my ass. Iris slumped down in her wingchair, watching the film roll on. She didn't feel that her life had been improved by being able to see this Deckard person's real face; he wasn't that interesting-looking. Plus, she already had the feeling, as she watched the film's Deckard character get pressured into going out hunting escaped replicants once more, that he was going to screw up the job. *Big time,* thought Iris. Tracking down and retiring replicants wasn't a career for the reluctant; the way she figured, you either put your heart into it or you might as well 'retire' yourself.

A few more minutes of screen time went by. And she knew she was right.

Way big. Iris shook her head as the images continued to flicker past. She felt both disgust and pity, watching Deckard go about his botched-up hunt. If he was alive at the end of the film, she'd be amazed.

11

She was wrong, as it turned out.

'What are you looking so pissed about?' Vogel had gotten up from his wingchair to switch off the film projector and relight the candles on the stand he'd brought into the private theater. The bright, empty rectangle disappeared from the screen. 'It wasn't *that* bad a movie.'

'It was okay, I guess.' Iris slumped down in the wingchair, still feeling annoyed with herself. 'But usually, I can call 'em better than that. I had a bet going with myself that Deckard would be iced by the end. And I lost.'

'So you did. I could've told you that Deckard's alive. Both in the movie and in reality. Real reality, that is.' Vogel fussed with the machine again, extracting the tail end of the film and winding it onto the take-up reel. 'He's not here in LA anymore, but he's alive. Just far, far away, is all.'

Iris wasn't sure how she felt about that. She went on gazing at the screen on the wall, dark now, where the last images had been of Rick Deckard and the Rachael character, the replicant who had thought she was human, furtively extracting themselves from Deckard's apartment and getting into the building's elevator. What happened to the pair of them after that, however they had fled from their pursuers both real and only feared, had been left to the imagination. If Vogel wanted to her to think that Deckard and the replicant he'd fallen in love with were still alive, on the run somewhere, that was fine with her. *I was half right*, decided Iris. *He did screw up the job.* The way Deckard had gone about normal blade runner operations, it would've been a matter of sheer dumb luck if any escaped replicants got caught and retired. If she'd ever had any doubts about being the best in the business, they were dispelled. The CGI'd face of Captain Bryant, down to his ugly yellow teeth, had been dead accurate; to have seen him cajoling and threatening a loser like Deckard to get back into harness as a blade runner had been somewhat baffling. Bryant could've brought the job, the whole business with the group of escaped replicants led by the charismatic Roy Batty, to her; he would've had a lot better chance of having gotten it taken care of, efficiently and without so much guff from the reluctant Deckard. At that level of incompetence, it was no great wonder that Bryant had managed to get himself iced, right in his own office, the one Meyer had been cleaning out when he'd given her the owl-tracking assignment.

'I don't know,' mused Iris aloud, 'just how much got explained. I mean, I know how Dr Tyrell got killed – not that his personal security measures were anything to brag about – but there wasn't anything in there about how these buildings got blown up.'

'Oh, this was only the *first* movie.' Vogel pulled the projector's electrical cord from its wall socket and coiled it into a loop. 'There was actually a sequel, called *The Edge of Human*. That explained a lot more.'

'God help us.'

'It's not that bad; technically very good, actually. The same guy – Urbenton – made it.'

'You're not going to play it now, are you?' Iris warily regarded Vogel. 'I mean . . . I don't know if I have time for it. Not in this life, at least.'

'Not right now, no.' Vogel laid the loop of electrical cord on the metal shelf beneath the projector. 'Eventually, though, you'll have to get up to speed on it. There's a lot of stuff you don't know yet that you're going to *have* to know. Or else . . .'

The way Vogel's words trailed off didn't sound good to Iris. 'Or else what?'

'Or else things won't go any better for you than they did for Rick Deckard. Possibly, they might even go worse.' Vogel sat down on the arm of the empty wingchair, facing Iris. 'Of course, that depends on how far you want to go with this. You still have the option of quitting now, of cutting your losses. Getting bounced off the blade runner division isn't the end of the world. You are, after all, still alive. That counts for a lot, even in a town like LA.' His thin, humorless smile showed again. 'Or better yet, outside of it. You could go on the run, like they did.' Vogel pointed to the empty screen. 'If you're worried about staying alive – and somebody in your position should be worried, given that you're no longer protected from your enemies by the LAPD – your chances would be improved, just about anywhere else.'

'You might think that's an option –' Iris's words grated in her throat. 'But I don't. I'd die if I ever left LA. You may as well cut off my air supply.'

'That's either a commendable loyalty to the place, or plain fear. About what's outside.'

'No.' Iris shook her head. 'It's just me.'

'Then you don't have a lot of choices left. Which is why you're here, isn't it?'

'Right now,' said Iris, 'I'm not really sure why I am. I was following a lead, that's all.'

Vogel's smile widened. 'Still looking for the owl? But you've been taken off that assignment, haven't you? It's not your problem anymore. There's a certain luxury that comes with screwing up a job as thoroughly as you have. Now you've got all the time in the world – or at least until what you're afraid of actually does happen to you.'

'It already has,' said Iris glumly. 'I *liked* being a blade runner. It suited me down to the ground.' Her mood darkened rapidly, no longer under her control; she felt as if the sheer tonnage of broken concrete and steel massed above her had given way, burying her in a lightless, airless tomb. 'That's why I was looking for that stupid owl. And following whatever worthless lead I could scrape up. I figured that maybe if I found it—'

'You could buy your way back into the department's good graces with it? A vain hope, sweetheart.' Vogel regarded her with true pity. 'You know the LAPD doesn't work that way. You get one chance, and one chance only. That's what was so hinky, to use the cop lingo, about Bryant leaning on Deckard to come back to the division and take on the job with the Roy Batty group of escaped replicants. Deckard should've known it was a set-up, that there was more going on than what Bryant had told him about – but you don't know about that part yet. That's in the sequel, which you haven't seen. But there's plenty of clues about it in the first movie. I mean, that whole business with the first cop you see, the one named Holden, the one interrogating the big ugly replicant named Leon – when Holden winds up getting blown away, it's obvious that he was set up to take the hit. Bryant had ID photos of all the escaped replicants in the Batty group; why didn't he give them to Holden in the first place, rather than send him here to get killed?'

'You're right,' said Iris. 'That seemed exactly hinky to me, while I was watching it.'

'Which proves my point, among other things, about the depart-ment not handing out second chances – not even when it says that's what it's doing. People like Bryant and your ex-boss Meyer . . . they're all liars.' Vogel's smile had long vanished. 'Believe me, I know. So when I tell you that you don't have the proverbial snowball's chance in hell of getting back in with the department, even if you did manage to find the owl for them, you can believe it. They're not going to trust you again, now that you showed you don't really trust them – which is what you showed when you didn't take the owl straight in to Meyer, when you did have it. You see what happened? What you did to yourself?' Vogel's penetrating gaze sharpened to a knife's point. '*You became one of them.* As sneaky and suspicious and double-dealing as anyone else in the department.'

'But I didn't have a choice about that.' Iris's protest raised her voice a notch. 'Like you said, they're all liars and cheats. Everybody in the world is – or at least in LA. You're toast if you don't match them at their own game.'

'Yeah, but you didn't, sweetheart. You wouldn't even have been in the game if it hadn't been for me.' Vogel tapped his chest with the forefinger of his good hand. 'You'd still be wandering around the *souk*, asking dumb questions, if I hadn't stepped in and bailed you out. So what'd you do then? You screwed me over, then held out on your boss and wound up getting your sweet ass fired from the police department. And you didn't even *get* anything out of it.' His hand gestured wide. 'Where's the owl? Huh? Tell me that, you're so clever.'

'I don't know.' Defeated, Iris slumped lower in the wingchair. 'If I knew that, I obviously wouldn't be here, getting reamed out by you.' The buried feeling came over her again; the private theater of the late Dr Eldon Tyrell was a like a candlelit bubble in an ocean of stone, the larger version of that which had encased her heart. 'I don't know *anything.*' Self-castigation rarely happened with her, but once started it couldn't be stopped; the entire *gestalt* of her usually confident personality flipped its polarity. 'The most basic stuff about the assignment; no wonder I wound up blowing it. I still don't even know why anyone wants the damn bird so badly. I mean . . . it's an owl. So what?'

'Maybe,' Vogel hinted darkly, 'it's a little more than that.'

'Yeah, probably, but if so, I don't know what *that* is. Maybe if I had figured out just what makes this owl so valuable, I wouldn't have been caught flat-footed by whoever took it off me. Waking up in the hospital, with my nervous system fried, wasn't exactly a treat, you know. But I was concerned about Meyer and some LAPD thugs showing up, and I wound up getting sandbagged by somebody – God knows who it was – who'd obviously been way ahead of me, with a phony chat already inserted into my apartment set to blow up in my face.'

'Now you're getting smart.' Vogel nodded in approval. 'It's not enough just to go looking for something; you have to know *why* you're looking for it. Why somebody *wants* it. If you don't know that, then you're blundering around in the dark. Anybody who does that in LA is going to find some pretty dark places, all right. And then you'll wish you hadn't.'

'Too late,' said Iris. 'At least for me.' She felt worse now, and closer to death, than when she had dragged herself out of the hospital, trailing tubes and wires behind her. 'Way too late.'

'No, it's not.' Vogel reached over and lightly placed the fingertips of his good hand on her knee. 'You're being too hard on yourself. You're making more progress than you realize.' He leaned back, pulling his hand away. 'You've already found out some stuff that you didn't know before.'

'Yeah, great.' Iris shook her head in self-disgust. 'Now I know what some other failed blade runner named Rick Deckard looks like. That's really going to help me.'

'As I said, you're being too hard on yourself. You now have an idea of what it is that you don't know, and how important that is. Whereas before, you went on without even being concerned about your own ignorance, and that's how you wound up in so much trouble.'

'Spare me the lecture.' Iris closed her eyes. The tonnage of ruins weighing on her shoulders hadn't moved. 'I feel bad enough already.'

'Self-knowledge is always painful,' said Vogel. 'You have to die to achieve it; die to your former self, that is. So that you can live again.'

She opened one eye just enough to try and see if he had been joking. 'What the hell are you talking about?'

'You're not there yet – but you will be. Whether you want to or not. That's what this is all about.' Vogel nodded toward the dark, empty screen on which the movie's images had slid past. 'Didn't you notice?'

'Notice what?'

'Something else a little mysterious.' Vogel tilted his head, alertly studying her responses. 'Something *you* should've noticed in particular. Not the business with Deckard and the other cop getting set up. Something about the woman; the one that Deckard fell in love with.'

'You mean the replicant?' Iris's brow creased in puzzlement. 'The one named Rachael?' She slowly shook her head. 'No . . . I didn't see anything. What about her?'

'You didn't notice?' Vogel lowered his head, like a predatory bird focusing on some small creature. 'Her face? That was what she looked like, in reality, when all of that stuff really happened.'

'So what about her face?'

Vogel leaned back. 'She looks exactly like you,' he said simply.

The rock encasing Iris's heart chilled, as though it had suddenly been exposed to the vacuum beyond LA's night skies. 'You're lying.' She could feel her pulse ticking faster. 'Now you're lying, too.'

'What's to lie about? It was there on the screen, where you could see it. Where you should've seen it.' With his free hand, Vogel reached into one of his coverall's pockets. 'I was afraid you might react like this. You've still got a long way to go. So take a look at these.'

Iris took a half-dozen glossy photo prints from his hand. Her own hand was trembling as she turned the photos around to look at them. 'What are they?'

'Stills. From the movie you just watched. Take a good look. And tell me what you see.'

She had to hold them tight with both hands, to keep them from shaking. The fear was lodged tight in her throat, as she looked down at the unmoving images. Iris could even remember the scene in the film, from which the still at the top of the pack had been extracted. It had been right at the beginning, when the Rick Deckard character had first encountered the enigmatic Rachael, and he had been requested by Dr Tyrell to run the Voigt-Kampff replicant-detection test on her. Which she had failed, of course. But in the meantime, she had sat there across the table from Deckard, with the softly breathing V-K machine between them, in the studio reconstruction of the Tyrell office suite in which Iris had found herself; smoking a cigarette and answering Deckard's rote drill of questions, in a curt and abrasive manner, her loathing for the cop in front of her readily apparent.

For a moment, Iris didn't see the still photos in her hand; instead, a memory flash of the movie opened inside her mind, the first scene

133

between Rick Deckard and the replicant Rachael playing in infinite slow motion on the even more private screen behind her brow. She could see the female replicant named Rachael, with her icy attitude and hard retro makeup and hair, like some ancient *film noir* temptress, a trace of blue cigarette smoke curling into the air above her, her clothes more expensive and tailored than any of the rough street-gear that Iris wore . . .

And then she realized that Vogel was right.

The still photos scattered across the floor as Iris leapt from the wingchair, her fists trembling convulsively at her sides. 'You're wrong!' She didn't know where the fear and anger inside herself had come from. 'You lying sonuvabitch!' The fury surged up along her spine and consumed every other thought. 'She doesn't look like me at all!' Leaving only the denial of what she already knew was true. '*She doesn't!*'

Then her vision cleared from the face she had seen in the movie to that of Vogel, regarding her with sad, calm patience. Waiting for her to admit it.

She looks exactly like you.

Iris collapsed into the wingchair, pressing her face against its soft leather, wet with her tears. Now she knew – or had just begun to know – why she had come here.

Intercut

'Damn.' The director leaned forward, shaking his head as he gazed at the monitor screen. 'He wasn't supposed to tell her that.'

The camera operator glanced over at the figure beside him. 'Why not? Wouldn't she have figured it out on her own?'

12

Pull yourself together.

She heard the voice inside her head. Her own voice, stern and unyielding, and without pity. For her pain, or anyone else's.

'All right,' said Iris. She pushed herself away from the soft leather upholstery of the wingchair, in which she had pressed her face in a vain effort to shut out both Vogel's words and the images that kept playing over and over on the screen behind her eyes. With the palms of her hands, she wiped away the tears that had dampened both her skin and the chair's. 'Tell me what you want.'

'What *I* want?' Vogel regarded her smugly. 'Maybe it's time to ask that question of yourself.'

'I just want out of here.' Iris stood up from the chair, wiping her hands across the front of her trousers. 'This whole thing is crazy. I don't know even know why I'm in this place.' The moment of revelation she'd experienced, sparked by the screen image of the female replicant Rachael's face, the mirror image of her own, had already faded. Her shoulders hunched with deep physical revulsion as she looked around the dark space, the glow of the candles barely able to push back the tonnage of ruins she felt weighing above her head. 'You're the one who dragged me in here for some godawful, idiotic reason. I don't care what your agenda is, anymore.' Anger tensed in her voice; the humiliation of having broken down in front of Vogel, weeping like a child as he'd regarded her in silence, took her resentment up another notch. 'I don't care about some stupid, fucking owl, I don't care who wants it, or why; I don't care what anybody's going to do to me if I can't find it—'

'You should care. There's some heavy people involved.'

'I'm *beyond* caring,' said Iris bluntly. 'I don't know if that's what you wanted to accomplish, if that was on your list of personal goals, but you've accomplished that much, at least. I'm going to walk out of here—'

'You wouldn't be able to find your way,' Vogel said.

'I'll *dig* myself out, then. Straight up and out of this mess.' Her trembling hands clenched into near-fists, as if her nails were poised to start prying at the rubble stacked above her. She headed for the private theater's door, making a quick, dismissive gesture at the empty screen on the far wall. 'One way or another. I don't have time for this.'

'It's all you have time for.' Vogel followed her out into the other room, brighter-lit with its massed ranks of candles. 'Don't fool yourself, now that you've gotten this close.' He reached out with his good hand, grabbing her shoulder to stop and pull her around to face him. 'Why do you think you're reacting the way you are? After all you've been through, what's the big deal about seeing someone who's got the same face as you?' Lowering his head, he peered closer into her eyes. '*That's* what you've got to ask yourself.'

'And that's what I told you I don't give a shit about.' Iris angrily shoved his hand away from her. 'I'm outta here. I'm not interested in any more of your home movies. Show 'em to somebody who cares.'

'All right,' said Vogel mildly. He stepped back from her and smiled, radiating a superior attitude that infuriated Iris even more. 'Maybe I'll show them to that other woman. The one named Rachael.' With a tilt of his head, he indicated the private theater and its blank, empty screen. 'The one your face really belongs to.'

'Yeah, right.' Disgust welled up in Iris, heavy enough to be felt on her tongue. 'You're going to run *that* old joke by me? It's the creakiest one in the book.' She stood with both hands on her hips, shaking her head as she regarded him. 'That whole business – what if the blade runners are really replicants themselves? – that's about as dumb as it gets.'

'Really?' Vogel looked as amused as before. 'What's so "dumb" about it?'

'Everything,' snapped Iris. 'For one, I've already heard that joke; it was maybe funny the *first* hundred times I heard it. For Christ's sake, that's one blade runners tell to each other; it's like basic cop-shop locker-room wise-cracking. "Hey, what if *we're* the ones who're replicants? Wouldn't that be a crack-up?" Granted, every once in a while somebody in the division has some kind of mental collapse and starts believing it's true. But by then they're usually so far around on the Wambaugh self-loathing Curve, they're about ready to eat their gun-muzzles, anyway. So it's no big loss. And it doesn't make the joke any funnier, or any less creaky.'

'What if it's not a joke?'

'Get real,' said Iris. 'It *is* a joke. It's nothing but the standard "set an old cat to catch an old rat" theory. What better way to catch replicants than with some other replicant, right? Like there'd be some special wavelength that they're all on together. The only problem is that there's a definitive physiological test for replicants, the bone-marrow examination. Replicants have a distinctive regularity to their bone structure that's only visible under exhaustive inventorying using an electron-scanning microscope. Which are still just a little too heavy for agents in the field to carry around with them, when they're trying to track down and retire some escaped reps – plus the amount of batteries you'd run through, keeping something like that powered up. Not to mention that it takes about two days to get the results cranked out. That's a long time to ask some suspected replicant to stand around and wait to see if you're going to put a bullet through his head or not. Impatient bastards that they are.'

'Considering that you're about to ice them,' said Vogel, 'maybe they've got a right to have something more accurate than the Voigt-Kampff run on them.'

'The Voigt-Kampff's accurate enough. Nobody complains about it afterwards, do they? But that's beside the point. You want to know whether blade runners are one hundred percent human or not? Fine – that's why when you join the police department, you do get one of those bone-marrow exams run on you. I still got the scar where the LAPD medics punched in for the sample.' Iris pushed the ragged sleeve of her jacket up past her elbow, turning her arm to display a dime-sized faded mark on her biceps. 'Hurt like a sonuvabitch, too, I can tell you. But when the results come back from the lab two days later, and you pass, and you're in, then you don't have to wonder about crap like that anymore.'

'No, you don't.' Vogel's thin smile was more unpleasant than it had ever been before. 'You just have to wonder if the LAPD would give you the real results of the bone-marrow test, or whether it would simply tell you whatever it wanted you to hear.'

'Shit.' Iris's right fist clenched tighter, as if she were about to launch it right into Vogel's insinuating smile. Which meant, she knew, that she didn't have an answer in words that she could fire back at him. 'Look,' she said finally, 'forget about proving whether any blade runners are human or not. You know why? *Because it doesn't matter.* They get the job done; that's what's important. *I* got the job done, when I was a blade runner. So what would it matter if I were a replicant?'

'You tell me,' said Vogel. 'You're the one who burst into tears when you finally realized that some other woman – supposedly a replicant – has the exact same face as you. One of you has a problem.'

'Yeah, well, it's not me.' Iris looked away, scanning the candlelit room and trying to reconstruct the route by which she had gotten there. 'I've been under a lot of stress lately – all right? And you took me by surprise with that one.' There seemed to be a confusing number of doors available, any one of which might open onto the tunnel through the piled-up mass of ruins. 'So I had a little breakdown. I don't know why, but it's over now. If you want to go around thinking that Rachael person, or whatever her name was, is the real human being and I'm the replicant – fine. Whatever. But I'm not exactly worried about my ex-boss Meyer sending the troops from the blade runner division out after me.' The thought, a belated retort to Vogel's insinuations, had just struck her. 'If I'm supposed to be a replicant, why didn't Meyer have one of the other blade runners retire me as soon as I was bounced out of the police department? Hell, Meyer could've done it himself, right there on the spot; he carries a piece around with him. And the way things are going for him right now, he could've used the money. So tell me, smart guy, if I'm a replicant, why am I still—?'

'Shut up.'

'What?' Iris was more pleased than offended by any evidence of getting under the smug Vogel's skin. 'What did you—?'

'I said, be quiet.' Vogel held up his good hand and made a gesture for silence. 'Listen.'

'I don't hear anything,' said Iris after a moment.

Vogel's gaze lifted toward the dark spaces at the room's lofty ceiling, beyond the reach of the candlelight. 'That's because you don't know what to listen for.' His voice had sunk to a tense whisper. 'You don't know this place; you've never been here before.'

'Yeah, and I don't want to be here again—' Iris broke off as she heard a distant noise, a faint scraping and thud of metal against concrete, somewhere above their heads. 'That's not good,' she said, her own whisper matching Vogel's. 'What's going on?' Her pulse ticked faster. 'Is this place coming down?'

Vogel remained silent as he listened intently to whatever was happening above.

'Look, I don't care for the idea of being buried alive in here. Or even dead.' Given the mass of rubble and the sheer tonnage involved, if the ruins were to settle further and snuff Eldon Tyrell's private quarters out of existence, the two of them would be crushed lifeless in a matter of seconds. 'Let's get going.'

'Don't move. They'll hear you. Then they'll be able to tell exactly where we're at.'

'"They"?' Iris looked up at the ceiling; the noises had stopped for a moment, then started again, fainter but also detectably closer. 'Who is it?' Of the possibilities that raced through her thoughts, none was pleasant. *Maybe*, she thought, *Meyer did decide to retire me.* Not only out of the police department, but for good. 'How did they know we're here?'

'They always know,' said Vogel. 'They know before you do. Or at least *he* does.'

'"He"?' Iris frowned in puzzlement. 'What "he" are you talking about?'

Vogel didn't appear to have heard her. 'This isn't supposed to be happening,' he muttered. The expression on his sharp-angled face darkened as he tilted his head back, slitted eyes focusing on some point beyond the room's ceiling. 'It's not in the script.'

'There's a script?' Iris peered closer at him. 'What's that supposed to mean?'

'Right now' – Vogel's distracted attention returned to her – 'you don't need to know. And there isn't time for me to tell you about it. We've got to get out of here.'

'Glad you agree,' said Iris. 'That's where I've been heading for a while now.' She nodded toward the room's tall, brass-fitted doors. 'Which one did we come in by?'

'Forget that,' Vogel said. 'We can't go out the same way we came in. You should know that by now. Nobody can ever go back; there's only forward, even if you don't know where you're going.'

Great, thought Iris disgustedly. *Always with the deep commentary.* 'Yeah, but if that's the quickest way out of here . . .'

'I said, forget it.' Vogel's brow creased with furious concentration. 'I've worked with the guy long enough to know how his mind operates. Especially, how he figures other people are going to react.' A long-simmering resentment tinged Vogel's words. 'He always

140

underestimates everybody else. He's got this godlike *über*-perspective on human affairs.'

'Who?' To Iris, the other's description sounded as though it were something personal. 'Is this the person who lifted the owl from me, back in my apartment? So now I take it that he's got a whole crew with him?' The burrowing and scraping sounds from the rubble above had become noticeably louder, indicating a number of unwanted visitors. *Maybe,* thought Iris, *they're the ones, or what's left of them, from the movie theater.* Which was not good; they wouldn't be likely to be in a pleasant mood when they found her here. 'Who is this guy?'

'Wrong guess,' said Vogel. 'Different kind of trouble entirely. But definitely trouble; when he starts deviating from the script, it's because he thinks he has to. That means he's going to be worried about having lost control of the project.' Vogel bit the corner of his lower lip. 'What it also means is that he must have caught *me* going off-script. Shit.' He glanced around the corners of the room, near the beamed ceiling. 'I didn't figure he'd have this place wired as well; this whole sequence was supposed to be off-camera.' Vogel's expression turned even more bitter and brooding. 'Which was what was in the script. So if he was able to catch me deviating, that means he didn't trust me from the beginning.'

'Why the hell should anyone trust you?' Iris flung her hands up in exasperation. 'You said you went off some script you were supposed to be following. And he caught—wait a minute.' She pulled herself up short, having found herself in Vogel's spiraling mental loop. 'I don't even know who we're talking about.'

'Figure it out,' snapped Vogel. He grabbed Iris's forearm with his good hand, and pulled her with him toward the darker reaches of Tyrell's private quarters. 'It's the director!'

'Director?' Iris let herself be led past the reach of the candlelight, as much to discover what Vogel meant as to find a way out of the buildings' ruins. 'You mean . . . the director of the *movie?*' She pointed with her thumb back toward the theater. 'That *Blade Runner* thing I just watched?'

'That's the one.' Vogel let go of her arm so he could fish inside the pocket of his jumpsuit for his flashlight. With its beam flaring ahead, he kept walking at a fast enough clip that Iris had to hurry to keep up with him. 'Come on. They're going to be on us pretty soon, if we don't get a move on.'

'Where we heading?'

'Like I said – I know how his mind operates. Urbenton will figure that we're stupid enough to go running out the way we got in here, and he'll have part of his production crew – the thug part – waiting for us. So we go another way.'

'If there is one,' said Iris.

'Don't worry.' Vogel kept the flashlight aimed ahead of them. 'I know my way around this dump pretty well.'

Beginning to have my doubts, thought Iris. The floor underneath her bootsoles had turned both broken, with the ends of bent steel girders poking through the once-polished planks, and sharply tilted to one side. Enough light bounced back from the flashlight beam hitting the walls to dimly reveal the condition of the ceiling overhead. The weight of the collapsed buildings' rubble had obviously hit this section of Eldon Tyrell's private quarters with enough force to warp the reinforced framework that had protected the other sections, twisting and flattening it like a lab rat's wire cage. Iris and Vogel had to duck beneath the bowed ceiling beams, shouldering aside dangling skeins of dead electrical wiring and data conduits; the stench of charred insulation sheaths was still strong enough to lodge choking in Iris's throat.

The private quarters came to an end at a sheer cliff-face of concrete rubble, bristling with lengths of corroded rebar. Crouching down, with the top of his head barely an inch away from the buckled ceiling, Vogel pointed up. 'We climb,' he said.

'Climb where?' Iris knelt beside him, in the scattered glow from the flashlight. The floor beneath her was now so tilted that she had to dig in her fingernails to keep from sliding into Vogel.

'You're skinny enough,' said Vogel. 'Shouldn't be any problem for you.' He swung the flashlight upward, revealing a narrow gap between the vertical rubble and where the ceiling had been sheared away. 'It's only tight for maybe twenty yards or so, then it opens up. It's easy; plenty of handholds.'

'Easy for me, maybe. But what about you?' Iris was close enough that she could poke the sling across his chest without even unbending her elbow. 'What are you going to do, stay down here and hold them off?'

'The hell with it.' Vogel pulled away the sling, now ragged and dirt-stained, wadded it in his hand and tossed it onto the loose rubble behind them. Flexing his fingers, he stretched out the arm that had been bound to the front of his jumpsuit. 'Thing was giving me a cramp, anyway.'

'Hey –' Iris frowned at the sight. 'You weren't hurt at all!'

'Not physically, no.' A quick smile flashed across Vogel's face. 'But your leaving me there, with those guys – that really cut me to the quick.'

Right, she thought in disgust. When there was time, she'd have to re-think her assumptions about what had gone down at the movie theater where she had managed to lay hold of the owl. If Vogel had been faking any detail about what had happened to him, then the chances were good that a lot of other details were phonies as well. *Maybe even the whole set-up* – though she had to wonder what the point of that would have been, what Vogel or whoever was behind him would have been trying to accomplish with that kind of elaborate ruse. But for all she knew right now, the moment she had slipped out of the movie theater Vogel and the other men had broken off their mutual gunfire and had stood around, smoking and exchanging small talk.

'You lying sonuvabitch.' Iris spoke the words almost without anger, except for that which she directed toward herself for having fallen for anything Vogel had ever told her. 'You know, instead of scrambling up this chimney-hole, I've got a notion that maybe I should stay right here instead. And have a little talk with whoever it is that's dropping in on us.'

'You don't want to do that.' Vogel emphatically shook his head. 'That's a way bad idea.'

'Yeah? Why?'

'Look, I know you're going through a spasm of distrust at the moment.' Vogel spoke with elaborate patience as he crouched beneath the buckled ceiling, with its dangling loops of wire and cable screening off the rest of what had been the Tyrell private quarters. 'I can understand that. And I can even admit it's somewhat deserved; I haven't been totally upfront with you about everything that's been going on—'

'Or anything.'

'We don't really have time to argue right now.' Vogel held up a mollifying hand, palm outward. 'You can chew my ass raw when we get out of here, okay? What you have to realize is that you are in deep, deep trouble.'

'Been there,' said Iris. 'Done that.'

'Worse this time; I promise you. If Urbenton has gone off-script, there's no telling what could happen to you. You don't want to trust me about that, fine. But look at it this way.' He brought his face close to hers, so that in the dim radiance of the flashlight she could see her own reflection in the dark centers of his eyes. 'As near as you've gotten to what you've been trying to accomplish – getting hold of that owl – it's all been made possible by me. For better or worse.'

'Mostly worse.'

'Regardless,' said Vogel. 'You don't *have* anyone else to trust, other than yourself – and you can't say that's gone any better. So it's me or nobody.'

'Maybe not.' Iris glanced up at the cramped space's ceiling, then back to Vogel. 'There's always this director guy and his friends who are about ready to drop in on us.'

'Sure. You got that option. I don't have any way of forcing you to get out of here. But just consider.' His voice dropped in pitch and volume. 'What if you guess wrong? About who you want to trust – and distrust. If I tell you that it wouldn't be exactly pleasant for you to meet up with Urbenton and his crew, and you don't believe me – it could get real ugly for you if you guess wrong on that one. Let's face it: people haven't been playing softball with you lately.'

That much was true, at least. 'All right,' said Iris. She sighed. 'So I go first? Up the chute, I mean?'

'Right.' Vogel's thin smile appeared again. 'That way I'll know where you are.'

'You're the boss.' She turned and inched forward, cautiously lifting her head into the open space where the broken ceiling ended. As Vogel had promised, the wall of rubble had plenty of jagged crevices that she could dig her fingertips into. The ceiling's edge scraped past her shoulder blades and spine as she kicked the toes of her boots into the crags below and started to climb into the narrow darkness.

Even without the occasional glint from Vogel's flashlight, a fraction of its beam sliding up past her face and hands, she could sense him below, climbing after her. Some of the handholds she found were fractured and crumbling, as though the concrete had been all but disintegrated by the force of the explosions that had collapsed the Tyrell Corporation headquarters. Bits of sharp-edged gravel slid under her palms and past her wrists; she took a certain wry satisfaction in imagining them raining down upon Vogel's upturned face.

The gap through which they crawled antlike opened up, after what seemed like a mile of scrabbling effort; Iris felt that the back of her leatherite jacket was no longer scraping along the cliff-face behind her. She could even breathe, taking in a complete lungful of the dust-laden, scorched-smelling air.

Iris suddenly felt something grab her ankle, and realized it was one of Vogel's hands, reaching up to snag her.

'Hold it.' Vogel had switched off the flashlight; his whisper filtered through the darkness to her. 'Don't say anything.'

She listened, and within a fraction of a second heard the same faint but distinct noises that Vogel must have detected. Whoever was burrowing down through the ruins, down to the Tyrell private quarters from which she and Vogel had just fled, the group was evidently within a few meters of their own position. Iris could hear the scraping sounds of smaller bits of rubble being shoved aside, clearing a parallel vertical shaft downward.

The space in which Iris clung to the rubble face was open enough that Vogel was able to climb partway alongside her. She glanced down and could just discern the sharp angles of his face, close to her elbow.

'They must think we're still down there,' whispered Vogel. 'Urbenton probably didn't wire all of the private quarters; must've figured that there was no need to do the crushed end, where we got out.'

She realized then that the dim glow by which she made out Vogel's face wasn't from his flashlight, but from the other group's worklights seeping through the network of crevices and fissures between herself and them. Holding her breath, she waited until the bits of stray light were swallowed up by darkness again, and the scraping and scrabbling noises had faded a bit, coming now from a point some meters below.

'We don't have much time.' Iris kept her voice as low as Vogel's had been. 'When they get down there, it won't take 'em long to figure out that we split on them.' She glanced upward along the rubble face, trying to discern any indicator of its remaining height, then looked back down toward Vogel. 'How much farther until we're at the surface?'

'Still a ways to go.' Vogel was completely hidden in the gap's darkness. 'Get moving.'

Without any aid from Vogel's flashlight, Iris was forced to grope around for each new handhold. The sheer face of crumbling cement ended, giving way to a tangle of metal reinforcing rods, knotted and twisted together into a steel rat's nest. She reached up and grasped a curved section of rebar and pulled herself up, bending her knees to bring her bootsoles flat against the concrete rubble.

That was a mistake, she realized immediately, as the concrete broke apart, her boots pushing through a thin layer to a hollow space beyond. Her entire weight tugged forcefully on the rebar section onto which she was holding, arms extended straight above her head. With a shriek of metal grinding across metal, the section stretched loose from the rest of the tangled rebar, dropping Iris several feet down. She dangled for a moment, twisting against the sheer rubble face, as though clinging to an immense elastic band; the unsteady motion, compounded by the surrounding darkness, sickened her to her stomach.

Iris saw the flashlight beam spring on, cutting across the gap and catching first her wildly kicking legs, then darting up to her face, dazzling and blinding her for a moment. 'Hold on,' called Vogel. There was no further point in whispering; the initial shriek of the rebar tearing loose would have penetrated every inch of the jumbled-together ruins, alerting the others to their whereabouts. 'I've got you—'

Holding onto the rubble face with one hand, Vogel leaned out and reached for her. Iris took her hand from the rebar section and grabbed tightly onto Vogel's forearm. Even as he pulled her toward himself, shouts were audible, though made faint and echoingly garbled by the intervening distance and the twists and turns leading down to the remains of the Tyrell private quarters.

With a sudden lurch, more of the tangled rebar came loose from above, instantly dropping Iris another couple of meters. Her grip instinctively tightened on Vogel's arm as she fell; that was enough to pull him off the rubble face. His other arm quickly grabbed around Iris's legs, stopping his own fall. Iris let go of his upward-extended wrist, letting herself be bear-hugged by Vogel around her knees, his head at a level with her stomach.

'Not . . . good,' gasped Vogel needlessly. Along with a quantity of loose concrete debris from the rubble face, the flashlight had fallen clattering down the gap beneath them. Its beam shot upward into their eyes, then was extinguished as the lens and bulb shattered against a jagged cement outcropping. 'This could've ... gone better ...'

She didn't bother replying. Her locked-straight arms, bearing both her own and Vogel's weight, were already beginning to ache. As she and Vogel swayed in the darkness, with the section of rebar that she grasped stretching and contracting with a nauseating elasticity, she could hear the others somewhere directly beneath them. That meant that the director Urbenton's crew – if that was who they were; she still had no way of knowing for sure – had reached the Tyrell private quarters, and specifically the crushed end of the rooms from which she and Vogel had ascended. It wouldn't be long before those others came swarming up the gap, through its initial narrow section and then where it opened alongside the rubble face, and found the two of them dangling here.

'I'm not waiting around,' announced Iris. 'Look, here's the deal. I can pull us up at least a little farther. Then you'll be able to grab hold of this bar yourself.' Her arms were beginning to feel as if they were being pulled out of their sockets. 'Then we can both climb up it, separately.'

'Don't know about that.' Vogel looked upward, past Iris's face. 'This thing – this metal stuff – it might not be too securely fastened.' He sounded oddly calm and analytical, given the situation. 'We're getting towards the surface, so a lot of the debris isn't weight-compressed and packed together as tightly as the lower strata. If we start jostling this around with too much body movement, it could come tumbling down real fast.'

'So what do you suggest?' She tried to keep her own irritation, triggered by Vogel's objections, coldly under control.

'Well,' said Vogel, 'the smart thing to do would be for one of us to let go and drop. That way, there'd be less mass and weight dragging on this metal stuff, and the other person would have a better shot of getting out of here.'

'Yeah, right; *that's* a great idea. And the person who lets go either gets killed in the fall, or gets whatever that bunch down below thinks should be coming to him – or her. Are you volunteering?'

'Not really,' admitted Vogel.

'Fine. Then we'll do it my way.' With Vogel's arms wrapped around her legs, Iris reached and grabbed higher on the rebar section, pulling herself up. She had no desire to wait around any longer, until their pursuers caught up with them; she could already

147

hear voices from down below, in the crushed end of the Tyrell private quarters. The knife-like ridges of the rebar cut into her palms and the bent joints of her fingers as she strained to drag herself and Vogel a few inches higher. Another lunging grasp, catching at a twisted angle in the metal, gave her a tight enough hold that she could wedge the horizontally slanting part under one arm; using her back and shoulder muscles, Iris levered herself onto the piece, leaning forward so that it was across her stomach. 'There . . . right in front of you . . .' Breathless, she gasped the words out. 'Grab it, for Christ's sake . . .'

She felt one of Vogel's arms let go, then a downward pull in the rebar section to which she clung as he transferred his weight to its vertical section. The circulation in her legs started up again, no longer cut off by his vise-like grip.

'You okay?' Vogel called to her.

'Yeah.' Iris nodded, even though she knew the darkness hid any such movement. She didn't bother to ask how he was doing; she didn't care, at least now that her arms no longer felt as if they were being yanked from their sockets by his added weight. 'Let's get going . . .'

Shifting position by grabbing the near-horizontal rebar section in both hands, then drawing up and getting one knee onto it, Iris climbed higher onto the tangled metal. Before she moved again, she felt one of Vogel's hands brush her knee as he grabbed the section above him—

The dark space in which they both hung suspended was suddenly lit up with glaring shafts of light. Iris saw her own and Vogel's elongated shadows leap upward, fracturing across the segments of the tangled skein of rebar to which they clung. The broken shadows danced for a moment, then were frozen into place as the searchlight beams, aimed from just below, found and locked onto the two of them, dazzling and blinding their shocked eyes.

Iris realized immediately what had happened. The sounds and voices she and Vogel had heard coming from the Tyrell private quarters had been only a distraction, to make them think that their pursuers were down there. When in fact a sizable number of the director Urbenton's crew had been silently creeping up the narrow gap and then along the rubble face, closing in on them.

Lifting her shoulder in a vain attempt to shield her eyes, Iris could barely make out the dark shapes behind the overlapping glare of the

148

searchlights. But she could see that they were moving, approaching as rapidly as possible, all stealth discarded.

She didn't bother saying anything to Vogel; he was already in motion as well, scrambling up onto the horizontal rebar section beside her, reaching at the same time as she did for the next piece that could be grabbed and used to pull themselves higher onto the tangled metal. Their parallel motion produced an ear-piercing, grinding shriek from the rebar as its rusted lengths scraped across each other, pulled taut by Iris's and Vogel's weight. The shriek went higher, a chorus bouncing and echoing off the ruins' angles as one of the pursuers grabbed hold of the bottom of the dangling metal and swung himself onto it.

Bad move. That was all Iris had time to think, before the tangled mass of rebar pulled free from whatever partial anchor it'd had on the outcroppings of broken concrete and twisted steel girders above. *Real bad move.* The additional weight of the pursuer, along with the force of his jump onto the dangling rebar, produced a deafening roar of metal scraping across metal; dime-sized rust flakes swirled and sifted down upon Iris's and Vogel's faces. She found herself falling backward, while still holding on to the tangled rebar.

'Go!'

Vogel's shout cut through the ear-bruising clatter and shriek, snapping her back to full attention. She looked up and strained to focus her sight through the confusing shafts of darkness and criss-crossing searchlight beams, finally managing to discern Vogel above her and scrabbling even higher on the interlaced metal – or at least staying in the same place on top of the hollow mass, as though he were some small animal racing across the surface of a wire-form ball, tumbling down an even wider crevice in the earth.

As precarious as his position was, Vogel was still able, between grabbing and pulling himself onto the next sections of rebar, to look over his shoulder and yell down to Iris. 'Come on!' His sharp-angled face contorted with the effort to make himself heard over the metal's noise. 'Move it!'

Before Iris could react, the breath was knocked out of her by a vertical angle of concrete rubble slamming against her spine and shoulder blades. Pinned by the tangled mass of rebar against one side of the gap in which it had fallen, she managed to free herself part-way by desperately clawing at the metal sections. She had gotten her upper torso free, but could go no further: the rebar, halted in toppling

149

down the gap, had shifted with the force of her exertions, with a diagonal piece pressing hard against her abdomen. Grimacing with pain, Iris pushed against the metal, feeling its sharp edges slice the shirt beneath her jacket to tattered ribbons and drawing parallel stripes of blood across her flesh.

A hand grabbed her under one shoulder and pulled; she knew without looking that it was Vogel, having come back down a few meters on the tangled rebar, clinging with one hand while reaching for her with the other. Instead of pushing down on the metal section against her gut, she was now able to instinctively push against it without fear of falling; her breath rushed into her lungs as the metal bar retreated a precious inch. She let Vogel drag her upward, until the rebar section was against the front of her hips, too far down for her to push against it anymore. That no longer mattered, though; she could grab onto the sections near Vogel and help drag herself free.

Just as the binding press of the metal flexed and cleared her knees, Iris felt another hand on her body, a tight grasp seizing one ankle from below. She looked down, catching one of the searchlight beams straight into her dazzled eyes, then managing to make out the faceless silhouette of the pursuer who had leapt from the rubble face onto the rebar. The man had reached through the metal sections and caught her; the rough, hollow sphere vibrated dangerously, threatening to dislodge itself from where it had momentarily halted in the ruins' vertical gap, as he locked his fist tighter onto her boot and pulled her toward himself.

She knew she had one shot left. Already free of Vogel's grasp, Iris let her arms go straight, dropping herself back down the mass of rebar. That took the pursuer by surprise; he was even more surprised when she pulled her ankle loose from his grip and, instead of trying to scrabble away from him again, brought the heel of her boot down hard into his face. Even through the overlapping noises of metal scraping against metal and both Vogel's and the rest of the pursuers' shouts, Iris could hear a satisfying crunch of splintering bone; a wet red flower blossomed where the bridge of the man's nose had been, and his eyes defocused as his mouth opened wide in shock and pain. His clutching hands jerked apart, then grabbed onto empty air as he fell away from her.

Not bothering to watch what happened to him, Iris was already scrambling back up alongside Vogel. Even as she reached that point, the tangle of rebar lurched again, twisting and rolling in the dark gap, and bringing both of them around to what was now its uppermost surface. Iris looked down through the center of the hollow shape and saw that the bloodied pursuer had managed to break his fall at the last possible moment, with one hand having grabbed hold of the metal section at the very bottom of the mass.

'It's going.' Vogel, alongside Iris, had also caught sight of what had happened below, then had quickly glanced over to where the rebar's jagged circumference scraped at the vertical sides of the gap. The angle of concrete against which the mass had been jammed tight was beginning to splinter and crumble, a loop of rebar acting like a horizontal chisel-point, driven harder by the struggles of the figure underneath. 'Jump!'

Iris felt a moment of weightlessness, as though gravity itself had been switched off, as she saw the cement outcropping explode into powdery dust and shards, and the rebar fell away beneath her scuffed knees and hands. Her unthinking animal reactions took over; her bootsoles thrust against the last remaining rebar section even as her fingertips stretched toward the rubble face opposite. With nails clawing into the face's crevices, and the toes of her boots kicking to wedge themselves in as well, Iris clung to the unlit surface, teeth gritting as she pressed herself flat against it.

'You're okay,' said Vogel quietly, from some place close to her. The vertical gap in the ruins of the Tyrell Corporation headquarters had gone completely dark again, the searchlight beams lancing from below having been extinguished by the tumbling fall of the rebar mass. 'Get up here.'

Guided by his voice, Iris climbed onto a narrow ledge of broken concrete, relatively flat and level, and crouched there, letting her pulse and breath slow once more. Keeping back from the crumbling edge, she glanced down and saw nothing. The tangled rebar had fallen with enough velocity to knock the pursuers back down toward the Tyrell private quarters; if the rebar had wedged itself in good and tight in the rubble-lined shaft, it would take them a while to find a way around it.

She turned her face upward, and felt something cold and wet upon it. For a second, Iris wondered if she had at some point torn her skin, perhaps a sharp edge of one of the rebar sections across her brow, and hadn't felt it during the chaos and disorientation in the ill-lit ruins. Still kneeling on the ledge, she reached up with one hand and touched her forehead, then drew her fingertips away and rubbed them together. The wetness wasn't sticky enough for it to have been blood, and it didn't taste salty when she put one fingertip to her tongue. *But if it's just water*, thought Iris, *then maybe* . . . 'It's rain,' she said aloud. Now she recognized the taste, only slightly acrid and chemical from its descent through the city's constant atmospheric pollution. Another sensation of damp and cold, seeping in from both the ledge and the surrounding rubble, and the slight noise of drops falling onto the hard surfaces, indicated that the rainwater was trickling all around her and Vogel. 'Look—' Iris fumbled to where his voice had come from, found his arm and pulled him toward her. She stood up, dragging him along with her, and craned her neck to peer beyond the outcropping of jagged cement above them. Through a narrow triangular hole, she could make out a wedge of the flame-lit underbellies of the stormclouds moving across LA's night sky. 'We made it,' said Iris, letting go of Vogel and wiping the rain from her face. 'We're at the top.'

'Of course.' Vogel sounded amused. 'That's what happens when you climb long enough. Even with this other stuff happening.' Enough dim light trickled into the space for him to be able to indicate a ladder-like slope of debris chunks threaded with the metal reinforcing rods. 'This part's easy.'

True enough, thought Iris, when she pulled herself out from the mouth of the shaft and stood upright again. The wind drove the rain and various pieces of sodden trash – newspapers with Chinese ideograms for headlines, tattered advertising banners even more obscurely coded – almost horizontal, with enough force that Iris had to brace herself to keep from being knocked over. As Vogel climbed out of the narrow opening behind her, she shielded her eyes and looked about the surrounding cityscape.

Like a mountain, thought Iris. Ringed by other, taller and spikier mountains. She and Vogel had emerged at what seemed to be the highest point of the Tyrell Corporation ruins, a slope-sided mound of concrete rubble and twisted steel girders poking up from them like the fingerbones of an ill-buried giant's corpse. Down in the shaft winding vertically through the debris, by which they had fled from Eldon Tyrell's private quarters, their lungs and tracheae had become so coated with inhaled ash and the other by-products of explosive combustion that they had no longer been able to smell or taste them. A few deep inhalations of the night's rain-wet air, however polluted, brought a black wad onto Iris's tongue, that she had to spit out to keep from choking on it. She wiped her mouth with the back of her hand as her eyes adjusted to being able to see once more, by the towering buildings' bright pinpoints of light and the intermittent gouts of flame that burst above them.

'Great,' said Iris. Vogel stood next to her on the uneven, shifting pinnacle, pointlessly brushing off the sleeves and front of his now-tattered jumpsuit. 'We took the long way out.' She had lost all sense of direction, at least as far as compass points were concerned; the direction by which she had first approached the ruins of the Tyrell Corporation headquarters, out on the edges of the surrounding streets, was extinguished from her physical memory. 'How do we get off this mess? Looks like a long walk, no matter which way we go.'

'I don't think,' said Vogel quietly, 'that we're going to get to make that decision.'

She saw that he was pointing to the sky; she turned and looked in the direction of his raised hand and extended index finger. A set of lights, that she had mistaken for stars dimly breaking through as the rain-depleted clouds thinned and scattered, grew suddenly brighter and agile, swooping down from above. Even before Iris discerned the trails cut across the night's darkness, the flaring lines closer set and visibly hotter than regulation police spinners, she knew they weren't LAPD. As they swooped lower and closer, the engine noises caught up with them, snarling lower in pitch than any cop vehicle, as though predators were already exulting in the catch their claws reached toward.

'These are Urbenton's?' Iris quickly glanced over at Vogel. 'How big a crew does he have working for him, for Christ's sake?'

'I don't know,' murmured Vogel. The expression on his face, lit by the glow of the spinner trails, was one of baffled dismay. 'I must've been wrong . . . down below . . .' One lowered hand gestured toward the exit hole behind him, and the Tyrell private quarters at its bottom. 'The ones down there weren't the only bunch after us; somebody had these waiting up here, too. But these *can't* be from Urbenton. He doesn't have anything like this . . .'

'Well, I'm not waiting to find out.' Freed of the soul-dampening claustrophobia of the ornately furnished rooms buried somewhere beneath her, as well as the even tighter press of the exit route she had just scraped through, Iris's normal temper flared. If she'd had the time, she would have decked Vogel with a fist to his jaw for needlessly dragging her through that entire vertical tunnel, and nearly getting

153

her killed in the process. *We could've stayed right there*, thought Iris as she started to run, *and saved ourselves the trouble.*

The slope of the ruins increased her speed. She caught herself with both hands against any outcropping of broken cement and steel that blocked her path, turned and kept her footing on the loose, sliding rubble, and kept running. The spinners, whomever they belonged to, were right above; Iris could hear the louder snarl of their engines as they swooped and banked only a couple of meters above her head.

Searchlight beams lanced around her, racing with the spinners' motion, in front and behind, then locking tight upon her, turning the rubble to a cold blue-white, blinding in its reflected glare. Her broken shadow vaulted across the glacier-like concrete floes.

Then her running stopped, as she skidded to a stop at a cliff's edge before her; she had to fall back and grab onto the rubble behind to keep herself from going over. The toe of her boot dislodged a piece of concrete small as a pebble; she heard nothing for several seconds, then far below the tiny sound of it clattering against the stratum of ruins at street level.

It was worth a shot, Iris told herself – though she had already known that she wasn't going to get away. *Just not in the cards.*

In the distance, blurred by the last of the rain, the lights of the city stacked up to the sky, all of them beyond her reach. Then they were blotted out by the brighter and closer glare of the searchlights as the anonymous spinners hovered down in front of her and trained their gaze upon the hard-shadowed figure pinned against the rocks, shielding her eyes from the glare.

13

'So when do I get to meet this Urbenton guy?'

'Who?'

At first, Iris thought that was supposed to be some kind of a joke. The other person sitting on a folding chair in the galvanized metal shed was one of the crew that had captured her on top of the Tyrell Corporation ruins; she recognized him, even though it had been dark then, with nothing more than the cold stars breaking through the clouds and the beams of the searchlights glaring into her eyes. His had been one of the voices calling out to the others, that this stage of the operations had been completed and objective secured.

'Don't make owl noises at me,' snapped Iris. It figured that they were all in on it, every one of them, right from the beginning. *The only person who doesn't know the whole story*, she thought irritably, *is me.* Just her luck – which, when she thought about it, had never really been the same since she had retired the Enesque replicant, as though that job had put some kind of convoluted, *Nacht und Nebel* curse on her. 'You don't have to rub it in.' She glared at the man guarding her. 'I want to know when we're going to segue onto the next tune, and I get to talk to the guy in charge.'

The guard peered at her, as though at some unexpected biological specimen that had crawled out of the surrounding desolate area and into the shack. 'And that would be . . . ?'

'Jesus Christ,' said Iris. 'No, don't go with that; I don't want to confuse you. I mean Urbenton. The director, or whatever the hell he's supposed to be.' She could tell, from the puzzled look in the man's eyes, that she wasn't coming across. 'Read my lips. Ur . . . ben . . . ton.'

'I don't know who the hell you're talking about.' The guard leaned back in his chair, tilting its front legs clear of the floor's splintery wooden planks, his arms folded across his chest. 'I've never heard of anybody named Bourbonton.'

Iris didn't bother to correct him. *Pointless*, she thought. She'd handled enough interrogations during her cop career, with suspects and perps both dumber and smarter than this guy, to know when things had reached a dead end. Either the guy really didn't know, in which case she was wasting her time by even asking, or he had been trained well enough to put up a convincing front, one that would take a long time to crack. Plus the ability to beat the crap out of him, which was more or less standard LAPD procedure in situations like this. She doubted if that much time was available to her, and she was sure that the other part wasn't, given that the guy was strapped with a big ugly piece in a shoulder holster, and she was weaponless. Her chair and his were far enough apart that if she tried anything cute he would have plenty of time to unfold his arms, pull the gun out and put its muzzle in her face before her butt was even off the curved metal seat beneath her.

Try waiting, Iris told herself. For her, it was a novelty, but she couldn't see that any other options were available at the moment.

'Thirsty?' The guard, unruffled by their exchange, pushed a plastic water bottle toward her with the toe of his boot.

'I'll let you know.'

Which wouldn't be long. The metal shack was already starting to heat up, from the desert-like sun hammering down on it. When she had been loaded into one of the spinners that had come hovering down on her, the first blood-red light of dawn had been starting to leak around the bases of the surrounding buildings. As the spinner had risen and flown eastward, away from the black-mottled ocean, the radiance had changed to a brighter and dirtier orange, textured and smudged by the constant ground-hugging pollution that silted the lungs of every Angeleno. Iris had spat out enough of it to know what the taste was like, waking in the middle of the night with the sensation that some invisible bedmate was sitting on her chest, hands tightening on her throat; that was the kind of repeating dream that came with the urban territory. So it didn't surprise her to see the black-brown inhalants lapping up against the low mountains, that surrounded the dense city basin like the tide of derelict oil tankers.

She turned and gazed out the single small window on one side of the shack, its lower left pane broken out, leaving one jagged triangle sticking up like a tooth. The rest of the window was too clouded with dust to see much, but through the hole she could make out a long vista of sand and scruffy, dried-brown brush clinging precariously to the dunes' hollow slopes. Dead machinery populated the area, right up to the distant limits of a sagging fence topped with rusting coils of razor wire. Most of the equipment looked like ancient earth-moving gear: bulldozers with their shovel-like snouts scraped into the dry rock beneath the sand, caterpillar treads snapped and draped off the giant metal gears, saurian cranes whose necks had been torn free of their sinews, their fanged scoops crashed down upon the little plastic-windowed booths where the human operators had once sat, a long time ago; steamrollers whose massive cylindrical wheels had become pitted with wind-driven gravel. Iris figured that the machines must have been used for road-building, not city roads but highways and freeways, back when there had still been open spaces anywhere near Los Angeles, before the metastasizing city had swallowed them up, oozing itself over them like some slowly and endlessly self-replicating unicellular organism.

Curious, passing time in the shack's heat and stilled air, she leaned to one side so she could look farther along the rows of defunct equipment. Her guess had been right, confirmed by hodge-podge stacks of what had been the signs mounted over the freeways – she had seen photos of them in some historical video documentary, part of her perfunctory civics classwork at the LAPD's training academy. Dark green backgrounds, with reflective white lettering, bright in the desert glare; it hurt her eyes to even look at them. Squinting, with the corners of her eyes watering, Iris could decipher the destinations spelled out on the old signs: places like Pomona and Glendale, Riverside and farther west to San Bernardino, farther north to Ventura and Oxnard. Nothing but names now, without meaning or reference; those places had been buried long ago, beneath the space-hungry city.

Which left no place to go to; not really. That was the true distinguishing feature of Los Angeles: every place in it was just like every other place. Something like the long-expected and even wished-for heat death of the universe had been achieved; with no place to go to that was any different from where someone had started from, why go at all? Instead, there was the constant milling about of LA's street crowds, like the random Brownian motion of molecules in suspension, without purpose or order, or even sensation. Iris supposed that was a big part of the reason for the characteristic blank-faced apathy of LA's citizens, and why she and other blade runners had always been able to run around in the streets with cannon-sized weaponry held aloft, and blow away things that looked like real people, and that died just as gruesomely, without any of the bystanders getting the least bit disturbed by what they were witnessing. *Someday*, mused Iris as she gazed out at the desert beyond the rusting machinery, *someday they'll invent a mass Voigt-Kampff test, one that somebody can run on a whole city at once. And LA'll flunk it.*

She reached down and picked up the plastic water bottle, unscrewed the lid and drank, tilting her head to let the luke-warm liquid slide down her throat. She set the bottle down between herself and the guard. 'So where's Vogel?'

The guard gazed non-reactively at her. 'Who?'

Iris rolled her eyes toward the sheet-metal ceiling of the shack. 'You know,' she said with forced patience. 'Vogel. The guy you picked up with me.'

'That his name?' The guard shook his head. 'We didn't bring anybody back here except you. That other person you were with – he got away. And we didn't bother to go chasing after him.'

'Yeah, right.' Iris considered the guard's statement with sour disbelief. *Expect me to believe that?* 'So why didn't you go after him?'

The guard shrugged. 'He's not important.' With a nod, the guard indicated Iris sitting across from him. '*You're* important.'

'Thanks. That makes me feel better, all right.' She turned again toward the bleak view outside the shack.

A tight-cell phone sounded its characteristic trill, muffled only by the leather of the guard's shoulder holster. As Iris watched, he dug beneath the holster and extracted the tiny device from his shirt pocket. 'Bolcom here.' He listened for a moment, then nodded. 'Got it.' The phone went back where it had come from. 'Let's go.'

Iris remained seated as the guard stood up. 'Go where?'

'Conference room.' The guard gestured toward the shed's door, indicating some place beyond it. 'Believe me, you'll like it better. It's got air-conditioning.'

'You got that right.' Her cowboy shirt, dirty and torn from crawling through the various passages of the Tyrell Corporation ruins, was starting to stick to the skin over her ribs. She stood up. 'Lead on, pal.'

As they were walking across the fenced compound, toward a distant set of larger buildings shimmering in the heat, the guard dug into his jacket pocket and held out something to Iris. 'Here,' he said. 'I was told you could have this back now.'

158

Iris glanced at the familiar object in the guard's hand. 'Really?' She was unimpressed. 'What good's an unloaded gun to me?'

The guard lifted an eyebrow at her, then halted. He raised the weapon and aimed it toward one of the ancient, half-buried bulldozers several meters away, then squeezed the trigger. The sound of the shot rolled out toward the distant, slate-colored hills, followed immediately by the bullet pinging against the bulldozer's concave scoop. Fresh, bright metal showed where the bullet had hit, knocking away layers of rust.

'It *is* loaded,' said the guard quietly, holding the gun out to Iris again.

I'll be damned. Iris stared at the gun, its black checked grip pointing toward her, then took it from him. The gun's comforting weight filled her hand, like a portion of her own anatomy that had been magically restored to her. She could tell there was a full clip inside it, minus the one shot that had just been fired off.

The guard continued walking, exposing his broad-shouldered back; a sweat stain darkened the area along his spine. 'Wait a minute,' Iris called to him.

'Now what?' The guard stopped and looked back at her. 'They're waiting for us.'

Iris leveled the gun at him. 'What's stopping me from blowing your head off, finding a spinner and leaving this cheap popsicle stand behind?'

'Why would you want to do that?' The guard appeared genuinely puzzled. 'You're among friends.'

He started walking again, without looking back. After a moment, Iris lowered the gun and followed him.

'Here you go.' The guard pushed open a battered steel door at the front of the complex's largest building. Air seeped out, several degrees cooler than the stuff rising off the desert floor. 'Make yourself comfortable.'

'I've been trying to.' She walked into the empty room. Hearing the door close behind her, she glanced over her shoulder and saw that the guard hadn't followed her in.

It took a moment for her to realize that she wasn't alone in the space. And that there were other eyes watching her. She'd had her senses attuned for human presences, somebody who wanted to talk to her, who wanted answers from her, and who she might – it was always possible – get answers from.

So she wasn't ready for the owls.

The surprise was enough that her hand actually darted toward the gun she had tucked into her jacket pocket, grabbing the checked metal grip and pulling the cold metal partway out before she realized what they were. Golden eyes, at least a dozen pairs of them, blinked and stared at her. Iris took a step back, so she could get them all into view. She saw now that one wall of the room was studded with bare metal perches, slightly higher than her own head, on which the animals perched. There was a variety of sizes and appearances, as though some retail aviary had been transferred intact from the *souk* in downtown LA. A couple of the owls were some pygmy breed, half the size of the others, but with the same sharp claws and predator's avidity; a couple had round faces, different in plumage from the rest of their bodies; one was almost pure white, with a few black flecks on its chest. Most of them were of the same goldenish brown, with black feathers as horns, as the one she had been pursuing for so long. For all she knew, one of the owls before her now might have been that elusive target.

'You like them?'

Iris turned and saw that someone else, as human as herself, had entered the room. Round-faced, elderly enough that the thinning fringe of hair brushed past his ears was completely white, infirm enough that he moved with the aid of the type of aluminum cane whose floor-end sprouted a set of widely spaced rubber tips. Carefully balancing himself, he pushed the door closed, shutting out the harsh glare bouncing off the expanse of sand, then turned his smile toward her again.

'They're okay, I guess.' An odd, ill-formed memory tugged at her thoughts; it took a few seconds to remember exactly what it was. Nothing that had happened to her when she had been asking questions at the *souk*, or anything that had really happened to her at all; instead, it was something from the movie Vogel had shown her inside the ruins of the old Tyrell Corporation headquarters. The bit where the cop Deckard first met the replicant Rachael; the first thing she'd said to him was to ask whether he liked the company owl, sitting on its perch in Eldon Tyrell's executive suite. And what had Deckard said to her? Iris couldn't remember the exact words; some stupid question about whether the owl was real or not. As if that mattered. Iris glanced back at the array of owls; a few of them were settling their wings around themselves again, as though the sound of human voices had startled them from sleep. 'I wouldn't know one kind from another, though.' She gave a small shrug. 'It's not exactly a topic I'm keen on.'

'So I understand.' The elderly man gimped his way farther into the room, extending the multi-footed cane and then dragging himself along after it. 'We know all about you – Iris, isn't it?' He smiled at her with teeth turned translucent with age, as he passed slowly before her. 'You may call me Carsten, if you like.'

'Why?' She stood with hands on hips, watching him. 'Is it your name?'

'Ho ho. Very cop-like of you, I'm sure.' He radiated a twinkly, grandfatherish persona. 'Young ladies shouldn't go into your line of work. It turns them cynical.'

'Wrong. I was cynical before I became a cop.'

'You're the exception, then.' Carsten didn't look at her, but stood directly in front of the owls, both of his gnarled and brown-spotted hands folded on the cane's rubber grip; he gazed upward, as if admiring the birds. 'But then, that's something else we do, in fact, know about you. That some things, that are for other people either optional – that is, a matter of choice for them – or the results of their formative experiences, are not so for one such as yourself.' He glanced over his shoulder at her. 'As you've indicated, on more than one occasion, you started out this way.'

'Christ, I don't even know what you're talking about.' Iris was beginning to think this was the essential element of the obscure, infuriating curse that had been laid on her. Since the replicant Enesque's death, everyone she encountered seemed to talk in riddles, weirdly profound on the surface, but balloon-empty once the words had been peeled away. *Like they're trying*, she thought irritably, *to screw with my head.* For what purpose, she hadn't yet been able to determine. 'Look, why don't you just tell me what you want from me?'

'*Want* from you?' The notion seemed to amuse the elderly figure. His smile, with its worn-looking teeth, grew wider. 'Why should anyone *want* something from you? That would indicate that you *have* something. Do you?'

'Only this.' She took the gun from her jacket pocket and held it up. 'Maybe I haven't used it enough. If you know what I mean.'

'I can guess.' Unruffled, Carsten returned to admiring the owls arrayed on their perches. 'This is undoubtedly another characteristic of your unfortunate profession. If you cannot figure out what you need to know, in the sense of determining the answers to your many questions, you believe you can force them to be produced. You can put your weapon to someone's head and then that person will tell you both what is true and what is necessary – which, of course, are not always the same thing, are they?'

'I'd settle for either one at this point.'

'The moderation of one's desires,' said Carsten, 'is the point at which wisdom commences. Come here, sweetheart.' He was no longer speaking to Iris, but to one of the owls perched in front of him. A russet-brown specimen extended its wings and flapped – audibly – down to Carsten's extended arm. Iris saw now that none of the owls was chained or otherwise fastened to the metal extension on which it sat. 'There's a good girl.' Holding one arm level, he stroked the owl's head with his other hand. The sleeve of his old-fashioned tweed jacket had no apparent padding or leather protection; the owl somehow managed to keep its sharp claws from penetrating the rough fabric and the skin inside, as though even its inadvertent potential for harm had been tamed away. 'Life's not so bad here, is it?' Carsten glanced at Iris, standing behind him. 'They can be very difficult creatures to maintain in captivity. They're sensitive to all sorts of conditions: humidity, degrees of light exposure, that sort of thing. But it can be done.'

'If you know what you're doing, I suppose.' Iris watched as the old man took from his jacket pocket a small plastic bag filled with scraps of meat; he transferred the bag to his other hand, then extracted the wet red bits from it and fed them one by one to the owl on his arm. The other owls regarded the process with keen interest, some of them partway flapping their wings, others shuffling back and forth on their metal perches. 'I never took care of an animal; I mean, like a pet or something. I had a chat for a while – until somebody messed with it – but that's not the same thing. They're designed to be low-maintenance.'

'Not at all the same thing,' agreed Carsten, feeding another scrap to the owl. 'Plus a living creature reacts to stimuli in its own way; they can be unpredictable, even the simplest of them. These' – he nodded toward the golden-eyed birds – 'are still essentially wild; they can never be truly domesticated.' His fragile visage seemed both sad and well-informed. 'At best, you could say that I've reached a certain understanding with them. They refrain from drawing my blood – they do so now, at least; it took a while, and quite a few scars, before we reached that point – and in return they get the little tidbits they desire.'

'Then they're lucky.'

'No, just smart,' said Carsten. 'Or smart enough. Smarter than human beings, at any rate. Smarter than you.'

'Maybe so.' Iris watched the owl take another scrap from the tips of the old man's fingers. 'You don't have to rub it in, though.'

'It's not meant to hurt, but to motivate. There are things you want to know; why not ask the questions?'

'Asking questions,' said Iris, 'is what's gotten me into this much trouble.'

'Only because you didn't ask enough of them. Or not the right ones. People so rarely do.' Carsten slid the plastic bag into his jacket pocket; with an empty-handed, tossing gesture of his arm, he sent the owl flapping back to its perch. 'But that's the chance you're getting now. So go ahead. Ask. Whatever is on your mind.'

'All right.' Iris looked from him, to the owls, then back again. 'Any of these Scrappy?'

'Pardon?'

'I'm not asking about their dispositions. Their names. What I want to know is if any of these owls is named Scrappy.'

'Ah.' Carsten nodded. 'As in Scrappy, the owl that at one time belonged to the Tyrell Corporation. And to Eldon Tyrell, in particular.'

'That's the one.'

'A worthwhile inquiry,' said Carsten, 'given the amount of trouble to which you've gone to find that particular owl. Unfortunately – and not just for you – none of the owls you see here before you is in fact the one Dr Tyrell so amusingly named "Scrappy". And let me answer your next question before you ask it: the owl you've been seeking has indeed never been here at our facility. As much as we would wish it otherwise.'

Iris mulled over the old man's words. As far as she could determine, he was telling the truth. Even though at least a couple of the owls, including the one he'd just fed, looked like the one she'd been sent to find, she wasn't enough of a bird expert to make a specific ID call – and the elusive Scrappy hadn't been in her possession long enough for her to have memorized any particular key feature. Except for it having been wild, with a chain attached to its banded foot to keep it from escaping; the ones here were conspicuously free of any such tether. As Carsten had claimed, they might not be exactly domesticated, but they had no inclination not to hang around and get their bloody treats handfed to them.

'Okay . . .' There had at least been one item of interest in what this Carsten person had told her. 'So I take it that you people out here are the ones who wanted to find Tyrell's owl? I mean, the ones who *really* wanted to and not just some front organization.'

'Of course we wanted to find it.' Carsten fastidiously cleaned his reddened fingertips with the handkerchief he'd taken from his jacket's inside pocket. 'But then, that is not an exclusive characteristic of our little group. There are others besides ourselves who would like to have possession of that same animal.'

Maybe, Iris thought to herself; at this point, she wasn't prepared to believe even that much. *For all I know, there's only one organization – or maybe only one person – who wants the thing.* And all the others were fronts for that mysterious entity. She spoke her next words aloud: 'Like who?'

'Oh . . . *many.*' Carsten's frail shoulders lifted in a shrug. 'You'd be surprised, I'm sure, if I were to give you an exhaustive list of everyone who is interested in the same thing – the owl – that you and I are. Or who have been in the past. It's an item of considerable value. Worth going to great lengths to acquire, I assure you.'

'Why? What's so valuable about it?'

'There now.' The old man nodded in obvious appreciation. 'That's the important question, isn't it? The question you should have ascertained the answer to *before* you started out on this so-troublesome quest. *Why* is always more important than *who* or *where*; inasmuch as to know the why of something is to know, *in potentia*, all the other questions and answers as well.'

The other part of the curse: these weird-ass lectures. Iris hoped she wasn't going to have to sit through another sermon, like the kind Vogel and the others had gotten into the habit of laying on her. 'All right,' said Iris. 'Same question, then: what's so valuable about Tyrell's owl?'

Carsten gave a slow shake of his head. 'That's not an easy question to answer.'

'I was afraid of that. Somehow I just *knew* I was going to get jerked around about this. Again.'

'Not at all.' Carsten's tone was both mild and amused. 'Your cop-type cynicism is getting the better of you. Though of course, given recent events in your life, I can well understand why that would be. Still, you should make an effort not to become embittered; it's not an attitude that suits you very well, considering the remarkable things that are in store for you.'

'What?' Iris gazed at him in perplexed amazement. 'You gotta be kidding. What the hell is *that* supposed to mean?' She could hear a couple of the owls on their perches, flapping their wings in alarm as her voice rose. 'If there's *more* in store for me, I don't want to know what it is. I've already gotten canned from my job – which I *loved*, and I don't need you telling me what was so wrong about it – plus, before that, I wound up getting my brain fritzed from a hot-wired chat – which I was also fond of – *and* woke up in the police department hospital – which I was *never* happy about. And all that was *before* I got dragged through the Tyrell Corporation ruins.' She knew she was stoking her rage higher, and didn't care. 'Let's not even go into what your bunch did to get me here. If all you wanted to do was have a chat like the others I've had recently, all of which didn't tell me a damn thing, and show off your bird collection, next time –' Iris jabbed her finger at the old man. '*Next time*, just *mail* me your invitation.'

'Really.' None of her angry words had disturbed Carsten's placid demeanor. 'And if I had, would you have accepted it? I think not. Please . . .' He extended a small, softly pink hand toward her. 'Why don't we start over? As if you had just walked through the door, having come here of your own volition.'

'That'd be the day.'

'Perhaps so.' Carsten gave another small shrug. 'I admit such would have required a prescient amount of wisdom on your part. We can't *really* expect that from other people, can we? So let's *pretend* that you had been smart enough to have done so.' Under his grand-fatherly mannerisms, a layer of steel was discernible. His small eyes didn't so much twinkle as glint with the edge of an instrument sharp enough to slice through another's tough demeanor. 'Look – there's coffee here.' He gestured toward a table at the side of the room. 'Real coffee, not any of that ersatzoid stuff. Those industrial by-products they sell from those street stalls will eat a hole in your lower intestine.'

'You're right about that,' said Iris. She knew a bunch of retired cops who'd gotten into the bad habit, when they'd still been on the force, of parking their spinners alongside one of those cheap xenoglot operations and draining a quart-sized polystyrene cup full of hyper-caffeinated junk simply to get through a couple of end-to-end shifts. They'd all wound up with colostomy bags in addition to their major-league Wambaugh Curve moodswings.

'Very expensive, of course – and just for you. We wouldn't do it for anyone, believe me. We have to work within our budget constraints. Unlike your former employers, we have to depend upon our own private sources of operational funds. Come on.' Carsten led her toward the table, where he poured out a cup from a thermal carafe. He handed it to her, then pointed to the other articles on the table. 'And surely you must be hungry, after all that expenditure of energy – and in the cold and damp, you poor thing! – at the Tyrell Corporation ruins. Please, help yourself. That's what it's for.'

Iris realized that she did feel both hungry and tired. The slight ebb of her anger had been produced by the old man's hospitality, however phony; enough to have exposed that pure adrenaline and temper had been keeping her going. She took the plate Carsten handed her, then watched as he deposited a jelly doughnut on it.

'That's such a cliché.' She shook her head.

'My apologies.' Carsten seemed genuinely apologetic. 'No simple cop inferences intended. But as I said, our resources are limited. And this –' He turned, gesturing at the building's interior. 'This is only a temporary set-up. Provisional. We'll be here only as long as we need to be. In order to get the job done. So we haven't established a proper kitchen. There aren't very many of us and we can get by, for the time being, without one.'

Iris took a bite. 'Who's this "we"?' She swallowed. 'Who are you people?'

'Another good question.' Carsten nodded approvingly. 'You're getting better at this. Some day . . .' His voice faded, almost to a whisper. 'Some day you'll know . . . exactly the right question to ask. And then . . .' He brought the gaze of his small, pale eyes around to her again, from whatever interior focal point it had fallen to. 'Then you'll have to decide whether to ask it or not.'

She froze in place, between heartbeats and the tiny, almost silent motions of the old-fashioned numbered clock on the room's wall. A red, viscous trickle from the half-eaten doughnut inched slowly down the inside of her wrist.

'Don't be frightened,' said Carsten gently. 'You might be lucky. That moment might never come.'

Frightened. She could remember when the same fear had touched her before. Then it had brought tears, a bout of weeping, of which she was no longer ashamed. Because she knew now that she had been right to be frightened. *She did look exactly like me,* thought Iris. The memory of that image, of the woman's face, the replicant named Rachael, filled the screen behind her eyes. There had been a question then as well, that she could have asked – but hadn't. Because she had been too afraid to.

Her hand came to her mouth, automatically, and she took another bite of the doughnut. She didn't want Carsten – whoever he was – to know how his words, and her memory, had scared her. Her mouth had gone so dry she could barely swallow.

'Drink your coffee.' Carsten had noticed her effort, close to choking. 'That'll help.'

She obeyed. She could feel her pulse start up again.

'Could you unfold this for me?' Carsten had pulled out a metal chair, like the ones that Iris and the guard had sat on in the other building. 'The joints are a bit rusty – like mine, I suppose.' The simulated twinkle appeared in his eyes again, as though they were some sort of cheaply artificial gemstone. 'And the other one as well. We might as well make ourselves comfortable. We have a lot to talk about.'

Iris set the chairs on either side of the table. She and Carsten sat down – creakily, in his case – with the thermal carafe between them.

'You asked a question.' Carsten refilled her cup, then poured one for himself. 'And as I indicated, one of the better ones available to you. So I feel duty-bound to answer it for you. I don't want you to think I'm wasting your time.'

'You wouldn't be the first,' said Iris.

'Ah. But with us – you and me, that is – it's different. I know how much time you have. And there isn't any to spare.'

She drained the cup in one go, head tossed back, then set it down empty on the table. 'Go on.'

'You wanted to know who we are.' Carsten wrapped both his hands around his own cup, as though trying to warm his thin, elderly blood. 'Our organization, such as it is, has no identifying name or other identifier. It's not even an organization; more of an amalgam, or an *ad hoc* committee.'

'For a committee, you seem to have an awful lot of members. That was a pretty good sized pack you had chasing me and Vogel through the Tyrell Corporation ruins.'

'Loyal employees,' said Carsten. 'As with most of the people you might find here. You see, the committee, such as it is, is made up of the other organizations – companies, a few research labs – that had been involved in the design and production of so-called "replicants", before the Tyrell Corporation established its monopoly in that field.'

Iris picked up her empty cup. 'There were other companies making replicants?'

'Several.' Carsten poured out a refill for her. 'Sudermann, Grozzi . . . in fact, the company for which I was the chief technical officer, Derain *et Cie*, held several key patents, without which no viable replicants could be manufactured at all.'

'Wait a minute. I thought Eldon Tyrell invented the replicant technology.'

'All by himself? That's a good joke.' The faint smile on Carsten's face showed no trace of amusement. 'Eldon Tyrell – and the Tyrell Corporation – certainly wanted other people to believe that. They put a lot of their public relations flacks on the task of implanting that notion, and they largely succeeded. But then, they had help: the Tyrell Corporation didn't achieve its monopoly in the replicant trade on its own. They were essentially given the monopoly, or rather, it was stolen for them.'

'Who did that?'

'Ah. As the ancient Romans would have said, *Cui bono*? Who benefits? An excellent adage, for helping determine the truth, and the culprits.' Carsten sounded both bitter and sarcastic. 'Obviously, the Tyrell Corporation benefited – but they weren't the ones who did it. They merely received the stolen goods into their hands; or, rather, into Eldon Tyrell's hands. You'll have to excuse my personal animosity toward the man; let's just say that I didn't shed any tears when I heard he had been killed by one of his own creations, the replicant known as Roy Batty.'

'I suppose,' said Iris, 'he got what he deserved.'

'You could say that. And you'd be correct. The mill-wheels of the gods grind slow, but they grind exceedingly fine.' A note of grim satisfaction sounded in Carsten's voice. 'Someday, certain UN bureaucrats, the ones in charge of the emigration program, will get what they deserve as well. They were the ones that handed the replicant monopoly over to the Tyrell Corporation. Eldon Tyrell was simply their lackey, following their orders, doing what they wanted done. Tyrell might have thought differently, but then, he was an egomaniac. And a deluded one.'

Iris sipped at the coffee. She looked over the cup's rim at Carsten. 'You're saying the UN was behind the Tyrell Corporation?'

'All the way.' The old man's temper had simmered down, but was still visibly present. 'It could even be said that the Tyrell Corporation was nothing more than a puppet organization, a wholly controlled subsidiary of the UN emigration program. In return for his complete cooperation, Eldon Tyrell was handed all the profits from the replicant industry, which was of course considerably enhanced by the ramped-up production orders placed by the UN for those slave-labor replicants given to the human emigrants. Something of a devil's bargain, I'm afraid, for poor Eldon; he became the master of the replicant industry, with all of his competitors eliminated – rather violently, too, by the UN's elite special forces military units; I remember when the blue-helmeted squadrons arrived on my company's doorstep. It wasn't pretty.' The small, pale eyes in the old man's face seemed to cloud with memory. 'And there weren't many of us that survived – of the Derain executives at the home office in Poitiers, I was the only one that got out alive. I had to go underground and rebuild the corporation from our branch office personnel, or at least the ones I was able to get to before the blue helmets did. That took a long time, and there was a limit to how much we could accomplish, even in league with the other replicant designers and manufacturers who had managed to survive the extermination process. Our little "committee" had its work cut out for it, just in trying to remain among the living. And all the while, Eldon Tyrell and the Tyrell Corporation were installed as the masters of the replicant industry – but as I said, at a price. Tyrell had the UN emigration program's leash around his neck from the beginning. And for an ego-driven type such as himself, that had to be galling.'

'I bet,' said Iris.

A thin smile showed on Carsten's face. 'Perhaps Eldon Tyrell made the mistake of trying to remove that leash; he might have convinced himself that he and his corporation had become more powerful than the UN, or that he was somehow able to protect himself from its retribution for his disloyalty. And as we know, he was wrong about that.'

'Wait a minute.' Iris warily regarded the old man sitting across the table from her. 'You're saying the UN was responsible for Eldon Tyrell's murder? That would mean that the Roy Batty replicant, the one who actually crushed Tyrell's skull, was operating under UN orders.'

'Not at all. It's almost certain that the Roy Batty replicant was acting on its own personal agenda when it killed Eldon Tyrell. But at the same time, there are some – shall we say? – *suspicious* circumstances about how Batty and the other replicants in his group of fugitives were able to both reach Earth and also penetrate the Tyrell Corporation's security systems. At every step of the way, things were made oddly *possible* for the Batty group. *Cui bono?* Hm? If the UN emigration authorities wanted to eliminate an associate who had become too troublesome to maintain a relation with, they didn't have to send any blue-helmeted hit squad after him; that would have been a little bit too noticeable, even in a place such as LA. How much easier and more secretive, yet no less certain and fatal, to simply make sure that a killer such as the Roy Batty replicant was able to gain access to Tyrell.'

'You don't have any proof of that, though.'

'True.' Another shrug from the frail-looking shoulders. 'You could even say that it might be no more than wishful thinking on my part; my personal animus toward the late Dr Tyrell is no doubt apparent. But I'm hardly alone in having wanted him dead; he had made himself a lot of enemies, both human and otherwise. And Tyrell certainly had the kind of devious mind – devious for the sake of being devious – that wouldn't have been satisfied with his privileged position as industrial lackey to the UN emigration program; they might have had to eliminate him to short-circuit any number of schemes he could've cooked up. But as to absolute proof?' Carsten smiled. 'Let's just say that, as I'm certainly older than one such as yourself, I might be at least a little wiser as well when it comes to the machinery of the universe.'

'Maybe.' It was Iris's turn to shrug; she wasn't going to argue the point with him. And if Carsten had actually killed his old rival Tyrell himself, or had arranged for it to happen, and was now trying to foist the blame off onto the UN, it wasn't any of her concern; that hadn't been anything assigned to her, even while she had been with the department. 'So you've got your committee of all the companies that were screwed by the Tyrell Corporation.' She gestured toward the old man with the rim of her cup. 'Now what're you trying to accomplish? Get back into business? Seems like now would be a good time for it, given that the Tyrell Corporation seems to be pretty much defunct.'

'It's not that simple,' said Carsten glumly. 'Nothing ever is. Even if the UN emigration authorities were aware of our existence – and we've gone to a lot of effort to make sure that they're not – they'd hardly be likely to turn the replicant industry back over to us. To do so would amount to revealing how they had attempted to wipe us out in the first place; that's something the UN itself, the administrative levels *above* the emigration program, might not even be aware of. There's every indication that the emigration program might in fact be a rogue element in the UN, operating on its own initiative, outside anyone else's oversight and control. They can only continue that way, and avoid being brought back under administrative discipline, if they keep secret the sort of illicit activities in which they've been engaged.' Carsten leaned across the table, his voice stripped down to utter seriousness. 'The emigration authorities are in too deep to let the truth come out about how they enabled the Tyrell Corporation to take over the replicant industry. They would rather destroy that industry, *and even the emigration program itself*, before revealing that.'

Iris didn't doubt the old man's analysis. It was an investigative truism. *The cover-up*, she told herself, *is always worse than the original crime*. Especially in that it created an endless cycle that got progressively more violent and ruthless as it spiraled downward, with one cover-up succeeding another to hide an original crime that became progressively smaller and less significant, by comparison.

'Okay,' said Iris, 'same question, then. What's the agenda? What do you guys want?'

'In practical terms? Very well.' Carsten laid his small, delicately manicured hands flat upon the table. 'We want the owl.'

I knew that was coming. 'The owl, huh? By which, I take it, you mean Eldon Tyrell's owl. Good ol' Scrappy.'

Carsten nodded. 'Of course.'

'What's the matter with the ones you've got?' Iris nodded toward the golden-eyed birds perched on the opposite wall. 'Or are you trying to complete a full set?'

'Very amusing. There's absolutely nothing wrong with them at all; they are, indeed, very valuable creatures. In many ways, and not just on the open market, where such things are prized for their rarity.' Carsten turned his gaze from her and regarded the owls. Some of them had closed their eyes, as though in apparent sleep; the others looked back at him without blinking. 'They have a specific and unique value to the committee of which I am a part. But the owl named Scrappy – Tyrell's owl, for which you have been so assiduously hunting – has an even greater, though similar, value.'

'Which is?'

'Well done.' Carsten nodded in approval. 'You're definitely getting the hang of it. Of asking the right questions, that is. You're doing very well. When you know specifically why the owl in question is so valuable to us, you'll have gone a great way toward answering a lot of the puzzles facing you.'

'That's why I asked.' Iris helped herself to more coffee from the carafe; there was only enough left to half-fill the cup. 'Not that I expect a straight answer or anything.'

'That's where you're wrong,' said Carsten. 'Everything has been arranged – at great effort, I might say – just so you'd be given that "straight answer". As much as it is important to you that you should find out these things, it is equally important to us that it be made possible for you to find them out.'

Iris had had enough coffee; she could feel the familiar, and comforting, jittering caffeine buzz down through her arms and into her hands as she pushed the cup away from herself. 'Prove it,' she said.

'As you wish.' Carsten stood up from the table. 'Follow me.'

14

'You sure you don't want to get some rest first?' The old man looked solicitously at Iris. 'We could set up a cot for you in one of the smaller, private buildings; the windows are already covered.'

'I'm okay.' Iris kept walking, head down to shield her eyes from the noonish glare of the sun. 'Don't worry about me.'

When they had stepped out of the building, with its coffee on the table and collection of perching owls, the daylight had hit her between the eyes like a hot fist. She could feel the sweat seeping out into the torn fabric of her cowboy-motif shirt as she walked alongside Carsten. His presence, and the gritty landscape beneath her bootsoles, was obscured by the shifting, molten after-images that had been burnt past her pupils.

'Seriously,' said Carsten. He could just be detected, peering into her face as he led the way to their destination. 'You've been on your feet for a long time. You might not even be aware of exactly *how* long. And there are matters of great import ahead of you. You'll need to be ready for them.'

He was right, she knew; her internal clock had lost its hands, a long – she assumed – time ago. The glowing digits inside her head that kept track of the course of hours had gone dark. She had entered the fatigue zone, familiar to her from days-long chases of escaped replicants, fueled by adrenaline more than any illegal stimulant. Tanking up on Carsten's coffee, genuine as it was, hadn't helped at all. The world seemed real enough to her – or too real, as though the dials marked Gravity and Mass had been turned up to eleven – but she had doubts about herself. Iris felt herself to have faded into some dim, nerve-eroded insubstantiality, as though she were her own ghost, coming back to haunt some locale vaguely remembered from her real life. *Like watching that damn movie*, she thought glumly. The images on the screen had been the real people; that irrational conviction moved uneasily through her mind.

'I'm ready,' said Iris. She raised a hand, palm outward, to keep

Carsten's blurry image at bay. 'Ready as I'll ever be.' That was the actual reason that she didn't want to go to sleep, no matter how tired and messed-up she had gotten. In her present condition, there was little Carsten or anyone else could tell her or show her that would give her a shock; the sensation of not really existing put a comfortable distance between her and this world she had found herself in. Here, the desert sun was hammering down on her and the rusting, decay-bent earth-moving equipment; but in her head, the cooling monsoon rains of LA continued to sluice away the dust and heat. 'Fire away.'

The after-images in her eyes had faded a bit; she could discern the old man's expression as he peered into her face. 'I respect your decision,' he said after a moment. 'After all – you've come a long way for this.'

'Not willingly.' She wiped the glare-stung tears from her eyes with the back of her hand. 'Don't forget that.'

'You know' – the old man sounded as concerned as before – 'you could be wrong about that.'

'And what's that supposed to mean?' Iris stopped and turned toward him. 'Let me guess,' she said irritably. 'What you're saying is that I *wanted* to come out here. And that I somehow engineered that into happening.'

Behind Carsten, the desert stretched past the machinery and the sagging fence, shallow rolling dunes and brown scrubby weeds dotting the vista all the way to the gray hills at the horizon. Little scratch marks on the cloudless sky moved in slow circles, revealing themselves as hawks – the last survivors in the wild – scouring the ground for prey with their razor-sharp scrutiny.

'In your heart of hearts.' Carsten spoke somberly, all possible irony drained from his reedy voice. 'When you were searching for something, that's the last place you would ever have looked.'

With her hands planted on her hips, Iris regarded the old man for a few seconds, then shook her head. 'I don't,' she said, 'keep either escaped replicants – or owls – anywhere near my vital organs.' She turned and started walking again, in the direction in which they had been previously heading.

Iris could hear Carsten murmur something behind her, almost inaudible. 'As far as you know,' he said. She ignored him.

With no idea of where they had been heading, she stopped and found herself gazing at the compound's fence, topped with razor wire, a few meters away. The low, metal-constructed buildings were somewhere behind them, as Carsten caught up with her. 'This is what you wanted to show me?' Iris gestured toward the fence and what lay beyond it. 'Looks like sand.'

'Not there.' Carsten touched her arm. 'You walked right by it. Without even seeing it.'

She turned and looked where the old man pointed. An angled trench had been slashed into the earth, dug and scooped out by a couple of the earth-moving machines, painstakingly resurrected for the purpose. Mounds of darker subsoil mingled with the buff-colored sand from above, sloped against the caterpillar treads of the crane and scoop-fronted bulldozer.

'A hole in the ground,' said Iris. 'I'm less than impressed.'

'It's what's *in* the hole that's important. Come on.'

The trench had been excavated in such a manner as to leave an earthen ramp leading to its bottom. Carsten started down it; after a moment, Iris followed him. She had to lean back as she stepped, hand against the loosely crumbling side of the trench, to keep the gravel from sliding out from beneath her bootsoles and spilling her backward.

At the lowest point of the trench, a battered metal door was incongruously mounted, its hinges set into a surrounding frame. The sun above had moved just far enough from its zenith so that the trench's floor had been hidden in deep shadow; standing or passing anywhere near the trench, she had been unable to see what lay in it.

A sepulchral chill pricked the skin on Iris's forearms. She and Carsten were far enough below the desert's surface – the trench's lip was at least a couple of meters above her head – that the air temperature had fallen several notches. That wasn't enough, though, to account for the degree of cold she felt crawling toward the marrow of her bones, or for the pearlescent layer of condensed moisture that had collected on the door. Iris reached out and laid her palm against the metal, letting the thermal differential pull at her own overheated blood for a moment. When she drew it away, the print of her hand remained, with clear drops of water collected and trickling down both from its base and her own wrist.

'Keep your groceries in here?' Iris wiped her damp hand on her trousers. 'Good idea. Things could go off pretty fast in this kind of weather.'

'A little more important than that.' Fumbling in his jacket pockets, Carsten produced a ring of keys, old-fashioned brass ones without blinking mini-lights or any other sign of digital security coding. 'As I'm sure you'll agree, in just a bit.' He unlocked the door, then turned with both hands a bar-shaped lever. A cloud of even colder moisture, like a little puff of Arctic wind released from an invisible bottle, blew across him and Iris as he pushed open the heavily insulated door.

Iris felt someone watching her, the weight of another's gaze falling from above, across her shoulders. She looked up and saw that it was more than one person: there must have been at least a dozen of them standing at the edge of the trench, like mourners at a burial service, regarding her with somber, unsmiling expressions. Iris recognized one of them as the guard who had sat across from her in the first small, metal-roofed building to which she had been brought; she supposed that the others, like the guard, had been part of the pursuit team that had tracked her and Vogel down, at the Tyrell Corporation ruins, back in LA.

'What the hell do they want?' Staring straight up into the watching men's eyes, Iris nudged Carsten with the point of her elbow. 'I mean, what do they want *now*?'

'What's that?' Carsten was fussily restoring the key to his pocket; he turned his gaze in the direction of Iris's, and saw the younger men standing above. Loose, sandy gravel trickled down the sides of the trench, dislodged by their boots. 'Oh . . . it's only natural.' He looked again toward Iris. 'You'll have to excuse some curiosity, and apprehension, on their part. They know how important your presence is here.'

'Yeah, right.' Iris wrapped her arms around herself, against the cold air that had rolled out of whatever space lay beyond the metal door. She had become so used to moving in virtual invisibility on her murderous errands through the distant city's streets, with none of the inhabitants paying her or her raised weapon any mind, that to be silently watched in this way was a novel and disconcerting experience. 'Let's get on with the show.'

'By all means.' Carsten pushed the door, with both hands this time, leaning into its thick weight. The frost cloud, bigger than before, momentarily eclipsed his face and upper torso, rolling past him like the breath off some antiseptic-smelling sea. 'Come on.'

It was dark inside, and even colder than Iris had expected, especially when Carsten pulled the heavy, insulated door shut, its edges meeting the surrounding metal as though a hermetic tomb had been installed here beneath the desert. The dark was sucked away and extinguished when Carsten flipped the light switch beside the doorway.

'Jesus Christ.' Iris hugged herself even tighter, fingers pressing through the torn sleeves of her embroidered shirt. She could feel the intense cold marching toward the center of her body, viscera contracting. 'What the hell is this? Some kind of a—'

She fell silent as the sensation of being watched, of eyes upon her, once again manifested itself. The room was empty, though, of all living things except herself and the old man; this time, she was sure of that. There was no wall of perching owls with their golden eyes regarding her, judging her as prey or threat. The gray concrete walls were lined instead with wide-diameter pipes and vents, layered with ice; minute crystal stalactites, frozen and glassy, extended from the ceiling. Blue fluorescent light, from tubes and flickering square panels, filled the chamber, dimly enough that it took her a moment to realize that the eyes whose presence she sensed, at the periphery of her own vision, were disembodied. The eyes existed, but the human – or human-like – bodies that might have once held them were gone.

Or had never existed. She turned slowly in the chamber's frigid air, looking around at the glass beakers and vessels sitting on top of industrial storage units and laboratory benches, with the spherical human eyes, complete with trailing optical nerve tissue, floating in some thick, almost gelatinous liquid. The eyes gazed back at her, unblinking and emotionless, as though possessed of some timeless perspective on human folly, beyond resignation or fear.

'I know this place,' said Iris aloud. Her words, and every breath she exhaled, hung in front of her in a little cloud. She could taste ice crystals forming on the tip of her tongue. 'I've never been here, but I know it.'

'That's right.' Carsten, standing beside her, didn't seem to notice the cold. It passed through his thin frame with no apparent effect. 'I'm aware that your friend Vogel showed you certain things. An old movie. About people like yourself: cops, blade runners. And about the other things, that are also like you, in their own way. Only they don't get to live. Not in the old movie, and not in this world. They have to die.'

'Too bad ... for them.' The cold made Iris clench her teeth, involuntarily. A shiver ran up her spine and across her shoulders, invoked less by the temperature than the unsettling aspect of the eyes floating in their glass containers. 'They should try for better parts the next time.'

'But you do recognize this?' Carsten gestured with upraised hand at the space surrounding him and Iris. 'From the movie?'

'Sure.' Iris nodded. The scene replayed itself in her memory, from what she had watched in Eldon Tyrell's private theater. It had been something with a couple of the escaped replicants that the blade runner named Rick Deckard had been tracking down, with intent to 'retire' them. Only Deckard hadn't been in the scene; it had been just the leader of the fugitive replicants, the one named Roy Batty and the big stupid one with the weak chin whose name Iris couldn't remember at the moment. Those two, and some kind of Asian-looking technician, with wispy Mandarin-like facial hair and pidgin English, an array of magnifying lenses turned up on his brow, and swaddled in artificial furs with heating tubes plugged in and trailing behind him. Which the Batty replicant had yanked out with a steam-like hiss, as he and the dumb one had terrorized the smaller figure. 'It was a real charming bit.'

I made your eyes. That was what the tech had said, in an odd transport of pride in his own work, as he had pointed with his gloved hand toward Batty's evilly smiling face. He had seemed happy to have had these walking evidences of his state-of-the-art craftsman-ship, his contribution to the Tyrell Corporation's manufacturing of products that looked just like human beings, talked and feared death just like humans, but somehow weren't human. *Your eyes . . .*

'Not, though, with a happy ending. At least not for old Chew.'

She supposed that had been the name of the eye technician, both in the movie and in real life, whatever that meant. If it meant anything at all, anymore. She couldn't remember at the moment if anybody had spoken the wispy-bearded man's name aloud, in the process of the replicant Batty and his partner extracting the information they had wanted from him. Information about Dr Eldon Tyrell, and how to get to him. Which hadn't resulted in a happy ending for Tyrell, either.

There were some differences to the scene she had watched in the *Blade Runner* movie. More disembodied eyes, to be exact. Chew had been happily fussing around with only a few of them, peering down a microscope and making little tweaky adjustments, probably on some deep-tissue, sub-cellular level, when Batty and the big dumb one had come strolling in—

At the back of her brain, Iris wondered – now – how the two escaped replicants had gotten in so easily, as if there had been no door locks or alarm systems hooked up at some Tyrell Corporation subcontractor's production area. In the movie, Chew had looked momentarily surprised to see the two figures standing there, like they shouldn't have been able to waltz right in and catch him at work. *Maybe this old guy is right*, thought Iris. *Maybe somebody did grease their way in*. Maybe not the UN, but somebody with some kind of inside access to the eye tech's workshop. Tyrell? Why would Eldon Tyrell have wanted to arrange this particular death? Iris could feel herself slipping, thoughts spiraling into another infinite regress of paranoia and true conspiracy.

The only thing she could be sure of at the moment was that in the movie she had watched deep inside the Tyrell Corporation ruins there hadn't been so many eyes, in so many jars and beakers and graduated flasks. Even the wall full of owls in the other compound building hadn't been able to creepily stare her down as thoroughly as what was happening here.

'What did you do?' Iris wasn't able yet – if ever – to unwrap her arms from herself. She used a nod of her head to indicate the vessels with their floating contents, like white, cycloptic tadpoles. 'Drag everything out of the dead guy's file cabinets?'

'We did more than that,' said Carsten. He still seemed unaffected by the chamber's cold, as if he had spent enough time here to get acclimated. 'This is more than old Chew's stock; our committee scoured all the other neuro-optical labs that had been subcontracted out to the Tyrell Corporation. There was a whole high-security district in Taiwan, with no other industrial production than that going on; the whole place was a virtual fiefdom, with Eldon Tyrell its absentee lord and master. None of the European operations, mainly around Neues Frankfurt and the Mont Blanc Tunnel sub-warrens, was as big as that, but there were more of them. It took quite a while, after the destruction of the Tyrell Corporation headquarters, to track those facilities down and clear them out.'

'What were you looking for?'

'Nothing,' said Carsten. 'Our committee's operatives were just making sure there wasn't anything going on elsewhere, with any of the other subcontractors, that was at the same level as what Chew had been doing in LA. Even before we moved in on what was left of Chew's neuro-optical facility, we'd had a pretty good idea that that had been where Tyrell's important design and prototyping work had been going on. For one thing, it was right under Eldon Tyrell's nose, practically speaking, so he'd have been able to keep an eye on it without having to leave the city or resort to potentially crackable communications links. The other indication was, of course, that Chew had been the best in his particular field; he had been chief technical officer and operations manager at the Taiwan facilities, building them up from scratch, before Tyrell brought him over here. That's why his English was so poor, the way you heard it in that movie you saw; he was hardly a native Angeleno. Even the ethnic sub-culture types can usually pull it out better than that, at least when they want to.'

'His language skills couldn't have been too bad,' said Iris, 'if he was as important to Tyrell's operations as you claim he was.'

'That's because the two of them, Chew and Tyrell, spoke a universal language, beyond English or pidgin, of design specs and prototype refinement. It's not as if they needed to socialize with each other; Tyrell was hardly the sociable type, was he?'

'Not from what I've heard.' Rubbing her arms in a vain attempt to create warmth, Iris glanced around the ice-bound space again. 'If you ask me, you and your bunch are a little on the obsessive side as well. Otherwise, you wouldn't have gone to so much trouble to re-create Chew's lab out here in the middle of nowhere.'

'Oh, we didn't *re-create* it; this *is* Chew's neuro-optical lab facility.' A note of pride sounded in Carsten's voice. 'Everything, right to the exterior walls. Even this.' Carsten leaned down and brushed ice crystals from a large, rectangular object propped against one of the workbenches. He flipped a switch at the back; with a faint, electrical buzzing, blue neon letters and back-lit plastic came on. The sign, when fully illuminated, read LA EYEWORKS. 'Just like in the movie – right?' Carsten smiled at Iris as he straightened up. 'It wasn't really the name of Chew's facility – as a matter of fact, it didn't even have a name, only an invoice code in the R and D section of the Tyrell Corporation's operating budget. Chew inherited it from some other business that had been there before, and kept it as his little joke.'

'Yeah, right; hilarious.' Iris couldn't keep from shivering; she felt as if the blood in her veins was starting to turn glacial from the chamber's cold. 'How'd you get all this stuff here?'

'That took some doing.' Carsten picked up one of the flasks, examined the floating blue-pupilled eye inside, then set it back down.

'Our little committee's operatives had to work pretty fast to pull it off. We had been keeping an eye on Chew for some time; we knew who he was working for, and how important that work was for the Tyrell Corporation. Soon as we knew that both Chew and Eldon Tyrell were dead – that Batty and the other escaped replicants had done their job – we knew we had at least a small window of opportunity before the Tyrell Corporation got reorganized enough to keep track of its subcontractors. Fortunately, buildings are constantly being demolished or being constructed in the city, so there wasn't any notice paid, even by the police, when our team took LA Eyeworks apart, boxed it up into half-a-dozen transport containers, and smuggled it out here. Twelve hours max, and it was ours.'

'Why'd you bury it?'

'Several good reasons.' Carsten gestured toward the walls. 'Out here in the desert, the thermal factor looms rather large. We've got a brace of generators going full-bore as it is, to keep this thing down to the appropriate temperature. Let's be practical – why should we make it even more difficult for ourselves, by letting it sit out in the sun? Not to mention what would happen if there were a problem of some kind, like the power supply going on the fritz.' He pointed to the flask he had set down a moment before; the eye's silent, patient gaze had swivelled around toward Iris. 'The stuff we're holding here is basically raw human tissue, or replicant tissue, which is pretty much the same thing, in terms of your basic spoilage effect. We don't have the temperature down all the way to Chew's operating conditions, but it's cold enough for our purposes. And we'd like to keep it that way. Down here, underground, things would stay basically cool at least until our tech crew got the generators running again.'

'That's one reason.' Iris reached over and turned the flask around so that the floating eye was no longer staring at her. 'What's the other?'

'We've got,' said Carsten matter-of-factly, 'what some other people would like to get hold of. Or to put it another way, we've got what other people would like to make sure we *didn't* have. We've got Chew's gear and stock out and hidden, but we don't want anybody else tracing it here. Our committee's operatives scanned everything as well as they could, when they were tearing it apart and boxing it up, but time was limited. There might have been bug elements, location devices, wired into the walls, right down at practically the molecular level. The Tyrell Corporation might have done that, to make sure that none of the work Chew was doing for them wound up in the wrong hands.'

'Well, you don't have to worry about the Tyrell Corporation any longer.' Iris balled her right hand into a fist; the flask had been so cold that it had stung her fingertips. 'From the looks of it, they're long gone.'

'Don't be too sure about that. The Tyrell Corporation wasn't synonymous with Eldon Tyrell. There were even elements inside the corporation that were actively opposed to the late doctor; the whole company was a rat's nest of intrigues and conspiracies. It's something of a tribute to him that he was able to keep on top of all that, right up until the end.'

'Maybe he didn't,' said Iris. 'If what you're saying is true, it might not have been any operation by the UN emigration program that did him in. It could've been some group right inside the corporation itself.'

'True.' Carsten raised an appreciative eyebrow as he regarded her. 'We've considered that as well. Which is another reason for our committee to be on its guard. The Tyrell Corporation had contingency plans for any catastrophic event, such as that which leveled its headquarters in LA. It's almost certain that a shadow corporation still exists, carrying out some kind of agenda aimed at restoring its power. If that shadow corporation is headed by the type of individuals who would have no qualms about eliminating their own CEO, then that indicates just how ruthless they are.'

'Yeah, well, that makes them about on the same level as everyone else. I don't see you and your bunch as being exactly non-violent.' Iris rubbed her upper arms even more fiercely and vainly. 'Look – how much longer is this going to take? I'm *freezing* here. I mean, I've seen your collection of owls, and now I've seen your collection of eyeballs in jars. What else is there?'

'Seeing those things is one matter,' said Carsten. 'Understanding them, and what they mean, is another. My committee's operatives didn't round up all the neuro-optical technology that the Tyrell Corporation had paid for, back when it had been a functioning, above-ground entity, just so we could have some entertaining souvenirs. There's a purpose to everything, even if it doesn't seem quite apparent to you yet.'

'Fine. Lay it on me before I get frostbite.'

'Impatience in the pursuit of wisdom might be foolish, but hardly something of which I can disapprove.' Carsten strolled away from her, his calm, unruffled breath hardly creating even the smallest cloud before him. He stood looking for a moment at a wall-mounted metal shelf, lined with more of the floating eyes and softly trailing optical cords. 'These little bits of flesh and nerve tissue – what do you think is so important about them?' He picked up one of the jars and tilted it slightly, studying the contents. The disembodied eye regarded him back with perfect equanimity. 'I mean, what do you think their importance was to Tyrell? Both the man and the corporation, that is. Why did the Tyrell Corporation go to such lengths to subcontract out this part of the replicant technology, instead of doing it in-house with all the rest of the bits and pieces that went into their products?'

'How the hell should I know?' Iris managed an irritable shrug, even with her arms wrapped around herself. 'Maybe it was cheaper that way, or something like that. Maybe the Tyrell Corporation was just keeping its production costs down. Eldon Tyrell might've been a smart businessman, on top of everything else.'

'He was all of that; there's no denying it. But he hardly needed to keep his company's production expenditures in line, since those were fully covered by the UN emigration program. The agreement that was put into place when he was handed the monopoly over the replicant industry was that he could pass along all costs to the UN, in any amount, and his company's profits would be added above that line, as a percentage of costs. So you can see, he would be motivated to keep those costs as high as possible, in order to maximize the profits flowing to the Tyrell Corporation.' Carsten shook his head. 'So it couldn't have been a cost-cutting measure, to subcontract out the neuro-optical prototyping work to Chew. Plus, you have to take into account that Eldon Tyrell, both by nature and by logic, was more than a little paranoid about letting any aspect of the replicant technology slip out of his grasp, once he'd gotten hold of it. That's why the Tyrell Corporation headquarters was such a monstrosity, with all of its design and production facilities in one location, virtually right beneath Tyrell himself. That was so he could keep an eye on it all, though that hardly did him any good at the end.'

'Fine,' said Iris. 'So it doesn't make sense. Then what was it with the eyes? Maybe Tyrell had gotten so paranoid that he couldn't stand being watched, and having all these loose eyeballs floating around, down in the factory, creeped him out too much.' She pulled one hand away from herself long enough to gesture at the shelf of flasks and graduated beakers. 'Hey, I don't particularly care for them, myself. As a decorating *motif*, they pretty much bite.'

'True.' One corner of Carsten's mouth lifted in a partial smile. 'But that was hardly the reason someone such as Eldon Tyrell would banish them from the company's headquarters. He had a more serious rationale for that.'

'Which was?'

'He was hiding them,' said Carsten simply. 'Or trying to. And before you ask, I'll tell you from whom: from the UN emigration program itself. Eldon Tyrell would have been a fool – which he most assuredly wasn't – if he had let himself trust the same organization that had wiped out his competitors in the replicant industry, merely because they had handed the monopoly on that industry over to him. Tyrell was fully aware that the UN emigration authorities hadn't done that because they were particularly fond of him and the Tyrell Corporation. They had done it because they found the Tyrell Corporation and its CEO useful for their purposes. And Eldon Tyrell also knew that if the moment came when he and his company *weren't* useful any longer to the UN, the emigration authorities would have little compunction about wiping him out in the same murderous fashion their blue-helmeted thugs had taken out my company and the others in our committee. More than that: the UN emigration authorities would have no choice about eliminating the Tyrell Corporation. They would have to do it, right up to and including the murder of Eldon Tyrell, in order to cover up their own trail of previous actions. They couldn't let Eldon Tyrell go on living after they had shut down the Tyrell Corporation; the only absolute way to ensure his silence would be through his death.'

'Okay, I got it.' Iris nodded slowly. 'So taking some part of the replicant technology off-site, away from the Tyrell Corporation headquarters, was Eldon Tyrell's way of buying himself insurance against the partners he no longer trusted. If he ever had trusted them, I mean.'

'Precisely,' said Carsten. 'Tyrell was trying to walk a fine line, between keeping the replicant technology under his control and splitting off just enough of it so that if the UN emigration authorities decided to shift it to someone else, they wouldn't be able to get it all. Or at least they would have a hard time doing it. Hard enough, and risky enough, that his friends at the UN might decide that it was easier – or at least a lot less trouble – to let him go on living, and for them to keep on doing business with the Tyrell Corporation, rather than try to make other arrangements. Arrangements that might not come off, if they weren't able to get hold of the piece of the replicant technology that Tyrell had hidden away at Chew's place.' Carsten glanced around at the icy walls of the chamber. 'And believe me, Eldon Tyrell had made plenty of arrangements to make sure that such a failure would have been a real possibility. When our committee's operatives took the LA Eyeworks building apart, they found all sorts of enhanced destructive capability charges laced throughout the structure, keyed to coded remote-detonation signals that would've been beamed in from the Tyrell Corporation head-quarters, while it still existed. In other words, Tyrell had made plans for either contingency, either taking out Chew and his facility or, if it was too late for that, then the big apocalyptic self-destruction he'd wired into his own building complex. Since you've already seen and been through the ruins, you know which one of those possibilities finally came to pass.'

'So where does that put the UN and its emigration program?' Puzzling over the things that the old man had told her was nearly enough to distract Iris from the chill pressing tighter around her. 'Why should you be concerned about the UN tracking you down because you've got Chew's stuff here? It wouldn't do them much good, anyway, what with the rest of the replicant technology having gone up in smoke.'

'The UN emigration program can replace everything that went up with the Tyrell Corporation headquarters – or it already has. Most of what they would need for that, the original replicant technology, they scooped up when the blue helmets raided and wiped out Tyrell's competitors – such as my company.' The bitter note was once again audible in Carsten's voice. 'They didn't just hand everything we had over to Tyrell; they kept enough of the redundant production-line machinery for themselves, in case they would ever want to go into business for themselves. Which is apparently what the UN emigration program is doing now. Our committee has other teams of operatives which have been monitoring various capitalization-intensive con-struction projects being run by UN front organizations, on the sly. There's a massive underground facility that's nearly finished beneath the Kansas crop-quarantine areas; the UN has got a couple thousand acres of geneticide-blackened landscape to play around in there, with a total perimeter lockdown in effect, supposedly to keep any traces of

GM'd wheat DNA from contaminating the still-productive areas farther west. Plus, it has a physical mirror site about halfway completed in a radiation-swept, former industrial zone in the Belorussian stump republic. The UN emigration authorities have obviously decided that if it's going to take over the replicant technology and run production itself, better to do it in non-populated areas rather than right in the middle of the biggest urban conglom outside of the Shanghai meldplex.'

'Yeah, I guess that makes sense.' Iris cupped her numb fingers in front of her mouth and blew into them, then shook her hands in an attempt to get the blood moving again. 'That way, if they decide to pull the plug, it wouldn't leave traces that are quite so public as that pile of rubble they've got sitting in the middle of LA right now.'

'But before they can pull the plug,' said Carsten, 'publicly or not, they've got to get their replicant-technology facilities up and running. The entire UN emigration program hinges upon the production and distribution of cheap slave labor – that is, the replicants themselves – to the outer colonies. With the Tyrell Corporation shut down, the program has been able to keep running on a severely minimized basis, drawing upon its stockpiled reserves of animation-suspended replicants. But those reserves are close to running out; Eldon Tyrell managed his company's production rates so that his only customer, the UN, could never get very far ahead in terms of long-term use and storage; it was always dependent upon current production to keep the emigration program going at the rate the UN deemed necessary. So it was obvious, right from the beginning, that neither side trusted each other. An arrangement like that, with mutual paranoia advancing exponentially, can't last forever. And that's why Tyrell squirreled away part of the replicant technology – in fact the most critical part, upon which everything else depends – in Chew's operation.'

'The eyes?' Iris shifted her own gaze to the mute, compound one held by the jars and their floating contents, then back to Carsten. 'What's so special about the eyes?'

'That depends, doesn't it?' Carsten's thin, fragile smile showed, as if once again indulging her. 'On what you think eyes are used for.'

'Is that some kind of a joke?' She wondered if the chamber's cold had at last frozen some vital synapse inside the old man's skull. 'What are eyes used for? For seeing, of course. You look at things with them. What the hell else?'

'And that's all?' Her answer appeared to produce even more mild

186

amusement in Carsten. 'You've never heard that old adage, I take it, that eyes are the windows to a person's soul.'

'I've heard it,' said Iris impatiently. 'It doesn't mean anything.'

'Why not? Perhaps because souls don't really exist?'

'Not enough to matter. Not on a practical basis. And even if they do exist, for human beings at least, that doesn't mean replicants have them.' Iris couldn't believe this; she was freezing to death, and also engaged in some obscure theological debate. 'That's probably why replicants flunk the empathy test, why their numbers come out so low when we run the Voigt-Kampff machine on them. If the reps had souls, then they'd be like human beings, and they'd have the necessary empathic faculty to pass themselves off as human. But they don't have that, so they flunk the tests, so they're not like human beings – not really – so they don't have souls, or whatever the word 'soul' is a figure of speech for. QED. *Now* can we get out of here?'

'In a minute. You've waited and searched for so long; why be impatient now?'

'Because I'm cold,' said Iris, 'and tired.'

'That might be so – but I've got your complete attention, don't I?' Carsten's smile turned even more knowing as, head tilted to one side, he regarded her. 'If you don't want to stay and find out why I brought you here, then you can leave. The door's right behind you.'

Iris didn't know why she hadn't left already. *Maybe because I'm frozen to the floor*, she thought. *I can't move.* But she knew that wasn't it.

'All right,' said Iris. 'You've got it, like you said. I don't have any choice about staying here. It's fate or something.'

'Those are the truest words you've ever spoken.' Carsten's smile had vanished. 'Truer than you know.'

She nodded slowly. 'Don't take all day about it, okay? Tell me what's so important about the eyes.'

'You don't just *see* with eyes,' said Carsten softly. 'There's more to them than that. People see *into* you through them; that's what is meant by their being the windows to your soul. It's an old saying – people said it long before there was a Tyrell Corporation, or replicant technology, or even a city called LA. People knew it was true, right from the beginning of time. They recognized that there was a *transfer of information* at that precise juncture; information relating to *identity*. Not just *who* that person is, into whose eyes you're looking – but *what* that person is as well. You can hardly deny that such is the case. After all – doesn't the Voigt-Kampff machine work, at least in part, exactly

187

on that principle? That the eye of the test subject reveals the ultimate truth? In fact, the individual on the other side of the machine lives or dies based upon what the operator – the blade runner; you, or someone like you – sees in that eye.'

'It's one factor.' Iris gave another shrug, even stiffer and more uncomfortable from the cold than before. 'Among many. The Voigt-Kampff machine measures pupil fluctuations and other involuntary stress indicators, weighs them together and sorts them out, then gives the operator, the blade runner, a reading that can be interpreted along certain set parameters. That's all.'

'A diagnosis, as it were.' Carsten's expression held no humor. 'Medically speaking. The blade runner being the doctor looking for a certain congenital, incurable condition. The treatment for which is very brief, and very final.'

'The LAPD doesn't make us take the Hippocratic oath when we sign on with the blade runner division. "Do no harm" is somebody else's job description, not ours.' A spark of anger flared inside Iris, hearing herself talk as if she were still a blade runner, and hadn't gotten canned off the force. 'That's how,' she said bitterly, 'I remember it, anyway.'

'But what you *don't* remember,' said Carsten, 'is ever taking a Voigt-Kampff machine apart, then tracing out its circuits to see if they actually worked as you had been told they did.'

'I was a blade runner, not some kind of service technician down in the LAPD basements.'

'Exactly. So you have no verifiable idea of whether the Voigt-Kampff machine did anything at all, or whether it was merely a prop in an elaborate scheme to make you think it did. Consider the manner in which it was designed; take the bellows component, for instance. What is that supposed to do?'

Just mentioning it brought an image to her mind's eye, the familiar memory flash of a V-K unit sitting on a table between her and some suspected replicant, the accordion folds of the bellows slowly compressing and expanding, as though the machine itself were alive. 'It samples . . .' It took a few seconds longer to remember what she had been told, back in the division training course. 'It samples the air, I mean the exhaled air from the suspect. His breath – or her breath. It detects minute traces of hormonal components and other stress indicators, and . . . let's see . . . metabolized catecholamines that have passed through the blood-brain barrier. Real sophisticated stuff; you're talking about counting molecules one by one.'

'Sophisticated, indeed. You're actually talking about detection and analysis procedures that would require a fully staffed laboratory twice the size of this chamber, and with a turn-around time from sample collection to final read-out of somewhere between twenty-four and forty-eight hours, if you want to get anywhere close to ninety percent reliability.' Carsten raised an eyebrow. 'Anything less than that kind of set-up, and the reliability falls to about the fifty percent line. Or about what you could achieve by flipping a coin. Hardly seems accurate enough to kill somebody over, does it?'

'Hey – did I make the rules?' The soft-pedaled accusation irritated Iris enough that she took her hands away from her body and spread them out in a mock plea for forgiveness. 'They told me the numbers to look for, and when those numbers came up somebody was toast. Too bad for them, but that's the name of *that* game.'

'More fool you, then. Because the design of the Voigt-Kampff machine isn't so much as to accomplish what they told you it was doing, but to make you *believe* that it was.' Carsten sounded smugly assured. 'If sampling the exhaled breath of a suspected replicant, even pulling the molecules right out of the air at a distance, was something that your testing procedure depended upon, it could be done a lot more thoroughly and effectively without some creaky eighteenth-century pump device doing the work. A sampling device using off-the-shelf parts wouldn't even be visible at all; the suspect wouldn't know that his exhalations were being analyzed, so there would be no test-related stress factors to deal with, and thus a greater chance of accuracy in the final results. So in fact, the design of the Voigt-Kampff machine ensures that whatever report it produces will have a considerably enhanced possibility of error, rather than less so.'

'Take it up with the department, okay?' Iris shook her head wearily. 'As far as I'm concerned, the thing worked fine. It's not like I ever got a lot of complaints filed against me about any of the readings I took from it. None of the suspects I retired were ever found out later, when the coroner's office did the post-mortems, to have been actually human.'

'And if they had, do you really believe the LAPD would have released that kind of information? That any of the cops it had given authority to kill, based upon the numbers read out from the Voigt-Kampff machines, had actually screwed up and blown away actual human beings? That's great public relations, all right. Even in Los Angeles, it's hard to get away with *that* many potential murders. Even if the local authorities had wanted to take the hit on something like that, the UN wouldn't let them. The emigration program, and its dependence on replicant technology, is premised to an essential degree on there being a way of telling real humans apart from the fake ones; the system collapses otherwise. Who's going to be stupid enough to sign up and emigrate off-world if there's no reliable way of detecting and controlling the slaves who do the work? Whether or not the Voigt-Kampff machines and the empathy testing protocols actually can tell if a suspect is a replicant, everybody involved, from the blade runner out on the streets right up to the top levels of the UN emigration program, has to pretend that it works.'

'You want to know something? I don't really care.' The ghostlike feeling, produced by the room's deep chill on top of her fatigue, rolled over her again like an invisible tide, in which she wavered with minimal gravity. 'If you want to make a case that all blade runners, including me, are murderers, blowing away real human beings because our V-K machines don't have anything inside them besides a couple of flashlight batteries – hey, knock yourself out. Whatever works for you.'

'Oh, there's plenty inside the Voigt-Kampff machines, all right.' With one of his pink fingertips, Carsten idly tapped against the side of a flask; its contents slowly rotated in response. 'Just because they don't do what you thought they did, doesn't mean they're functionless. In fact, the V-K devices have some pretty impressive innards. If you'd ever taken one apart, you'd know what I mean.'

'The next time I have a couple free hours and a set of screwdrivers handy, I'll do that.'

'It'd take a little more than that, I'm afraid. Specifically, several advanced degrees in micro-circuitry implementation, and a reverse-engineering team with a few decades of combined experience in the field. Not to mention the ability to get around the melt-down charges that are trigger-wired into the Voigt-Kampff machines. Those are real tricky to deal with; they're designed to keep anybody from figuring out just what it is that the devices are really for. Break the seal on the circuit-board casing and you're basically looking at a puddle of charred silicon and polycarbonate scrap. It took our committee's techs a long time to find a way of bleeding off the thermal charges before they wiped out the circuits underneath.'

'Good for them,' said Iris sourly. 'I hope they kept their fingers intact as well.'

'We lost a few, actually. Techs, not fingers; some V-K models have wired-in charges up in the lethal range.'

'So was it worth it? What did you find?'

'We found . . .' Carsten's voice trailed off for a moment, as if the thoughts in his brain took a few moments to sort and assemble. 'We found that the Voigt-Kampff machines are definitely not fakes; that is, they're not empty boxes, with a few colored lights and meaningless dials to make people think they're doing something real. They do something, all right. Specifically, the Voigt-Kampff machines *look* for something. And interestingly enough, the same thing we're looking for.'

'Sure they do.' Iris didn't bother to filter the skepticism from her voice. 'And what is it? Something to do with eyes? Or owls?'

'Both.' The expression on Carsten's face had achieved an oddly somber mischievousness, as if he enjoyed teasing someone about deadly serious matters. 'As you've undoubtedly noticed and filed away in that inquiring police-mode brain of yours, we have an interest here in exactly those categories.'

'No kidding.' The cold had penetrated deeply enough into Iris's flesh that it was no longer painful. An anesthetic numbness had taken possession of her. 'They do seem kind of important to you. Given the effort you folks have gone to, just to round up so many.'

'Important to others as well, and for much the same reasons.' With a gesture for her to follow him, Carsten turned and walked farther into the chamber, away from the door by which they had entered. 'Let me show you something really interesting.'

She stumbled as she let him lead her, all sensation gone below her knees; ice crystals seemed to crunch beneath some other person's bootsoles, a truly invisible ghost inhabiting the exact same space that she did.

Several meters beyond the laboratory workbenches, with their beakers and flasks occupied by the silently floating eyes, Carsten stopped by a row of rectangular objects resting on low trestles. The sight didn't dispel any of Iris's bleak mood, as the objects were the dimensions of coffins; the rear section of the icy chamber appeared as though it had been prepared for a public mourning ritual, with the victims of some mass tragedy arranged for viewing.

A thick layer of snow-like frost had accumulated on top of the coffin-like objects, obscuring any other indicators of their nature. Carsten stood beside one, looking across it toward Iris. 'What do you suppose we've got here?'

'God knows.'

'I'll help you out.' Carsten leaned down and with the flat of his bare, pink hand, brushed the white crystals away from one section of the top. The glittering crystals drifted down to the toes of his shoes. 'There.'

His clearing of the ice was enough to show that the object's horizontal surface was made of glass or some other transparent, durable substance. And that it was indeed a coffin; Iris could make out a human form lying inside, face upturned, hands crossed on its chest, with the utter tranquility of the dead.

'Great,' said Iris. She supposed the other coffins held similar contents. 'I'll have to hand it to you. You've got all sorts of keen collections here.'

'For someone who has been in the business you have – getting paid to kill things that look like human beings, and who could very well have been human beings, for all you might have known – you sound a little disapproving.'

'I just retired them; "killed", if you prefer. Then I got paid and that was the end of it.' She glanced down at the coffin between herself and the old man; the face of the body inside was too blurred, by the smeared ice crystals still adhering to the glass, for her to make out its features. 'Maybe this was even one of them; I wouldn't remember something like that.' She looked back up at Carsten. 'That's because after they're dead, they don't really matter to me anymore. Maybe I'm lacking in the same necrophile leanings that you and your committee seem to have, from the looks of things around here. I never even kept a scrapbook of my completed jobs, with pieces of paper and photos and stuff; I know some blade runners did, though. And they wound up far out on the Wambaugh Curve, where there was no way for them to come back. So I sure as hell wouldn't have kept the bodies around, either, even if I'd had room for them in my apartment. Not my notion of interior decorating, I guess.'

'Please – you can forgo the sarcasm.' Carsten held up one of his hands, its palm turned out to ward off her stream of words. 'It hardly becomes you. But since you insist on demonstrating how callous one can become from working as a blade runner, I'm sure you won't mind if I show you a few more things.' He reached down, toward a metal latch at the side of the coffin's glass lid. 'You've seen worse, I expect.'

'Feel free. Like I said before, there aren't a lot of things left that can surprise me.'

'Don't be too sure about that.' The latch clicked apart, metal from metal; with a hiss of air, like a vacuum-pack of standard ersatz coffee being popped, the coffin's lid unsealed from the silicon gasket around its edge. Vapor clouded the glass, turning it completely opaque as Carsten tilted it back on its concealed hinges. 'This universe is *made* for surprises.' He reached over, still grasping the edge of the lid, then let it drop on the other side, where Iris stood. 'Now what do you see?'

She peered down, then shook her head. 'Oh, this is good, all right.' In some ways, the sight of the coffin's contents, and being able to see clearly the face of the human figure within, had genuinely surprised. But not so much that she wasn't able to conceal her reaction from Carsten. 'Eldon Tyrell, taking a long-deserved rest. That's cute.'

It had taken her only a few seconds to recognize the corpse, though she had never seen the living man. *Only in the movie*, Iris reminded herself. The one Vogel had shown to her, appropriately enough, in the late doctor's private theater, deep in the ruins of the Tyrell Corporation headquarters. It was a relatively easy match, between that remembered image and the face of the glass-lidded coffin's inhabitant, even with its eyes shut and the rectangular-framed glasses missing. Tyrell had looked so close to death, like an animated corpse, in the *Blade Runner* movie, that the evaporation of whatever remaining vital spirit he'd once possessed had hardly changed him at all.

'Indeed,' said Carsten. 'I'm glad Dr Tyrell's face is familiar to you.'

'I'm not. I could've gone through my whole life, happily, without ever seeing him, either live, on a video screen, or dead like this. Let's just say he doesn't exactly set my pulse racing, okay? In this mode or any other.' Iris glanced back down at the face in the coffin; it appeared as if Tyrell were asleep, his thin-lipped mouth set as though he were savoring some dream of corporate empire. 'Though somebody in your outfit did a good job, putting him back together. From what I saw in the *Blade Runner* movie, and how Tyrell got iced by the Roy Batty replicant, I would've expected the remains to be in much worse shape than this.'

'Oh, he's in good shape, all right.' Carsten seemed even more ironically amused than before, the delicate, pink crepe of his face wrinkling with a wider smile. 'You might be surprised at exactly *how* good. Here, let me show you.' With no apparent squeamishness, Carsten reached down and fastened his hand upon the wrist of one of the hands folded on the body's chest. He lifted it and held it toward Iris. 'Go on.'

After a moment's hesitation, Iris let the old man place Tyrell's wrist in her own hand. Carsten's fingers pushed hers into place, on the underside of the cold flesh. The slight weight of the dead's hand and forearm rested against her fingertips, as though she were to try to read by Braille the delicate lines of the tendons there.

'Charming,' said Iris. 'But I already knew what corpses felt like. It's not much different when they've been put on ice like this one. Still feels dead.'

Carsten didn't say anything, but went on gently smiling at her. And waiting.

That was when she felt it. Faint, almost imperceptible; slow, with seconds between each trembling occurrence.

A pulse. The heartbeat of the dead. Or not quite dead enough.

'You see?' With her eyes closed Iris heard Carsten's voice, only subtly mocking. 'I told you that there would be a few surprises left for you.'

Intercut

'That was great.' The camera operator nodded in appreciation. 'Did you catch the expression on her face?' His own image was a ghostlike reflection on the glass of the monitor screen. 'Moments like that make it all worthwhile.'

'Not bad,' said the director, beside him at the control panel. 'It'll do.'

Don't knock yourself out. From the corner of his eye, the camera operator gave the other man an irritated glance. Nothing was ever good enough for the sonuvabitch; it made for a bad working atmosphere, in a situation where things were already not exactly bright and cheerful. *Show a little appreciation, why don't you?* He knew, though, that it would only make things worse if he'd said something like that out loud.

And it hadn't been exactly easy to get the shot down on tape; the camera operator's hands had been darting over the board, punching up one angle after another, his brain moving even faster in its circuits, trying to anticipate where the POV would have to go next. He hadn't been able to depend upon somebody on location, the way he had before with so many of the remote set-ups, to get the female and the surrounding action in line for him. This old man, out wherever they were in the desert, was unreliable; he couldn't be counted on to get things right. He was into the scene all the way, completely in character, with no consideration for technical matters.

'Watch out.' The director nodded toward the monitor before them. 'She's going to snap out of her funk any second now.'

'Don't worry; I'm on top of it.' Firing back at the director was something that the camera operator could afford to do. *He'd have a hard time finding somebody who could replace me.* Which wasn't a matter of digging up another operator with moral standards so diminished as to have no objection to working on a job like this one – the notion of moral standards in the video business being more a conceptual item than a real one – so much as the high-level skills to pull it off. Half the hidden cameras out in that walk-in refrigerator, buried somewhere beneath the sun-baking desert surface, had had their lens defrosting units go out seconds before the old man and the female blade runner had stepped into the set. The camera operator had looked up at the ranks of monitors before him and the director and had seen every other rectangle of light blurring out beneath a gray fog. There was no way the shoot could be scrubbed until after a tech crew had gone in and fixed the problem; the big difficulty with working *faux-vérité* style with a lead character who wasn't in on the joke, such as this female blade runner, was that re-shoots were out of the question. Once the set-up was rolling, there was no turning back. The director might get a kick out of a high-wire act like that, but it mainly put knots in the bellies of the people having to do the actual work. *Like me*, groused the camera operator to himself. He'd wound up, at a moment's notice, having to figure out a way of pulsing the switch-on power surges for the afflicted cameras, generating enough heat from the overloaded micro-circuitry to dispel the mist from their lenses, giving him a thirty-second scan time before they clouded up again. When the tapes got uploaded to the post-production booth, the editors would be cursing him, but at least they'd have something to work with.

'Make sure,' ordered the director, 'that we've got both a wide and a tight close-up when she speaks. I might want to do something fancier here, get her location re-established and personal situation isolated.'

'You got it.' The camera operator had anticipated the request; there were no adjustments he had to make yet. Making the female blade runner look small, dwindled at the center of the chilly environment, was such a classic way to go that he would've been surprised if the director hadn't asked for it. 'They're live now, on seventeen and thirty-two.'

'Get ready.' The director leaned toward the monitors, scanning across the different angles of the woman's face and the darker corners of the ice-encrusted chamber in which she stood. 'Now . . .'

The director spoke as if he were personally willing time to start up again, some place where it had become embedded in an invisible glacier. The two figures, fragmented and reassembled on the monitor screens, might as well have been caught in that frigid stasis, their hearts slowed down to synch with the mired tempo of the corpse in the glass-lidded coffin. Which was, of course, the trouble that came from doing business with the dead, getting caught up in the affairs of those who had spent their time among the living and had no change coming to them. The camera operator sensed that in his bones, as if the chill from the distant subterranean chamber had seeped through the wires and out of the monitor screens, then across the short pseudo-synaptic gap between the illuminated glass and his hand. His arm suddenly felt bloodless and numb, a bent stake hammered into his heart.

That's what I get, he thought morosely. The same advice he had silently given to the female blade runner, he should have taken himself. She was as good as dead, in more ways than one; the whole business of her having the same face as the replicant named Rachael, who the poor doomed bastard Deckard had fallen in love with, had implications just as fatal for her. *And now*, mused the camera operator, *I'm nose-deep in her business*. Watching her, getting her into focus, watching his hands move across and work the controls, as if they were an infinitely variable substitute for the more sensitive points of her anatomy, his actions falling somewhere between seduction and rape. He wondered of whom; she didn't even know he existed, let alone was watching her by remotely controlled and hidden cameras. His own concerns were moving from mercenary to obsessive. Which was a bad sign, considering for whom he was working. The director's agenda, to the extent it had been revealed, didn't seem to allow for a lot of happy endings.

He could warn her; it was a possibility that had occurred to him already, back when the nature of the job had first started making itself clear to him. It would take only a few punches of the buttons in front of him to start up the fog-clearing overload pulses he'd jury-rigged into the hidden cameras and let them go unchecked, long enough so they'd blow up with a satisfying spatter of lens glass and smoking circuits. The female blade runner was a smart enough cookie to realize on her own, given that kind of tip-off, to figure out that something was unkosher about the set-up with Carsten and his so-called committee; maybe she'd be smart enough to turn tail and run, right out the frozen chamber's door, away from the glass-lidded coffins and their creepy contents. Maybe she'd be smart enough to keep running, out into the desert, toward the slate-gray mountains to the east, even farther away from LA's drizzling rains and neon-lit darknesses and whatever they concealed. *Forget the owl*, he told her; he tried to make the words penetrate the monitors' glass and travel across the wires to her. *Just go . . .*

The female blade runner didn't seem to hear his silent warning. And his hands stayed professional and restrained, away from doing anything with the controls that might have given the game away.

'All right,' said the camera operator. He spoke to himself as much as to the director sitting beside him. He had spotted the shift in the woman's face, the eyes that had widened slightly when she had perceived the pulse inside the supposed corpse's wrist, now narrowing in the next stage of her reaction. She had recovered herself, ready to speak and move again. *Worse luck for her*, thought the camera operator as he tweaked the gain on the spot mike hidden closest to her. 'Let's roll . . .'

15

Cold, thought Iris, *and timeless*. For a moment, and a seeming eternity, she felt the way she had at the movie theater in LA, when she and Vogel had ingested the thermatos. *World without end. But no amen.* Both clock time and her own pulse had come to a halt, frozen in place, while waiting for a signal from somewhere in what was left of that other world, the one outside her skin.

She felt the signal, another's pulse, and it took all her self-control to keep herself from dropping the cold wrist she held, and snatching her hand back to herself, as though the icy flesh had suddenly flared with heat. For a few moments longer, Iris kept her fingertips poised against the blue vein threading snake-like among the tendons that disappeared under the sleeve of the jacket in which the late Dr Eldon Tyrell had been dressed. *Or not so late*, she corrected herself. Once again, the slow, fragile pulse made itself known.

'That's a good one,' said Iris. 'Real good one.' Still holding the body's wrist, she glared across the coffin, its glass lid thrown back; her slitted gaze narrowed even further as she regarded Carsten. 'You must live for little jokes like this one. What kind of reaction were you hoping to get from me? Screams or a dead faint?' She shook her head in disgust. 'Sorry I can't oblige. I'm too stiff right now to collapse.'

'Your reaction was pretty much what I expected.' Carsten's attitude of mild amusement hadn't ebbed. 'You're a professional, after all. In many ways. In the line of work to which you're accustomed, the difference between the living and the dead is merely a matter of what stage of the process you're in.'

She ignored the comment. 'So what is this supposed to be? A practical joke, or something?' She gestured with the dead man's hand. 'What did you do, wire him up with a subcutaneous pump? There's a lot that can be done with hydraulics. Or at least until the batteries run down.'

'You know it's not a joke.' Carsten took the late doctor's hand from her, as though Tyrell were a dance partner being turned over to the next in line. 'If it were a joke, I don't think you would have gotten quite so angry; really, it's written there in your face. You look as though you'd like to kill me.'

'That's accurate.'

'But you're not going to,' said Carsten. 'That's what I mean by professionalism. There are still questions to be answered, and you figure I can tell you what you want to know.' His childlike shoulders lifted in a shrug. 'So ask away.'

'All right; I'll do that.' Her voice got louder and harder, bouncing off the ice that coated the chamber's walls. 'What's the deal here? Eldon Tyrell is dead. I saw him get killed in that stupid movie Vogel showed me. Which is why the Tyrell Corporation is *ganz kaput*, or at least the reason why it's not put back together the way it used to be. And put back together is what Tyrell himself would have to be, if you want me to believe that somehow you've got him here, and he's got his ticker going, only turned down low. What I saw the Batty replicant do to him in that movie was like an egg getting crushed. Skull-wise, the prognosis was not good for the poor bastard.'

'No, it wasn't.' Unperturbed, Carsten leaned down and fussily restored the hand and forearm to where it had been lying folded on top of the other, across the body's chest. 'If you thought the number you saw the Batty replicant perform on Eldon Tyrell was a fatal one, you'd be absolutely right.'

'So what's the deal?' Inside her head, she tried to pick apart the old man's words, trying to find a clue in their tangled connections. 'Are you trying to tell me the movie I watched, that *Blade Runner* thing, was a fake? And what I saw happen to Tyrell – that *didn't* happen to him?'

'Oh, it happened to him, certainly enough. Eldon Tyrell had accumulated enough, shall we say, bad karma in his lifetime that such a fate was inevitable for him. In many ways, it could be postulated that he had done his own part to bring about exactly the death he had wished for himself. In the machinery of the universe, a guilty conscience is one of the teeth on the gears that mesh with such flesh-rending precision. When the Batty replicant's hands closed around Eldon Tyrell's skull, just as you saw in the movie, the result was rather like Humpty Dumpty, in the old children's rhyme.'

'I take it you mean that was an egg which was not going to get put back together any time soon.'

'Not with all the duct tape in the world.' Carsten exuded a grim satisfaction. 'The Batty replicant should be admired for its thoroughness; that was a good kill, if a messy one.'

'So then, like I said before, this has to be some kind of a fake.' Arms wrapped around herself once again, Iris nodded toward the unmoving figure in the glass-lidded coffin. 'And frankly, I don't get the point of it. If that's not Dr Eldon Tyrell in there, what is it?'

'Oh, it's Tyrell, all right.' Carsten nodded slowly. 'But not the one you saw in the *Blade Runner* movie; not the one that got killed by the Batty replicant. Let's just say it's a *different* Eldon Tyrell.'

'I think,' said Iris after a moment, 'I know where this is going. And I don't like it. Not one bit.'

'Really?' The attitude of mild amusement returned to Carsten. 'Why should it bother you to consider that this' – he pointed to the body in the coffin – 'might in fact be a replicant? An Eldon Tyrell replicant, to be exact.'

'It complicates things.' Iris spoke with barely contained fury. 'And things are complicated enough already. I don't need this.'

'Why should it be such a problem for you?' Carsten's words gently but relentlessly needled at her. 'I thought you blade runners were supposed to be the experts at telling the real from the fake, human beings from replicants.'

'Don't start with me about that.' Iris turned the flat of her hand toward him. 'It doesn't matter whether cops like me can tell humans from replicants or not. But if Tyrell was having his labs make a replicant, using himself as the templant, the master that the copy would be based on – then it takes everything up another notch, headache-wise.' Her own head actually was beginning to throb, as though, by some sympathetic magic, it felt the trauma the late Eldon Tyrell's had undergone. 'Why would he have even *wanted* to do something like that?'

'A good question,' Carsten said. 'You're getting better and better at this game. But you're slightly off, regarding the details. It's not "replicant", in the singular. We're talking about more than one.'

'Okay, that does it.' Iris turned and took a step back the way she and the old man had come, past the shelves of silently staring eyes and toward the door. 'I don't care about any answers. I'm not hanging around for this.'

'Yes, you are.' Surprisingly strong, Carsten grabbed her by one arm, stopping and pulling her around to face him. 'If you didn't want to know things like this, you shouldn't have started asking questions.

Going right back to the beginning, when you were trying to find a certain lost owl, and you didn't have any idea where it was going to lead to.' He let go of her and stepped back beside the glass-lidded coffin. 'If this is where the trail winds up, you're going to have to face it, no matter what it means. That's what a *real* cop would do, at any rate.'

The old man's words stung her. Inside her jacket, the gun the guard had returned to her had chilled into a small sculpture of black ice. Though one that could both silence the old man, and still the slow pulse ticking through the veins of the coffin's occupant, once and for all. *You're taking an awful big risk*, she thought as she glared at him.

'You see,' continued Carsten, elaborately helpful, 'in some ways, it should have been obvious to you.' He gestured at the other coffins, lined up on their short trestle supports. 'I thought that, given the business you were in, you would know more than you apparently do about the exact mechanics of the replicant industry. What I suppose looks to you like funeral caskets, standard cemetery furniture, are in fact shipping containers – though, of course, not of any ordinary kind or function. They're what had been used when the UN emigration program had been in full swing, for transporting the products of the Tyrell Corporation, the completed replicants, to the colonies in the outer star systems.' His smile turned wry and ugly. 'That's the problem with canned meat, you might say. Any time you're shipping perishables, you're faced with a spoilage problem. And since the Tyrell Corporation's replicants have only a four-year life expectancy, your customers aren't going to be too happy if you use up a good percentage of that shelf-life getting the products out to the colonies. Even with the UN transport ships' enhanced light-speed capabilities, by the time the Tyrell Corporation would have warehoused the replicants here on earth, shipped them out to a central distribution point, then from there to the separate colonies and finally into the hands of their new owners, there would have been at the most a few months left of the replicants' lifespans. Hardly an economic proposition, even for an entity with the resources of the UN emigration program. Thus the need for shipping devices such as this.'

Carsten reached down and touched a control pad, near the latch of the opened coffin. A string of red digits lit up on a small black read-out panel; as Iris watched, the last digit in the sequence changed from a seven to a six, in a glacial countdown process.

'As I said,' continued Carsten, 'without something like this, the

Tyrell Corporation's merchandise would have been just about dead by the time it reached its ultimate destinations. Using suspended-animation technology to slow down the replicants' life processes en route resulted in a loss of a couple of months at most; still significant, which is why the Tyrell Corporation's manufacturing practice was to stuff the replicants into these boxes as soon as they came off the assembly line and before they were shipped off-planet, to absolutely minimize such losses in usefulness. The UN emigration program wouldn't have gone on paying the Tyrell Corporation, and allowing it to maintain its monopoly on the replicant technology, if it hadn't.'

'So what?' Whatever other emotions Iris might have felt were now swept aside by her exasperation. 'Why should I be concerned about how the Tyrell Corporation shipped its goods? What's it got to do with me?'

'Perhaps more than you realize,' said Carsten mildly. 'With you and all the other blade runners. None of you ever stopped to think about the time-based logistics of the so-called escaped replicants you were supposed to hunt down and "retire". Most of them were at the ends of their four-year lifespans when they showed up back here on Earth. As you saw in the *Blade Runner* movie you watched, the Batty replicant and its group returned to LA specifically in an attempt to shake some sort of hoped-for extension of their lives from their creator – which, of course, Eldon Tyrell was unable to grant them.'

'So?' Iris managed a near-frozen shrug. 'The replicants were out there in the far colonies, doing whatever crappy jobs they were given, for close to four years. Then some of them escaped and came back here. Big deal. Like you said, they could be in the colonies for that long, since they were basically on ice when they were shipped out there.'

'Ah – but the suspended-animation containers, like the ones here, were supposedly only used on the journey *out* to the colonies. But what about the journey *back* here to Earth? How did any of the escaped replicants manage that, without coming to the ends of their allotted lifespans and dying en route, if they had already used up most of their four years off-planet?'

'How the hell should I know?'

'Exactly,' said Carsten. 'You *don't* know. It's a mystery, if you stop to think about it. For any of the Batty group, for example, to have made their way back to Los Angeles and the Tyrell Corporation headquarters, they would have needed access to suspended-animation containers such as these, identical to the ones in which they were shipped out to the colonies. Otherwise, they would have expired by reaching the ends of their programmed lifespans, before they ever got here.'

'Okay.' She mulled it over for a few seconds. 'Maybe they *did* have access to these things. They killed the crew and took over some ship, didn't they? That was what was said in the movie, about Batty and his group. So it was a UN emigration program freight ship, returning a load of these empty containers to the Tyrell Corporation. The Batty rep and his bunch put themselves into suspended animation inside the containers and sent the ship on an auto-pilot program to Earth. That way, they still had whatever was left of their original lifespans to try shaking down Dr Tyrell for the extension they wanted, but didn't get.'

'A nice theory, but impossible in practice. Even if they managed to pull that off on their own – these containers can't be sealed and their animation-suspending processes initiated from inside them, and the UN ships can't be brought into Earth orbit on auto-pilot – any escaped replicants would still need the assistance of other parties to be brought out of the suspended-animation state.' Carsten pointed his thumb toward the coffin-like devices. 'These things don't have alarm clocks built into them. Once you're in, you need somebody else to wake you up.'

'Fine. Then they had accomplices or something. Maybe the rep-symps did it for them.' Iris had never had any run-ins with organized groups of human replicant-sympathizers – they had apparently faded away in the couple of years she had been with the police department – but she supposed they might still be active. 'Giving a bunch of escaped replicants the chance to mess with Eldon Tyrell and the whole Tyrell Corporation – that's exactly the sort of thing that some underground rep-symp cell would get a kick out of pulling off.'

'It's much more complicated than that,' said Carsten. 'The operation of these suspended-animation shipping containers is a highly technical affair; they were developed solely for the use of the replicant industry, and there's no expertise from other areas that can be applied to them. In fact, the members of our committee who keep these up and running are former Tyrell Corporation employees, on whom we had to expend considerable resources in recruiting and then extracting from their positions with that company. For the rep-symps to have aided the kind of conspiracy you imagine, for the

204

purpose of aiding escaped replicants in their attempts to reach Earth, they would have to have recruited *and kept in place* similar, highly trained operatives. And not just here, at the escaped replicants' destination, but at the outer colonies as well, so the replicants could be both placed into the suspended-animation state as well as taken out of it. For such parties to have been rep-symps, as you theorized, would mean the rep-symp underground and its activities had spread all the way to the far colonies. Not very likely, given that the only human beings out there are either UN emigration program personnel or the emigrants themselves, all of whom had been carefully screened to eliminate anyone with rep-symp tendencies.'

'Okay. Then who the hell *did* help the escaped replicants get here to Earth, alive and kicking?'

'I don't know.' The smug attitude had evaporated from Carsten's wrinkled face. 'I wish I did. It's something our little committee is working on, trying to determine exactly that. But our resources are limited, and we have other things that take up the lion's share of our attention. The only thing of which we feel reasonably sure – and it's a matter of logic more than hard evidence – is that whoever was behind the traveling assistance provided to the escaped replicants, it must have been some entity with connections going right to the top, either in the Tyrell Corporation itself or the UN emigration program.'

'Yeah, right,' said Iris sourly. 'Like Eldon Tyrell would finance an operation that was not only going to make his company look bad – dangerous escaped replicants running around in the streets of LA – but would ultimately get him killed. How likely is that?'

'Eldon Tyrell was a complicated man.' A sliver of Carsten's humorless smile returned. 'And as I indicated before, one carrying a large karmic debt – or bad conscience, to use a more old-fashioned term. He was capable of anything.'

'Like having replicants made from himself?' Though her breath was still a white plume from her nostrils, her rising anger managed to generate something like heat inside her gut. 'Why would he do that? Replicants were supposedly manufactured in order to provide slave labor for the colonists out there. If I were one of them, and I got stuck with a rep as ugly and scrawny as some Eldon Tyrell model, I'd demand a refund.'

'That's hardly why he did it.' Carsten shook his head, gazing down the line of unopened coffins. 'His reasons were more complex than that: he wanted more than to be the templant for some production

205

line of replicants, to be shipped off to the colonies. He might have had a considerable ego, but not one that would have considered his physical form worth duplicating.'

'Then why?' Something in the way the old man spoke had chilled Iris, far beyond a matter of her blood growing thick and heavy in her veins. His voice had gone so soft and quiet, as if he had begun to whisper of secrets that even the replicant sleeping its long, slow hours and years inside the glass-lidded coffin, dreamless behind the withered face of Eldon Tyrell, was afraid to hear aloud. 'What's the deal, then?' She peered closer at the figure standing on the other side of the coffin. 'Or is that something else you and your committee don't know?'

'We know plenty.' Her words appeared to have needled a flash of anger out of Carsten. His pale eyes looked like ice chips as he regarded her. 'It's *your* ignorance that we need to remedy.'

'So what is it that I don't know? Either tell me, or let me go out and play in the sunshine.' Iris visibly shivered. 'I can't even feel my feet anymore.'

'It's not what you don't know. It's what you *think* you know. And that you're completely wrong about.'

'Sure –' Iris stamped one bootshod foot, in a vain attempt to get its circulation going again. 'You already ran that number past me. All that business about the Voigt-Kampff machine being a fake, and blade runners actually "retiring" real human beings instead of the replicants we thought we were putting away. Whatever.' She shook her head. 'Maybe everything you said is true; I don't know. I don't even know if it matters to me anymore. That was another world.' She spoke the realization aloud, before she knew herself what it meant. 'I used to live in it, I used to have my job there, and I *loved* that job. But I don't have any of that now; I don't live in that world anymore. So if you want to go ahead and tell me that everything I knew about that world was a lie . . . go ahead. Why should it matter to me now?'

'Because now,' said Carsten, 'you're lying to yourself. If it didn't matter to you, you wouldn't have followed the traces to the ruins of the Tyrell Corporation headquarters. You could easily have died there. So you must have wanted something from that rather arduous process you put yourself through.'

'No kidding. I wanted my old job back. I thought maybe I could get it, if I found the owl I had been assigned to locate in the first place.'

'And you stuck around there, watching old movies with your friend Vogel, long after it was apparent that the owl in question was hardly to be found in a place like that. Or even any further clues as to its whereabouts. But you stuck around because Vogel had other things to tell you and to show you; things you apparently wanted to know.' Carsten raised one of his snow-white eyebrows. 'So it seems you weren't searching for the owl at all – perhaps not even from the beginning of your quest. Whether you knew it or not, or were prepared to even admit it to yourself, you were searching for the truth. And now you have to face the possibility that you're about to find it.'

'Because you're going to tell it to me, I suppose.'

The old man nodded. 'That's what you're here for.'

'All right,' said Iris. 'Tell you what.' She reached inside her jacket, her hand forcing its way past the leatherite stiffened by the chamber's cold. The gun was colder than her fingers; the nearness of the metal to what was left of her heart had done nothing to keep it warm. She drew the gun out, raised it and sighted directly along its black barrel toward a point between Carsten's pale eyes. 'You say you've still got some big secrets left to lay on me. That you know what it is I've supposedly been looking for. The real truth, and all that other bullshit.' Iris curled one forefinger around the gun's trigger. 'I'm going to give you a chance to prove it.'

'Really?' The sight of the gun, aimed and rock-steady, didn't appear to alarm Carsten. 'And what's that?'

Iris shifted the gun a few millimeters and squeezed the trigger. The flash from the muzzle lit up the chamber as though a streak of lightning from one of the thunderstorms preceding LA's monsoon season had transferred inside the ice-covered walls. At one side of Carsten's head, the wispy white hair fluttered as the bullet passed just above the top ridge of his ear.

The echo of the shot had slammed against the limits of the chamber hard enough to temporarily deafen her. As her hearing cleared once more, Iris could hear the minute, bell-like tinkling sounds of ice crystals, dislodged by the shockwave, drifting like bright stars and diamonds from the ceiling and settling across the grim face of Eldon Tyrell and the glass lids of the other coffins, as though the chamber held a depiction of a winter's mass funeral from a child's illustrated storybook. The thickly viscous liquid in the various glass beakers and jars had shivered with the impact, their contents disturbed enough to slowly turn inside, as though the bodyless eyes had been aroused by events and had brought their silent gaze around to watch.

'Maybe that wasn't such a good idea.' Carsten reached up and touched the side of his head, then checked his fingertips to see if there was any blood on them. 'To have given that weapon back to you. Your emotional state is obviously a little shaky.'

'Too late now.' Iris raised her voice against the shrill whistle of escaping refrigerant; the shot had penetrated one of the larger pipes at the far end of the chamber, releasing a gray jet of condenser gas. 'But don't worry; it's not a hormonal thing. I've got a proposition to make you.'

'I'm listening.'

'Here's the deal.' Iris kept the gun dead-level between herself and the old man. 'Whatever revelations you've got lined up, they better absolutely blow me away. So to speak. Or I blow *you* away.'

'But I was going to tell you everything, anyway.'

'Now you'll really be motivated to make it good.'

Carsten considered for a moment, then nodded. 'It's worth a shot,' he said. 'So to speak.'

'Exactly.' Iris raised the gun a little higher. Her arm felt both weightlessly numb, and solid as a carved extension of ice. 'So go for it.'

'The truth? The real truth, as you spoke of? Here it is, then.' Carsten took a step backward, spreading his arms wide to indicate not only the row of glass-lidded coffins, but the ice-bound chamber itself. 'Everything you see here, everything you thought you knew about replicants – it's all wrong. You don't even know the real *purpose* of replicants. Why they were created. What they're made for. You just don't know.'

'So tell me, then.' Iris was beyond impatience. 'What's the purpose of replicants?'

'Batty knew,' said Carsten. 'When that group of escaped replicants went to Los Angeles, to confront Tyrell – they knew. Somehow they had found out the secret about themselves, about all replicants. So you tell me something. You saw the *Blade Runner* movie; what did the Batty replicant and his band go to LA for? What did they want from Tyrell?'

'Life. Or more life.' The gun didn't move. 'What else would they want? When you're at the end of a four-year lifespan, getting a postponement on your death is pretty much going to be your number one priority.'

'And why would they go to Eldon Tyrell to ask for that kind of extension? It would seem a pointless quest to ask that from the very same creator who had dictated the moment of your death to begin with.' Carsten folded his arms across his chest. 'If Eldon Tyrell had decided upon what was to be the pitifully short length of their existences, why would the Batty replicant or any of the others have thought they could change his mind about that?'

'Maybe they didn't. Maybe they just hoped they could get something out of him. A reprieve. They would be equally dead if they *hadn't* gone to LA and confronted their maker. The odds didn't matter. They didn't have anywhere else to turn.'

'Which raises the question about why they would have thought it was even possible for them to be given longer lives; to have their own deaths pushed a little farther away. When you watched the movie – when you saw what actually happened between the Batty replicant and his creator, Eldon Tyrell – didn't it strike you as odd how quickly Batty folded?'

'What do you mean?'

'Batty was a determined individual; he was designed to be. The original Roy Batty, the human being who was the templant upon which the replicant Batty was based, had been a real piece of work. I know that for a fact; I knew the man. If the replicant Batty had possessed even half the human Batty's ruthlessness, he wouldn't have simply accepted Eldon Tyrell's quick explanations, one techno-buzzword after another, about why it was impossible to extend the escaped replicants' four-year lifespans. But since the Batty replicant was in fact a true duplication of its original's nature, the fact that he seemingly accepted getting brushed off by Tyrell indicates that possibly something else was going on. That whatever else the other escaped replicants in the group might have been led by the Batty replicant to believe, he at least had some other agenda.'

'If he did then he wasn't any smarter than the rest of them. If somebody is coming to the end of his four-year lifespan, what could be more important than trying to get some kind of extension?'

'That depends,' said Carsten simply. 'Upon the nature of the replicant – that is, the nature of the human templant that the replicant was duplicated from. And as I said, the original human Batty was not an easy-going kind of person. In fact, he could be downright vicious; that's why he was considered so valuable at what he did, and why the Tyrell Corporation used him as the templant for a production run of military-aggressor model replicants. Basically, the original human Roy Batty felt, deep within what passed for his soul, that whatever problems he was confronted with, the best solution consisted of killing somebody else.'

'Charming.'

'You should talk.' Carsten's pale eyes gave her a wry glance, above the barrel of the gun leveled in his direction. 'You've never made your living any other way than that. The only difference between you and the original Roy Batty, the human one, is that you and he have had different problems. You thought all you had to do in this world was retire a few escaped replicants, and the original Batty never had any problem with killing humans as well. Perhaps he even preferred it; at least you haven't gotten around to that stage yet. Though in some other important ways, you and the original Batty were even more alike than you might think.'

'Really?' Her hand and the raised gun had frozen into one solid construct. 'And how's that?'

'Neither one of you knew what was really going on. What you were really doing as you went about your deadly jobs. You didn't have the slightest idea – didn't even care, probably – about what the real purpose of the replicant technology was. The Roy Batty *replicant* knew; somehow he had discovered the truth, out there somewhere in the far colonies, among the stars. Maybe he was told the truth by whatever parties they were who helped him and the other escaped replicants reach Earth. Maybe those other individuals – humans or other entities; who knows? – and organizations had their own agenda about why they wanted murderous replicants such as Batty to return to the Los Angeles where they had first been created. But the suspicions remain, and the facts behind them, that the Batty replicant wasn't in any way interested in groveling to his creator, pleading for a few more days of life. Whatever he did along those lines might have been nothing more than an act, a subterfuge that pulled along with him the other escaped replicants whose help he needed – plus fooling Eldon Tyrell himself. Tyrell's personal quarters at the Tyrell Corporation building were laced with security and alarm systems; with the number of enemies he had made in his lifetime, he would have been an idiot not to have had them. Right?'

'I suppose so.' Iris gave a stiff nod. 'Rich people in general tend to be on the paranoid side. Especially when they live in the middle of a hole like LA. Everybody wants a piece of them, and they've all got knives.'

'Exactly. Yet Tyrell didn't trigger any of those security alarms when he was confronted with an intruder like the Batty replicant, even though he knew from the design parameters for one of his company's own products that Batty wasn't likely to have been there on a social call. Things could get really ugly, really fast, when either a human or a replicant Batty was around. So to keep Tyrell from calling for security, whole divisions of which were available right there in the building, the Batty replicant would have needed a cover story, some explanation for why he had come there that would distract Tyrell from the actual purpose of Batty's visit. That's what the business of wanting more life, an extension to his paltry allotted span of four years, was about. The Batty replicant knew all along there was no way he or the other escaped replicants could get that from their creator; he'd always known that. Useless to ask. But useful, as I said, for a cover story. Something to divert Eldon Tyrell from the real reason the Batty replicant was there. And it worked.' A thin smile showed on Carsten's face. 'As you saw, in the *Blade Runner* movie. It worked long enough for the Batty replicant to take care of the business he had come there for.'

'You're saying,' said Iris slowly, 'that the Batty replicant went to the Tyrell Corporation headquarters . . . just to kill Eldon Tyrell?'

'Does that surprise you?'

'Not much.' Iris still kept the gun leveled at the old man's forehead. 'I suppose it was a matter of who got first crack at him. Eventually, somebody had to.' Both her arm and the gun felt weightless; she held them in place without effort. 'But what would the Batty replicant have gotten out of it?'

'The same thing anybody would have gotten, if they had been cheated of all but four short years of existence, lied to and sold as slave labor to the humans in the far colonies. The same thing you would have wanted if it had been you that had made your way to your creator's private quarters. What else but revenge?'

She had to admit the old man was right; that was exactly what she would have wanted. *If I'm going* – she addressed an invisible Eldon Tyrell inside her head, as though she had inserted herself into the movie she had watched in the ruins – *then you're going with me*. She was so angry about merely losing the part of her life her job as a blade runner had been, that the frozen gun in her hand seemed to thaw a little bit from the heat of her brooding. But at least she'd had the life; Batty and the other replicants had been cheated out of even that much.

'But he got his revenge,' said Iris aloud. 'He did kill Tyrell.' The images from the movie, of the Batty replicant crushing Tyrell's skull between his hands like a withered egg, were still bright red in her memory. 'He got what he wanted.'

'And he came a long way for it.' On the other side of the gun, Carsten nodded in agreement. 'Risking what little bit of his life was still left to him. When you only have four years in total – and you're aware of that – then any single day is infinitely precious. Whereas real human beings, who don't know when they're scheduled to die, think therefore that they're immortal; we can waste all the days we care to. An unlimited supply – but replicants know better. In that way, the old Tyrell Corporation motto is true: "More Human than Human." They *are* better than us.'

Iris was unimpressed. 'But not so much better,' she pointed out, 'that someone like me wasn't able to settle their hash for them.'

'True.' Carsten's thin smile appeared on the other side of the gun. 'But that might mean something slightly different from what you think it does. But never mind that, for the moment. One secret at a time. We were talking about what it is that the replicants knew, which was so important that their leader Batty would risk the few remaining days of his oh-so-short life to make sure their creator Tyrell wouldn't have any more of *his*. After all, when the Batty replicant and his followers climbed into the suspended-animation shipping containers' – Carsten gestured toward the row of glass-lidded boxes between himself and Iris – 'they had no way of being sure they would climb *out* of them when they reached their destination – *if* they did. They could just as well have been lying down in their real coffins, the ones nobody ever exits, or at least not alive.'

'Maybe their souls would've climbed out,' said Iris sourly. 'Assuming they had any.'

'Assuming that anybody does. We're talking about Los Angeles here. If such things existed, they'd be for sale somewhere. But the secret, the truth, the escaped replicants knew – that somebody either told them or they had found out on their own – made such things as souls unnecessary. Or at least unnecessary as far as actual life is concerned.' Carsten's reedy voice grew subtly louder and more emphatic; his pale eyes brightened with a feverish spark. 'Because in a way the *Blade Runner* movie you watched with Vogel was right: Eldon Tyrell did have the ability to stave off death, to grant more life – even immortality. But not to his own creations; not to replicants such as Roy Batty and his followers. But to himself. That was the secret, and the truth. And that's what the replicant technology was about, before it was stolen by the UN emigration program and handed over to the Tyrell Corporation. It had nothing to do with providing cheap slave labor for the emigrants in the far colonies; that was merely what the UN, with Eldon Tyrell's connivance, had twisted it into. Its real, true purpose was life itself. Eternal life.'

'You're joking.' The fervor in the old man's voice had sent a creeping sensation across Iris's chilled skin. *And I don't think it's very funny,* she told herself. If it were only some kind of joke, it would be better than the nut-case religious tone that had seized upon Carsten's words. She didn't relish the thought of dealing with a religious fanatic, which was what he sounded like now; the fragile, white-haired figure had been transformed into some latter-day Savonarola, right before her eyes. *Which means,* thought Iris, *I'll have a hard time with the rest of this bunch out here.* The rest of his 'committee' and its operatives were probably as crazy as he was. If she popped him, there was no telling how the ones up above, on the sunlit desert surface, would react. Not well, was her best guess.

'Immortality,' said Carsten quietly, 'isn't something to joke about. Except when you don't think it's possible. Then everything is a joke, isn't it? – because everyone dies, eventually. Humans and replicants alike; it's just a matter of how soon. The Batty replicant wouldn't have had to do anything to have his revenge on Eldon Tyrell, except wait. Even if that waiting had taken place after Batty was dead, his brief four years over – he'd have died with the comfort of knowing that someday, soon or late, his creator would join him in the grave. As all men do.'

'But somehow – that's what you're saying – the Batty replicant knew that wasn't going to happen. Not with Tyrell.' She studied the wrinkled face on the other side of the gun. 'Somehow he wasn't going to die. Ever.'

'That's correct.' Carsten gave a single nod. 'Because even though Eldon Tyrell and the UN emigration program had stolen and perverted the replicant technology, turned it into an assembly line for manufacturing slaves, *its original purpose still existed.* The replicant technology could be used for exactly that for which it had first been devised. But in this case, not for the sake of all humanity, but for one human being: Tyrell himself.'

'If,' said Iris, 'it actually could work that way. Which you haven't proved to me.' She extended the gun a little farther, emphasizing her doubt. 'You haven't shown me anything, except a corpse in a glass coffin. A corpse which has some kind of way-slowed-down heartbeat. And that looks like somebody I saw get murdered.' She shook her head. 'I don't think much of the evidence so far.'

'That's because you haven't seen all of it.' Carsten stepped away from the open coffin, with the Tyrell-like figure inside it. 'Let me show you something you might find more impressive.' He stopped beside the next coffin in the row, all of them mounted on the same knee-high trestles. With one hand, Carsten reached down and unlatched the glass lid and eased it back, the way he had done with the first of them. He took a step away. 'Take a look.'

She had tracked him with the gun as he had gone through his showman routine. Now she stepped forward and glanced down into the newly opened coffin-like container. The twin of the other figure, the occupant of the first coffin Carsten had flung open, lay in this one. The exact same sleeping face, the grimly withered visage of Eldon Tyrell, was gently touched by a few ice crystals that had been dislodged from the rim of the glass lid.

'Not much of a surprise,' said Iris. 'Replicants come in multiples; that's what a production line is all about.' She didn't need to check the slowed pulse of this one; she had spotted the tiny, glacial tick in the vein at the side of the inert body's throat, indicating the same deep state of suspended animation the first one had been sunk into. 'How many duplicates of himself did Eldon Tyrell have his lab run off?'

'Enough for his purposes.' Carsten continued down the line, unlatching and tilting back the glass lids, revealing a dozen or so Tyrell replicants; Iris lost count as the process continued. He left the last one in the row still closed; standing beside it, he looked at Iris. 'It was a limited production run; we're pretty sure we've accounted for all of them. Our committee had its operatives right inside the Tyrell Corporation, most of them close to Eldon Tyrell himself, so we could keep an eye on what he was up to. When the Tyrell Corporation headquarters building was destroyed, we knew exactly what had to be extracted from the structurally secure chambers inside the ruins. We didn't want to take any chances on these particular items falling into the hands of any Tyrell loyalists – though in fact, we have no idea of whether the shadow corporation elements had any idea of this part of Eldon Tyrell's plans. He was rather a secretive individual – but then, he had a lot to conceal. *No one else in the Tyrell Corporation knew what he did.* Other than the few lab operatives Eldon Tyrell needed in order to carry out his personal agenda, there was nobody except Tyrell himself who knew the real purpose of the replicant technology. And like some ancient Egyptian pharaoh, murdering the architects of his tomb, once Tyrell had gotten the labor he needed out of those few lab operatives – once he had gotten the replicants for which he had been the original templant – he simply eliminated them. In as final a manner as possible. Let's just say that Eldon Tyrell saw no irony in attempting to achieve his own immortality at the price of other people's lives.'

'I still don't get it.' Even though her target stood a few meters farther away now, Iris kept the gun raised and leveled at his forehead. 'What's the point of running off a batch of physical duplicates of yourself? What would Tyrell have thought he was accomplishing with that? You take 'em out of these boxes and wake 'em up, then four years later they're as dead as anybody else.'

'Ah. But you see, you're making the same erroneous assumption that so many others make about replicants.' Carsten spread his hands wide, indicating the row of coffins before him, and their eerily similar contents. 'And always have made, since the original replicant technology was first stolen, and the uses suppressed for which that technology was created. You assume that a production run of replicants, no matter who was the original templant on which they were based, were meant to be created and animated *simultaneously.*'

'Well, yeah; of course.' Iris made a slight gesture with the gun in her hand. 'What else? If you're cranking out slave labor, or expendable troops for some suicide military operation, then you're naturally going to put as many as you can into the field, all at the same time. There's no point in rationing them out, not if you're planning on winning whatever battle you're fighting, or getting as many emigrants as possible to sign up and ship out to the far colonies.'

'No point at all,' agreed Carsten, 'as long as those are the uses to which you're putting the replicant technology. But as I said, the original purpose of the technology is entirely different. If you're using

215

it for purposes of achieving immortality, then the replicants, even if created at the same time, are not animated simultaneously, but *sequentially*, one after another. A chain of lives, as it were, amounting to one potentially endless life.'

'Wait a minute.' From over the raised gun, Iris skeptically regarded the old man. 'Let me see if I've got this right. What you're saying is that as one replicant wears out – one of these, let's say' – she nodded toward the sleeping figures in the glass-lidded coffins – 'then the next Eldon Tyrell model in line is animated, or woken up, or whatever you want to call it. And then the next one after that, when its turn comes. All the way down the chain, for however long you want to make it. But so what?' Iris shook her head in exasperation. 'That's not immortality. If the original Eldon Tyrell is dead, he's still dead, whether there's some physical copy of him running around or not.'

'You're correct about that. The physical copy, in and of itself, is nothing. It is merely the container; the contents are what is important.' Carsten reached down and placed his hand on the brow of one of the figures, deep in its suspended animation. 'It's what is in here that counts, that determines whether the original Eldon Tyrell would be alive or not. Of course, for that to be the case, we must dismiss another erroneous assumption about the nature of the replicant technology. Individuals such as yourself, blade runners and others most concerned about replicants, have always thought that the personalities and minds, even the souls, of the creatures with which you dealt were only fictional constructs, a matter of elaborately developed but still false memories and other *gestalt*-forming mental contents downloaded into the newly hatched replicants' cerebral cortices. Entire phony biographies written on blank slates, as it were; life histories that seemed real to the replicants, even when they knew logically they were false, that none of the events and emotions they thought they remembered had in reality happened. Perhaps the cruelest deception of all; for no other reason, the replicants might have wished to have had their revenge on their creator. *Know thyself* is a vicious maxim, when to discover the truth is to discover that one's very nature is a lie.'

'That's the way it goes,' Iris said. 'Everybody finds out they've been lied to, eventually.'

'True,' said Carsten. 'And you, and the rest of the blade runners, were certainly lied to when you were informed that the replicants' mental contents, their minds and memories, were *necessarily* fictional.

But they're not; the nature of the container, the physical form, doesn't dictate such falsehoods, anymore than an empty glass dictates that water or wine be poured into it. The glass doesn't care; neither does the blank slate inside a newly created replicant, waiting for information to be inscribed upon it. Truth, to the degree that such exists in this universe, can be placed there just as readily as lies. And that, of course, is what the original purpose of the replicant technology was about: the immortality achieved by transcribing the actual mind and memories, and even the soul, of an original human being into a newly created physical duplicate of that original.'

'Assuming it could be done,' said Iris, 'why a physical *duplicate*? If I were Eldon Tyrell, and I wanted my mind and memories and the rest transferred to a new body, I'd certainly want to trade up. Physically, that is.' She nodded toward the withered visage in the coffin-like container closest to her. 'Surely the Tyrell Corporation could come up with something better-looking than that.'

'Of course it could. But it couldn't be used for what you're talking about. The container might not dictate the contents, truth or a lie, but the contents do dictate the container into which they can be loaded. All Eldon Tyrell's mind and memories were based upon events that happened to a body just like these.' Carsten had taken his hand from the brow of the sleeping replicant; now he gestured with it toward the rest of the figure in the glass-lidded coffin before him. 'To put that mind and those memories – that dark soul – into some nobler, more heroic form would create a fatal discrepancy between the inner *gestalt* and its new physical manifestation. Believe me, it's been tried; I imagine Eldon Tyrell tried it himself at one time. The best result is total paralysis of the replicant that receives the mismatched download; the usual result is convulsions and death from an overload feedback in the connections between the spine and the major muscle groups.'

'Okay; scratch that, then.' A few ice crystals had drifted across Iris's hand and the black barrel of the gun; there they looked like minute stars in an inverted night sky. 'It still doesn't strike me as much of a process. What kind of immortality would you get out of this? It's not a chain; it's a loop. Just the same thing over and over again. The same damn Eldon Tyrell, or anybody else, starting up again at the same place and living his same evil little life once more. But that's not immortality; it's a definition of hell.'

'So it would be,' said Carsten, 'if that were all there had been to the original replicant technology. But there was more to it than that; much more. What my companies and the others had been trying to achieve was a refutation of the Newtonian law of thermodynamics that so harshly applies to information theory: the one that states that in every exchange some data loss inevitably creeps in.'

'Not if the information is digitized. Then it's a string of ones and zeros. You can't screw those up.'

'A typical mistake, to worship the almighty bit.' Carsten's disdain was apparent in his pale eyes. 'You're overlooking the fact that such information, however it is recorded outside of the human body, must still be transcribed back into an analogue container, the raw bloody pulp and gristle of the brain. To get beyond the loop you spoke of, to ensure that Eldon Tyrell or any other physically duplicated person wasn't simply going through the same dismal life over and over again – to achieve an actual *cumulative* immortality, an ongoing life – then the basic *gestalt* information would have to be transcribed into and back out of an analogue form that would in fact allow data errors to creep in. Worse: the process would create a cascading error effect. The errors would increase at a geometrical rate, rather than merely an arithmetical one. And of course, the farther back the information in the individual's biography, the more contaminated by error it would become every time it was transcribed into and out of the fallible, fleshy recording medium. Only the most recently recorded information, the events that had happened to the most recent, previous replicant in the sequential chain, would be even relatively free of such transcription error; everything else would be progressively lost to a deepening dementia and progressive loss of fundamental memory – leading to what my own company's psychiatric technicians termed "*gestalt* collapse", the catastrophic implosion of all personality-based functioning, similar to a building crumbling in on itself due to the erosion of its foundation. When that happens, it doesn't matter how fresh and well-preserved the top floor is; it goes along with the rest.'

'Congratulations,' said Iris sourly. 'You've just proven that this whole immortality shtick could never work.'

'On the contrary; I have merely shown you what the problem is, what my company and the others were working on before the replicant technology was stolen from us. We knew very well what we were up against; we were attempting to defeat entropy itself, the inevitable principle of disorganization and loss of form that is a constant throughout the universe. The cruel part of having our work stolen from us is how close we had come to our goal.'

'How close is that?'

'Close enough so Eldon Tyrell was able to grasp the prize that had been inches from our fingers.' The seething resentment sparked brighter in Carsten's eyes. 'Close enough for others, whether the UN emigration program or whoever has been working with the escaped replicants, to have realized he had managed to create the last missing piece of the puzzle. To have achieved true physical immortality, using a sequential chain of replicants for which he had been the templant, without the entropic decay of the *gestalt*-forming contents of his mind and memories. And having put the puzzle together at last, Eldon Tyrell had become too dangerous to live. Somebody – some agency, some force, some entity, either from outside or from within his own circle of confederates, even possibly from within the Tyrell Corporation itself – decided that rather than allowing him to live forever, it had become imperative he die. Immediately.' Carsten folded his arms across his chest. 'And so it was arranged.'

Iris could see the pieces of the other puzzle assembling themselves. 'Through the Batty replicant.'

'Just so,' replied Carsten. 'Somebody took the necessary steps, from the far colonies all the way to Los Angeles, to make sure that a murderous escaped replicant would be able to reach the Tyrell Corporation headquarters in LA, penetrate its defense systems with laughable ease, as well as be coached in the one cover story that would distract Eldon Tyrell from alerting the security agents who would have been seconds away from coming to his aid. Instead of immortality, all that Eldon Tyrell wound up with was an endless future as a skull-crushed corpse, until such time as his bones were blown away by dust.'

'Now you've lost me again.' Iris gestured with the gun she held aimed at the old man. 'What would it matter if the Batty replicant killed Tyrell? You said he had already created the missing piece to the puzzle, some way of using a sequential chain of physical doubles of himself, replicants modeled after his templant – but with some kind of cumulative mind and personality which didn't decay and fall apart the way it otherwise would. And he had done so to the point that these other mysterious forces you're talking about, that had been somehow keeping track of what he was up to, would have known he had succeeded in achieving a method of immortality. That's why they sent the Batty replicant to knock him off. But what's the problem with that?' She made a dismissive flick to one side with the gun's dark barrel; ice crystals shook from her numb hand and drifted down onto the face of the Eldon Tyrell figure in the glass-lidded coffin before her. 'It just means that the lifespan of his original physical body got terminated a little earlier, and maybe a little more uncomfortably, than he had been expecting to happen. So what? He'd already had the next links in the sequential chain made up; they're lying right here in front of us. And if he had the magic key ready also, the way of getting the contents of his head into his replicant double without any information decay, then whatever Tyrell Corporation flunkey he would've had standing by in case of emergencies like this – and of course he had one; paranoid guy, right? – then that flunkey could've pulled the switch or whatever was involved and done the job. And Eldon Tyrell would've been up and running again, mean and ugly as ever. Why didn't that happen?'

'There's a lot of reasons it could have failed to happen.' Carsten looked unimpressed with her arguments. 'Primarily, due to Eldon Tyrell having been surrounded by far more conspirators and traitorous elements, right inside his own corporation, than he had any notion of. Whoever had been designated with the responsibility of "throwing the switch," as you put it, could have been one of those traitors. Let's face it, Eldon Tyrell hardly had the kind of charisma that inspired universal loyalty among his employees. Any one of them might have preferred to see him as a corpse rather than as an animated replicant. One has to be careful about making enemies; they tend to multiply in the dark, like insects. However, as much as something like that could have or should have happened to Eldon Tyrell, it is not in fact what occurred. His death – his true death, all chance of immortality gone – wasn't accomplished by the mere failure to throw the switch that would have put the transcription of his mind and memories into a waiting replicant receptacle. That would have been too easy – and not nearly final enough. For, of course, if the transcription that had been made of his mind and memories still existed, who could say the switch might not have been thrown later?' Carsten shook his head. 'Better to make sure Eldon Tyrell stayed dead. After all, it's what the Batty replicant wanted, as well as the conspirators who arranged for his passage to LA. And the only way to do that was to destroy the channel by which the transference of information, from the dead Tyrell to the new replicant Tyrell, was to have been made. And that's exactly what the Batty replicant did.'

Iris regarded the old man sidelong once more; the creepily fervent tone had crept into his reedy voice again. 'Yeah?' She was glad she had the gun hanging in her numb hand between herself and Carsten. 'How'd he do that?'

'You already saw how it was done,' said Carsten. 'You saw the *Blade Runner* movie. And it wasn't just a movie: as your friend Vogel told you, it was in fact the actual taped record of what happened. So the way you saw Eldon Tyrell die in the film – the way you saw the Batty replicant kill him – was the way Eldon Tyrell did indeed die; in reality, in the world as we know it. You understand that, don't you?'

'Sure.' Ice crystals sifted from Iris's close-cropped hair down the back of her neck. 'I've got the picture.'

'I'm sure you do. I'm sure you're watching it right now, on the screen of your memory. And you can in fact see – in all its red detail – the whole sequence of Batty's murder of Tyrell. Am I right?'

Iris made no reply. The mere mention of the sequence had been enough to bring it up vividly inside her head, with no necessity for her to close her eyes to appreciate its somber beauties. She had felt no distaste the first time she had seen it, on the much larger and external screen of the private theater in what had been Tyrell's personal quarters in the ruins of the Tyrell Corporation building in LA. Watching the sequence again, in her memory, produced no new queasiness. *Only a death*, Iris told herself. Exactly like others she had seen, like others she herself had been responsible for. The only difference was the hands-on nature of this one; literally so. She watched, in memory, as Batty's hands settled on either side of his creator's age-creased head.

'A very detailed shot, isn't it?' From down the row of glass-lidded coffins, Carsten's thin voice hectored at her. 'When the makers of the film edited down the shots from the concealed video cameras, they went for the tight close-up, to make sure that we could see exactly what happened. What the Batty replicant did to Tyrell, other than simply kill him. Tell me; what do you see? What *did* happen then? What did the movie show?'

'The hands . . .' Iris spoke slowly, as the images unreeled in similar motion in her thoughts. 'And Tyrell's head . . .'

'The hands, yes; very good.' Carsten leaned forward above the

221

coffin closest to him, watching her as intently as might any bird of prey. 'And the thumbs . . . Batty's *thumbs* . . .'

His words seemed to be coming from infinitely far away, like the faint cry of some winged creature circling in a cloudless sky above. She could barely hear him, though she knew precisely what he had said to her. *His thumbs.* Iris could see them, the exact small motion pressing into Tyrell's face, and the blood that had welled up from beneath them.

'The eyes.' Iris spoke quietly, the gun in her hand forgotten for a moment and drifting downward. 'Batty crushed his *eyes* . . .'

'Now you know,' said Carsten. His voice had turned gentle, almost kind in its soft tones. 'Or at least a bit more than you did previously. Look at me.'

She turned her gaze away from the bloody images of memory and toward the old man in the ice-bound chamber.

'You've got your hand – at last – upon the end of the thread that will unravel the rest of the secrets.' There was no fervor in Carsten's words now, only the simple authority of fact. 'That's the trick, the switch to be pulled, as you put it. That's what is so important about them, and the way the Batty replicant killed Eldon Tyrell. Watch.'

With the cold gun hanging at her side, Iris watched as Carsten reached down toward the face of the figure sleeping in the open coffin before him. With a gentle motion, he drew his fingertips across the eyelids of the Eldon Tyrell replicant. When he raised his hand from the figure's creased brow, there were two black holes where none had been before.

Carsten walked along the row of opened coffin-like containers, reaching down and repeating the same simple action. As he passed, the faces all gazed upward with the same empty stare. When he came to the one in front of Iris, he drew his fingertips across its face as he had done with the others, then stepped back and regarded her in silence.

She looked down at the empty eye-sockets, emptier than any night sky could be. The hollowed-out sockets looked like twin wells, into which one could fall, and keep falling, without ever hitting bottom.

'The eyes . . .' Carsten's words came from somewhere close by her. 'They're the secret . . .'

Intercut

'Okay,' said the director. He leaned forward, peering even more closely at the monitor screen. 'She's onto it now.'

The camera operator scanned across the other screens before them, row after row of fragmented images from the icy subterranean chamber, the set beneath the desert's surface. *God, that's ugly,* he thought, wincing at the views of the suspended-animation containers and what they held. He could have lived a long time without any need for seeing one eyeless Eldon Tyrell, rather than a whole platoon of them.

But in some way, the view from the prime monitor, the one that the director was so intently studying, was even worse. The look on the female's face, as the camera operator had zoomed in on her, was that of someone on the verge of waking from her own troubled sleep, from bad dreams, into—

He didn't know. The director hadn't shown him the script. Everything had been live, real-time improv, the camera operator working the controls with virtually no respite for hours on end. *But it's almost over,* he told himself. Even for a job like this, with so much left so irritatingly mysterious, a certain instinct for pacing had kicked in; he could tell when the end was coming.

Whether the female they had been tracking, the one whose face filled the monitor screen, would be as relieved was another matter.

'Stay on her,' instructed the director, swiveling his chair away from the bank of glowing images. 'We're going in for the kill now.'

From the corner of his eye, the camera operator watched as the director reached for the tight-cell phone sitting on the top shelf of the wheeled equipment cart. He had no idea what the director meant by that, but it didn't sound good to him.

The director had his wide, overfleshed back to him, so he couldn't hear what was being said into the phone, what new instructions were being given, and to whom. *Not your department,* the camera operator told himself. *All you have to do is watch.*

He looked back toward the monitor screen. The female's eyes seemed to gaze right back into his own, as though waiting for him to speak, to warn her somehow . . .

16

'The eyes,' said the old man. He didn't look down at the sleeping figure in the glass-lidded coffin. 'That's the secret.' The row of Eldon Tyrell duplicates dreamed whatever slow dreams they might, without benefit of eyes to see them. 'From the beginning, that was the secret. That was what you needed to know.'

Iris closed her own eyes and stepped backward, away from the coffin between her and Carsten. 'I don't want to hear anymore.' She held up her free hand, palm outward, as though to fend off both him and the hollow-eyed figure in the coffin. 'I've heard enough.'

'No, you haven't.' Carsten's voice was cruelly blunt. 'You have to hear it all. Every bit of it. You don't have any choice about that.'

'Why?' She looked at him now. The fear that had sent her heart pounding, trying to force her cold-thickened blood through her veins, had been evoked by the Tyrell figures' empty eye-sockets; she had no idea where, from what part inside herself, that flinching terror had come. 'Why me?'

'You'll find that out as well, soon enough.'

'Really? You'll tell me?' The hope in her voice shamed her. Iris felt something colder than before on her face, stinging sharper than the ice crystals that had drifted down from the chamber's ceiling. She touched her face with trembling fingertips and found frightened tears, already at the point of freezing. With the back of her hand, she wiped them away. 'Don't screw around with me anymore,' she pleaded. 'I can't take it.'

'Just listen, then.' Carsten lowered his voice, knowing she would still be able to hear every word. 'Here's the deal. This is how it works. The eyes are how the transfer of information is made; it's an optical process. The windows of the soul, right? When those windows are thrown wide, things can enter as well as exit. That's how the chain is forged, link by link, as it were. And it's different from the download process used in the manufacture of ordinary replicants, the ones with fictional biographies and memories instead of real ones; those false memories are loaded in during the actual cellular construction of their brains, on top of the base material transcribed from the minds and memories of the human templants upon which they're based. But what's loaded through the eyes is the new material, that the original human or the most recent replicant duplicate has experienced, and that has become part of the human's mind and memories, in whatever interval of time since the base *gestalt*-forming material was laid down. Plus – and this was the breakthrough Eldon Tyrell achieved, since the original replicant technology was stolen and handed over to him – a *counter-entropic* signal, based upon wave-cancellation theory, ensuring that with each new subsequent transfer of information, data errors from previous transfers are identified and eliminated. Essentially, instead of a cascading pile-up of data errors, eventually resulting in paralysis or idiocy, the transcribed information is constantly renewed to a pristine state. And the result of *that* is true immortality; an unbroken chain. If everything had gone according to his plans, Eldon Tyrell would have lived forever.'

'If you say so,' murmured Iris. The words had come streaming past her, with only a few catching in her thoughts, like scraps of paper written upon in an incomprehensible language, swirling in the gutter of an LA street. 'If he'd wanted to . . .'

'There's no doubt about that. Eldon Tyrell wanted everything; that was the problem. And to never let go of it. That was why even his associates, such as the officials of the UN emigration program, turned on him at last. They had to; that much greed and hunger couldn't be trusted, even by those who were nearly as greedy and hungry. It's one thing to want, as the Batty replicant did, more than a meager four years of life. It's another to want eternity.'

'He didn't get it, though . . .'

'No,' said Carsten. 'He didn't. No one does. At least, not yet.'

'I don't get it, either,' said Iris. She brushed the last of the ice crystals from her face and looked direct at the old man. 'If the eyes are the important things – and that must've been why Tyrell had somebody else working on them, outside the Tyrell Corporation, right? – then why the mysteries beyond that? What was all that for?'

'Mysteries?' Carsten appeared amused; he raised one white eyebrow. 'I'm not saying there aren't any – in fact, there are plenty – but which ones in particular are you referring to?'

'Come on. I said before, don't screw around with me. The owl,' she said bluntly. 'What was the whole business with the owl? Why send me, why send anybody, off on some hunt for it? What has a stupid bird to do with Eldon Tyrell's eyes?'

'Everything,' replied Carsten. 'Do you really imagine that someone like Eldon Tyrell would keep an animal of any sort, a mere living thing, around for no reason? He was hardly the sentimental type. And if there were any sort of genuine test of empathic capability, if a Voigt-Kampff machine could be made to work and discern whether someone was human or not, the chances of his passing the test would have been slight indeed. So if the owl was there in his personal quarters in the Tyrell Corporation building, there was some purpose for it. And the owl's purpose was that it was Eldon Tyrell's back-up survival system.'

'Say again?'

'It's simple enough.' Carsten gestured toward the figure sleeping in the glass-lidded coffin. 'Tyrell was realistic enough to know that he had enemies. He knew something might happen to him that would prevent the transfer – the throwing of the switch, as you put it – between him and the next intended link in the chain. Given the situation, he would have been a fool not to have created some kind of a back-up, a way of somehow increasing his chances, giving himself at least a shot at survival in case the worst came to happen. And that's why the Tyrell Corporation's owl, so amusingly named Scrappy, was – or perhaps is, given that the creature might still exist, alive, somewhere in the city. We don't know who took the owl from you, or what that person might have done with it. Or even why anyone else might have wanted it; it's useless without one of the replicants you see here, after a new set of artificial eyes are surgically grafted in. Because all that Scrappy the owl contains, encrypted into its limited cortical matter, is a *minimal set* of Eldon Tyrell's basic mind and memories, a highly compressed version, with some considerable amounts of data eliminated, of the *gestalt*-forming mental contents that would have been transferred optically from him to the next waiting replicant in the sequential chain, if the Batty replicant hadn't gotten to Tyrell first.'

'I don't get it.' The tips of her fingers felt like icicles as Iris rubbed her aching brow. 'Why put something like that inside an owl? What was the point of it?'

'The owl served Tyrell's purposes admirably; it is, in fact, the perfect medium for the transcription of the minimal set, the essential back-up of Tyrell's mind and memories. As a predator, it has a complex enough neuro-cortical system for there to be excess circuit space for that set, even if, as I said, some material had to be discarded. If the minimal set were used to animate one of the waiting Tyrell replicants, there would be undoubted gaps in Tyrell's memory, but the essence, the *gestalt*, of the man would be there. As well as his most recent memories; Tyrell was apparently in the habit of updating the contents the owl carried on a weekly basis. That's why he kept the owl so close to him, in his personal quarters, feeding and taking care of it on his own; in effect, he was merely taking care of an exteriorized part of himself, and not another creature at all. That would have required the exercise of some empathic function on his part, a function he lacked. And of course there were other, physiological reasons why the owl was used; other than the now-extinct primate species, the owl is one of the few creatures with true binocular vision. Both its eyes look straight forward, as do those of a human being; the optical-based transfer of information is impossible to perform, otherwise. Then there are reasons beyond that: beside the conven-ience of the owl being a relatively small and easy-to-handle animal while in captivity, given Eldon Tyrell's fussy meticulousness at doing so, there is the survival factor. With its own owl mind and instincts still operational, and the Eldon Tyrell minimum set merely carried as non-functioning neurological baggage, as it were, the owl has at least some ability to look after itself, should circumstances arise when Tyrell would no longer be able to do so. And as you've found out for yourself, that turned out to be the case. The vermin-ridden back alleys of Los Angeles were a perfect hunting ground for the escaped owl, until it was captured by the people from whom you managed to take it.'

'I didn't have it for long,' murmured Iris. A memory image arose, of the great-winged bird of prey in her tiny apartment. 'Not long at all.'

'Not your fault.' Carsten's voice was tinged with pity again. 'You were up against forces of which you could, as yet, have little understanding. You're still up against them. There have been reasons for the things that have happened to you; those reasons are still undisclosed to you, but they were real, nevertheless. Going all the way back to the beginning – and perhaps even farther than that.' He watched her for any reaction. 'Tell me – why do you think you were chosen to go hunting for the owl? Why were you given the job?'

'Because . . .' Iris was no longer sure, but came up with the only answer she was able to. 'Because they thought I could find it. Somebody thought I could.' She shook her head. 'But I don't know who it was anymore. Maybe I never did.'

'There's more to it than that,' said Carsten. 'Do you want me to show you?'

'Do I have a choice?'

'I'll give you one. Now I will. You've come this far, but we won't go the rest of the way – unless *you* want to.' His voice had dropped almost to a whisper. 'I'll let you decide. I can show you, or you can walk out of here right now. Out into the sunshine, where it's nice and warm. And you won't have to know.'

Iris thought it over. As much as she could; her thoughts seemed frozen in place, as though they had become as chilled as the numb flesh of her limbs.

'All right.' She gave a single slow nod. 'Go ahead.'

'You have to come over here.' Carsten reached across the coffin between them and took her free hand. He stepped around the head of the container, closer to her. 'This is what you've been waiting for. From the beginning.'

He led her down the line of coffins, each with its glass lid thrown back, revealing the grimly sleeping contents within. All the way to the end of the line, close to the ice-covered wall of the chamber. The last coffin-like container was there, the one that Carsten had left unopened. The flat surface of its lid was frosted white with an accumulation of ice crystals, like a shelf of snow.

Carsten let go of her hand and reached down to the latch at the side of the coffin. Once again, Iris heard the tiny, breath-like sigh of the container's pneumatic seal being breached. Carsten grasped the edge of the lid and, with greater care than he had used with the others, lifted and tilted it back.

'Now tell me what you see.' Carsten stepped away, letting Iris come forward, reluctantly but inevitably. 'This time.'

She stood at the side of the coffin and looked down. And saw herself.

It had happened before. The memory of watching the movie and seeing the woman up on the screen, the one who had looked exactly like her. The one named Rachael who the blade runner Deckard had fallen in love with. She had been able to deny it to herself then, that she had been looking at her double, the face the same as her own. Deny it until Vogel had pointed it out to her, had made her admit the truth. And fury and tears had burst forth, from some unknown place inside her, for some reason she couldn't fathom. Fury at being frightened, frightened by not knowing what it meant; tears at knowing it meant everything, even though she had yet to discover why it did . . .

'You see her, don't you?' Carsten's soft voice came from behind Iris. 'It's like a mirror, isn't it?

Iris had only time for one slow nod of agreement, before the mirror shattered.

She heard the cry from the sleeping woman, the one with her face but a different name, the one named Rachael. As if the woman were suddenly waking up from her long sleep, woken by bad dreams, bad enough to make her cry out in pain, mouth wide and back arching up from the padded, silken lining of the glass-lidded coffin. The cry broke louder, echoing from the icy walls, until it was just as suddenly silenced by the blood that welled up and filled the woman's throat and mouth.

And the echo wasn't that of her silenced cry, but the ringing of the gunshot which had brought a smaller red flower blossoming at her breast, with a dark center where the bullet had smashed through the collarbone below, stopping the infinitely slow beat of her heart.

The next shot from the gun in Iris's raised hand slammed the woman with her face back down into the coffin. The woman's arms flung wide, hands spread, as if she were trying to embrace a bullet big as the world. And then she was only a crumpled dead thing in the red-spattered box, the backs of her wrists against the metal of its edges.

'You poor fool,' said Carsten. No shock, but only sadness sounded in his voice. 'That won't do any good. It won't stop anything. It's too late for that.'

Iris let the gun, warm enough now to thaw her frozen hand, drift downward from its own weight. She felt dizzied and unsure as she turned away from the coffin and its dead contents to look at the old man. 'I don't know why . . . I did it . . .'

'It doesn't matter.' Carsten reached out and touched her shoulder, with almost paternal kindness. 'Not for you . . . or her. Which is the same thing, really. You know that, don't you? It's like suicide, only you're still alive afterward. You can't kill yourself that easily.'

Not for lack of trying, thought Iris. She wondered if she had been trying to, from the beginning. The beginning before the owl. She

230

raised the gun in her hand, its metal chilling again to the temperature of her cold flesh, and regarded it—

The sound of another gunshot came, distant and muffled by the chamber's ice-laden walls. More shots, the distinct stutter of automatic-rifle fire, filtered though from outside and above, at the surface of the surrounding desert.

Carsten turned away from her, his slight body visibly tensing into full alertness. 'That's not supposed to be happening,' he muttered.

'What?' Iris could hear more shots, still muffled but louder and closer. 'What's happening?'

'Stay here,' ordered Carsten. He plucked the gun out of the stiff fingers of her hand, then headed with it toward the door by which they had entered the chamber. The disembodied eyes, in their fluid-filled vessels, watched him pass without comment.

Carsten, gun poised in one hand, pulled open the heavy door. Bright sunlight didn't pour in; Iris realized that she and the old man had been down there for hours, long enough for evening to have set in above, in the real world. There was enough dim light from outside to silhouette another figure in the doorway, just past Carsten.

Should've let me do it, thought Iris; a measure of her former hardcore professionality returned as she saw what happened next. Carsten's reaction time was too slow; even with the gun already raised into position, he wasn't able to get a shot off in time. A snarling flare burst from the silhouetted figure's automatic rifle, braced against his hip; the impact of the bullets was enough to lift Carsten's slight form off the floor and send him flying backward into the chamber. Before he landed, the clenching of his fist upon the gun he'd taken from Iris sent a single bullet upward; it hit one of the bare fluorescent light fixtures. With a sparking sizzle of electricity, the entire chamber was plunged into darkness.

With the first shots, Iris had scrambled behind the row of suspended-animation chambers. Crouching down, she watched as the figure in the chamber's doorway switched on a flashlight; its beam swept across the space, illuminating the eyes floating in their gelatinous liquids, then passing on. The figure stepped over Carsten's body and walked cautiously past the lab benches.

Silently, Iris crept farther behind the row of coffins, away from the armed figure's approach, until she was hidden by the first container Carsten had opened. The flashlight beam swept across the row, then settled on the coffin at the far end, the one holding her own double.

231

With his automatic rifle slung over his shoulder, the figure held the flashlight directly above the far coffin, then leaned forward to examine the dead female replicant it held. Enough of the beam caught his own face, and Iris was able to recognize him. *Meyer*, she thought. *My old boss.* Somehow, she found herself unsurprised.

It took only a few seconds' examination for Meyer to assure himself that the female replicant in the coffin was dead. Switching off the flashlight, he turned and strode toward the exit, the doorway illuminated by what was left of the fading twilight outside and above the trench in which the chamber was buried.

Iris slowly crept forward, so she could keep an eye on Meyer for as long as she could. She ducked behind the corner of one of the workbenches when she saw another figure outside the doorway.

The second figure said something she couldn't catch, though she thought she could recognize the voice. But Meyer's words, as he was still inside the chamber, were plain enough.

'Yeah, I found her.' With a tilt of his head, Meyer pointed toward the unlit interior. 'I worked with her long enough when she was alive; I should be able to tell.'

The other figure started to make some protest, but Meyer cut him off.

'I don't *care* what happened to her. Just that it did.' As Iris watched, Meyer pulled the automatic rifle up into firing position, braced against his hip. 'You earned your pay.'

Another quick burst of rifle fire sounded, then Meyer stepped across the corpse sprawled outside the doorway.

Iris waited until Meyer had climbed out of the trench, then she crept forward and found her gun beside Carsten's outstretched, motionless hand. She picked the gun up in both her numb hands, holding it close against herself as she listened to the distant sound of spinners lifting from the desert's surface. The vehicles' jet exhausts snarled, then faded in the night sky above.

Enough stars had come out that, in their cold blue radiance, Iris was able to look down at the face of the corpse outside the chamber doorway, and recognize the sharply etched features of Vogel. Her capacity for surprise was exhausted; she stepped over the body and out into the trench. Looking up, past the hole's crumbling rim, she could discern the luminous scars of the spinners' trails, heading to the west. Toward Los Angeles.

They did a good job, thought Iris as she walked across the bare sand of the compound. *Very thorough.* She appreciated their work on a coldly craftsmanlike basis: the area around the low buildings and rusted earth-moving equipment was littered with the bodies of the committee's operatives, most with their own automatic weapons inches away from their outflung hands. The peacefulness of dead things, their agendas terminated, lay over the star-illuminated patch of desert like a benediction.

She found her guard, the one who had given her both water and her gun, face down outside the main building. Stepping around him, Iris pushed the door of the building open. No lights – the raiders, whoever they had been, had apparently taken out the chugging generator on which the compound had been running. She had already taken a flashlight off one of the corpses outside; she switched it on and sent its beam across the building's interior.

Thorough, all right. This time, disgust tinged her estimation as she saw the dead owls scattered across the building's floor, their feathers raddled with blood, looking like unfortunate stuffed toys that had been dragged through the machinery of some slaughterhouse. She turned away and walked back outside.

A shadow, a moment darker than the blue night, passed across her.

Iris looked up and saw tiny sections of starlight blinked out, as something flew above. Something much smaller than a spinner that moved in silence and swooping curves, thrust by the beat of its widespread wings. She swept the beam of the flashlight up into the night sky, and caught, for a fraction of a second, the reflected glow of two golden eyes. That was all it took for her to recognize the owl, the same one she had hunted and captured before.

The owl flew out into the open expanse of the desert, toward the jagged shapes of the far hills. Her own eyes had become so adjusted to the partial spectrum laid down by the stars that she could follow the creature's rapid shadow across the flat landscape. In the distance, beyond a broken, flattened section of the fence ringing the compound, she saw the owl dart down toward the ground. The figure of a man, barely discernible, stood waiting for it, one forearm raised. The owl's wings flared outward to brake its plummet, its talons reaching for and catching upon the perch of the man's arm. Once settled there, the owl wrapped its wings close against itself.

As Iris watched, the man started walking across the luminous sands toward her; the owl remained on his raised arm. When the dark figure had approached only a few yards closer, Iris realized that there

233

was someone else with him, a smaller figure walking at his side; a child.

Both figures, separate now in her gaze, strode unhurriedly toward her. When they reached the toppled section of fence, the man had to stretch his free hand toward the child and help her across; Iris could see that it was a girl, with dark hair drawn back into a single braid. With the gun dangling loose in her hand, Iris waited as they crossed the interior of the compound, past the inert machinery and the corpses face down in the sand.

'You won't need that,' said the man. 'The gun – it's not necessary.'

The bright gold eyes of the owl regarded her without blinking. From where the owl perched on his raised arm, its eyes were at the same level as his. Eyes, and a face that Iris had recognized, even before he spoke.

'You're Deckard.' A statement, not a question. 'The blade runner.'

'Sure.' He didn't even have to nod to let her know she was right. 'You should know. You saw the movie.'

Deckard looked older than he had in the movie, the close-cropped hair flecked with wiry gray stubble at his temples. His face, with the tiny scar on the chin, was creased and weathered, but definitely the one that the female replicant in the movie had fallen in love with.

He and the girl had stopped a yard or so away from her. The gaze of the dark-haired girl was nearly as unblinking as that of the owl; she still held onto Deckard's hand. 'And my name,' she announced in a quiet voice, 'is Rachael.'

'Of course.' Iris didn't know what else to say. 'Of course it is.' What she couldn't say, but knew in her heart with absolute certainty, was that she was looking at the child that the woman in the movie, the one also named Rachael, had once been. There was no mistaking the resemblance between the child and the adult.

Or, Iris also had realized, between the child and herself.

'You've come a long way,' said Deckard. 'Farther than you realize. But in some ways' – the same lopsided, ironic smile from the movie showed on his face – 'you haven't gone anywhere at all.'

'I don't know what you mean.' Fatigue had washed across her again, like some invisible tide across the desert, the surge of its waves bearing her on the surface, without will of her own. 'Really . . . I don't.'

'You will. Everything gets revealed, eventually. Whether you want

234

it to or not.' Deckard let go of the child's hand and took hers. 'Come on.'

'Wait a minute.' Iris resisted the pull of his hand. 'You were the one, weren't you? You had to have been.'

'What do you mean?'

'The one who took the owl from me,' said Iris. 'When I had it in my apartment. I can tell. When you're standing this close to me, I can tell.'

Deckard waited a moment before replying. 'It was necessary,' he said finally. 'And it was for your sake as well. If I hadn't taken the owl from you . . .' He glanced at the golden-eyed creature perched on his raised arm, then back to Iris. 'You wouldn't be alive right now.'

'Maybe not.' She couldn't decide whether that would have been better.

She let the blade runner and the child lead her across the compound, toward the fence. In the distance, out where the owl's shadow had led her gaze, she saw now an unmarked spinner parked in the hollow of one of the dunes.

'Where are we going?' After all that had happened, Iris knew she had no way of stopping anything else from overtaking her. 'Back to Los Angeles?'

'Don't be silly,' said the little girl, trudging beside Iris. 'How could we? It's not possible.'

'Why not?'

Deckard kept walking, leading her toward the spinner; he had let the owl fly ahead, the beat of its great wings audible in the desert's silence. He glanced over at Iris. 'You can't go *back* to LA – not the real LA – if you've never been there in the first place.'

'What do you mean?' Iris stopped in her tracks, pulling her hand away from his. She had tucked the gun inside her tattered jacket, its weight against her ribs. 'What're you talking about?'

'She doesn't know,' said the girl Rachael. 'You have to tell her. *Everything.*'

'Soon enough,' said Deckard. He raised his hand, pointing up to the night sky. 'Look. Take a good look. Those aren't the stars you see from Earth.'

Iris tilted her head, gazing up at the disordered constellations. None of which she recognized; in the farther corners of her memory were the bright images of other stars, other wordless patterns that she had never put a name to. *But maybe I never saw them*, thought Iris. There had always been the clouds and the rains, in LA. In some LA.

'That doesn't prove anything,' said Iris. She could hear the desperation in her voice, the attempt to hold onto at least one thing she had thought was true. 'It doesn't—'

'Nothing does.' Deckard started walking again, with the little girl beside him. He didn't look back. 'Then you find out for yourself.'

Iris waited a moment, feeling the desert winds slide through her jacket and across her skin. She glanced up at the unfamiliar stars once more, then lowered her gaze and followed after the man and the girl, toward the waiting spinner.